Praise for
IF THE DEVIL HAD A DOG

"In a word? Un-put-down-able. The characters are so carefully delineated you can hear them breathe. Even the secondary characters, both good and bad, are so alive that you feel as if they are part of your world. The story reels you in, from the smashing first line and delivers until the end. Readers won't want to shelve these characters. More books, please!"

I. Eishen – Amazon Reader

"The new psychological thriller by T.K. Lukas will touch a lot of people in many ways. Far too many of them, from the most feminine to the hardest of veterans, will be able to closely relate to the distress and anxiety detailed in Lukas's new novel. Some of the chilling-but-thrilling scenes may leave you wondering how much of what you're reading is fiction, and how much of it is a shared, terrifying moment in history. However, as if to help you recover from the moment, the next few words might make you laugh out loud, or stop for a bit to consider a thought-provoking idea. *If the Devil Had a Dog*: full of surprises and highly recommended."

Gary B. Haley – Author of *The Attunement* and *The Scrapbook Lectures*

"I am SO TIRED! And it's all Lukas' fault. I seriously could not put this book down. I could not stop reading it and loved the story so much I didn't want it to end. There was an added layer of fun in reading a book and knowing places and recognizing names. I'm so glad Lukas is thinking series, because no one who enjoys this book is going to be ready to let these characters go! T.K. Lukas has a hit in this one."

S. Miles – Amazon Reader

"I finished reading *If the Devil Had a Dog* two days ago, but I can't stop thinking about the story! While reading the book, I felt conflicted, wanting to get to the end so I could know the resolution, but not wanting it to be over. I highly recommend the book to anyone who loves suspense and great characters."

B. Maybe – Amazon Reader

"What a thrilling story of romantic suspense. Loved the flawed characters. Would love to know that the storyline will continue. I would recommend this story for anyone who enjoys suspense, assassins, crime with a touch of romance. 5 stars with hopes to see a book 2 soon."

S. Danzer – Amazon Reader

"I could not stop reading it...aside from the fascinating story, I was pleased with the writing, structure, and proper grammar. As a retired editor, I am oftentimes distracted -is there a shortage of good copy editors out there? I thoroughly enjoyed this book and look forward to another one soon."

A. Kourany – Amazon Reader

"The story was believable and the characters delightful. Markus' PTSD was very real and Sidney's attempts to escape domestic violence and other extreme dangers were on point. Even Trevor and Eli were people that were broken in some way but all of them exhibited strengths that is often rare. Perfect story!"

A. Williams – Amazon Reader

"Good plot, continuous action with little down time and terrific writing with great descriptions and minimal filler. Loved that the chapters were labeled, which should be a requirement for all authors all books."

G. Mache – Amazon Reader

"I picked this book up for a quick read on a plane ride. I couldn't put it down! I was gasping and snickering on the plane; the woman next to me even asked what I was reading since I looked like I was enjoying it. The wit and charm are no less than you'd expect in a Texas themed novel. I loved the cowboy/rodeo themes and the main character is so smart and inquisitive. You won't be disappointed in this book!"

R. Choo – Amazon Reader

"This was one of those books that hit the ground running. Not a boring moment. Could hardly take a break. In this complex world we live in now, we can only thank God we have not had to endure a life like this. Great job!"

J. Shirley – Amazon Reader

"I really liked this book! I was swept along to the extent that it was difficult to stop reading when it got so late in the evening. Excellently written with twists and turns I didn't see coming, and fully fleshed characters to boot. The subject matter is timely, the locales are described accurately, and the conclusion is satisfying in oh, so many ways. Top notch writing!"

W. Reader – Amazon Review

"This was a suspense filled read that had me dying to get back to it every time I had to put it down. It wasn't like any other book I ever read. More twists and turns than a pretzel."

S. Goodwin – Amazon Reader

IF THE DEVIL HAD A DOG

By

T.K. Lukas

Chevalier Publishing

ISBN: 0-9962356-4-7
ISBN-13: 978-0-9962356-4-8

Chevalier Publishing

Note:
This book is a work of fiction. Names, characters, places, and incidents either are the product of the author's imagination or are used fictitiously, and any resemblance to actual persons, living or dead, business establishments, events, or locales is entirely coincidental.

Dedication

*For Baron, who taught me to believe in heroes,
who taught me to believe in everlasting love,
who taught me to believe it's never too late
to live happily ever after.*

From My Heart

Writing this novel, while sometimes an excruciating exercise in fortitude, was ultimately cathartic. I am closely acquainted with women who've found themselves in frighteningly similar circumstances as the heroine, Sidney. Fearing their partner's "till death do us part" vow, they've combated domestic violence, both mental and physical. These are smart women— strong women—women who got sucked into their abuser's sick world.

My fictitious heroine flees her violent marriage. However, she's put through hell and her life is still in danger. Sadly, in real life, many women haven't the means to escape. This story is not meant to be a blueprint for how every woman should handle her individual struggle. This is fiction based on fact. If you are in a domestic violence situation, please reach out for help. While not a personal endorsement, a possible place to start is genesisshelter.org or another such organization in your community.

Now, a word about the "hero." I use that term with immense pride and familiarity. The lead male character, Markus, is patterned after a few men I know, one quite personally. If you are acquainted with the quote attributed to George Orwell, you'll know my male lead character and understand his motives without further explanation: "People sleep peaceably in their beds at night only because rough men stand ready to do violence on their behalf."

While Markus handles his PTSD in an atypical manner, those with PTSD can surely identify with his emotions and his decision to deal with his situation in his own way. Post

Traumatic Stress is a very real and very serious mental health issue. If you are suffering, please don't carry the burden alone. Again, not an endorsement, but organizations such as the [Wounded Warrior Project](#) and their Warrior Care Network may provide helpful resources.

I'm hopeful that strong, smart women and courageous, rough men who find themselves in situations similar to those of my characters will gain a sense of strength and feel a shoulder of sympathy in the words of this novel.

Always faithful,
T.K. Lukas

CHAPTER 1

Alpine

"Friday's as good a day as any to run for your life," Sidney McQueen said aloud for perhaps the hundredth time since fleeing Fort Worth. *But where the hell have I run*? She slowed her truck and horse trailer to a crawl as she approached the tiny town that looked like it belonged in the middle of the previous century. She'd hoped for a better first impression of the place that was supposed to provide a clandestine refuge—a safe haven —to hide away from the man she referred to as "the devil."

Yet her initial glimpse of the small, west Texas town appeared to be nothing of the sort.

Alpine, Texas appeared to be in a confused struggle to uncover its true identity. She noticed contradictions at every turn, juxtapositions underscoring the intricate nature of the community. Native American art galleries and sleek photography studios were as equally represented as tattoo parlors, livestock feed stores, and saddle makers. High-end jewelers, chic boutiques, and antique book dealers were nudged up against Mexican taquerias and gourmet restaurants, all sharing a few city blocks of awning space.

Even the name of the town and the name of the main drag pointed to contradictions. Beyond Holland Avenue, one might expect to see a collection of windmills irrigating rows of tulips instead of acres of cotton. Edelweiss did not thrive in this land better suited for ocotillo and yucca that grew in spiky abundance on the twin peaks overlooking the town. By all appearances, Alpine was a mishmash of clashing, complex personalities.

But clashing and complex was not what she needed. To Sidney's hypervigilant mind, everything in this tiny town seemed to be in a skirmish. Not even close to her image of an idyllic refuge, Alpine provoked disquieting thoughts.

She considered heading on down the road. But where would she go, with darkness only a few short hours away? Practical matters must be considered. She decided to explore further. Driving past the downtown shops, she noticed business owners sweeping their sidewalks. A few offered a perfunctory wave before going on about their tasks. Shoppers strolling along the storefronts ignored her. A matched pair of golden retrievers napped in the afternoon sunshine on a porch next to a gourmet hotdog stand.

Upon giving it further consideration, she realized she could blend right in. Her tensions and misgivings eased somewhat. This speck on Texas's western horizon might prove ideal after all.

After making a second sweep around the downtown loop, she drove back to the edge of town where visitors and residents were greeted by a vibrant billboard that looked like a ten-foot-tall picture post card. It read *"Howdy, Welcome to Alpine."* Across from the sign stood the Maverick Inn, a collection of low-slung, tan adobe buildings reminiscent of an old roadhouse-style motel. An adobe wall surrounded the complex, while gigantic desert yucca, with stalks of white flowers shooting up from clusters of sword-shaped leaves, grew as tall as the flashing neon sign.

Clean and well lit, it appeared safe. It was on the main road with a straight shot out of town, in case she needed to drive away in a hurry. *Perfect.*

She pulled her truck and horse trailer next to the In.

Sidney grabbed her handbag and her cellphone, double-checked that she'd locked the cab of her truck, before walking around to the side of the three-horse trailer. She lowered the middle window and the dark, chocolaty brown mare stuck out her head and nickered.

"I won't be long, Mocha. I think I've found us a place to stay for the night." She stroked the mare's velvety nose, rubbing the large star that swirled on her forehead. "I'm sure you're as ready as I am to stop driving."

Glancing at the life-sized plastic statue of a horse standing in the first stall of the trailer, a "horse" wearing a traveling sheet matching Mocha's, Sidney decided that buying the fake horse was a stroke of genius. If someone were pursuing her, they would have been told to keep an eye out for a woman matching her description pulling a trailer with only one horse in it.

From behind, the shrill sound of a long, drawn-out wolf whistle followed by vulgar catcalls startled her. She twisted her head around and noticed that the noise erupted from a rusty old pickup truck overflowing with eager, denim-clad testosterone. In a metropolitan city, the truck would be considered a prized, vintage find. Here, it was a ranch vehicle, something used for working, like the hard-calloused cowboys spilling over the bed's railings and hanging out of the cab's windows.

Sidney rested her forehead against the trailer, squeezing her eyes closed and wishing the pickup truck would roll on by. She considered climbing back into her truck and being the one to keep rolling on, but she'd been on the road almost ten hours and was exhausted. Ignoring the rude taunts would be impossible—the truck had slowed to a crawl. She decided playing it cool but smart was her best option to avoid a possible confrontation that might escalate into something she'd have to handle publicly. Flying under the radar was crucial.

"Hey, blondie. Save a horse, ride a cowboy," shouted the tall, sunbaked beer drinker who stood in the bed of the truck and leaned against the cab's back window. He swilled the last drop and tossed the bottle in the general direction of a grassy field.

The amber glass shattered against the curb.

His white athletic jacket bore numerous rodeo patches for saddle bronc riding. A thick mixture of dirt and manure smeared the coat, almost obscuring the "2012" patch sewn on the sleeve. The patch was from Sul Ross State University, which was known as the birthplace of collegiate rodeo.

The driver, wearing a similar jacket, leaned out the window. "Say, sexy mama. Wanna swap your shiny truck for this old heap? This'd sure be easier for you to drive. You're too small to climb in and out of that huge rig."

Sidney turned on her cellphone and whirled around behind their truck. She snapped a picture of the license plate and another of the occupants' surprised faces. A record of evidence, just in case.

She gripped the phone, her thumb hovering over the photo button, ready to snap another picture if needed. "You boys run along. Go find someone your own age to play with."

Her petite frame, long, blond ponytail, hip hugging jeans, and pink flannel shirt belied her thirty-four years, giving her the appearance of a younger girl. From the mass of rodeo team letter jackets, Sidney guessed them as either in college or fresh out. A little cougar action, or action of any sort, was not on her agenda.

The truck's lowered tailgate was a crowded perch where four cowboys squeezed shoulder-to-shoulder with their legs dangling over the edge, their booted feet hovering inches above the pavement. When the driver shoved the truck's gears into park, one rider slid off the tailgate, his slight frame emerging from the midst of his beefier companions. All wore their cowboy hats pulled low enough for the brims to shadow their eyes.

With his hands planted on his hips, he jutted his chin in defiance. "You *boys*? I haven't been called a *boy* since I was ten." Insolence dripped from each word.

He was a compact, lean bull rider, the half-dozen patches sewn on his jacket attesting to his sport. The emblems depicted a bucking bull ridden by an arched-back rider, one arm cocked high above his head. It was the only jacket clean enough to read the logos.

"This ain't no *boy's* toy here." He unbuckled his belt. His jeans and boxers dropped to his boots.

Encouraged by the uproarious laughter and shouts of admiration and jealousy from his buddies, the exhibitionist added a few hand pumps and hip thrusts to accentuate the crudeness of the action.

Sidney snapped another picture of the raunchy scene as she backed toward the hotel. Tension from her gritted teeth and clamped jaw shot a pulsating wave through her head. She knew the signs. It was a migraine. It would wedge just above the base of her skull. She hated those—those were the bad ones that usually lingered for days.

"Hey," he shouted, pulling up his jeans. "I expect royalties if that photo goes viral."

"Fucking jerks," Sidney muttered under her breath as she pocketed the phone. Hurrying toward the Inn's office, she let the cowboys' crude comments hang in the air, willfully ignoring their unwelcome verbal assault.

"Welcome to the Maverick, a roadhouse for wanderers. I'm Ruth. What can I do for you?" A friendly lady sprang from behind the front desk to greet the stranger.

Her pleasant smile and cheery voice were as earnest as the west Texas wind. She was dressed in a plush jogging suit and sequined running shoes, both the same silver-gray as her lively eyes and her shellacked, bouffant hair. Ruth was a monochromatic burst of warmth and energy.

"Hi Ruth. I'm Sidney. I need a room for the night. I'm pulling a horse trailer, and I've got portable panels to make a small turnout pen. Is there room out back to accommodate that?"

"Oh, honey, I wish I could help you. I'm booked solid right through the holidays." Her eyebrows drew together in genuine concern.

"The holidays? Oh, right. I almost forgot." She hadn't really forgotten; she just didn't want to be reminded of or to think about what used to be her favorite time of the year.

"Thanksgiving's six days away, hon." Ruth pointed to the calendar on the wall, as if for proof.

"And you're booked? Way out here in the middle of nowhere?" Sidney tried to quell her rising panic. There was no need for alarm. There might still be time to get settled someplace before dark.

"All kinds of things bring people to Alpine in the fall and winter. Game hunting's a big draw." Ruth poked her pencil up at the taxidermy mounts of a variety of animal bodies, heads, and antlers on display.

Sidney glanced up at a full-figure mount of a glassy-eyed mountain lion staring down on her. She shivered. "Would you happen to know of a place called Yeager Stables? It was recommended to me, but I don't have directions or a phone number."

She had left Fort Worth in a hurry. There'd been no time for written directions, only time for an urgent agreement of more information to follow. All she had was a name and a destination. The promise of further instructions was yet to be fulfilled. Her anxious mind raced over the many possible reasons she had not been contacted.

"Sure—I know the place. It's a short drive north of town past the airport, like you're going to Fort Davis. The guy runs a hunting lodge, too."

"Great. Is it close enough that I could make it before sundown?" Her shoulders rose and fell with her sigh of relief.

"If you hurry. Here's the number, but you might not be able to get through. Cellphone coverage is sporadic, at best. You're welcome to call from the landline in my office."

"I'm kind of in a hurry. I'll call once I'm on my way. If you could just write down the address, I'm sure—"

"I'll draw you a map." Ruth grabbed a piece of paper, scribbling with a fast hand.

"Thanks. If you just write down the address, I'll put it in my GPS." Sidney didn't want to sound unappreciative, but she wanted to be back on the road—quickly.

Ruth snorted laughter through her nose. "Hon, ain't no GPS going to find this place. It ain't on the map. Better I write you some directions. I'll email Mr. Yeager for you to let him know you're coming. We wouldn't want to surprise him."

"Oh. Uh—sure. Okay." Sidney busied herself by riffling through the free literature in the rack from the Visitor's Bureau, tapping her foot, and glancing several times at Ruth as she scratched out a map and directions. "What kind of a place is Alpine, if one were considering staying longer than just a short visit?"

"I came here in fifty-six to attend college—loved it so much I never left. It ain't changed much, except there are more artsy-fartsy folks than we used to have. But I enjoy that. I draw and paint, some." Ruth pointed to the expansive oil on canvas taking up most of the wall behind her.

The scene was a dramatic sunrise washing over a field of dewy bluebonnets, with a broken-down windmill covered in thorny catbrier vines. However, it was the deer standing next to the windmill that drew Sidney's attention. Alert, ready to flee, a whitetail doe stood with muscles tensed, her tawny hide gleaming from the reflection of the sun's rays. The doe returned the viewer's gaze with an intense, suspicious expression that seemed real. The wary animal appeared as if she might leap off the canvas and bound away at the first hint of danger.

I know exactly how you feel.

Empathizing with the apprehensive doe, Sidney took a step closer to inspect the masterpiece. "Ruth, this is gallery worthy. I'm impressed. Signed 'RAY.' Is that your artist's signature?"

"Thanks, hon. Yes. Ruth Ann Youngblood. The little *ray* of sunshine behind my initials was my late husband's idea."

"I can see it suits you," said Sidney, tracing her finger over the signature.

"My husband was born in Alpine. He loved it here." Ruth paused for a moment and then bent to her task. "It's usually quiet and laid back. Most folks are the hard working, salt of the earth types. With the college, though, we get our share of rowdies. And when there's a rodeo in town, the atmosphere can get a bit *spirited*."

"I'm guessing there's a rodeo tonight. I think I met some of the contestants when I drove up." Sidney craned her head to peek out the window, relieved that her rowdy welcoming party had chosen to carouse elsewhere.

"Rodeo's tomorrow night," said Ruth, putting the finishing touches on her map. "And I'm familiar with the truck that pulled up. Everyone in town knows *that* truck."

Sidney took the paper Ruth held out, impressed with the detail. "The occupants were, as you put it, a bit *spirited*," she said, arching her eyebrows.

"Most of them are on the rodeo team and are good boys, but the group has a few mischief makers. My grandson, Victor, is on the team," said Ruth, walking Sidney to the door.

"Your grandson. Ah, I see. In what event does Victor compete?" She stood with her hand gripping the doorknob, her eyes scanning the road.

"My grandbaby's the best bull riding champion Sul Ross has had in decades. On a full rodeo scholarship, too. He was blessed with natural ability. You ought to see him ride, sometime, if you decide to stick around Alpine."

"Thank you, Ruth, maybe I will. And thanks for all your help." Sidney bit her tongue, keeping her thoughts in check. She'd already seen far more of Ruth's grandson than she cared to.

Before driving away from the Maverick Inn, Sidney secured Mocha's window, all the while reassuring the mare that it wouldn't be much longer before they were settled. In the cab of her truck, doors locked, she took a quick glance at the last photograph she'd taken. She shook her head, thinking that bull riding wasn't the only thing Ruth's grandson was naturally blessed with. Her thumb hovered over the "delete photo" option a moment. She hesitated. Would she need this for evidence? Evidence of what? She wasn't sure. She kept the photo.

CHAPTER 2

Alpine

Passing Sul Ross University, Sidney turned north onto Highway 118. As she drove by the small municipal airport, she made a mental note to check the runway configuration, wondering if *his* Citation X might have room to land. His Falcon Fifty would be doubtful. Her stomach pitched and rolled at the thought of seeing *that* custom jet on the runway.

Chasing twilight, Sidney watched the sun sinking nearer to the horizon. She glanced at Ruth's hand drawn map and eyed the odometer. Road signs that matched the drawing were easy to spot, thanks to Ruth's artful hand. Past the Roadrunner Ranch on the left, then beyond a mile marker sign for Fort Davis, Sidney approached the most obvious landmark. The drawing indicated to turn right at the red, white, and blue Texas flag mailbox just past the Meriwether Ranch Road cutoff. She braked slowly, turning onto what seemed more like a cattle trail than a road.

The truck and horse trailer took up most of the winding caliche lane that twisted into dangerous, blind curves. Sidney took her foot off the accelerator, hoping no one tried to pass on this narrow and rutted track.

"Jeez, this is a butt-puckering drive," she said, carefully negotiating the hairpin curves. Despite the road's narrowness and the difficulty of keeping the truck and trailer in a safe position, at least no one could sneak up on her in a hurry. That thought brought some comfort.

Three more miles of dusty gravel brought Sidney to her destination. On the right side of the road sat a wide entryway marked with two massive granite boulders. Parallel lines of twelve-feet-tall timber posts, each sharpened to a point, flanked the driveway. It looked more like a stockade than the entrance to a ranch. Overhead, a horizontal beam connected the heavy timber posts. From the beam, a carved wooden sign dangled high above the closed, locked gate. The sign matched Ruth's drawing. Both depicted a winged red dragon, talon claws ready for action, a forked tongue snaking from its wide jaws, and an arrow tipped tail curving around powerful haunches.

Sidney slowed, braking to a halt. "Well this looks uninviting. A dragon? Really? How about a sign with a horse, or a Texas star?"

She dialed the cellphone number Ruth had written for her. It went straight to voice mail. She dialed again. Same. After getting out of her truck, she walked up the drive to the locked gate, looking for a security box with an intercom or a press-to-talk button. She pressed, talked, got no response. Looking up, she waved at the security camera hovering over the double padlocked, heavy wrought iron gate.

"Hello? Anyone there?" She pressed the button again for good measure, waiting for a response, then several times more in rapid succession.

Walking back to the horse trailer, she sat on the wheel well and sipped from a bottle of water while contemplating a plan. Mocha poked her head out of the lowered window, dropping hay from her mouth onto Sidney's head.

"Thanks, girl. This hair looks bad enough without your help." She stood and dusted the straws of hay from her head and shoulders.

Mocha stomped in the trailer and whinnied in the way horses do when nervous. Shrill. High-pitched. The trailer rocked back and forth as the agitated mare continued to stomp in the confined space of the interior stall.

"What is it, girl? What's wrong?" From her peripheral vision, she caught a slight movement—dark and silent—creeping through the thick brush. As it drew nearer, she heard twigs snapping and leaves rustling. Closer and closer it came, its low growl vibrating deep within the tangled thicket.

Sidney held her breath. She inched her way toward the cab of her truck where her mace-spray keychain dangled from the ignition switch. The glove compartment held her Taser stun gun. She had not practiced the act of carrying the weapon concealed inside her boot or under her shirt sufficiently enough to feel natural. She swore under her breath, promising herself the next time she felt threatened, her Taser would be within inches of her grasp.

In a rush, a mammoth black creature sprang from the woods. It landed in front of Sidney, blocking her path. Prepared to leap, the animal leaned forward in an attack stance, the hair along its spine bristling on end. Its lips, drawn into a menacing snarl, revealed lethal fangs. Unblinking yellow-gold eyes held her in surveillance.

With slow, deliberate movements, Sidney backed toward the horse trailer to close Mocha's window. With each step she took backward, the creature inched a step closer. Once up against the trailer, Sidney realized she had nowhere to go. She considered making a run for the back of the truck and leaping inside, but the animal was big enough to leap in, too. Thinking quickly, remembering what she'd read about soothing savage beasts, she began humming a lullaby.

After several long moments, well into the second verse, she noticed the animal's posture soften; its tail, once rigid, began a slow, side-to-side wave. Its ears, no longer flattened against its skull, were now pricked in curious attention. Fangs disappeared behind lowered lips. Eyes, though less menacing, were still watchful.

Taking a chance, she held out her hand and crooned in a hushed, soothing voice. "There, now. You're a good dog. Please, be a good dog."

The animal eased closer. Leaning forward on its massive front paws, claws digging into the dirt, it sniffed.

"Holy shit," said Sidney, taking a deep, shaky breath. "If the devil had a dog, you'd be it. But I know the devil. He hates dogs."

The imposing canine wagged its tail as it stepped closer, sniffing Sidney's jeans and boots. It circled around and sniffed her hand again, allowing her to scratch its head and ear. Then the huge dog sat close, leaning its weight into her, heaving a contented sigh.

"So, you know the devil personally, do you," said a voice from behind.

Sidney jumped and spun around, letting fly a string of curse words. The dog jumped too at the sound of its owner's voice. The animal bound around in circles, then dropped its frontend low to the ground, its backend high in the air in the 'let's play' invitation.

"Sorry, ma'am. I didn't mean to frighten you. That's Rex's job, frightening people. Usually, he eats little girls like you."

Sidney's eyes grew wide. She took a step back.

"I'm kidding. Unless you're really Little Red Riding Hood, then all bets are off." The man grinned, seeming to enjoy the situation. "Seriously, it appears he's taken to you. I've never seen him behave this way before."

"He's intimidating." Sidney looked back and forth between the dog and the man; her comment easily applied to either one. "He must weigh a hundred fifty pounds. What is he? Wolf?"

"A hybrid. And good guess. One twenty-five, give or take, depending on how many Red Riding Hoods he's eaten."

"Very funny." She stroked the dog's muzzle, allowing him to lick her hand.

Sidney wondered why she didn't have red lights and warning bells going off about this man. In the back of her mind, she knew she must keep her guard up, despite the fact that this wild creature seemed to adore and respect its owner. Gathering her wits, she assessed the situation, as well as the man standing in front of her. She was quick and thorough, just as she'd practiced in her career. As a psychologist and a jury consultant, it was her job to determine a potential juror's influence on a case, and if that juror might be hiding his true beliefs. Identifying the liars was a valuable skill, both on and off the job.

Despite the cool, late afternoon temperature, the man standing in front of her wore only running shorts and a tight USMC T-shirt. He was muscular and well built, though not the bulky, weightlifter type. He moved with a grace more like that of a dancer, but the dancers she'd known didn't have ghastly scars on their legs from what appeared to be bullet wounds.

Good looking—sexy, really—but not the typical movie star handsome type. Pushing six feet with dark brown hair cut military short, and he projected confidence. She guessed him to be in his late thirties or early forties. His manner was direct, yet not threatening, and she noted his use of humor to diffuse this tense situation. Easy smile, charming dimples. Intense, smoky gray eyes—but sad eyes. And, his dog-creature worshiped him.

"I rescued Rex, plus a dozen more, from a puppy mill that breeds these German Shepard-wolf hybrid trophy dogs. Owners who wouldn't take the time to learn how to handle these animals would send them back. The puppy mill would then resell them, and so on." Markus gave a hand signal and the dog dropped to the ground on his belly and froze, awaiting the next command.

"Oh, poor Rex," she said, the thought of puppy mills making her cringe.

"I found good homes for the others. Rex needed some serious rehab, so I ended up keeping him. He was too unpredictable to rehome."

"He's magnificent. I'm Sidney McQueen, by the way. I'm looking for a Mr. Yeager. Yeager's Stables? Ruth at the

Maverick Inn pointed me in this direction. I tried calling—"

"Yeah. Cellphone coverage sucks out here. I'm Markus Yeager. You've found the right place. What can I do for you?" He held out his hand.

"I was expecting someone older." She shook his hand, returning the firm grip, noticing the rock-hard callouses on his fingers and along the outer edges of his palms.

"I wasn't expecting anyone at all." His serious expression was transformed when he smiled, his dimples giving him a youthful appearance. However, the expression dissolved quickly, reverting to its somber state. "So, I guess we're even."

"You weren't expecting me? I met a friend of yours in Fort Worth. Trevor Nolan? He told me about you and suggested I come to Alpine. He was supposed to email or call you." Sidney hadn't heard from Trevor either, which made her sick with worry. She chose to keep *that* information to herself, at least until she figured out whether or not she could trust this Markus character. Her gut said "yes," but trusting her gut this past year had almost proved deadly.

"Trevor Nolan?" Markus shook his head, his expression curious, yet puzzled. "Hell, I haven't heard from Trevor in months."

"Yes, and Ruth at the Maverick Inn also said she'd send an email to let you know to expect me. I'm gathering that you've not been in front of a computer in a while. I'm pretty intuitive."

"Intuition's a nice asset, if one is perceptive enough not to disregard it." Markus ran his fingers through his sweaty hair as he steadied his eyes on hers. "Repairing fences and checking feeders left no time for sitting at a computer today."

"Any excuse will do for staying outside on a day like today?" asked Sidney, understanding the feeling full well.

Looking down at his running shorts, he caught her meaning. "Rex and I love being in the woods. If I don't take him for his daily run, he goes a bit stir crazy."

"I'm a runner. I can identify." An overwhelming sense

that if she didn't take off running at that very moment—running and not stopping for anything—*she* might be the one to go crazy.

"Rex got distracted. Something caught his attention and he took off. Otherwise, I'd have been back at the lodge by now, probably looking at my computer."

"Sorry. I hope I didn't get him in trouble." Sidney called Rex over, giving both ears a good scratch.

"Nah—no worries. What can I help you with?" Markus looked on as his wolf-dog bonded with this complete stranger, and he shook his head, his expression registering disbelief.

"I'm needing a place to stay for the night, maybe longer, if it's a good fit. My trailer has living quarters I can sleep in. I just need a place to park it and to put up a small portable pen."

"I can do better than that. There's plenty of room in the barn, stalls with run-in paddocks. You're welcome to the caretaker's apartment above the barn."

"An apartment?"

"It hasn't been used in months. It's probably a little musty, but it's nice. How long are you planning on staying?"

"I'm not planning on anything, yet, just pondering. I'll take you up on the offer of the barn for Mocha, but I think I'd rather sleep in my trailer, for tonight anyway, while it's still light and I can see what I'm doing." Sidney took note of the orange and pink streaks melting across the western sky, while to the east, a few stars made a faint appearance.

"There is electricity. All the modern conveniences. Even indoor plumbing." The boyish charm of his smile contrasted starkly against the sad intensity of his eyes, as if both features belonged to two separate people.

Sidney laugh nervously. "I'm sure it'd be fine. I just like to be settled before it gets dark."

"Suit yourself. I'll open the gate. After you pull through, I'll hop in and ride with you, show you the way to the barn, if that's okay."

"Yes, sure. Come on, Rex. You ride shotgun." She

opened the door and the big dog jumped into the cab. He settled his haunches on the seat, his front legs on the floorboard.

"Don't embarrass me, boy," said Markus as he sprinted to unlock the gate.

After the truck and trailer cleared the entryway and the padlocks were secured, Markus slid into the rear passenger seat behind Rex, giving the dog a scratch and a pat. "The drive curves around that tree line to your right, then you'll see the outdoor riding arena. Beyond that are the stables."

"Okay."

"So, you heart scuba diving? Your bumper sticker—I noticed it when you pulled through the gate." With his index fingers, Markus drew in the air the shape of a heart.

"Oh," she glanced in the rearview mirror. "Of course. Love it. My favorite hobby, besides horses." Sidney's flat voice sounded unconvincing.

"Really? I love scuba diving, too. Australia. Belize. Fiji. Dubrovnik, if you're not dodging bullets. Where's your favorite place to dive?"

"Oh—uh—Belize, for sure. Good water, there, in Belize." Something about his way of questioning made Sidney uncomfortable, almost as uncomfortable as her memory of coming close to drowning in Belize.

"Yeah, the Blue Hole. Fantastic. That sucker's one hundred forty-five or so meters deep. Challenging, but worth the effort. How deep are you rated?"

"Rated?"

"Yeah, how deep do you dive? Eighteen meters, thirty meters?"

She glanced again in the rearview mirror and caught Markus studying her. The feeling he was reading her, challenging and testing her, caused her breath to catch. Shifting her eyes straight ahead, she put on a casual air. "I'm a beginner —more into snorkeling than into scuba."

"You hate it."

"I—hate it."

"So, why pretend? Why the "I heart scuba" sticker?" Markus's voice was as smooth as a detective interrogating a serial killer.

"It's a long story. I'd much rather ride than dive, anyway. So, how many horses do you have at your stables? And Ruth mentioned something about a hunting lodge, too?" Not too obvious with the smooth changing of the subject, she told herself. But one glance in the rearview mirror at his amused expression told her otherwise.

"There're about ten or so locals who board their horses here. I have twenty of my own I use to pack clients out for overnight or weekend hunts. Off season, I lead mounted sightseeing and photography expeditions into the Davis Mountains." He shifted his position in the back seat, allowing him to view Sidney's face from both the rearview and side view mirrors.

"You keep your horses busy." That he watched her from all angles was not lost on her. A studier of people knew when she was being studied. Her eyes met his in the mirror for a brief moment before she looked away, chilled by the hint of something dangerous in the intensity of his stare.

"Drive past the arena. The stables are just around the bend."

"Okay." On one side of the arena, Sidney noticed a ramped platform such as those used to allow a person in a wheelchair to be placed in a saddle. "Do you cater to disabled riders?"

"Sometimes."

Sidney waited for more of an explanation. It was not forthcoming.

Markus nodded toward the rearview mirror. "Do you have a dog? Is that its collar hanging there?"

"I used to, once upon a time." The black and red plaid collar reminded her of more than just the skin-and-bones yellow Labrador she'd found in Breckenridge, Colorado. It also served as a reminder, every time she looked in the rearview mirror and saw it dangling there, for her to watch her back.

"I'm so sorry." He didn't ask or say anything more. He could see the tears welling in Sidney's eyes.

And she didn't offer anything more.

Behind the tree line, the stables came into view. Situated in a "U" shaped footprint, the fieldstone and rough cedar plank building housed twenty stalls along each parallel arm. The front facing section contained tack and feed rooms, restrooms, a vet and wash rack, and an office. Adjacent to the office, the focal point was a seating area for guests to view the arena. An apartment on the second floor overlooked the indoor arena situated in the interior of the structure.

"Wow, this looks impressive. Mocha won't know what to do, staying in a place this opulent."

"Mocha's been traveling in style. That's a nice trailer you have." Markus twisted around in the seat, looking out the back window at the trailer and strumming his fingers on the headrest. "Is it my imagination, or did I notice two horses in there when you pulled through the gate? Won't you need two stalls?"

"No, just one. The '*horse*' in the first stall is a fake, you know, like the full-sized plastic replicas tack stores use to display saddles and blankets. It's a long story." She waved her hand in casual dismissal. "Is it okay if I park there?" Sidney pointed to the opposite side of the barn where several empty trailers were lined in a neat row.

"Either side's fine," he said, letting slide her quick dismissal about the fake horse and her second awkward segue into a change of subject. "There're monitored cameras all around—you should feel safe. I've never had any mischief or theft out here, but I won't take any chances."

Sidney backed the truck and trailer into place and unloaded her horse while Markus grabbed two buckets and a bag of sweet oats she had indicated were in the trailer's storage compartment. He led them into the barn, taking them to the first empty stall on the west wing.

"This corner stall has the largest turn-out paddock, which looks like your girl will appreciate. That's one tall mare. Is she a Thoroughbred?"

"She's a Thoroughbred, Hanoverian cross. Fearless, super easy to ride, and she can jump the moon."

"Are you a competitive jumper?" Markus eyed the leggy mare with admiration.

"When I have the time. Thanks for the roomy stall and paddock. Mocha loves to roll."

"Sure. It used to belong to my stallion, who is no longer with us. You can also see this side of the barn from where your trailer's parked."

"Thank you. This is perfect. I'm sorry about your stallion. How long ago?"

"Last year. Hunting camp. Mountain lion. End of story."

"Oh my God," she gasped. "The taxidermy mount in the Maverick Inn?"

"That's the one. Well, if you don't need anything else, Rex and I'll leave you two to get settled. It's another half mile's jog to the lodge."

"Want me to drive you?"

"Thanks, no, you get settled. I'd rather run. I'll be here at sunup to feed. My barn crew is off until after Thanksgiving, so it's nice and quiet around here. The down side is all the chores are mine for a while. See you in the morning."

She watched as Markus backed out of the stall and toward the door as he spoke, as if he were suddenly in a big hurry to leave. That was fine with her. She wanted to hurry and finish her barn chores, too. Get inside her trailer. Lock the door.

"Sounds good. I'll feed and brush Mocha, get all this road dust off her before I turn in. See you tomorrow."

Sidney removed Mocha's black and gold sheet and draped it over the stall's door. The mare dropped into the deep pine shavings, rolling like a dog scratching her back. Standing and shaking from nose to tail, she sent up a cloud of dust.

With a currycomb in one hand and a brush in the other,

she groomed the dusty horse while Mocha munched her oats and hay. Sidney kept one eye on the western facing stall window and on the darkening horizon, the sinking sun no longer visible in the sky.

CHAPTER 3

Alpine

Markus hurried to Sidney's truck and silently opened the rear passenger side door that he'd rigged with his gate key to remain unlocked. He opened the front passenger door. Inside the glove compartment, he found a pink leather holster with a shiny Taser that appeared brand new. Behind was a matching accessory bag. He unzipped it, his eyes widening at the discovery of what was inside—twenty individual bundles of one hundred dollar bills. If each bundle held fifty bills like the one he thumbed through, a hundred thousand in cash meant serious business.

A passport bearing the name *'Sidney A. Knight'* was secured inside the accessory bag with a yellow sticky note reading, *'Change ASAP.'* The photo resembled the Sidney McQueen he'd just met, despite a few alterations to her appearance. The truck's registration papers and insurance card were issued in the name of a Trust. After carefully putting everything back into place, he depressed the door lock button, shutting the door without making a sound.

As he sprinted to the hunting lodge, thoughts tumbled around in his head. Who the hell is Sidney McQueen, or Sidney Knight? He'd seen better disguises on cheap Russian spies— even on amateur American spies, for Pete's sake. And how did the Mountain Princess Trust fit in?

After locking Rex in his kennel, Markus took the stairs

two at a time to the suite he occupied at the end of the hall. The other dozen rooms were empty until the day after Thanksgiving when the first of his deer hunting clients would arrive. He turned on the faucets for a quick shower and let steam fill the room. The hot water washed over him as he collected his thoughts.

He reflected on his movements—his actions—the past days, months, years. Had it been two, going on three already? People he'd met. Conversations he'd had. Clues he might have missed. Had he become complacent? Too confident his '*John Walker*' identity had been buried and forgotten? Markus knew he'd been as careful as if he were still an active member of the Company. It was unlikely someone used Trevor to get to him— Trevor didn't know about his past as '*John Walker*,' Trevor only knew the real Markus Yeager. Surely no one had sent this woman here.

After toweling off, he pulled on a pair of black jeans and a black, long sleeved shirt, checking the clip on his custom Glock before tucking it into his waistband. With his laptop powered up, he clicked open his email, scanned down the inbox, read the brief note from Ruth at the Maverick Inn, and scanned farther until he saw one from Trevor.

> *Hey Markus, I'm sending someone your way. A damsel in distress. She's in serious trouble. I won't go into detail—she'll tell you what she wants when she wants, but bottom line is she's fleeing a dangerous domestic situation —husband's a monster, and that's being kind. Among other suspicious activities, her soon-to-be-ex-husband is involved in south of the border pharmaceuticals—no Rx required. My cellphone was compromised along with hers. Long story. I'll get in touch with you as soon as I've got a new phone number. I just met her (Sidney Knight), but instinct tells me she's the real deal. Mama concurred. I'm positive you*

will, too. Otherwise, I would not have sent her your way.

Watch your back.

Later buddy, Trevor

What the hell have you gotten me into, Trevor?

Markus leaned back in his chair and stared at the monitor, the words of the email a blur. Leaning forward, he read the message again, the knot in his gut tightening each time he skimmed the short note. He knew this was way over Trevor's head. Trevor had some experience and was a smart guy, but young; how reliable were his instincts? His mother may have concurred, but how could either of them truly understand the sad reality of what humans were capable?

They haven't seen what I've seen.

Trevor's email said her name was 'Knight,' yet she'd introduced herself as 'McQueen.' Was it possible that someone connected the dots between 'John Walker' and Markus Yeager? If so, they could have connected Trevor to Markus. But who, and how? He closed his laptop, grabbed his night vision goggles, and slipped outside. Sprinting along the deer trail, moving quieter than a shadow, he took the back path through the woods that led to the stables.

A light was on in Sidney's trailer. Ten feet away but hidden in the inky darkness, Markus caught a fragment of a glimpse of her behind the trailer's lowered blinds. In such close proximity, his night vision goggles were unnecessary.

Unexpectedly, as if the security cord broke free, the door's blinds flung upward. Framed in the window, she stood at the small kitchen counter as she poured a glass of wine, her tomboy clothes having been cast aside. She wore only her bra and panties. Very sexy, lacy, see-through bra and panties.

Markus sucked in his breath, held it. *Damn. Wasn't expecting this.*

Sidney dashed to the trailer door's full-length window and stretched her arm up, struggling with the distance as she reached for the cord to close the blinds. The end of the cord dangled just out of reach. Up on tiptoes, she managed to grasp hold of it. She gave the cord a tug and shuttered the blinds closed, just before giving the man in the shadows a full-frontal view.

Markus eased closer. He slipped behind the trailer and came up the far side, his back pressed against the aluminum siding. Out in the paddock, Mocha whinnied. A horse in the barn returned her greeting. More nickering. More whinnying. Soon, several horses joined in, a cacophonous welcome to the new mare on the block.

Markus moved closer to the barn's west wall, muttering curses under his breath for the horses to be quiet.

The trailer door opened a crack. Sidney peered out, inching the door open a bit more, sweeping a flashlight over the darkness. She aimed the beam toward the paddock adjoining Mocha's stall. The golden light settled on a crouching, dark figure that melted into the shadows. She shrieked and slammed the door shut.

Markus slinked into the barn and hurried to the feed room, grabbing the bucket of horse treats. The night vision goggles were shoved into a drawer in the supply cabinet. A red and white Sul Ross rodeo team jacket hung from a hook by the door. He shrugged it on as he moved swiftly, flicking on the main overhead light and covering the ground to Mocha's stall with long strides. Stepping inside, he closed the stall door.

Flashlight in one hand, baseball bat in the other, Sidney burst into the barn. She stopped short when she saw Markus standing in her horse's stall. Mocha, munching on a pile of alfalfa treats, looked up and nickered.

"I wasn't expecting to see you here." Her voice sounded high-pitched and breathless. "Something spooked the horses. I saw—I don't know—maybe a mountain lion in the shadows. It ran away when I shined my light on it."

"I heard the horses, too, and thought I'd come check on things. I was out for a walk, anyway." He swallowed hard, imagining the sexy bra and panties hidden under the gray gym sweats she'd pulled on. "It may have been a stray dog. I didn't see a mountain lion. But you never know, after what happened."

"Exactly." Sidney relaxed her grip on the bat. "Nice letter jacket. It seems everyone in town wears one."

"Not my usual attire. It belongs to one of my barn staff."

"I gathered that. Unless your name is Aubrey and you are the 2012 Women's Barrel Racing Champion." Sidney pointed to the insignia and logos on the jacket.

"Ah. Aubrey. She's fast, all right." Markus's expression gave nothing away.

"Is that so?" Sidney raised an eyebrow, wondering if he meant fast in the rodeo arena, or someplace else.

Markus gestured with his chin toward Sidney's bat. "If there had been a lion, were you going to beat it to death? A gun would offer better protection."

"That's true. But I have a fear of guns. Actually, it's beyond fear. It's paranoia. It wouldn't be safe, owning a gun but being afraid to handle it."

"I teach courses in gun safety. I can help you turn your fear into a healthy respect."

Offering to help this woman learn to shoot a gun when his spy radar was on high alert made perfect sense, he told himself. If she was an operative, she would know damn well how to use a gun and her coy ruse would soon be made evident. It wouldn't take much to challenge her bluff, if she *was* bluffing.

"Thanks. I'll consider your offer." She turned to leave, then paused. "I've been told you're the person to come to for protection. For my own personal reasons, I'd like to know more about you. Trusting people has become, problematic, for me."

"I understand."

"I just opened a bottle of wine. Would you humor me and share a glass, share some information about yourself? Before you go back to your lodge?"

"All right. Sure. A glass would be nice. Before I go back to my lodge." No hint of an invitation to stay longer, he noted.

Not that he would have.

Three glasses later, Markus stood to leave. "Thank you, Sidney. It's been an enjoyable, enlightening evening."

"You've enlightened me about the glories of Alpine. However, I'm disappointed I didn't learn more about you. That was the purpose of this exercise." Sidney pushed herself out of the chair, her body's slight sway hinting at the empty bottle of wine.

"Conversations have a funny way of taking their own course." Markus set the empty bottle of wine on the kitchen counter.

Together they walked to the door, the tight quarters making it difficult to not touch or not bump as they said good night. The image of her in her lacy lingerie that revealed intimate secrets tugged at his mind. He decided to play his card.

"May I make a bold, personal observation?" he asked, his expression once again giving nothing away. Though it was a question, he was prepared to make a statement.

"Yes. Be bold." Sidney was feeling bold. Wine did that to her.

"Red freckles on your nose and emerald green eyes— I'm guessing that blond is not the color you were born with." Markus imagined her again in those see-through panties, knowing full well that the best evidence, this woman's unwitting intimate disclosure was a clue he should keep to himself. He would try to throw her off balance, to make her falter. See if there was a flaw in her story. A chink in the armor.

"Wow. You're either bold or rude." Sidney took a step back, giving him an arched-brow, wary look. "If not blond, what color do you think my hair is?"

"Oh, I'd say you're definitely a redhead," he smirked.

"What? You want a gold star for guessing?"

"What makes you think I'm guessing?"

"Look, I don't know what your game is, but I'm not amused. What are you trying to—?"

"I love red hair. Don't you?"

"I—yes—most of the time." Sidney shoved both palms outward in a physical blockade, backing away. "You need to leave. Get out of my trailer."

"Why cover it up? You can take that off, if you want."

"Excuse me? Take what off?"

"That silly blond wig." Markus spun out the door, leaving it and her mouth wide open.

*****

Upstairs in his private suite, Markus pushed a wall tapestry aside, revealing a door hidden in the wood paneling that could be seen only if one knew where to look. He located the four secret strips of wood and pressed them in the required sequential pattern, each for the correct length of time. The wooden panels shifted outward, allowing the bulletproof door to slip silently into the wall. He stepped inside the stark room large enough for only a table with a computer and monitor, a state-of-the-art printer, and a shredder. He secured the door behind him.

He slipped a key from his pocket and opened the top drawer of the desk, taking from it another key hidden underneath the drawer. That key opened a small, rectangular black box containing an encrypted one-way phone capable only of dialing out. With the coded numbers entered, he waited, gave the password when asked, and when prompted further, replied with his request.

"Need background check ASAP on female, age thirty-four, current residence Fort Worth, Texas. Name on passport is Sidney Knight, spelled K, N, I, G, H, T. May also go by Sidney McQueen. See what you might find on a Mountain Princess Trust, while you're at it. Need info as well on her husband, no name available. Suspected of Mexican cartel involvement. Acknowledge."

A pause—Markus pressed the off button and re-secured the phone into its black box. The same steps were repeated in reverse order until he secured the door and pulled the tapestry into place. It swayed back and forth on its black silk cord before slowing to a stop.

Made of black silk, the hand-woven piece was simple, and the painted lettering in bold white script was written in Japanese Kanji. *"A warrior is worthless unless he rises above others and stands strong in the midst of a storm."*

Below the script and spanning the width of the tapestry was a white circle bordered in red. Painted in the circle was the same fiery red dragon that hung over the gated entryway to his ranch. Markus read the quote aloud as he did each time he exited the secret room, his hands pressed together, body bowed at the waist. Then, with eyes closed, he silently repeated the words painted on the tapestry. He visualized the petite figure who had crafted it, the slender hands that wrote the words. He saw clearly the woman with the long black hair who had brought to life the sacred message—who had inspired the man he would become.

CHAPTER 4

Fort Worth (One Week Earlier)

Sidney sat at a bistro table on the rooftop patio of Reata's Restaurant. She gazed over the railing at the swarm of holiday shoppers crawling the pavement far below. It seemed to her that everyone was sipping coffees and laughing and chatting—an entire cross-section of downtown Fort Worth behaving as if it didn't have a care in the world.

Sidney let out a doleful sigh. She used to count herself among them. She checked her watch for the fourth time and drained the last of her margarita, running the tip of her tongue around the rim of the glass and licking it clean of the lime-flavored salt. Her platinum Rolex strapped to her wrist confirmed again what she already knew.

Five o'clock. Happy hour. How ironic.

The sound of the elevator doors whooshing open and sliding closed drew her attention to the alcove across from the bar. Whether male or female, every patron sitting at the bar turned and stared as Sidney's cousin, Jessi, made a grand entrance. An inch shy of six feet and rail thin, she wore her long black hair in her signature style, a tousled ponytail. Jessica Cordoba was used to turning heads. Her chiseled bone structure and full lips made her a favorite with the photographers and makeup artists who worked for the Dallas modeling agency that had represented her for the past dozen years. Despite being thirty-four years old and well past the prime age of most models in the industry, Jessica Shea Cordoba was in high demand.

"Hey, Sid, sorry I'm late," Jessi hugged her cousin in a warm embrace. "The shoot ran long. Same story. They always run long. I finally put my foot down and said 'enough.' I mean, how many takes does one really need of a white sofa, a bottle of vodka, and a naked girl draped in a mink coat? If the art director can't get it shot in six hours, he's not going to get it at all. I knew you were waiting for me and that your nerves must have been on edge."

"No problem. I'm grateful that you're here. Where's Rafael? He's still coming, isn't he?"

Jessi bit her bottom lip and shook her head. "That was the plan, I know, but we had a big fight about it this morning. Rafe said he couldn't risk possible repercussions. Thanks to the high-roller clients Winston sends his way, Rafe's import-export business has doubled in revenue this year."

"I thought it was the other way around, that Rafe's firm sent clients to Winston." Sidney shrugged away her confusion.

"Either way, he's not coming." Jessi fidgeted with the ring on her left finger. "Don't worry about it, Sid. We can handle this without him."

"I can't believe he's putting business before family. And today of all days." Sidney pressed her fingers against her temples, feeling certain this was a bad omen.

"Winston and Rafe go way back, and he's considered Winston part of the *family* since you two got married. Also, Rafe introduced you to Winston in the first place—I'm sure that makes him feel awkward about being here today."

The memory of that first meeting, when she'd walked into Winston's law office escorted by her cousin-in-law, seemed eons ago, yet it was only last year. Rafael had been insistent that the two were perfect for each other and she should meet his longtime friend and attorney. Although she had barely had time to get used to being a widow, she'd agreed. If anything, it might turn out to be profitable for her jury consulting business. To break the ice, Winston had called her a few days before they actually met in person. It was a pleasant conversation, and he asked her for advice on jury management. He read many of her articles, he said, and his comments about what she'd written had been eloquent, knowledgeable, and flattering. In fact, he was so excessively complimentary—to the point of obsequiousness—that she had a momentary urge to call off the meeting. Sidney shuddered at the memory.

"I wish I could blame this mess on your husband and his poor cupid skills," said Sidney. But this is mine. I own this. I should have listened to my gut. Now, I'm *unmessing* my life."

"Rafe meant well," offered Jessi. "But you're doing the right thing, and I support you one hundred percent. On the bright side, you don't have to worry about how to support yourself."

"Fortunately, money has never been an issue."

"Speaking about money, Rafe must be raking in the dough with his new client in Spain. Even though he's got plenty of other international clients, he insists this is The One that will set us up for life. It's either ego or avarice." Jessi wagged her finger. "Look at this ridiculous ring. When I refused to put it on, he got pissed. It's so ostentatious—I'm embarrassed to wear it."

"Jesus Christ, Jessi. That's huge." Sidney eyed the square yellow diamond set in platinum and surrounded by a cluster of white baguettes. "At least it can double as a weapon. You could kill someone if you punched them with a left hook."

Jessi laughed nervously. "The thought has crossed my mind. Besides his becoming so materialistic, Rafe is behaving like a jealous maniac lately. He accuses me of flirting with other men, even with other women, for Christ's sake. I mean, if he doesn't give me a little breathing room, this pretentious ring *may* become a weapon."

"Seriously Jessi—are you guys having problems again?"

"Not really problems, just—issues. But, I can deal with it. It's not half as bad as what you've been going through. Anyway, since we've been talking about starting a family, Rafe has been, I don't know, nicer?"

"Rafael is a dick. Sorry, but he is." Sidney waved the waitress over and ordered another margarita. "Top shelf, please, double shot of tequila, and a sparkling water for my cousin. And if you have one, a brawny male who has the *cojones* to sit at our table while I serve my husband with divorce papers. My cousin's husband was supposed to act the role of the brawny male, but turns out he's an asshole who puts money before family."

The waitress snorted. "If a brawny male with *cojones* was a menu item, our 'take out' crew wouldn't be able to keep up with the orders. Chips and salsa? Appetizers?"

"I couldn't eat. Do you want anything, Jessi? A leaf of lettuce?" Sidney laughed at their old joke, knowing what Jessi would order.

"Buffalo rib eye, rare. Loaded baked potato, extra butter. Don't come near me with a salad. Instead of the sparkling water, I'll take a glass of your house pinot noir. I might as well indulge. With what's planned for this evening's agenda, this may be my last supper."

Sidney tried to shrug off the image of da Vinci's painting of The Last Supper. But she had no answer as to who might play the role of Judas. She watched as Jessi spoke to the waitress, and she noticed how tired her cousin appeared. Or, maybe Jessi's expression was more worried than tired.

"Hey, are you okay?" Sidney leaned in and gave Jessi's arm a squeeze after the waitress left with their order. "You seem a bit—I don't know—tired?"

"I am tired, but I'll be fine when this advertising campaign is over. Long hours." She returned the gesture, giving Sid's arm a squeeze. "So, everything is in place? You've taken care of all the details? The money, the bank, the safety deposit box, a post office box, a hotel for tonight until you can get your stuff moved in with Rafe and me?"

"Everything's in order. I moved Mocha today to a private barn in Weatherford a friend-of-a-friend owns. I left the truck and trailer Winston bought for me at the ranch for him to keep. I took a taxi into town and then rented a car."

"Good," said Jessi, nodding. "What else?"

"I've cashed out everything I could get my hands on that was mine to cash out—what was mine before we got married. I put into the vault at my new bank the valuables I knew Winston would go ape shit over—the gifts he'd given me and nothing more. All that remains at the ranch means nothing to me. He can have it. I'm walking away with my life and my horse. I don't care about the rest. I'll let my attorney hash it out."

"I'm sure Winston will represent himself."

"Of course, with a full team of assistants at his beck and call. He'll leave no stone unturned when it comes to winning. I've seen him in action too many times in court. He'll play dirty. That's why I hired Aleck Stavros."

"Thank God he was willing to take your case. I was worried that no attorney between Dallas and Fort Worth would touch it, knowing they'd be going against *him*."

"Aleck Stavros isn't intimidated by anyone, let alone Winston. He said he'd welcome the opportunity to face off with *him* again." Sidney sipped her margarita, steeling her resolve. Winston's reputation was well known, but it was based on unequal parts of respect and the fear of retaliation, the latter part of the equation tipping the scales in its favor.

*****

Charles Winston Knight, III acquired things. One thing he wished to acquire was the stunning redhead sitting in his office. The cousin of his business associate's wife, she was everything Rafael had said she was, and more. She was a brilliant psychologist. That might come in handy.

Prior to entering the working world, the brainy beauty had been a doctoral student at Southern Methodist University's School of Psychology in Dallas. Her PhD thesis, *'Neuroscience-based Credibility Assessment for Jury Management – Is Your Juror a Liar?'* had led to numerous articles being published in legal journals. As a result, her services as a juror manager kept her in high demand. She charged accordingly.

C. Winston Knight became a regular client.

The first time Sidney consulted for Winston's firm, it was a personal injury case in which his firm's client, the plaintiff, was suing a drunk driver who'd had multiple DWI's. It should have been a simple matter of putting a multiple offender behind bars. Sidney soon learned that life in Winston's world was seldom simple.

It had been mid-morning, just after ten o'clock, when the plaintiff and his wife, experiencing car trouble, pulled over to the side of the road. The husband went to the front of the car to lift the hood and check the engine while the wife had gone to the rear of the car to retrieve the orange emergency cones from the trunk. It was a bright clear morning with very little traffic. The date was December twenty-fifth.

The elderly gentleman didn't remember the crash. He couldn't recall hearing a horn honking, or, brakes screeching. Since there'd been no evidence of skid marks, there'd probably been no attempt to stop. What he remembered was waking up in a field of grass several yards away from his car and seeing scattered about him the wrapped Christmas presents they were taking to their grandchildren. The car was slammed so hard from behind, the impact so crushing, that it severed his wife's legs just above both knees. She bled to death before paramedics arrived. The drunk driver fled the scene, leaving behind his crumpled, bloody license plate as evidence.

The passion and intelligence Winston employed in his arguments, the way he had the jury crying and hanging on his every word, the charisma he displayed in and out of the courtroom, impressed Sidney. The genuine tenderness Winston showed to the grieving husband moved her. Like the female jurors she selected for the case, Sidney was smitten. He won her over, too.

However, winning the case wasn't enough for Winston —justice was not yet served. While out of jail on bond and awaiting an appeal, the defendant was brutally beaten, his legs broken, and both of his eyes gouged out. Whoever did it made sure the man would never again get behind the wheel of an automobile.

Police suspected two drug-thugs who happened to be former clients of Winston's; however, due to lack evidence, no one was ever charged for the crime. Although he denied any involvement, Winston was emphatic that the drunk driver got exactly what he deserved, no matter who inflicted the punishment. He argued that the cash settlement the insurance company paid wouldn't give the old man his wife back.

Sidney ignored her internal red flags. She'd seen Winston speaking to the two whom police suspected—had seen money exchange hands and whispered words nodded to. She asked Winston point-blank if he was involved in any way with the attack. She accepted his tear-filled apology that followed his angry and vile denial during a loud argument that ended with her against a wall, him in her face yelling at her to never again accuse him of misconduct.

Three months later, after a tumultuous romance, she was Mrs. C. Winston Knight. It was supposed to have been a simple weekend get-away—a mini-vacation. But when they arrived in Lake Tahoe, a short and sexy Modern Bride wedding dress just her size was hanging in the closet. He had planned everything— flowers, cake, champagne, preacher, and a diamond ring as big as a doorknob.

When Sidney protested, saying she wasn't ready, wasn't sure if marriage was what she wanted, his anger flared. "After all I've done—this is the thanks I get? When you're in love, marriage is the next logical step. I've gone to all this trouble to surprise you, and you're going to embarrass and hurt me by turning me down?"

She admitted to having deep feelings for him—but the word 'love' had been difficult for her to say. Beyond the initial animal attraction to a handsome man, Sidney was attracted to his brilliant legal mind. She respected his ability to debate any topic—although he *did* always insist on having the last word.

But it was his carefree spontaneity out of the courtroom and his enthusiasm for living life to the fullest that she had fallen for.

He made her laugh. But, he also made her cry, something she had not experienced in her previous marriage. Life with Peter Dollar had been devoid of emotion, devoid of a passionate connection that Sidney craved and Peter avoided.

Winston insisted she change her name, despite her logical arguments against it. "This is my third marriage," she reasoned. "Changing my name is such a hassle. My professional career, the few patients I still see, getting them used to a different name—"

"If you love me, you'll change your name," he had cajoled. Then, when the cajoling and pleading and pouting and giving her the silent treatment all failed to persuade her, he resorted to shouting. "Goddammit. I don't want to be introduced as Winston Knight and his wife, Sidney Dollar. I want to be introduced as Mr. and Mrs. Winston Knight. You must still love your dead husband. Otherwise, you'd want to share my name."

Though she denied still harboring feelings for Peter, it was no use, especially when the subject of starting a family came up—he didn't want his children having "Knight hyphen Dollar" for a last name.

With tears in his eyes, he'd appealed in a sorrowful tone, "I want you to be proud of me—proud of who I am—proud to be called Mrs. Winston Knight. If you're ashamed of me and my last name, why did you marry me?"

Sidney wavered. She was learning that in order to maintain a sense of control over her own decisions, it was critical to pick wisely which battles to fight. She reasoned with herself that changing her name wouldn't alter her identity. Resigned, yet resentful, she chose to concede to his attempts to manipulate the situation. What meaning was there in a name, after all?

They had flown to Lake Tahoe on his favorite private jet, the custom Falcon Fifty. Staying in an acquaintance's mansion overlooking the lake, they argued the entire weekend after his big surprise wasn't as romantically accepted as he anticipated.

Nothing she did was right, or good enough. Her dress was too tight, too short, too pink, even though he'd bought it for her. She flirted with the busboy. She texted her cousin when she should be paying attention to him. He preferred scotch before dinner, cognac after—she should've known that by now. Her clothes in the closet crowded his freshly pressed shirts; her toiletries took up too much space in the bathroom. Her easy use of vulgar language grated on him—ladies shouldn't talk that way. The heart-shaped rock he found on their walk and presented to her wasn't given sufficient praise—so he threw it in the lake. She wanted to go dancing after dinner, he didn't. There was a scene in front of the country club, loud and ugly, and people had stared.

As soon as the jet touched down at Meacham Field in Fort Worth, bringing them back home, Winston left for his downtown law office, Sidney to her home office. She called her cousin before unpacking, thinking her suitcases might stay packed, that she might be leaving.

"Jessi, I've made a huge mistake. I need out of this marriage. Winston has some serious issues. I mean—serious. I'm so stupid. How could I not have seen? Hell—I'm a *psychologist*."

"You're not stupid, Sid. You were vulnerable."

"I can spot a juror lying from a mile away, yet I was blind to my own husband's lies. And his being dishonest is the lesser of the issues."

"I'm sorry, Sid. I don't know what to say. Why isn't there a fairy tale ending for every '*I do*'?"

"Why isn't there a Patron Saint of You Should Have Known the Fuck Better?"

"Don't beat yourself up over a mistake."

"It's my third, *my third*, mistake. Three strikes, I'm out."

"Your first doesn't count. You were eighteen and it lasted a day, thanks to Grandfather getting it annulled quickly. The second wasn't a mistake. We all loved Peter, but he didn't love himself. You confided to me that your marriage was empty —loveless. You were on the verge of divorce when he committed suicide."

"It may have been an accident. Guns go off sometimes when they're being cleaned."

"Sid…"

"I know…"

Sidney resolved to not give up on the marriage. Surely, she could put every effort into making it a success. Perhaps this was how relationships between husbands and wives were, in real life. She was a jury consultant, not a marriage counselor, and certainly not a relationship expert. Anyway, the only happy marriage she'd ever witnessed was between her grandparents. From what she remembered, even her parents' relationship had been rocky. She decided she would give it at least a year. At that point, she'd know whether or not being Mrs. C. Winston Knight, III was sustainable. If it didn't work out, a divorce wasn't the end of the world; it was simply the end of a relationship. And after every ending was a new beginning.

*****

The waitress brought their order, and Jessi cut into her buffalo rib eye. "Perfect. So rare that if I slapped it, it'd start mooing again, or whatever sound buffalo make." She lifted her wine glass, "Here's to you mooing again, too, Sid, and getting your life back."

"I'll drink to that." They clinked glasses, and Sidney's margarita tumbler let loose a sprinkling of lime green salt onto the tablecloth.

When Sidney heard the sound of the elevator doors opening and closing, a shiver ran up and down her spine. Without looking, she knew who would be rounding the corner by the familiar sound of his deliberate, unhurried boot steps. He stopped along the way to greet and glad-hand business associates and acquaintances, laugh at jokes, give a friendly slap on the back, a hug and an air-kiss, before making his way to the corner table at the rail.

Standing with his arms crossed in front of him, he tilted his head and peered down at Sidney, frowning. His large brown eyes were expressive, and today they showed impatience and anger. "I see we have company. I assumed you called me here to have a romantic dinner at 'our place' and to apologize for the way you've behaved all week. I was prepared to forgive you, after a sufficient amount of groveling on your part, of course."

Turning, he said curtly, "Jessica." He nodded his acknowledgment of her presence.

"Winston." Jessi nodded in return.

When not in court, Winston wore the standard Fort Worth businessman's uniform accepted in boardrooms, bars, and at the ballet: spotless denim jeans with starched, razor-sharp creases, white dress shirt without a tie, sports coat, cowboy boots, and a western belt that usually clasped with a silver star buckle. In Winston's case, his initials were written in gold and inlaid across the center of the shiny silver star. Winston never settled for standard. His wardrobe was custom tailored, French-cuffed, and special ordered to suit his impeccable taste.

One thing Winston never wore, however, was a hat—it would mess up his hair. Spiked in a modern flattop and sprayed in place, his shiny black hair gave him at least an additional inch and a half to his height. The lifters inside his boots, which already had two-inch heels, added another two inches. At five feet ten inches tall in his bare feet, appearing to stand well over six feet infused him with the confidence to strut, chest puffed and shoulders back, in front of juries or to loom over those he wished to intimidate.

Winston lowered himself onto a seat and turned to Jessi. "Since Rafael won't be joining us, I guess I'll have the pleasure this evening of a *ménage a trois*." He flashed a smile, showing off perfect teeth, his seductive tone flirtatious.

Bewildered, Jessi replied, "How did you know Rafe wouldn't be here tonight?" She ignored his threesome remark.

Winston paused and smirked, as if studying Jessi's expression. "You know Rafe and I are like brothers. Brothers talk."

"Your usual, Mr. Knight," the waitress interrupted, setting his double scotch, no ice, no water, on the table. "Will there be anything else?"

"Well that depends on you, sugar. What else did you have in mind?" His eyes cast a lascivious look that slid up and down the server's body, as if mentally unsnapping every one of the pearl snaps that held her blouse closed.

"Oh, Mr. Knight, you're such a flirt," she said, throwing Sidney an uneasy smile. She twirled away, her short denim skirt flaring out high above her turquoise and brown cowgirl boots.

"Winston," said Sidney, after swallowing the rest of her margarita and setting the empty glass down by her cellphone. She took a deep breath, gathering her courage. "I didn't ask you to meet me here so we could have a romantic dinner. I asked you here so I could tell you in public, with a witness present, that I filed for divorce this morning."

"Actually, Sidney, I already know why you asked me here. I'm not stupid." Winston's anger was barely contained, his voice a low growl.

Sidney drew back in surprise. "What do you mean you know—"

"Let's just say I have a suspicion. Tell me in your own words why you filed for divorce."

"Let's just say it's because of irreconcilable differences. I'm leaving with what I brought into the marriage. I'm not asking for anything from you, other than my name and my life back. This divorce will be short, sweet, simple. Just like the wedding."

Winston glared at her, swirling his scotch in the glass before tossing it back in one gulp. "I know what you've been up to this week. I thought maybe you'd had a change of heart when you asked me to come here—*our place*." He slammed the empty glass down on the table, leaning forward and stabbing his finger into Sidney's face. "No woman has *ever* walked out on me. I'm the one who does the leaving. Women beg me to stay."

"Well here's one who's not begging. Here's one who's doing the leaving."

"You're an idiot if you think you can get away with treating me like this. There won't be anything short, sweet, or simple about it, if you plan on seeing this through."

"I'm seeing it through. I want my life back. The suit's been filed in Tarrant County. My attorney will contact you, or the sheriff can serve you the papers—your choice. We'll part ways, older but wiser. You'll move on to your next conquest, and I'll just move on."

"You conniving bitch. You've been planning this all along, haven't you? Marry a rich man, take him for all he's worth?" Winston leaned in closer, his nose inches from Sidney's face. "If this is the game you want to play, Sidney, game on. But listen to me and mark my words. I'll demoralize, dehumanize, and destroy you."

"Fine. I just want to divorce you. Now, leave me the fuck alone."

"I've always hated your easy use of vulgar language—I find it so unattractive." He shook his head disapprovingly. Then, pushing back from the table, he drew himself up to his full height, looming over Sidney. His nostrils flared in anger. Pounding his fist onto the table, he sent the silverware bouncing into the air. Spoons, forks, and knives clattered back down in a metallic, musical crash.

Sidney held her reaction to his physical outburst in check. She knew it was best to not react. She counted her measured breaths, calming her nerves. Her expressionless eyes stared at him, waiting for his next move.

Winston jutted his chin and rocked back on his heels in a defiant posture. "You want me to leave you the fuck alone? I'll leave you alone when I'm good and ready. Until then, you best be on your guard."

"It sounds to me, Winston, that you're threatening me." Sidney kept her voice flat and devoid of emotion.

"There's a fine line between a threat and fair warning.

In the meantime, I'm filing a restraining order against you. You are not to set foot on *my* ranch. Everything behind the gate and inside the fence is mine. That means your horse, too." He paused for effect. "I sure hope nothing happens to your precious Mocha while we're sorting this out."

Sidney gave Jessica a silent, knowing glance. Her heart pounded against her ribs. She was sure the noise it made could be heard by others. She wanted to scream hateful insults; she wanted to grab Jessi's steak knife lying on the white tablecloth and turn this son-of-a-bitch into a eunuch. With concerted effort, she calmly stated, "My attorney will sort things out for me."

"We'll see about that." Glaring at Jessi, he said, "Give my best to your husband." Turning, he stormed away from the table. On his way to the elevator, he shoved past the waitress. She stumbled. The tray she carried, loaded with cocktail and wine glasses, crashed to the floor.

"That went well," said Sidney, giving Jessi a wide-eyed, deer-in-the-headlights look.

Jessi's eyes were as wide and as astonished as her cousin's. "That was one hell of a threat, Sid, and we both know he was dead serious. Thank God you recorded the conversation —and *thank God* you've already moved Mocha."

"No kidding." Sidney's hand trembled as she stopped the audio recording on her cellphone. "And, why in the hell would Rafe say anything?"

"I don't know. But you can bet I'll find out." Jessi fidgeted with her half-empty wine glass.

"Winston said he knew what I'd been up to this week." Sidney shook her head, trying to make sense of that disclosure. "I wonder if he's been spying on me. Remember the note from the former Mrs. Knight?"

"I remember the note quite well." Jessi drained the wine in her glass and signaled to the waitress for a refill.

Upon returning from Lake Tahoe and after news of their wedding had been formally announced, Sidney received a gift from Winston's most recent ex-wife. Nicely wrapped in bridal paper and delivered via courier was a box containing one extra-large condom. Included was a hand-written note that read: *Keep your eyes wide open. Keep your business to yourself. And above all, wear this on your heart—it WILL be fucked.*

CHAPTER 5

Fort Worth

The hotel suite Sidney booked for the weekend, chosen for its well-known private security, was a few blocks from Reata Restaurant. Its year-round heated swimming pool on the rooftop level with a million-dollar view of downtown Fort Worth was an added bonus. Late November in Texas called for a heated pool, especially for an evening swim.

After checking in at the lobby and hugging Jessi goodbye, Sidney dropped her suitcases in the room's closet. She quickly changed into her bikini, threw on a robe, and slid her feet into a pair of flip-flops. Before heading for the roof, she grabbed a single-serving bottle of chilled white wine from the in-room bar, a plastic glass, and tucked them inside her tote bag.

With the rooftop to herself, Sidney floated on her back for a short while in the warm waters of the infinity pool, watching the striated, pastel colors of the early evening sky. After swimming laps until her arms and legs felt like weights and her lungs stung, she hefted herself onto the ledge and toweled off. She poured the wine and raised her glass in a toast. "Here's to you, brave girl, and to getting your life back."

"May I join in on your toast?" said a man's voice.

Sidney jerked, spilling her wine. Turning around, she saw a dark figure approaching her from the opposite side of the pool. He was silhouetted against the setting sun, creating the startling effect of a shadow emerging from a glowing, orange orb. She blinked her eyes hard, trying to focus. As the figure drew nearer, Sidney relaxed a degree when she noticed the dog.

"I hope I didn't frighten you, but it seems like I did. Sorry about that. I'm Trevor Nolan. This is Gunner. He helps me get around." He stuck out his hand and waited, smiling, dark shades covering his eyes.

The next thing Sidney noticed, after the dog and the dark Wayfarers, was how ruggedly handsome he was, despite the bright pink scar running in a zigzagged line across his forehead. The scar was as sharp and shiny as his blonde, buzz-cut hair. Her eyes were drawn lower to the prosthetic leg emerging from pressed khaki shorts. From the right knee down, a shiny mechanical device was fitted with a Nike tennis shoe. He wore a red T-shirt with a United States Marine Corps logo and a slogan stating, *"Pain is weakness leaving the body."* She reached for his hand and shook it.

"I'm Sidney Knight. Pleased to meet you. I see Gunner's service dog vest says it's okay to pet after asking permission. Is it okay?"

"Sure. He likes pretty girls."

"And I like a man with a sense of humor. How do you know I'm not a toothless old hag?"

"Gunner's trained to detect toothless old hags. He'd have pulled me in the opposite direction, if you were."

Sidney laughed. "A guide dog that doubles as a hag detector. Sweet. He's lovely. He reminds me of a dog I used to have, but my yellow lab was female. Breck, short for Breckenridge where I found her on a ski trip in Colorado. She was the best dog."

"I'm sorry to hear you say 'was.' So, may I still join you in what you were toasting to? I overheard your toast."

"I spilled most of my wine, but there's enough left to finish the salute."

"I brought a bottle. I can fix that problem, since I'm the one who created it." He swung a backpack off his broad shoulders, pulling from it a plethora of items, from a French-to-English dictionary to a roll of plastic bags for picking up dog poop. Finally, he retrieved a bottle of cabernet, red plastic drinking cups, and a corkscrew before setting them aside.

"Ah. Always at the bottom." He stowed everything else back inside except for a bowl he filled with water from a canteen. He placed the bowl on the ground for Gunner.

"Wow. You're well prepared," Sidney marveled.

"I was a good Boy Scout."

They sat in lounge chairs facing west, and Sidney described for Trevor the sunset as it put on a dazzling display worthy of a poem. "I hope soon to be riding off into the sunset, or somewhere, I'm not sure where. Just anywhere far away from here. West gets my vote, especially if the sunsets are this spectacular."

"Your description sounded like an impressionist's painting. Thank you for that. My distance vision is almost zero, just fuzzy shapes. Up close, it's what the docs call *limited,* or *legally blind.* So, is that what your toast referred to? Getting your life back?"

"Yes, but I'm not getting it back, as in receiving a gift. I'm taking it back, as in it's mine and he doesn't deserve it anymore. Not that he ever did."

"From whom or from what are you taking your life back? If that's too sensitive, you don't have to answer, but sometimes telling a nosy stranger your troubles can help. Unload, unburden, say what you want, and you don't have to worry about the person judging you because you'll never see him again. Stranger therapy. It's really pretty damn brilliant. And it's free and comes with complimentary wine."

Sidney warmed to Trevor, her residual misgivings abating. She needed someone to talk to, and his offer seemed genuine. Since it couldn't be Jessi tonight, a stranger might be the next best thing. But first, she needed a little reassurance. "All right. Let me consider that. But tell me something about yourself, so we're not complete strangers."

49

"Okay. I'm from Fort Worth. I live with my mother and two younger brothers about five miles from here, but I'm taking a few days for myself to decompress before I go home. I've spent the last month at Brooke Army Medical Center in San Antonio with Gunner helping other wounded warriors learn to walk on prosthetics, use a service dog, get back into the game of life, that kind of stuff. I love doing it. I go once a quarter, but it's an emotional drain. So is living with my mom and two little brothers. No, not really, they're great. Connor and Colton, the twins, are seniors in high school. They're badass soccer players, international level, and are currently spending a semester in England, by invitation only, at the York Soccer Symposium. I moved back in with Mama—we kind of help each other out when the other needs a hand—but I'm looking for an apartment close by. When you're twenty-six, living with your mama can cramp your life style. How am I doing? Want me to keep going?"

"You're doing great. Please—keep going."

"Let's see—these scars and mechanical moving parts are from Iraq, two thousand and nine. They said they replaced my left eyeball with a realistic replica, but I told them 'If it's realistic, you need to figure out a way for it to get as bloodshot as my right eye when I get stinking drunk.' I thought it was funny."

"That *is* funny." Sidney laughed.

"So, my right eye can see shadows on the peripheral with limited vision in the center. I can't drive a car or sink an eight ball, but I can pour a glass of wine without spilling a drop. Most of the time. I was with the eighth Marines. Infantry officer. Now, Gunner and I attend college. I'm in the Master of Fine Arts program at Texas Christian University." He broke off, giving Sidney a sideways glance. "Whew. That's as much as I've talked about myself in one sitting. Ever."

"And you did a fine job. Wow, an MA in Fine Art— that's impressive. What's your medium?"

"Sculpting. My undergrad was in graphic design, but

staring at a computer screen gives me migraines these days. I've found that if I work in a semi-dark studio with no fluorescent lighting, just a little ambient sunlight, my head doesn't split open. I'm working on a life-size bronze of a combat soldier with his service dog."

"Is Gunner your model?"

"Indeed. I figure even if I end up losing the rest of my eyesight, I can still see with my hands and feel my way around the sculpture. I practice doing that. I blindfold myself to see what happens. I definitely need more practice, though. My figures come out looking very Picasso-esque. Oh—and I'm gay. I've not said that out loud before. Stranger therapy *is* brilliant. Very freeing."

Trevor took off his sunglasses and looked at Sidney, his right eye flashing an expression that seemed both relieved and grave at the same time.

"Ah—that's an extraordinary disclosure. I'm honored to be the one you shared that with. Have you been in denial, or —?"

"Oh, yeah. All my life. My dad was a Marine. I've always tried to be him. He died four years ago right after I got my commission. He was so proud. He was a great man, but it would have killed him to know his son was gay. That was the way of his world—very black and white. All right, enough about me. Tell me about you and the life you're taking back."

"Quick and abbreviated. I was born in Dallas. Live and work in Fort Worth. I'm a psychologist. Besides seeing a few patients suffering from traumatic brain injuries and reestablishing how they deal with daily life, I work for attorneys to help them select jurors. That's how I met my husband. Actually, my cousin's husband, Rafael, introduced us. Rafe and Winston are business associates and Rafe thought we'd be a good match. Anyway, I'm ashamed to say that this is my third marriage. It seems I have a talent for picking good horses, just not good husbands. Anyway, we've been married for all of eight months. Today, I served him with divorce papers. It's going to get ugly. I may end up with scars and mechanical moving parts myself when it's all said and done. If I'm lucky."

"Your hands are shaking. So was your voice. You're serious. Tell me about him—what happened—why you're so scared of him."

How much should she tell this kind stranger? How much could she reveal? There were so many reasons why she feared her husband—so many reasons for leaving. She shuddered, thinking about all that had occurred this past week. She decided to start her story with the dogs.

*****

Sidney pulled on her pink hoodie and set the jogging program on her phone to 'Start Run' as she stepped onto the back porch of Winston's Fort Worth ranch house. She still thought of it as *his* ranch, even though he'd insisted she redecorate right after the wedding to make it feel like her own. Whistling again, she called to her dog. "Breck! Here, Breck."

Damn it, where are you. The dog had never been gone longer than a few minutes. It had now been several days.

The early morning fog had lifted and the riding trails that ran along the black pipe fence line at the back of the property were muddy from the previous night's rain. Sidney took care to watch where her feet landed, not wanting to step in a hole or trip over a rock or a tree root. She loved jogging alone on the trails cut for horseback riding, but they could be treacherous if one was not paying attention to the rough and undulating terrain. She covered four miles each run, taking first the path along the perimeter fence line, followed by the switchbacks that were cut diagonally throughout the back pasture. The last segment was the path that took her into the deep woods. Preferring the sounds of nature, she didn't listen to music when she ran.

When her running program indicated she'd covered two miles, Sidney looked at her watch to check her pace. As she did, she momentarily took her eyes off the ground. She tripped and stumbled on the uneven pathway. Her hands outstretched, she braced to catch herself from doing a face plant. The ground, softer and looser than the rest of the trail, gave way where she landed to the side of the path.

A sickening, sweet odor arose from the wet leaves heaped in a pile. She pushed aside the leaves and loose dirt scattered over what appeared to be a shallow grave. Her heart sank to her stomach. She recognized her dog's red and black plaid collar.

Oh… Oh, God no.

Despite covering her mouth and nose with her hand and pinching her nostrils closed, escaping the putrid smell was impossible. A closer look revealed what appeared to be a bullet hole that formed a perfect dark circle in the back of the dog's skull, and a fragmented, shattered hole gaped in the front where the bullet must have exited. Breck's yellow coat was matted with blood. Maggots crawled in and out of the wounds, the nostrils, the eyes and mouth. Her jaw was fixed open, as if in an everlasting howl.

Sucking in a deep breath and holding it, Sidney quickly covered the dog with the fallen leaves. She crawled away from the grave on her hands and knees, retching. Vomit covered her shirt and left a sticky trail to the gruesome scene. Still on all fours, she heaved again and again until nothing more came up, until her ribs and muscles ached and her throat burned.

She sat back on her heels and wrapped her arms tight around herself. Salty tears streamed down her face. She tried to imagine who could have done something so horrifying. "I'll come back for you, Breck. I won't leave you—I'll bury you deeper."

She wiped the tears from her face and glanced around, making a mental note of her location. Then, she remembered to hit the "stop run" selection on her jogging program to set the GPS, which would record the exact coordinates.

As she pushed off from the ground to stand on wobbly knees, she dusted the wet grass and leaves from her leggings. Then, from the corner of her eye, something caught her attention. A small mound of white peeked up from the fallen leaves under a post oak tree. It appeared to be a heap of sugar or a dollop of cream, the item incongruous with its woodland surroundings.

Odd.

She slipped over and knelt down, brushing the grass and dirt aside. Digging with her bare hands, she uncovered more of the object. It was the rounded top of another skull with bits of white hair yet attached.

Her hands became raw as she clawed away at the dirt, the wet soil becoming embedded underneath her manicured nails. Soon, the entire skull emerged. Around the skeletal vertebrae was a gold bandana with the ranch's logo—a medieval knight dressed in chainmail and riding a black warhorse, with the letters CWK Ranch in bold red script. She had tied it around the neck of a stray white terrier that had wandered onto the property soon after she'd moved in with Winston. Cotton, as she had named him, disappeared within the week.

"I don't want a homeless stray around here," Winston had said the day the puppy showed up in the barn, frightened and hungry. "We have working dogs. The Doberman's provide security. That mongrel is a worthless piece of shit."

"I'll find a home for him. He's sweet and adorable. He looks like a West Highland Terrier. Someone will want him," Sidney pleaded. The dog soon disappeared.

Later that evening, her hands raw and scratched from digging in the dirt, Sidney lay in bed wondering how to confront Winston about her earlier discovery. Any confrontation had to be handled with restraint and moderation. A wrong word, a misplaced phrase, or an ill-timed glance from her could cause his violent temper to erupt. He'd had the usual pre-dinner double scotch followed by a bottle of wine with dinner. Two generous cognacs were dessert. Her instinct told her to wait until he was sober, but her anger and revulsion over what she'd discovered on her morning jog overruled her better judgment.

"Winston, darling," she whispered, choosing her words carefully. "I need to ask you something."

He rolled over. "I'm half asleep. What is it?"

"On my run this morning, I came across…" She took a deep breath, steadying her nerves. "I came across the graves of two dogs. Not really graves, just shallow holes they were dumped into. One was the stray puppy I named Cotton, the little skinny terrier that showed up when I first moved here. The other was Breck."

"You said you needed to ask me something. That wasn't a question. That was a statement. Do you have a question or not?" Winston propped his head in his hand and stared at her, waiting for a reply. The beginnings of a sly smile pulled at the corners of his mouth. He enjoyed a good cross-examination.

"Do you know anything about it? Do you know how both dogs could have come to be buried on the trails or how they could have died in the first place?" Sidney's pulse raced. She fought to keep her voice even, despite the adrenaline pushing it higher.

"What are you accusing me of, Sidney? Are you saying I killed those dogs?"

"No. I'm not accusing. I'm not saying. I'm—asking."

"Dogs run away. Dogs get lost. Dogs on ranches die due to any number of reasons. It's a tough life for a dog on a ranch. Who knows what happened."

"The person who put the bullet in the back of Breck's head knows damn well what happened." Sidney rolled over, turning her back to Winston.

Sharp fingers on her shoulders jerked her around to face him. He kept her shoulders in a vice-like grip. "Look at me. What the hell are you saying? Are you implying that I killed those dogs?"

"Stop—you're hurting me. I need to know if—"

"That's a slanderous thing to say about your own husband. Any evidence? Eyewitness accounts? Can you prove that in a court of law?" The playful smirk on his face and twinkle in his eyes revealed his heightened level of enjoyment. Drawing Sidney into an argument he knew he'd win aroused him more than foreplay. It was an act he performed often.

"Let go of my shoulders, and let go of the attorney-speak. Just talk to me. Tell me you had nothing to do with killing those dogs."

"I had nothing to do with killing those dogs."

"Say it like you fucking mean it," Sidney screamed. She tried to pull away from his grasp, but his fingers dug into her shoulders.

Winston spun over on top of her, pinning her arms above her head with his hands. He forced her legs apart with his legs and entered her with rough, brutal force, each thrust a punitive stab. "I hate it when you use such filthy language. It's beneath you—makes you sound like a common whore. If that's what you are, I'll treat you like a common whore."

"No—don't—"

The punishment, harsh and humiliating, lasted minutes, yet seemed like a lifetime.

When it was over, Winston scooped Sidney up in his arms and carried her to the front door. He opened it and dumped her onto the porch. Shutting the door, he secured the lock. The house went dark. Inside, his footsteps echoed as he retreated down the hallway to the master suite.

Shocked by the rush of cool air on her naked skin, Sidney banged on the door and pounded the bell. "Open the door. What are you doing, Winston? Let me in." She banged until her fists hurt, then picked up the cast-iron boot scraper and used it as a doorknocker. Gouged splinters of wood from the heavy oak door stuck to her skin.

She waited, ear pressed to the door, listening, hearing nothing.

"Winston," Sidney shouted, her mouth pressed against the doorjamb as she pounded with both fists. "At least toss me some clothes. Asshole!"

A light in the barn in the ranch manager's apartment

flicked on. Curtains slid apart. Roberto stood silhouetted in his window, looking toward the main house. Sidney ducked behind the potted palm trees on the porch, trying to conceal her nakedness. She waited until the light in the barn went dark.

Barefooted, she sprinted to the horse trailer parked next to the barn. She high-stepped over sharp stones and prickly grass burrs, trying not to cry out from the injuries to her bare feet. After opening the tack room door, she found a horse blanket and wrapped it around her shoulders. Sitting in the dark, confined space of the tack room, breathing the familiar smell of leather, horse, hay, and oats, she held a hand over her mouth and quietly wept.

After a long while, the smell and the presence of all things horse—for her, all things good—calmed her. She began to gain control, to start the mental process of centering herself. Soothing herself. Thinking. Figuring out a way to break free from the grip of a dangerous man.

A momentary stab of panic threatened her composure before clarity set in. She knew what she must do. Make a plan. Be smart. Prepare to fight for her life. Set herself up for a day to get the hell out—and resolve to make that happen soon. She understood that to stay in this marriage was perilous. He would hurt her worse than he already had.

CHAPTER 6

Fort Worth

The night air cooled as stars poked through the darkened sky. They twinkled and reflected against the pool's smooth surface as Sidney reached for her robe. She didn't know if she felt more like crying or curling up in a little ball in a corner somewhere. Or both. Hearing herself speak out loud the things she'd endured, the things she'd denied, the things she'd finally come to face head-on, made her realize how much she hated the wreck her life had become. She needed to take her life back. She needed to regain control.

I've lost myself somewhere along the way. How did I let that happen?

"Jesus H Christ, Sidney. And I thought Iraq was scary. What the hell did you do?" Trevor refilled the wine glasses and gave Gunner a chew toy from the backpack.

Sidney smiled, ignoring the little bit of wine Trevor spilled. "I stayed in the horse trailer the rest of the night. Wide awake—planning. The next morning when the maid came, I slipped inside the house behind her. Winston was eating breakfast. He glanced up from his newspaper, but never said a word."

Trevor raised his glass, clinking it against hers. "To you. You've got more balls than a lot of men I know. So, then what?"

"Then, I showered, dressed, and went upstairs to my

59

office. I called a divorce lawyer, my banker, my trust fund manager, and then my cousin. I put my plan in motion. I gave myself one week to get out. It's been one hell of a long week."

"Was he always that crazy?"

"No. Yes, I guess. I don't know. He's the most complicated human being I've ever known. He's smart. Energetic. A workaholic, really—he has a passion for law."

"What else?" asked Trevor.

"He was fun. He had an insatiable appetite for adventure. He could be very charming, was often quite generous, to me, anyway. He could be kind, too, when it benefited him. When I first met him, I was impressed with the compassion he showed toward an elderly client of his. But, strange things would happen, like people he held grudges against would end up hurt. Badly hurt."

"And you served this man divorce papers today? Why the *hell* don't you have a bodyguard? Do you carry?"

"I don't carry. I'm terrified of guns. He's not. He had them all over the house, at least one in every room, often more, just in case."

"In case of what?"

"Some of his clients are not whom I would call the upper crust of society. In fact, it dawned on me why he married me after a dinner party he'd hosted for some very wealthy foreign clients. I was a tool for his trade. He asked me to study and pay specific attention to these four particular dinner guests. Afterward, I had to give him a detailed accounting on each one, what I thought about their personalities, their strengths and weaknesses, et cetera. He wanted an inside advantage in knowing how to handle them—how to pressure them into doing business his way. He was, *is*, a master manipulator."

"And these wealthy foreign clients—"

"Were the reason for the guns Winston kept all over the house. He's a great attorney, makes a ton of money, but not enough for two private jets, a ski chalet in Breckenridge, and a ranch in Fort Worth with a barn full of expensive show horses.

Besides the stacks of cash in the home safe, there's no telling how much money he has invested in stocks."

"I'm assuming you think he's got a little illegal somethin'-somethin' going on with these foreigners."

"I can't prove it, but I have a feeling he's involved with one of the Mexican cartels. Among other clues I won't go into, I've overheard him talking about Juarez in reference to some of his clients. Perhaps there's some money being laundered through bogus Texas businesses. At least, I'm guessing that's what's happening. He brags too loudly on the phone, especially when he's talking to my cousin's husband. Drops names. Flashes money like a big shot when he's not one."

"Sidney. Those are bad dudes. They make al-Qaeda look like lambs. Again, why don't you have a bodyguard? I'm serious."

"I'm making this divorce very public. Winston's shiny image and reputation mean everything to him. He won't do anything to me that would cause people to suspect him of wrongdoing." Sidney knew that Winston had a very lopsided view of good and bad, right and wrong. He saw himself as being the defender of good and right; he just invented his own rules to suit his game.

"Do you suspect your cousin's husband is involved, too?"

"No. I've known Rafael a long time. He and Jessi have been together since they were high school sweethearts and he was a foreign exchange student from Spain. Even though they've been business associates for years, Winston still has a need to impress Rafe—he's like a hoarder when it comes to amassing people's admiration."

"Wow. What a nightmare. You're one tough cookie." Trevor stroked his dog's ear while Gunner slept, the chew toy tucked between his front paws.

"I hate to be rude, but this tough cookie's exhausted. It's been a long day and the wine's gone to my head. I hope you don't regret suggesting 'stranger therapy.' I probably shared more than I should have, and you should probably forget everything I told you. I will say, however, I'm glad I met you and Gunner."

At the sound of his name, the yellow lab sat up and looked at Sidney, then picked up his chew toy and placed it on her lap. Sidney laughed and hugged the dog, playing a quick game of tug, letting the dog win.

"I don't regret it at all. It looks to me like you needed someone to talk to, and I doubt very seriously that I'll forget anything you said. That's some pretty scary shit you've been through. I'm walking you to your room. No. Don't argue."

"All right. Thank you."

Trevor fished around in his backpack. "Here, take my card. That's my cellphone number. I know this was supposed to be 'stranger therapy,' but I don't want to stay strangers. If you need something, someone to talk to, someone to put a bullet in someone's head, call me."

"Don't tempt me." Sidney took his card and gave him one of hers from her bag. Collecting her things, she led the way to her room. In the hallway, she hugged Trevor, thanking him again. Grateful for this chance encounter, she was glad she'd decided to trust this person and indulge in a harmless session of stranger therapy.

"Stay in touch, lady. I want to know that you're okay." Trevor hugged her in a tight embrace. "I'm serious."

"I will—I promise. Good night. Good night, Gunner." She patted the dog and let herself into her room, locking the door behind her and fitting the security chain in place.

Sidney hung her bag on the hook behind the bathroom door and slipped out of her robe and bikini. Showering off the chlorine from the pool, she let steam from the hot water fill the room. She took her time, enjoying the luxury of the scented body oil she rubbed onto her wet skin. As the water began to cool, she reached her arm out of the curtain, searching for one of the folded towels stacked next to the shower. Patting her hand on the counter, she stretched her arm out farther, but she couldn't find it.

I know it's there. She pulled back the curtain.

Winston walked toward her, towel in hand. "Need this?"

Sidney gasped. "How did you get in here?" she asked, her voice a harsh whisper.

"When you left earlier in your robe, a sympathetic housekeeper enjoyed a very generous tip for helping this forgetful husband who'd supposedly lost his room key. It took you long enough to get back. I was about to come looking for you. You know I don't like being kept waiting."

Frozen in fear, she felt goosebumps erupt along her arms. Trapped, with no way out, she knew she would have to remain calm—think fast—outsmart the devil.

"Don't divorce me, Sidney. I love you." Winston approached her with the towel outstretched, a helpless look in his bloodshot eyes. "I know you love me, baby. We can work this out."

CHAPTER 7

Fort Worth

The room felt suddenly chilled. Sidney tried to wrap the shower curtain around herself, as if for protection. Goosebumps now covered her naked flesh. She told herself to stay calm—play it cool. She mustn't let him know that she was scared. He would be like a circling shark, having smelled blood in the water, looking to rip flesh to shreds.

Breathe.

"Don't be modest. I'm your husband. I know what your body looks like naked. I know what you feel like. Smell like. Taste like. Come here. I'll dry you off." Winston, towel in hand, held out his arms.

"Please, darling," she said, both her smile and her carefully chosen words forced. "Hand me the towel. Once I'm dressed, then we can talk." Keeping her voice even, calm, and soothing was difficult, but critical. She noticed his eyes were bloodshot, his speech slurred.

"I like my idea better." He moved toward her.

"No. No talking unless I'm dressed. Afterward, we can discuss everything. Hand me the towel." Sidney forced another smile. She would try anything, say anything, to placate this monster. "Darling. Please."

Winston handed her the towel. "Have it your way. Can I pour you a cocktail? I found a bottle of Crown in the guest bar."

He turned and stumbled from the bathroom.

"No. Thank you." She hurried the towel over her body.

"I'm making you a Crown and coke. I'm not drinking alone." His voice was loud and demanding.

It appeared that's exactly what he'd been doing, she thought. "Fine. Be right out."

She knew better than to take a sip—it might be drugged. But what the hell to do? Let him get drunk and pass out. That usually worked. Usually. Could she call the police without Winston hearing? Where was her cellphone? Robe pocket—look there.

She eased the bathroom door closed. Grabbed her robe. The robe felt light. She ran her hands down the terrycloth fabric. No phone.

It must be in my bag.

She clawed through the clutter inside of the bag, but her hands came up empty. Then, she remembered she had tucked it into the outside pocket along with Trevor's card. Panting with fear, she slid the zipper open.

"What are you doing?" Winston pushed open the door and handed her a cocktail glass. "I thought we were going to talk."

"I'm looking for something for my upset stomach. I thought I had some in my bag." Sidney shoved the tote behind the door, her phone peeking out from the now half-zipped pocket, and slipped into her robe.

"Drink up. That'll settle your stomach." He pulled Sidney into the bedroom.

Winston led her toward the sitting area in front of the bay window where an oversized chair sat in the neon glow that filtered in from outside. Sidney stole a glance at the bed. It had been turned down, the pillows fluffed and propped against the headboard. Countless one hundred dollar bills were strewn across the mattress like rose petals.

"Some women prefer flowers," said Winston, following the path of Sidney's gaze. "But I know my baby. I know what gets Baby hot."

She shuddered.

A half-empty bottle of Crown Royal whiskey sat on the nightstand along with Winston's opened briefcase. Lying next to it was his ever-present Ruger semiautomatic pistol. She knew he kept it fully loaded.

Plopping down onto one of the chairs, Winston pulled Sidney onto his lap. "Look at me and tell me you don't love me. Look at me and tell me you want to leave me. You can't, Sidney. I know you can't. We belong together. I need you. I'm not losing you."

"Winston, please, let go of my wrist. You're hurting me."

He kissed her wrist before letting go. "There. Done. I'm sorry, Sidney. I'm not myself. The idea of you leaving me is driving me mad. I seem to… I'm a better man when we're together. I know I've made mistakes, but I'll make it up to you. I promise."

"I need time. Space. Please, Winston—" She turned her head, averting his kiss.

"You can't leave me. Don't go through with this divorce. I'll do whatever it takes to make this marriage work. You have my word."

Pulling free, Sidney pushed away from his lap. "Winston, I don't want to fight. That's all we've done for eight months—fight. It's exhausted me. I can't think straight. Can you please just give me some time to rest? To try and work things through in my mind? I'm so tired. I'm…"

Involuntary spasms took over, and she began to shake uncontrollably. She squeezed her eyes closed to staunch the flow of tears. The attempt failed. The tears splashed down her face.

"Baby, baby. Come here. Don't cry. I hate it when you cry." Winston stood, enfolding her in his arms. "I love you, Sidney. You still love me. You're my wife. That's all that matters. We'll get through this. You don't want to divorce me.

You know that you don't."

His attempted persuasion, with the soft, hypnotic voice that he once used to seduce her, now caused her blood to run cold. For full measure, he kissed and caressed each manipulating word against her ear, her neck. "Call your attorney first thing tomorrow. Put a stop to this nonsense. We'll take the Falcon and fly somewhere romantic. Anywhere you want to go."

Sidney felt herself being lifted, carried, and laid down on the bed. The strong desire to slip into her shadow-self tugged at her. It was her secret haven when there was nowhere to run, nowhere to hide. Eyes closed. Teeth gritted. She longed to disappear into her out-of-body self. To reach that safe place of nothingness—of not feeling.

Disconnected. She is a voyeur. As if watching through a camera lens…

Her robe was pulled open. Rough hands on her breasts claiming her flesh felt foreign—a mouth on hers, biting her lips, tongue probing her mouth, teeth raking her neck—the weight of him pressing down, grinding, thrusting his way into her. It all felt illusory. Her panicked breath, shallow and fast, seemed to come from another's body. His sounds and his smell were a faint tie to a world once tangible. The fists her hands made—the deep crescent marks her nails inflicted into the fleshy parts of her palms—felt as though they belonged to another. The word 'why?' echoed in her mind—was the sound real, or imagined? The tears were real. The pillow was wet.

*****

The feel of cold steel on her bare stomach startled Sidney from a troubled dream—or was it a trance? She blinked, trying to make sense of her surroundings. In slow inching increments, she raised her head and stared down at the dark outline of the Ruger on her belly.

Winston sat on the side of the bed, a glass of straight whiskey in his hand, and watched her through bloodshot eyes. "Go ahead and do it," he slurred. "If that's your intent."

"Take the gun away." Sidney's voice was barely audible. An icy panic ripped through her body like a bullet shot from the gun. "Please…"

"You were mumbling. I could make out what—only a few words. Leaving. Divorce. Finished. If you're leaving me, divorcing me, if we're finished, you might as well pick up that gun and shoot me. I'd rather be dead than be without you."

"Don't—do—this."

"But you're going to have to get over your fear of guns first. I'm going to help you with that, Sidney. Pick up the gun."

"No." She choked on the word, gasping for air.

"Pick up the goddamned gun." Winston poured another whiskey, the bottle now empty. He drained the glass.

"I—I can't. Don't do this." Her eyes grew wide with fear.

Winston reached for the gun and picked it up, brushing the end of the barrel lightly over her skin. He skimmed it up and down over her stomach and between her breasts. Lingering, taking his time, he swirled the tip of the pistol over each nipple. Grabbing Sidney's hand, he forced it around the barrel. He pressed the cold metal into her palm and squeezed his hands around hers.

"Feels good, doesn't it? Gives a person power. The ability to take a life. The ability to save a life. What's it going to be? Leave me—take my life. Stay with me—save my life."

Sidney felt her fingers growing numb where he clamped her hand vice-like between his hands and the barrel of the gun. Her mind raced as she tried to think of what to say, what to do, how she might defuse this powder keg. Shallow, fast breaths made her mouth dry and cottony. She was prepared to agree to anything. Prepared for whatever he wanted until she could find a way to get out of the room and run like hell.

The long moment stretched on. She knew he was waiting for her answer, and patience was not his virtue. She quickly considered her options before stammering, "I'll do whatever…"

A pause—but the moment felt different, the air suddenly less charged.

Winston's eyelids began to droop; his head nodded forward and snapped back. He swayed. His grip weakened. His hands fell away from hers and the gun dropped onto the mattress. The pillows against the headboard cushioned him as he fell back, passed out, mouth open and snoring.

Sidney slipped out of bed and hurried to the bathroom. She searched for her bag in the darkness, finding it on the floor behind the door. Hands trembling, she fished Trevor's business card and her phone out of the front pocket. Fumbling with her hurried text, she managed on the second attempt to hit the send button.

911. Husband broke into my room. Has gun. Drunk. Passed out. Help. Hurry. Sidney.

Her wet bikini felt cold against her skin when she pulled it on. The robe offered slight warmth. She grabbed her noisy flip-flops and stuffed them into her bag, flinging it over her shoulder. With her suitcases out of the closet and sitting by the door, she stopped and listened for snoring.

Good.

She reached for the safety chain, pinched it between her finger and thumb, and eased it from its slot, careful not to jingle it against the metal door. Then, without preamble, a thought as explosive as a lightning bolt, flashed into her mind.

His briefcase was open.

This opportunity, however dangerous, however risky, begged not to be wasted. A chance this potentially valuable must be acted on swiftly. The significance of learning what Winston hid in that briefcase could not be underestimated.

Sidney tiptoed back into the bedroom. She eased her way to the nightstand. Pried the briefcase open wider. A mouth, spilling its secrets. This was not the formal, hand tooled leather briefcase he took to his office or into court. This was the plain black satchel he carried everywhere else.

Thin curtains filtered the dim neon light. It was enough

to see what she was looking at—files with names she recognized—the names of the dinner guests he'd asked her to assess that one evening at the ranch. Scanning the files, Sidney's hand flew to cover her mouth. The documents confirmed her assumptions. Those names had been all over the media in recent weeks. They were in the hierarchy of one of the most brutal of the Mexican drug cartels.

Next to Winston's snoring body, she spread open the files. Clearly legible were names—dates—amounts of money—scribbled notes. She eased her phone out of her pocket and selected the video application, chose high-resolution for low lighting, and began filming. She passed the phone's camera over each file, then made a quick pass over the gun, over Winston lying passed out and naked, and over the sea of one hundred dollar bills now scattered on the floor.

Breath held, she replaced the files, making each movement as soft as possible. Just as she was about to ease the briefcase back to its original half-open state, Sidney's eyes were drawn to one file that stood out from the others. The last file in the back had a blue tab instead of the white tabs of the others. The label spelled out S. A. D., her initials when she had first met Winston. Sidney Alexis Dollar. She eased it out and slid the file inside her tote bag and stood to leave.

But something had changed. Winston had stopped snoring. His breathing was measured and slow.

Leave. Get out.

Sidney tiptoed to the door as fast as she dared. She turned the deadbolt—*fuck, that was loud*—and depressed the door latch with her thumb. Pulling the door toward her a fraction of an inch, she listened for squeaks in the hinges, for someone behind her. She continued to ease the door an inch at a time. A noise coming from the bedroom rattled behind her—the snoring had resumed, louder than before.

She released the breath she'd been holding through lips pulled into a tight slit. Her lungs begged for more air. She pulled air in through her nose, quickly refilling her aching lungs.

With her suitcases in hand, she stepped out into the hallway and saw Trevor hurrying toward her. She set the cases down as quietly as she could and placed a finger across her mouth in the 'shh' signal.

"Are you all right?" he whispered.

"I will be."

"He's still in there?"

"Yes. Can't you hear the snoring?"

"No. Another gift from Iraq. Did you get the gun?"

"I didn't. I don't—"

"No problem. I'm armed. If he wakes up and comes out shooting, I'll put a bullet in his black heart. Let's get the hell out of here."

At the look of surprise on Sidney's face, he gave her a quick 'trust me' nod, motioning for her to follow as he grabbed her suitcases. She reached into the room to close the door. Carefully. Quickly. Silently pleading for the door not to squeak as she tugged it shut.

Trevor hurried down the hall as swiftly as a man with two flesh and bone limbs, Sidney on his heels. The elevator was slow to make it to the top to retrieve them, and then slow to set them on the bottom floor. Sticking his head out into the hallway, he looked left and right before moving to the door adjacent to the elevator. He swiped the plastic key and pushed Sidney into his room, locking the deadbolt behind him.

Gunner jumped off the bed and leapt up to greet him as if he'd just returned from a year's deployment. Trevor scratched behind the dog's ears and kissed the top of his head. "I love you too, now settle down." Retrieving his pistol from his waistband, he checked to make sure the safety was engaged before placing it on top of the bureau.

"I saw the look you gave me," he said, turning to Sidney. "My right eye sees enough that I can shoot someone if I have to. Aim for thoracic center mass. I may have lost a lot, but I haven't lost the ability to defend myself, or others, if called to do so."

"You're unbelievably… brave doesn't seem descriptive enough. Valiant? Heroic?"

"Hey, I said I was gay. I didn't say I was a pussy."

*****

Sidney paced in front of the window as Trevor took care of business with the hotel staff. Moments before, she had peeked into the S. A. D. file and put it away, horrified of what else she might find when she had time to delve into it with her full attention. What little she saw when she thumbed through the file was shocking. Copies of texts and emails between Jessi and her. Her client list. Her personal contact list downloaded from her computer and printed on her own office letterhead. A copy of her driver's license and social security card. Eight-by-ten glossy nude photos of her—some she had posed for, some she had not.

"All right. Mama's on her way," said Trevor as he came back into the room. "Hey, are you okay? You look sick."

"Thanks. Just what every girl wants to hear. I'm fine. Are we set to go?"

"Yes. The valet has our suitcases waiting at the curb. I dropped your rental car key off at the front desk and they notified Hertz. You've been checked out of your room. The cleaning staff can do what they wish with the passed-out body in the bed."

"I think that's adorable, your calling her 'Mama.' What did she say about being awakened in the wee hours of the morning for a ride home?" Sidney tugged the USMC ball cap lower. Trevor's shirt hung to her knees, fitting more like a dress; it was his idea to disguise her before they left.

"You missed a strand. That red hair of yours would be easy to spot a mile away." He pushed the loose hair up into the cap. "Well, she was a bit confused at first, especially when I mentioned I had a female companion. But I told her it was an emergency and that I didn't have time to explain. She's probably just happy I'm finally bringing home a girl. Come on, let's not waste time in vacating the premises."

Trevor checked to make sure the hallway was clear.

Seeing no one, they hurried past the lobby and out through the automatic doors. As Trevor tipped the valet, a white Range Rover pulled to the curb.

"Perfect timing," he said, waving to his mother. Opening the passenger side door, he unclipped his dog's lead. "Load up, Gunner. Scoot over—leave room for the pretty girl. Mama, this is Sidney—Sidney, this is Mama."

The yellow lab hopped into the back seat and Sidney followed, the ladies greeting one another with pleasantries and curious smiles. Trevor made sure their bags were loaded into the back compartment before coming around and getting into the front passenger seat.

"Mama, you're a honey for picking us up, but we're in a mighty big hurry. We need to get the hell out of Dodge. Story to follow."

"All righty then." She gunned the gas pedal, tossing everyone back in their seats with a whiplash effect.

CHAPTER 8

Fort Worth

Sidney leaned her head against the headrest and turned her face toward the window. Cars and trucks streamed by. Trees swayed in the cool breeze. Buildings stood stoic, some already adorned with holiday decorations. A young couple embraced on the street corner while an elderly man sat at a bus stop feeding a skinny dog. A suspicious police cruiser sneaked down a side alley, lights off. Nothing remarkable, just the fixtures of normal, everyday life.

Her heart was seized in a cold grip at the realization that her life had catapulted far beyond the realm of normal. She looked at her reflection in the car's window and stared into her own eyes, trying to see if they might reveal something to her, give her any advice, tell her what to do. She saw nothing.

Voices from the front seat pulled her from her reverie. She listened as Trevor gave his mother an abbreviated version of her story—how they met—why she needed their help. It was a sanitized recounting.

If only it were really that simple.

As she listened, it dawned on Sidney that Trevor's mother wore a pink scarf wrapped around her head, the word *survivor* emblazoned in bold white letters across the back. No hair hung from under it, which left the skin on her thin neck exposed. Watching the woman from the vantage point of the

75

rearview mirror, she also noticed that Trevor and his mother looked remarkably alike. While their features shared a genetic component, it was their eyes that flashed identical expressions. Both had the eyes of a fighter, though Trevor had been left with only one.

"Here we are. Mistletoe bungalow. It may need a little TLC—it was built over one hundred years ago—but it's been a special home for my family since my husband and I were newlyweds." Trevor's mother smiled into the rearview mirror at Sidney. "By the way, you can call me Eli. I pronounce it like the man's name, Ely. Everyone I know who's named Elizabeth goes either by Liz, Liza, or Beth. I thought I'd be different and claim the first three letters."

"I go by my first three letters, too, sometimes. Sid—also like a man's name. Thank you, Eli, for picking us up at such an inconvenient hour. I'm sorry I was zoning out back here and not joining in on the conversation. My mind is on other things." She offered a weak smile.

"I gathered as much, from what Trevor said. Sweetie, we may be new friends, but we're true friends. We'll help however we can."

*****

After Eli passed out hugs and goodnights, Trevor and Sidney retreated to the front porch to sit and sip hot tea. The quaint, tree-lined street was dark and quiet, the lawns well-manicured, the bungalows along the lane offering wide porches for friendly chats with neighbors or for teenagers to steal their first porch swing kiss. Gunner lay across Sidney's feet like a warm, yellow blanket. In the distance, downtown Fort Worth's skyline glistened in the thin autumn fog rolling in below a sliver of a moon.

"All right, you've had a hell of a day. Do you want to sit for a while longer or do you want to turn in? Mama has your bedroom all fixed up. With the twins off at soccer camp, Mama now has someone else to fuss over. You've done her a favor."

"I'm ready to go to bed—I'm exhausted. Eli's a darling.

You're lucky to have her, and vice versa. I noticed the breast cancer scarf she wore on her head. Recent?"

"Double mastectomy last year. Just finished her last chemo a few weeks ago. She's a strong lady. But proud. The hardest part for her was losing her long blond locks. She has a closet full of wigs in different styles she always wears. Except for when her son calls her in the middle of the night and needs an emergency ride home."

"You're both exceptionally strong people. I admire that."

"I get it from her. Come on, I'll show you your room."

*****

Before turning off the nightlight, Sidney sat on the bed and pulled the S. A. D. file from her tote bag. She poured over each page with growing alarm. The opening document detailed the encounter she'd had with Winston the first time they'd met. The last entry had been made only yesterday. Some pages were copies of personal, handwritten notes she'd thought she'd thrown in the trash. There were printouts of text messages and emails, transcripts of phone conversations, details of credit card charges, photos of her lunching with friends and clients, even daily entries of mileage driven on her car.

Realization of what the file contained washed over her like an ice-cold shower. She dropped the file, the pages fanning out over the rose and white chenille bedspread.

She gasped for breath. Copies of text messages. Pages and pages of them. He saw *all* of her text messages. He must have bugged her cellphone. She realized that, at some point, Winston would see the text she sent earlier to Trevor's number. Phone numbers can be traced.

Trevor was in danger.

She threw on her robe and ran down the hall to his room.

*****

Trevor and Sidney sat at the breakfast bar while Eli paced the kitchen floor, waiting for the coffee to finish brewing. Given the dire circumstances, Trevor argued that it was best to wake his mother and bring her in on the situation. Sidney agreed.

"I feel like I've invited potential disaster into your lives. I'm so sorry. I don't know how to fix this or how to make it right." Sidney's hand trembled as she took the offered cup of coffee from Eli.

"It's not your fault, dear. And we're not certain that anything will happen. Let's not buy trouble where there is none." Eli sipped her coffee. "Trevor, what do you think?"

"What I think is I walked into your life, Sid, and invited myself into your private moment—that toast to yourself of getting your life back. Remember, brave girl?"

Sidney offered a thin, weak smile.

"If your husband does trace the number and confronts me, I'll say I've never met you before, that it must have been a misdial. Simple. In the meantime, Sid, you can't use your cellphone, your computer, or your email accounts again. You'll have to buy a pre-paid phone and use that for a while. I'll set you up with a new computer and email account. As soon as your attorney's office opens... I'm sorry. I'm just taking over. Do you want me to go on or mind my own business?"

"You *are* taking over. However, you're doing a fine job." Sidney's face was as pale as the cream she stirred in her coffee. She hated feeling needy, but at this moment, she knew she needed help.

"Call your attorney from our home phone and explain what's happened. Set up a meeting for him to come here ASAP. You can't leave this house until we have a safe place for you to go. You can't go to your cousin's—Winston knows that's your plan. Are we missing anything?"

"I told you about the file I took. I need to tell you about the video I made, too. I don't know what to do about it. If my phone's bugged, will he know I filmed him? I'm not savvy about these tech things."

"Not unless you emailed it or texted it to someone from your phone. It probably depends on what type of bugging device he used, though. I'll check on that. What's on the video?"

"It implicates him with the people I told you about. It seems to confirm my suspicions about the '*foreign business clients.*' And for the record, I haven't sent the video to anyone." Sidney pulled her phone from her robe pocket and handed it to Trevor.

Eli came around behind Trevor, leaning over his shoulder to watch, too. The footage was clear enough to see the names on each file, and with the video stopped, to read every page, amounts of money entered next to dates, and business names and addresses. Notes in Winston's handwriting revealed his personal thoughts regarding the client or a particular matter about a meeting. Restarting the video, they watched the graphic scene unfold as the camera zoomed in on the crumpled one hundred dollar bills strewn across the floor before panning across the bed, the gun, and Winston's full-frontal exposed body.

"Hm. Exactly what I suspected," said Eli.

"What's that?" asked Sidney.

"Bullies usually are compensating for something *small*."

"Mama!" Trevor burst out laughing.

*****

At noon, Eli ushered Aleck Stavros into the dining room, where the table was set with a light lunch. She excused herself, shutting the French doors, leaving Sidney and her attorney to speak in private. Trevor had taken a taxi on a mission to secure a pre-paid phone and a new laptop for Sidney. The bigger mission, however, was to pay a visit to a tech buddy to learn what he could about cellphone bugging devices.

Aleck eased his immensity into the armchair at the head of the table, his bulk barely squeezing into the limited space. He was not a fat man. He was a giant of a man. At six feet nine inches tall and weighing in at three hundred pounds, all who saw him assumed him to be a football linebacker. Strangers often asked for autographs. Sometimes he'd oblige and sign when they insisted they recognized him, laughing at their disappointment when they read his signature, signed *Aleck*

Stavros, Attorney at Law, Clueless about Football.

"Thanks, Aleck, for coming. I… I'm in a terrible mess. I don't know what to do." Sidney wrapped her arms around herself. The panic she felt as a small seed in her stomach was swelling, pushing up into her chest, making breathing difficult.

"We're going to do what we set out to do." He gave Sidney's arm a gentle squeeze. "We're going to get you out of this marriage, quickly, safely, and as you wish, taking nothing but your last name back. However, with our newfound knowledge, we must proceed with extreme caution. May I see the file you told me about on the phone?"

"I made you copies. Or, Eli did. Minus the nude photos of me. I didn't think you needed to see those. I'll keep them in the original file with me." She handed him a stapled stack of papers and watched his eyebrows work up and down as he flipped through the file, frowning and pursing his lips.

At the light tapping on the door, Sidney looked up. She waved Trevor in and introduced the two men. Gunner nosed the new party at the table before lying down at Sidney's feet. "Please stay, Trevor. I want your input. Is that all right with you, Aleck?"

"Your call, Sid. But it's fine with me."

"OK. Thanks." Trevor pulled out a chair and sat. "I'll show you what I picked up later, but your new phone and laptop problem is solved. And, I learned some cool stuff about bugging cellphones. Your pictures and videos are safe. But he's probably been listening in on every phone conversation you've had, and we know he's copied your texts and emails. If you've used your phone to make a call from this location, which I'm sure you haven't, he'd be able to track it here, via GPS technology."

"Sidney, what about this video you made?" Aleck reached for the plate of sandwiches and poured a glass of iced tea. He passed the plate to Trevor and indicated with a nod that Sidney should eat something, too. "You said it implicated him with a connection to, how'd you put it, some very bad men."

"Yes, it clearly does." She shook her head 'no' when

Trevor offered her a sandwich, afraid she'd choke if she tried to swallow.

"If Winston, *when* Winston, learns your file is missing from his briefcase, he'll know that you saw the other files. If they're as bad as you say, you could be in danger for having seen them. I think it would be appropriate, as your attorney, for me to have all the facts. Wouldn't you agree?"

The video was replayed, three times over.

"If what I'm seeing here, in addition to what you told me when we first discussed your divorce, all add up…" Aleck ran a hand down his face, trailing fingers through his gray mustache and goatee. He leaned in and gave Sidney a stern look, his piercing blue eyes steady on hers. "We've got one shitty situation on our hands. Yes, that's a legal term I learned in law school. This has gone beyond a simple divorce. This has become a situation where I recommend we get the DEA and-or the FBI involved. It's no wonder you're scared. I'm scared for you."

"I was afraid you were going to say that." Sidney crossed her arms on the table and leaned her head down, trying to hold back the tears.

Trevor rubbed her back with one hand. His other hand was busy drumming against the table. "Stream of thought here … Sidney needs to get out of town—"

"—and disappear for a while. I couldn't agree more," said Aleck. "I'll give her a few days head start before I turn that video over to the DEA. Trevor, make a copy and download it onto a safe hard drive or a flash drive before I leave. Oh, and include the audio recording of the threat he made, too. I'll take the phone and lock it in my office safe until Monday. I've got a friend in the Agency whom I want to call and ask a few questions about how best to handle this."

"Yes sir. She needs to be disguised when she leaves. I'm sure Winston's already looking for her."

"I'll need a truck and trailer. I won't leave without Mocha. He's already threatened her safety," Sidney mumbled, her head still resting on her arms crossed on the table. Lifting her gaze, she looked from Trevor, then to Alec. "If Winston were to find her, he'd kill her, just to get to me. I couldn't bear that."

"Is that doable?" asked Trevor. "Can you get away safely, pulling a horse trailer?"

"Yes. I don't think Winston would expect me to flee with my horse, especially since I left my truck and trailer at his ranch."

"OK. Good used truck and trailer from a private party is easy to come by. Do you have the funds?" asked Trevor.

"She has the funds. Cash is not a problem," said Aleck. "If you can locate a truck and trailer today, I'll have the funds ready. We can't delay. I want her out of town no later than noon tomorrow. Do you have a place in mind where she can go— where she'll be safe and far away from here?"

"I have the perfect place in mind," said Trevor, scrolling through his contact list on his cellphone.

"Tell me why you think it's perfect." Aleck leaned back in his chair and folded his arms across his chest, eyes to the ceiling to visualize Trevor's description.

"Markus Yeager, former Marine Officer with Force Reconnaissance Special Operations Unit. After he was wounded, he left the Marines and went to work for a private security company that specialized in offshore oil wells in the Middle East. I met him when he came to San Antonio to volunteer with the Wounded Warrior project. I was his assigned wounded warrior."

"So far, so good." Aleck lowered his eyes, settling his gaze on Trevor. "Where is Mr. Yeager's place?"

"He has a remote ranch and hunting lodge in Alpine. It's about an eight-hour drive, give-or-take. I've been several times with other Marines. Man, this place is not easy to find, but that's what we want."

"Yes," Aleck nodded.

"If I needed a place to hide, that's where I'd go. Markus

is the one I could count on to have my back. He's been out of the Marines several years, but men still talk about him. Stories about him are legendary."

"Sounds perfect. I agree. Let me have his contact info, too, after you call."

"Hell. My phone's probably been traced by now. I should have gotten a replacement for mine, too. I don't know how these James Bond bugging devices work, but if her husband thinks my number is the one she sent her 9-1-1 text to, I don't want him somehow being able to spy on who I call."

Don't call him my husband, Sidney thought, one part of her wanting to enter the conversation, the other part wanting to remain silent. The silent part won.

"It's wise to play it safe, Trevor. And, email me her new number and email address when you get it set up. In the meantime, I'm sending a friend of mine over here—Sidney, are you listening?"

"Yes, Aleck, I'm listening. Sorry." She raised her head from the table, feeling like a small child, with the adults talking about her as if she weren't in the room. "And one other thing— Jessi needs to be contacted. She's expecting me to move in with her and Rafe. If I don't call her soon, she's going to be worried sick."

"I'll take care of that. And, I'm sending a policeman friend of mine to give you a crash course on personal protection. I'd feel much better if you knew the basics on how to defend yourself, maybe how to aim a gun."

"No guns."

"All right, a Taser, then."

Sidney nodded. That was the best she could manage.

*****

The plan went off without a hitch. Leaving earlier than anticipated, Sidney pulled out of Fort Worth at eight on Friday morning, making one stop in Weatherford to pick up Mocha before heading west. Eli and Trevor insisted on escorting her that far, to see that she safely made it away with her horse.

The truck and trailer were ideal. She'd asked Trevor to make sure the truck had a powerful towing package, and he came through. He found a low mileage truck that had been used to haul a yacht from the Gulf of Mexico to Dallas. It came with a red and white scuba diving sticker on the back bumper—ironic, because Sidney hated scuba diving. She'd tried it once at Winston's insistence, but with the mask on her face, her claustrophobia sent her into a panic. She'd almost drowned, trying to get the mask back on. Her ineptitude infuriated Winston who loudly hissed insults, humiliating her in front of the people at the Belize Yacht Club's dive shop. He sure wouldn't suspect she'd be driving a truck with a sticker on it announcing her love for scuba diving.

Trevor, on a spur-of-the-moment act of ingenuity, had purchased the trailer dealership's plastic, life-sized display horse along with two matching sheets. *What a brilliant guy*, she'd said, and kissed him full on the mouth. If Winston was on the lookout for her and suspected she'd fled with Mocha after all, he'd be watching for a trailer with *one* horse.

Taking Sidney into her closet, Eli had pointed to a long shelf and said, "These wigs give me confidence and make me feel like the woman I used to be. Invincible. Strong. Brave. And not to mention sexy, with never a bad hair day. Choose your favorite."

The goodbyes were difficult but she knew she must leave—she couldn't stay and risk putting Eli and Trevor in more danger. In addition to the personal protection techniques she'd been taught by the police officer, she added a few safety tips of her own: be wary of everyone, use her camera to document trouble, revert to using her maiden name, 'McQueen,' and don't let the sun go down without being behind a locked door.

With Mocha loaded in the trailer and with Fort Worth's skyline shrinking behind her, Sidney began to breathe a little easier. Money that Aleck had secured from the trust account would allow her to pay cash for everything. She would not leave a paper trail. Once he had a new phone, she and Trevor would reconnect as soon as it was safe. He would call and give her exact directions and a phone number for where she was to go. For the time being, all she had was a name and a place, and that she was to drive to Alpine, Texas.

On the road for an hour, Sidney wondered how long it would take for Trevor to get his new phone. She picked up her cellphone, checking the volume, checking to make sure the battery was charged, checking to see if she'd missed his call. She didn't doubt that he would call, as soon as he felt it was safe. She shivered with an accompanying thought—would *she* ever feel safe again?

CHAPTER 9

Alpine

Markus pushed back the silk tapestry, and going through the memorized ritual, pressed four wooden slats in the correct order. The camouflaged panels shifted outward. The bulletproof door slid into the wall. He stepped into the safe-room, secured the door behind him, and powered up the computer, eager to see if there had been an overnight response to his request for an ASAP background check on Sidney McQueen/Knight.

There was. He sat and read.

> **Found**: **Sidney Alexis Knight, PhD, age, 34. Maiden name, McQueen. Married to Fort Worth, Texas attorney Charles Winston Knight, III, age 42. His fourth marriage, her third. Petition for divorce filed in Tarrant County, Texas, Wednesday, November 14, 2012. Plaintiff: Sidney A. Knight. Defendant: C. Winston Knight.**
>
> **Other Pertinent Information**: **Her parents died when she was eight—private plane crash in Alaska. Father, Dallas plastic surgeon Dr. Marshall McQueen, was piloting the plane; mother, Kay, the only other passenger. After crash, returned to Dallas, lived with her paternal aunt, Margaret McQueen, single**

mother of daughter Jessica – same age as Sidney.

Education: Highland Park High School, Dallas, TX. Undergrad degree in World Literature, PhD in Psychology, both degrees from SMU, Dallas, TX.

Cousin: Jessica Shea McQueen Cordoba, married to Rafael Cordoba. Reside in Southlake, TX.

Special Note: Rafael Cordoba was high school foreign exchange student from Madrid. He remained on a student visa. Married Jessica Shea McQueen January 1, 1998.

Found: Mountain Princess Trust, established by Patrick Donavan McQueen, now deceased, grandfather of Sidney. Initial proceeds: four million from life insurance policies paid upon death of parents, plus inheritance of father's personal wealth, which was sizeable. With interest, sizeable investments, and real estate holdings, Trust is currently valued at forty-seven million, according to IRS. Trustee: Sidney A. McQueen, Beneficiary: Jessica S. Cordoba.

Alert: Charles Winston Knight, III, on several "watch" lists, including FBI, ATF, and DEA. Multiple contacts with the Río Negro cartel, a splinter group of the original Juarez cartel. Activity suspected: money laundering, drug smuggling, and weapons trafficking. (Arm of cartel that controls weapons also deals in human trafficking, mostly children. However, no known involvement he's dealing in *that* dirty business. Not that he gets a gold star for that.)

Shall I close out this background search or

leave it open and active?

Markus leaned back in his chair and clamped his hands behind his head, gnawing on the inside of his cheek. All right, he thought, Sidney's a smart little rich girl with the devil on her tail, assuming she was referring to Winston Knight as being the devil that hated dogs.

That alone was reason enough for Markus to hate the man—he didn't trust anyone who didn't like dogs. Taking out his notebook, he jotted down a few thoughts from what he'd read. First, Winston was a successful attorney with three ex's probably bleeding him dry, with a fourth soon-to-be-ex in the works. He'd be desperate for cash.

But, if he *was* in bed with the Río Negro cartel, he's probably got cash gushing as hot and heavy as a teenage boy's semen. He wouldn't need to get to Sidney's money. Unless it wasn't the money he was after.

As always, Markus wrote in large letters: *WHAT AM I MISSING?* The act of writing, coupled with the act of reading the prompt, always jogged something loose in his brain. He sat and waited for the enlightening moment to occur.

Before turning off the computer, Markus answered the email with the cryptic reply: 'O & A,' thinking to himself, *definitely, open and active*. On a second thought, he added:

> **Find net worth of CWK, III, along with info on his previous divorce settlements and any other debts. Also, extensive background checks on both Jessica and Rafael Cordoba. Much thanks.**

With the hidden door secured and the tapestry in place, Markus began his daily workout routine. It was ten minutes after four in the morning. An hour of aikido, karate, and ninjutsu would still allow him time to shower and get to the barn to feed the horses by six o'clock.

*****

Beyond a bend in the road, the barn came into view. Markus saw Mocha's paddock was empty and no lights glowed in

89

Sidney's trailer. A sense that something was not right tugged at him. He quickened his steps, the only outward indication of his concern, yet his mind raced over several possible scenarios for that concern, nearly all of which disturbed him. Upon entering the barn, he saw that Mocha's stall door stood wide open, the stall empty. Hurrying around to Sidney's horse trailer, he knocked on the door. Banged again, harder. No answer.

He tried the handle and found the door was locked. Striding to the rear of the trailer, he checked the tack room door —it was locked, too. There was no sign of Sidney or her horse. An alarm began vibrating along each taut nerve. A cold apprehension filled his gut. Instinctively, he swept his eyes across the ground for signs of a struggle—signs of blood.

Rex growled low, followed by an abrupt, short bark. He took off toward the wide and dense tree line separating the barn from the riding arena. The big dog plunged right in and disappeared into the thick brush.

Markus sped off at a dead run behind Rex. He pulled the Glock from the holster concealed under his denim jacket and followed the dog into the shadowy thicket. While creeping through the dewy undergrowth and trying to discern things outside his field of vision, he was raked across the face by a thin, thorny branch. It drew blood. Markus ignored the sting and the red drops oozing down his cheek. He gripped the weapon tightly in both hands, holding them near his chest in the tactical posture. Pushing forward, he emerged from the other side of the tree line.

And there was Sidney. She cantered Mocha in the arena, making sweeping circles and figure eight patterns, the mare executing perfect lead changes at the center. All the while, a watercolor wash of pink and lavender teased the eastern horizon.

Markus pulled up short, holstered the Glock, and allowed his breathing to normalize. "Jesus Christ, you scared the hell out of me. I didn't see you or your horse. Your trailer was dark and locked. I thought someone had—"

He physically shook the thought out of his head as he walked to the arena. With his booted foot propped on a middle rung of the pipe fence, he ran his hands through his hair, relieved to see she was safe and sound. Rex barked another greeting, playfully running up and down the fence line.

"Were you going to shoot me? Is it a crime to go for a morning ride?" Sidney's manner was serious, her face conveying her annoyance. She trotted over to where Markus lounged against the fence.

"No, of course not. I just—"

"How dare you! Do you treat all guests at your stables with the same rudeness that you showed me last night? Who do you think you are? Your behavior went *way* beyond being a jerk. What if I'm a cancer survivor? What if I have a disease that's robbed me of my hair? What if I've been injured by something or *someone* that's caused me to have to wear this— how did you put it last night before you bolted out the door— *this silly blond wig?*"

With that, Sidney peeled the hairpiece off her head and flung it at him. "There. Are you happy now?"

Reining Mocha around, Sidney cantered to the opposite end of the arena where the wide gate dipped lower by a few feet than the top rails of the fence. With a touch of heel and a forward change in her body position to cue the horse, Sidney and the mare jumped the gate with fluid effort. They sailed over it with room to spare, then disappeared from sight around the tree line.

Having caught the long blond wig, he juggled it in his hands. Markus gaped after her, this time the one to be left with his mouth hanging wide open. "Rex, I believe I had that coming to me. What do you think, boy?"

Rex looked up at Markus and tipped his head left and right. His intent eye contact was evidence of the intelligent animal trying his best to understand. He gave a single loud bark, as if agreeing with his human.

Markus set off walking toward the barn, the big dog at

his side. "Damn, if she's not hot, and I'm not talking only about her temper."

Moments later, Sidney heard the pair as they approached, but ignored them. She continued with her business of unsaddling and putting tack away. With brush and curry comb in hand, she worked over the sweaty mare's coat, as if the sleeker the horse became, the less frustrated she herself might feel. She groomed at a feverish pace, not letting on she knew Markus was standing close behind. Not an easy task, for his presence overwhelmed her.

"Sidney, I owe you an apology," he said, speaking to her back. "You're right. I had no idea why you wore a wig. I had a notion that something was off about you and your story, and my suspicion caused me to act inappropriately. I hope you'll forgive me. Are you a cancer survivor, or a survivor of any of the other issues you mentioned?"

Sidney kept up the unrelenting pace with the currycomb and brush, refusing to make eye contact or to acknowledge Markus's apology. Begrudgingly, she said as little as she felt was necessary. "It's really none of your business, but no, I'm not. Trevor's mother is the cancer survivor. She loaned me the wig. Why were you suspicious? What were you thinking?"

"Ah. That's the million-dollar question. I wish I had a million-dollar answer."

"I counted two million-dollar questions. Why, and what?"

Sidney flung the brush and curry comb into the grooming bucket and turned around, fists on hips, ready to launch an attack against the man who'd insulted and humiliated her. Instead, she dropped her chin to her chest and scrunched her eyes closed, letting out a heartfelt belly laugh.

"Now that's funny," she said, and meant it. "Sorry, but you're no more of a natural blond than I am."

"How do you know I'm not a natural blond? Care to test that theory?" He fluttered his eyebrows up and down in a comical fashion, removed the wig from his head and handed it to her. "I could be one of those guys who dyes my naturally blond locks to a mousy brown, just to throw off the chicks."

"I seriously doubt that," Sidney reached for the wig.

"What? That I have naturally blond locks, or that I have chicks chasing me?"

"That you have naturally blond locks. But you're definitely not mousy brown. I'd say chocolate."

"Dark chocolate, I hope. It's healthier to eat." He gave her a look that could have been interpreted any number of ways. "So, will you forgive me for being a jerk? Can we start over?"

"It's forgiven, but there's no need for starting over. I'm leaving."

"Leaving—why?"

"Alpine's not right for me. From the minute I pulled into town, I've experienced, for the most part, hostile intimidation. That's the last thing I need in my life right now. I'll load my trailer and look for someplace else to stay. How much do I owe you for boarding Mocha overnight?"

"I wish you'd reconsider. I had an email from Trevor when I got back to my lodge last night. He told me enough about your situation, including some pertinent details, to know you could be in serious danger."

Sidney locked eyes with him, the stare-down moving beyond inquisitive to uncomfortable. "When did you see Trevor's email? Was it when you went back to your lodge after I first arrived? Or, was it the second time you went to your lodge after telling me to take off my silly blond wig? Because if it was after the first time, and then you came back to the stables, you'd have known at that point why Trevor sent me here. So, which was it?"

Markus chewed the inside of his cheek and took a deep breath, his hesitation giving him time to put his thoughts in order. "After the first time. My suspicions were already ar— aroused," he almost choked on the word.

"Your suspicions? What are you talking about?"

"I became suspicious about you almost immediately.

The obvious wig, the fake horse in the trailer, the 'I love scuba diving' bumper sticker but you know nothing about diving and profess to hate it. The evasive answers. My intuition said something was way off."

"Intuition's a nice asset, as I've been told, if one is perceptive enough not to disregard it." Sidney folded her arms across her chest and cocked her head. She wasn't about to let him avoid her eye contact—not that he was trying to. The intensity of his stare was palpable.

"Touché." Markus held her challenging gaze. "Trevor's email mentioned the serious trouble you're running from, but he said he'd only just met you and doesn't really know anything about you. I felt compelled to make sure your story added up. Oh, and Trevor's email said that your name is Sidney Knight. You introduced yourself as Sidney McQueen." He shrugged his shoulders, palms out in an innocent gesture.

"What about my story are you trying to add up? And who is it that you're trying to protect, you or Trevor?"

"I protect people." His severe tone matched the sharp look he gave her, one that sliced the air between them. "You'll be safe with me. Why do you think Trevor sent you here?"

Sidney heaved a deep sigh. With her back leaning against Mocha for support, she thought about why Trevor *had* sent her here—what his exact words had been. "Trevor said this was the perfect place for me to 'hide out.' I hate that phrase. That's what criminals and gangsters do. I'm neither."

"No. But the people you're hiding from are, if Trevor's email is correct. An abusive man on the verge of becoming your ex-husband with possible ties to a Mexican cartel. Is that the crux of it?"

She nodded, not sure she could trust her voice.

"I can protect you if you stay here. You should reconsider leaving."

Sidney untied Mocha's lead rope and made her way toward the paddock. "I do my best thinking when I'm on a horse or when I'm running. Since I've already unsaddled my horse, a quick run's in order. I'll let you know my decision when I get back. Deal?"

"Deal. This lane goes past the hunting lodge to the top of the ridge before dropping down into a straight shot to the duck pond. Exactly two miles. You'll add a mile and a half on your return if you stop at the lodge for coffee and-or breakfast. Will a three and a half mile run give you enough thinking time?" His fleeting smile held a hint of persuasion.

There go those sad, gray eyes again. "I can get a lot of thinking done in that distance. It's Knight, by the way, but I'm going by McQueen, my maiden name, until it's changed legally. Until then, I'm mentally and emotionally distancing myself from *that* person and *that* name."

"Probably a good idea. Another good idea—I want you to take a GPS tracker with you. I send all my hunters out with one. It has a panic button they can press that alerts me if they have trouble reloading their gun, or they need me to bring them another beer, or they run out of toilet paper."

Sidney's eyebrows arched in surprise. "Beer *and* shooting?"

"Beer *after* shooting. Anyway, I can set it to activate a panic alarm if the wearer stops moving for a preselected amount of time. It depends on the type of hunting they're doing—deer stand, bow hunting, duck or quail—it varies. For example, if they fall and break a leg and forget to hit the panic button, I'm alerted to their location so I can find them. Since you're running, I'll set your stop movement alert for, what, five, ten minutes?"

"I don't stop when I run, so, three minutes I guess? But, is it necessary?"

"Rattlesnakes, wild boar, mountain lions, and you don't carry a gun?"

"I get the picture."

"I've got one in my truck. I'll bring it to your trailer."

It was seven-fifteen, the sun now fully engaged in washing the morning with its golden warmth when Sidney stepped off to begin her run. The GPS panic device Markus gave her was on a band around her wrist. She felt it was over-cautious, but at the mention of snakes and mountain lions, she'd relented.

"Which color?" he had asked, but before she could answer, said "Obviously, pink." He'd taken hold of her arm and strapped the pink leather band around her wrist, the color matching her bright pink and black running shoes and outfit. He took his time showing her how to use the device.

"Be careful. See you back at the lodge. Coffee or tea?"

Sidney turned around, jogging backward, "Coffee. Cream—no sugar. Thank you." She forced a smile and waved. Anxious to clear her mind and looking forward to the solitude, she turned and ran up the inclining lane that led away from the stables.

"Rex, first it was hug-the-ass jeans, then sexy, see-through lingerie, then grey gym sweats, which I have a personal weakness for. Then those tight English riding breeches which gave me thoughts of 'tally ho.' Now it's pink and black leggings that leave no doubt."

The dog barked and cocked his head.

"A weaker man would've run up the white flag by now. It's a damn good thing I'm not a weak man. Come on boy, I've got breakfast to cook. I'm thinking quiche." He set off up the hill at a fast pace, Rex bounding alongside him.

CHAPTER 10

Alpine

Taking her time, running a slow pace, Sidney tried to clear her mind of distractions. Her safety was the primary focus. Should she decide to leave Alpine, where would she go? She could keep driving west, but north seemed safer—the more miles between Texas and herself sounded best.

There had not been time for a full explanation why Trevor *had* sent her to Alpine—he just said that this was the perfect place for her to go. Trevor said that he knew Markus from the work they did together helping wounded warriors at the Brook Army Medical Center, that Alpine was within a day's driving distance, and that if Trevor were in need of help or needed a place to hide out, this is where he'd come. No doubt about it, he had said, Markus was the person he could count on who would have his back.

What Trevor failed to mention, she thought as she looked back over her shoulder at the stables disappearing from her view, was that the sadness in Markus's eyes ran deeper than the fear she tried to conceal in her own.

As she passed the hunting lodge, Sidney noted that it was built much like the stables, crafted of cedar and stone, elegant, yet understated. It had a definite European flair, almost Bavarian in style, yet was right at home in Alpine, Texas. The irony made her smile. She checked her watch and slowed her pace further, wanting to allow more time to think.

When she reached the top of the ridge, she paused for a moment, cognizant of the time and the automatic panic alarm that would go off if her body stopped moving forward for longer than the preset three minutes. But the view was breathtaking.

The Davis Mountains dotted the horizon to the north, and turning to the south, another smaller range jutted across the skyline. She made a mental note to look up its name. To the east and west lay a valley of mixed grasses that grew in pastel shades of yellow, green, and lavender. A variety of cacti in various prickly shapes and heights poked up among a scattering of scrub oak, purple sage, and desert willow. Yucca, prickly pear, and agave thrived; the succulent vegetation was stark and beautiful in its desert surrounding. Sidney breathed deeply, filling her lungs, the air's smell reminding her of freshly mown hay.

Farther off the trail, dense stands of oak, cottonwood, and juniper created dappled shadows on the stony earth. The oaks and cottonwoods were well into the process of coloring their leaves for autumn. She lost herself in the moment, in the harsh beauty of this surreal landscape. For that brief pause, her heart felt light.

Two minutes plus—better get moving.

Setting off, she dropped down off the ridge, purposefully slowing her pace as she made her way toward the duck pond. As she neared the large oval of dark water surrounded by tall cattails and reeds, she spied a lesser trail that snaked off to the right. On impulse, she took it. The sunlight speckling the shady trail invited an investigation.

Scrub oak and willow gave way to a variety of taller cottonwoods and oaks. The woods grew denser, the underbrush thicker and thornier, the trail narrower, until Sidney realized there was no longer a discernable trail at all. She turned around, then around again, trying to gain her bearings, and farther into the woods she spied an opening. There, the earth was bathed in a pool of sunlight flooding that one spot of the dense forest. She moved toward the sunlight. As she did, a sound she'd never heard before, a sound indefinable, stopped her in her tracks.

Thwap. Thunk.

What the hell was that?

The strange noise was followed by the sound of voices —two men congratulating each other—*good job*, one voice said —*damn right*, the other voice said. Then, both men turned toward her when they realized they had an audience.

One voice said, "Bitch, don't you even think about moving."

The other raised a menacing contraption and pointed it at the intruder, but said nothing.

Take a deep breath. Stay calm. Play dumb.

"Hey, no problem. Is that a bow and arrow? Or, like, what do they call those things… like, crossbows, or something? That's *way* cool. You're like Robin Hood, you know, like in the movies? I'm so lost. I just got in about midnight last night from L. A. where the movie *I'm* shooting's like, on break for the holidays, and I'm, like, how'd I get way out here?"

The first voice asked, "Exactly what the hell *are* you doing out here?"

Sidney clasped her trembling hands together to keep them from shaking. "I'm, like, supposed to be jogging this scenic path that the hotel gives guests a map of, you know, to see interesting things about the area and all? But the mapped trail ran out in the middle of freaking nowhere, and now I'm lost. But my money's on you two gentlemen. I'll bet you can help me find my way back to Fort Davis. Isn't it like somewhere over that way?"

Sidney pointed in the opposite direction from Markus's lodge and put on her best helpless pout. She ignored the glassy-eyed deer with the arrow protruding from a bloody wound to his chest cavity. The dead animal was splayed on the ground not ten feet away from where she stood, his magnificent antlers a sure prize for any trophy hunter.

99

"Just stand right there and shut your trap," said the second voice, deeper and more menacing than the first. Turning to his companion, "What the hell is someone from L. A. doing in Alpine?"

"Don't be an idiot. How do you know she's from L. A.?"

"Look at her. Who wears that shit in Alpine?"

"Who cares where she's from? She's a witness to poaching. You know what that means for us. Parole violations will send our asses away for a long time."

The man with the menacing voice sounded pissed. "You stupid bastard. You just told her we're violating parole and we're poachers. Miss Air-head Valley Girl would never have figured that out if you'd kept your mouth shut, you big dumbass."

"Dumbass? I'm smart enough to know she's never going back to Fort Davis—or to L. A.," said the high-pitched voice, taking a threatening step toward Sidney.

Sidney took a step back—stole a peek at her watch—wondered how long she'd been standing still. Was it long enough for the stop movement alarm to have activated? Not wanting to draw attention to her actions, she surreptitiously slid her hand around her wrist, her fingers in search of the panic button on the GPS.

*****

Markus stood at the kitchen sink and peered out the window as he sipped his coffee. He looked at his watch and crosschecked the time against the clock hanging above the pantry door. *Damn, that woman's a slow runner.*

"Well, Rex, I'd guess Miss Fancy Pants wouldn't eat quiche. Women who run and drink their coffee sugar free eat yogurt and granola." Markus set two cereal bowels on the table, the canister of homemade granola and the tub of Greek yogurt on a tray. As he placed the tray on the table, the GPS monitor in his back pocket began vibrating.

He fished the device out of his pocket and flipped it open. The numeral "two" flashed red—the number assigned to the GPS Sidney wore—a stop movement alert indicating she was at the top of the ridge. Out of habit, he patted his shoulder holster as he sprinted out the door, Rex following.

The Jeep sped up the gravel lane toward the ridge, bouncing and churning up rocks and dust. He scanned his eyes left and right of where she should have been, but he couldn't see her. According to the GPS, she had stopped just beyond the peak of the crest. Maybe she was injured and rolled down the hill to the pond. He eased the accelerator forward. As he approached the top, Markus reached over with his right hand and held Rex steady by the collar, keeping him from bouncing out of the seat. The Jeep's tires barely cleared air as he topped the crest. He sped down the hill toward the duck pond.

He shoved the gearshift into 'park,' stomped on the emergency brake, and then flew out the door. Rex was on his heels, the hair along his spine standing on end as he sensed the heightened anxiety. Markus scanned the perimeter of the pond, looking for any sign of disturbance among the reeds and tall grass, any sign of Sidney, when a sickening noise split the air.

Thwap. Thunk.

His trained ear recognized the unmistakable hiss of a crossbow releasing its instrument of death, followed by the repellent sound of the high-powered weapon's deadly arrow penetrating flesh and splitting bone.

The sound jerked him around. It came from over his shoulder. Cautiously—bent low at the waist—he sprinted toward the shaded deer trail that angled off of the gravel lane to the right. Glock in hand. Listening for sounds of distress—a yell for help—a whimper—anything.

Voices. He slowed, listening closely. Two males speaking—one twangy, one husky. They seemed to be arguing. And then he heard Sidney's—but—it sounded different. It was her voice, he was certain, and he had a good idea of what she was doing.

Good girl. Stall them.

A steady buzzing noise like the sound of a hornet came

from the pocket holding the GPS tracking device. He didn't need to look at it to see what the alarm was. The long, drawn out signal vibrating in his pocket indicated the panic button had been pushed.

He grabbed Rex by the collar, and with silent commands, kept the dog by his side. Knowing that Rex would instinctively run to Sidney, he feared that whoever held the crossbow would use it on this dog that looked like a vicious wolf. Markus circled wide. He kept to the patchy shadows of the junipers and madrone. He came up behind the two men, swift and silent like a darkening cloud, wasting no time rushing in.

"Drop to your knees and put your hands behind your head, fingers laced." Markus pushed one to the ground who didn't comply quickly enough. He walked around to face them. "One at a time, take your belts off. You first, Mr. Twangy." He indicated with the point of his gun which one.

The man with the high-pitched voice yelped, "Don't shoot," and removed his belt with unsteady hands. Markus growled out instructions for the other man to use the dropped belt to secure Twangy's hands behind his back.

"Now you Mr. Husky, take yours off. Drop it next to you, and then clasp your hands behind your back. I'm walking behind you. If you make a move, I'll blow your fucking head off." Markus stepped behind Husky. With the Glock in his right hand, he eased down, picked the belt up in his left hand, made a loop, and slipped it around the man's wrists.

In a sudden burst, the man flung his body backward and knocked Markus off his feet. The Glock slipped from his grip and tumbled to the ground. The big man yanked his hands free from the belt and dove for the gun. Before he could reach it, Markus was on Husky's back. He hammered both fists into the base of the man's skull, sending his face scraping into the dirt. In one fluid motion, Markus grabbed the man's left arm and twisted it behind his back at an awkward angle. Gripping the man's elbow with both hands, he thrust upward. The loud "pop" was the sound of the man's shoulder as it dislocated from its joint.

The man screamed, his guttural roar ripped with pain. He cried out a noise that sounded close to the word *stop*, his gravelly voice registering several octaves higher.

"You have another shoulder. Want to keep it in place?" Markus twisted the man's right arm behind him and shoved the elbow upward, holding it in a position that elicited excruciating pain.

"Stop. Yes." The big man pleaded, his voice trembling.

Markus stood and picked up his gun. "Go kneel down by your buddy over there." He smiled when he saw Sidney and Rex keeping a close watch on the other poacher. Rex looked as if he might eat the man alive.

Husky did as he was told, cradling his left arm against his belly.

"This time put your hands together in front of you." Markus looped the belt around the big man's hands, "I'll try to be gentle with this…" He yanked the belt to tighten the loop around his wrists.

"Oww! You son of a bitch." Husky spewed forth a slew of curse words.

"Sorry. I forgot about your dislocated shoulder." Markus threaded and knotted the leather strap, making sure it was secure. "On your bellies, both of you."

The two men sat down and rolled onto their stomachs as instructed. Slightly off balance, the big man toppled more than rolled, letting out a high-pitched yelp as his injured shoulder smashed against the ground.

Stepping aside of the two, Markus motioned for Sidney to follow, signaling for her to keep her voice low. "Are you okay?" he asked.

"Yes. Fine," she whispered. Her voice no longer trembled, although her breathing continued as shallow pants.

"My Jeep's at the duck pond. Keys are in it. Take my cellphone and drive to the top of the ridge. There's usually good cell reception up there. Call 911. Have the sheriff bring the Game Warden, too. Give a brief description of what you saw using your Valley Girl voice I heard before. That was a pretty good stalling technique, by the way. Don't give them your name even though they'll ask for it. Leave my phone in the Jeep on the ridge. Then run to the lodge. Wait for me there."

"I have my phone—"

"Don't use your phone or your name. I don't want you having to give a statement to the police that'll become a matter of public record or tomorrow's headlines. Sidney McQueen can't be traced to Alpine. Understand?"

"Yes, of course." She slapped her palm to her forehead.

"I'll tell the Game Warden that Miss Valley Girl took off after making the phone call for me while I held these two at gunpoint. It would be logical she was scared that she was trespassing or something. Now, get going. Take Rex with you."

*****

Sidney stood in the great hall of the lodge and sipped coffee, admiring the collection of Ruth Ann Youngblood oils adorning the walls. The paintings were as glorious as the masterpiece she had seen hanging in the Maverick Inn. The landscapes varied in background and mood, from wintry rocky ridges with lavender skies, to orange and brown forests infused with autumn's golden glow. The one constant in each painting that pulled Sidney into the drama of the scene was the animal.

The puma, stalking atop a rocky ridge. The pheasant, camouflaged against fall's vibrant leaves. The mountain goat, balanced on a precipitous crest. The buck, leaping across a meandering stream. The coyote, trotting through bending wheat grass. All were either hunting or being hunted. Their eyes gave everything away.

Car tires chewing up gravel drew her attention away from the paintings. She walked into the kitchen and peered out the window to see the sheriff and the game warden drive past on their way to the gate. The dead deer lay in the bed of the warden's pickup truck. In the back seat of each vehicle sat a prisoner. Markus's Jeep, the third in line, pulled up the short drive to the lodge. He got out and waved, giving her two thumbs up and a satisfied smile.

He took the cup of coffee she held out as he walked into the kitchen. "Thank you, Sidney." He smiled and leaned against the sink, stroking Rex's muzzle.

"You're welcome." She sipped her coffee and watched over the rim of her cup the man she'd just witnessed brutally displace another man's arm from its socket. Threaten to blow that man's head off—and he meant it, she had no doubt.

That Markus now seemed so calm and relaxed registered in two different places within her—her fight-or-flight gut said this man himself might be dangerous, while her rational mind said this man and his ranch might provide the refuge she needed. She wasn't sure what to make of it. Both her gut and her mind seemed to be flipping a coin.

"Man, those two played right into a script, almost as if I'd written their lines." Markus shook his head, chuckling. "I told the Game Warden I'd asked the L. A. airhead something about trespassing, and she took off like a scared jackrabbit. Those two idiots jumped right in about your being a bubble-headed actress from L. A. who probably didn't want publicity, and since the witness to the crime fled the scene, they should be let go."

"Seriously?" Sidney asked, eyes wide.

"What dumbasses. The Game Warden said the dead deer with their crossbow arrow buried in its thoracic cavity was witness enough, along with my statement."

"Thank you for keeping my name out of it. I'm curious, though. I'd just pressed the panic button and out you came from the shadows, gun in hand. How'd you get there so quickly?"

Markus pulled out a chair for her at the breakfast table and she sat, waiting for his answer. He moved to the chair across from her and spooned granola and yogurt into their bowls as he spoke. "I unleash my superhero on special occasions. This seemed special enough."

She studied him as he finished mixing their breakfast, wondering what superhero name she'd give this smoky-eyed Johnny-on-the-spot. "Seriously, how'd you get there so fast?"

"You said you didn't stop when you ran," he said, handing her a bowl. "I set the alarm for ninety seconds instead of three minutes. I figured that if you stopped for a minute and a half, you were probably in trouble."

"Ninety seconds?"

He nodded. "The stop movement alarm showed you were on top of the ridge, but when I got there, I didn't see you. At the duck pond, I heard the release and contact of their arrow striking the deer. I thought you'd been hit. I headed toward that sound. I also heard voices. Then, the panic alarm buzzed and I was already there."

"Ah. I guess it was lucky I stopped up on the ridge to admire the landscape."

"Yes." Markus nodded at her. "Lucky, indeed."

"You got pretty rough with that one guy…" Sidney's voice faltered.

With both hands, Markus gripped the edge of the table and leaned forward, closing the space between them. "When I arrived on the scene, that *guy* was going to kill you for witnessing a crime that would send him back to prison. Who knows what they would have done to you first." He paused, letting his remark sink in. "I was *gracious*, leaving his other shoulder intact."

Sidney stared up at the ceiling. She felt chastened by the brutal truth of his words and the intensity of his demeanor. "You're right. I'm grateful you showed up when you did."

"Look at me, Sidney." His eyes locked on to hers as she lowered her gaze. "Sid—you have no idea of the level of badness—of pure evil—that's in this world."

"In this world? I'm a psychologist with a cushy office and a few clients who count on me to help them put their broken lives back together. I hand-select jurors. I've got a manicurist and hair stylist, both of whom make house calls. My jumping coach hauls my mare to competitions where I show up, ride, and then I leave to go home with my trophies." She paused, gulped air, and tried to swallow the panicky feeling of hyperventilating.

"I didn't mean to insult you. I was trying to point out—"

Sidney held up both hands. "Let me finish. This is about *my* world. I've never had much *badness* in my life, until—my husband... *Badness*, for me, had been the occasional snotty cashier at the dry cleaners who insisted my Hermes blouse was already ruined when I brought it in. You're right. I had not run across this kind of *badness* in my daily life. But, I'm beginning to understand pure evil on a personal level..."

Sidney threw her head back and stared up at the ceiling again. Sucked in deep breaths. Struggled to keep from bawling her eyes out. It would be so easy to let go and to allow the tears to flow. She closed her lids tightly, squeezing back the tears. She bit down on her lip and brought her emotions under a semblance of control. She knew she'd gone far beyond simply beginning to understand evil. When she felt confident in her voice, she leveled her gaze at Markus.

"There's no beginning about it. I understand full well, on an intimate *and* personal level, the danger I'm in. It frightens the hell out of me."

Markus reached his arm across the table and took her hand. "I don't mean to frighten you further, but the men you're dealing with are far more dangerous than a couple of poachers, if Trevor's email was correct."

"His email was correct."

"Trevor said someone—your husband—has hurt you. I won't let that happen on my watch. Have you come to a conclusion about leaving, or staying?

"Yes." Sidney gripped his hand, her voice decisive. "I'm staying in Alpine."

CHAPTER 11

Alpine

As much as she could be certain of anything, she felt it was safe to remain in Alpine. With that decision behind her, she forced down what little she could manage of her breakfast, disregarding what felt like a huge stone in her stomach.

Markus had carried her suitcases up to the apartment, indicating the two well-appointed rooms for her to pick from. She'd chosen the "Retro-Cowgirl" suite instead of the "John Wayne" suite, although sleeping with "The Duke" watching over her had a certain protective appeal. She quickly unpacked what little she had brought, shoving the two empty suitcases under the bed. That task complete, she made a quick check of what supplies she would need to buy on their trip into town.

While she waited for Markus to return, she wandered around the apartment. Though a two-bedroom suite built above the barn for the manager's use, it seemed as spacious and elegant as a custom-built home. A floor-to-ceiling window on the north wall allowed an unrestricted view of the indoor riding arena below. Sidney thought the place looked like an advertisement straight out of a glossy, high-end magazine. There was nothing musty about it, despite Markus describing it as such.

With an hour to kill before their trip to town, she had plenty of time for pacing the floor. Sidney checked her watch.

For the fourth time, she pulled her cellphone from her pocket, looking for a missed call. She sat by the fireplace and flipped through the pages of a random book. Jangled nerves and anxiety interfered with breathing. With concerted effort, she tried to push her apprehension aside.

Call me, Trevor, for God's sake.

A sharp knock at the door jolted her. She jumped like a frightened rabbit. She hurried over to it on quiet feet and pressed her eye against the peephole. Breathing a sigh of relief, she opened the door.

"Hi, come on in," Sidney stepped aside, allowing Markus to enter. "You're a bit early. I wasn't expecting you just yet."

"Sorry, but I thought you'd want to see this." Markus handed her a sheet of paper. "An email from Trevor. I printed it out for you." At the look on Sidney's face, he added, "He's been trying to call you, but couldn't get through. He's fine, but, well, go ahead and read."

She scanned the email, her lips pursed, her eyebrows knitted with worry as she read. "Now I understand why he didn't call yesterday while I was driving here. Spending the day at the emergency room with his mother trumped buying a new phone. Poor Eli. Sounds like she'll be all right, though."

The email explained that Eli, weak from her last chemotherapy treatment, had fainted. She fell, and the gash she received above her right eyebrow had required several stitches. She was fine, more worried about Sidney than anything else. Trevor had left emails for Markus as well as for Sidney, in hopes that one or the other would see it. The email also included his new cellphone number, *"just in case the damned cellular gods decide to bless the connection."*

"I should get my laptop out and shoot him a quick email," said Sidney, handing the paper back to Markus.

"I replied and told him you arrived safely. I gave him a brief run-down of this morning's encounter with the poachers. I told him you'd contact him ASAP. Here's the Wi-Fi password."

Markus wrote out the code on Trevor's email and handed it back to Sidney.

"Do I have time to email him before we head to town? Are you in a hurry?"

"You have time. I'm in no hurry. Just the opposite. In fact, I've changed our plans, if you'll indulge me."

"Oh, really? What's up?"

"I want to show you around the ranch first, before we go to town. When you're through emailing, meet me down in the barn and be ready to ride. Does that sound okay to you?"

The expression on her face might have been enough, but she added, "Yes. That sounds like a welcome distraction."

*****

Markus rode in the opposite direction from where the poaching incident had occurred. He wanted to steer clear of the bad memory or of anything that might cause Sidney to feel anxious. With almost 3600 acres belonging to Yeager Stables and Hunting Lodge, there were plenty of other trails to choose from. His goal was for Sidney to relax and enjoy the ride. He wanted her to understand she could trust him. Once that was established, he needed her to confide in him.

He had to get her to tell him—in her own words with no holds barred—what the hell was going on.

The information he'd gleaned from the background check about her and her husband couldn't be divulged. Those facts would have to come from her. He knew from experience that this might prove tricky, that a frightened woman would seldom bare her soul to a man she'd just met.

Markus turned around in his saddle to look back at Sidney. "Blue is a little different than your mare. Not as tall as Mocha, but you look good on her. Do you like her?"

Sidney patted the roan mare on the neck. "I love her. She handles like a dream."

"She's one of my favorites. When the trail opens up a bit wider once we cross the creek, we can ride side by side."

"Sounds good. So, how long were you in the Marines?"

"Six years before being medically discharged."

"Ah. The scar on your leg." She paused before proceeding. "I, uh, I noticed it yesterday when I first pulled up at your gate. Is that why you were discharged? Am I being too personal?"

"You can ask me anything." He hoped she'd be as amenable to answering his questions once the tables were turned. "And yes. The bullet that ripped through my leg, taking my knee with it, made being a Marine a bit difficult."

"I'm so sorry."

"I'm good as new, now, thanks to the bionic knee. I run faster, jump higher, and ride longer than I ever did before." He tried for a light tone, yet not flippant.

Sidney rode her mare up next to his as they crossed the creek. They stopped midstream, allowing the horses to drink. "Any other wounds?"

"A few."

"Are you all healed up and scarred over?" Her expression conveyed unmistakable sincerity.

A long silence hovered between them like a thin cloud, dark enough to cast a shadow but transparent enough for the truth to shine through. "Yes. I'm healed up and scarred over. Completely."

"Good. I'm glad." Sidney's puzzled look let Markus know she wasn't convinced. "And then what? Did you move to Alpine right away?"

"No. After I was medically discharged and recovered from my wounds, I hired on with a private security firm. My assignments were mostly on high-risk offshore oil platforms for clients in the Middle East."

"Sounds risky."

"It was."

"Did you burn out? What brought you to Alpine? And how long have you been here?"

Markus laughed. "I expected I'd be the one asking questions. Now, I'm being interrogated."

"Questions about what?"

"Nothing. Never mind."

They rode their horses up out of the creek and followed the wide deer trail, the two mares walking shoulder-to-shoulder. The blue sky and warm sunshine seemed more suited to a spring day rather than one in late November. Adding to the moment, a constant chattering of mockingbirds, swallows, and sparrows filled the air.

Markus removed his water bottle from its holder attached to the pommel of his saddle and offered Sidney a drink. She took the bottle and drank, mouthing '*thanks*' as she handed it back. He noticed that her fingers lingered on the bottle, allowing his fingers a longer moment of contact. He wondered if that were purposeful or accidental. The notion she had done that on purpose, had let his fingers linger on hers, aroused him, and he reproached himself for thinking like a schoolboy. He took a gulp of water from the bottle and returned it to its holder.

"I didn't mean to sound like I was interrogating you."

"No worries." Markus spurred his horse into an easy trot. Sidney followed his lead. "Did I burn out? Yes, sort of. I've been in Alpine almost three years. And, you'll meet the reason I came to Alpine later when we go to town. I'll take you to my favorite place for lunch."

"You moved here for a restaurant?" Sidney trotted alongside Markus.

"No. For a person. Come on, let's gallop." Spurring his horse into a run, he threw slack to the reins, giving the mare her head. The need was strong to gain distance from the creek where the horses had watered—from the place where he'd had sexual thoughts about Sidney and been reminded that he was still a man.

It was that same distraction that had almost cost him his life on his last mission in Sarajevo. It *had* cost Sonja hers. He'd allowed his carnal desires to interfere with the mission. He would never forgive himself. He would never forget. And, he'd never let it happen again.

*****

They walked their horses toward the barn at a slow, lingering pace. The closer they neared to the stables, the slower the pace became, as if neither wanted the conversation to end. Sidney appeared to enjoy the brief respite from her desperate situation, while Markus continued to hope she would open up and share her secrets.

"I'll unsaddle the horses," Markus offered, "if you need time to freshen up before we head to town.

"Thank you. I also want to send a quick email to my attorney, and check to see if Trevor's responded to my earlier message."

"Rex and I'll be down here waiting. No rush." He watched as she skipped up the stairs, taking them two at a time, and he wondered how she could appear so carefree on the outside, when on the inside, he imagined she must have been holding back a tsunami of emotions.

His earlier assessment proved correct. Sidney was too frightened to bare her soul. The ride had been pleasant, and she shared stories of her childhood, talked briefly about her grandfather and her cousin, of her dreams and aspirations as a young girl, and of her love of horses. But she did *not* tell him what he needed to know most: why she was running from the man she was divorcing, a man she called "the devil." He also wanted to know if this devil acted alone.

Markus's gut told him the answer to the second question was a definite "No. There must be others." As to the first question, he had a good idea why she was divorcing and running from her husband. But that information was sparse—almost clinical—and privately obtained. He had to hear the inside story from the woman on the run.

After unsaddling the two mares and turning them out to pasture, Markus strolled over to the wash bay where horses were bathed, groomed, and vet-checked. He washed his face and hands in the industrial sink normally used for soaking bandages, leg rolls, and veterinary implements. He could have gone to the more elaborate restroom in his office, but this was quicker, more convenient, and he used it often.

"I should have invited you up to use the guest bathroom. That was rude of me." Sidney had changed into skintight jeans that she'd tucked into knee-high black boots, and the black sweater she wore showed off her curves.

"No worries. This gets the job done." He snatched a section from the roll of paper towels and swiped it over his face. "I see you've gone blond again."

"I think it's the right call, don't you?"

"It was absolutely the right call, putting on that silly blond wig." He winked and smiled, his dimples registering the depth of his amusement. "Seriously, remaining incognito everywhere except for here where it's safe for you to—"

"Let my hair down?"

"I was going to say, 'be yourself,' but, yes." Markus took Sidney by the elbow and guided her toward the Jeep.

He took the scenic route, his tour-guide-worthy description of the flora and fauna impressive in its thoroughness. The road twisted and turned past rocky outcroppings and stands of spiny green and red ocotillo before landing them on the western edge of town. Markus eased his Jeep onto Holland Avenue, and then took a side road over the Amtrak rails to Murphy Street. On this side of town, the art shops and cafés were smaller, quainter, the facades grittier. Here, the bars, porches, and patios were stuffed with more locals than tourists.

"Edelweiss?" Sidney shot Markus a wry look as they pulled into the parking lot.

"Would an alpine setting be complete without edelweiss?" Markus hopped out of the Jeep, Rex on his heels. "I thought we could have lunch. I'll introduce you to some friends. Then, I'll take you to the store for whatever supplies you need."

"Sounds good." Stepping out of the Jeep, she eyed the number of cars and trucks in the lot. "It must be a popular place. Good food?"

"Authentic German cuisine and the best *kirschwasser* money *can't* buy."

"*Kirschwasser? Can't* buy?"

"Cherry water. But don't let the name fool you," he said as he opened the screen door bearing a sign announcing that well-behaved dogs were welcome if their owners were equally well-behaved. He stepped aside for Sidney to enter. "It's a secret family recipe that's not sold in stores. If we're lucky, there'll be a bottle hidden behind the bar."

The interior, decorated in the traditional blues and whites of the Alps, was light, bright, and cheerful. With no more than a dozen tables plus a row of stools pulled against the long mahogany bar, Edelweiss was a cozy hangout. Opposite the dining area, three pool tables and a jukebox shared space with a small dance floor and bandstand.

Markus waved to a few people sitting at the dining tables as he guided Sidney to the back of the room. "You should recognize her," he said, nodding to a lady at the bar.

"Ah. A friendly face." Sidney visibly relaxed. "Hello, Ruth. It's nice to see you again."

Ruth twirled around on her barstool to face Sidney. Her gray jogging suit and glittery running shoes were similar to those she sported the first day Sidney had pulled into Alpine and inquired at the Maverick Inn about a room.

She took both of Sidney's hands in hers. "Oh, I'm so happy to see you again, too. And I'm glad to see that my map helped you find your way to Yeager's Stables." Turning to Markus, she said, "You're taking good care of her, I hope. The Maverick was booked solid, otherwise I'd have kept her myself."

"Yes, ma'am. How are you, Miss Ruth?" Markus gave her a kiss on the cheek.

"I'm well, thank you. Y'all having a late lunch—early dinner? Care to join me?

"Late lunch. We'd love to join you." Markus pulled a stool out for Sidney next to Ruth. He leaned his elbow against the crowded bar, waiting for another seat to become available. Rex curled up on the floor at his feet and rested his nose on his paws.

A set of double doors opened outward from the kitchen. A tall, voluptuous, dark-haired beauty wearing a tight fitting, low-cut dirndl emerged. Singlehandedly, she carried a tray over her head, the tray laden with steaming plates of spaetzle, schnitzel, red cabbage, and a variety of sausages. As she passed Markus, she slapped him on his buttocks and planted a quick kiss square on his mouth.

"Ja, I think another twenty pounds you should gain. Then you'll be suitable." Her German accent and deep, silky voice gave a seductive quality to her words. She flashed a winsome smile and nodded at Sidney, saying, "Hello," before hurrying off to deliver lunch orders to waiting customers. Her round, well-formed derrière drew admiring stares and suggestive remarks from the males sitting at the bar.

"Hello to you." Sidney called back to the woman with the hourglass figure who bore German delicacies to appreciative diners. She turned to Markus, amused at the embarrassed look on his face. "I'm guessing she's the person—the reason—that brought you to Alpine. She's very pretty. What's her name?"

"Heidi."

"Of *course,* it's Heidi. I should have guessed."

CHAPTER 12

Alpine

Sidney forced a thin smile. The tiny pang of jealousy knotting her stomach made her feel ridiculous, as if she were a silly, young girl. Although, she admitted to herself, that was exactly how she felt. The psychologist in her quickly analyzed the situation, labeling the feelings something akin to the Stockholm syndrome. Though she wasn't technically a captive, and Markus wasn't holding her hostage, she empathized with him on some level close to that. She *was* under his armed protection.

And those gray eyes captivate me.

"And that," Markus pointed to a robust, muscular man walking toward them from the pool tables. "That is Dieter, Heidi's fiancé." The man wore leather lederhosen, a blue-checkered shirt, and red suspenders embroidered with edelweiss. He appeared as if he'd magically tumbled into Alpine, Texas, directly from the Black Forest.

Sidney's eyebrows darted upward. "Fiancé? I see." Her face relaxed in an easy grin. She understood how this handsome man with the mahogany colored hair and the bright blue eyes would attract a girl as striking as Heidi.

Dieter, who towered several inches over Markus, shook his hand and clapped him on the back. The two spoke in German, and they shared a brief conversation and a hearty laugh before Markus made introductions.

"Sidney is a guest at the stables, and of course, you know Ruth." Seeing that her tray was unloaded, Markus waved Heidi over and restarted the introductions.

"Heidi and Dieter moved here about six months ago from Achern, in the Black Forest region of Germany. Heidi is the great-grandniece of Otto Webber. Otto is the owner of this fine establishment. I'll connect more dots later."

Both Heidi and Dieter embraced Sidney and air kissed both cheeks, their European greeting and welcome to Edelweiss. Stepping behind the bar, Dieter brought out a bottle of crystal clear liquor and five shot glasses. The bottle bore a simple white label declaring it "Webber's Wasser," with a realistic sketching of two plump red cherries on stems with bright green leaves.

Dieter gave Sidney the first glass, then passed one to the others. "This is how we toast to new friendships back home." His lively eyes sparkled as he raised his drink. "Prost."

"Prost," was toasted all around as glasses clinked together. Sidney took a shy sip, barely touching her lips to the rim of the glass. Her eyes watered as the warm liquid bathed her throat.

"I was expecting sweet," she said, making a bitter face. "This… is not sweet."

Markus laughed. "You're not a lightweight, are you?"

"No." She tried another sip. "It just took me by surprise."

"It's fermented complete," said Heidi.

"Complete?" Sidney sniffed the liquid in her shot glass and took another small sip.

"How do you say in English?" asked Heidi. "Um. Not undone without the inside, um, stone."

"She means the cherries are completely whole—the pits aren't removed before fermenting. That's what gives *kirschwasser* its bitter almond, cherry flavor." Markus poured both Dieter and himself another shot glass, clinking and prosting again.

"Bitter almond cherry flavor. Perfectly described."

Sidney pushed her glass away. "I like it, but one's plenty for me."

"Me, too," said Ruth, handing her shot glass to Dieter. "I'll have a glass of that red monkey wine, though, if you have it."

"Coming right up." From under the bar, Dieter pulled a bottle of wine that had a label with a golden monkey clinging around the neck of the bottle. "Affentaler pinot noir for Miss Ruth. Sidney? Heidi?"

"Monkey wine? Sure, why not?" Sidney's expression was a mixture of amusement and curiosity.

Dieter poured the wine, explaining as he did. "*Affental* means monkey valley, though Germany's Black Forest is not known for its wild monkeys. The word '*Affental*' originally came from Ave Tal, meaning Ave Maria valley—for the pilgrimages that occurred there. But that was way back in the thirteenth century. I guess the Germans drank so much wine that they confused the spelling of *Maria* with *monkey*, hence the name change."

Sidney, Heidi, and Ruth clinked their glasses. "Prost," they all said as they sipped their red monkey wine before Heidi hurried off to tend to a beckoning customer.

Sidney turned to Markus, prepared to ask him a question, but she hesitated. The look on his face caught her off guard. It was a look that said he wasn't embarrassed she caught him staring at her. It took a moment for her to gather her thoughts.

"Yes?" Markus inquired. "It appeared you were ready to ask me something."

"I, uh, yes…" she stammered. "The way you were staring at me, I forgot my question."

"I have that effect." Markus grinned, seeming to enjoy the moment.

"Another of your superhero powers?"

"Perhaps. But, I promise to use it for good and not for evil."

"I like your friends, Heidi and Dieter," she stalled. "Oh, I remember. I was going to ask you to connect more dots. Who is Otto Webber? Is he—?"

"*He* is right there." Markus pointed to the front door.

An average sized elderly man entered through the front screen door. Yet, there was nothing middling about his presence. With the bearing of a proud soldier, Otto Webber strode across the room. A thatch of cropped gray hair stood thick on his head, and his clear, blue eyes took in every detail as they scanned the crowded café. He nodded as he smiled and greeted the regulars, stopping to say hello and *welcomen* to those he didn't recognize. Otto wore Levis instead of lederhosen, but his Bavarian embroidered shirt and red suspenders matched those worn by Dieter. An enormous white wolf-hybrid stuck close to his side.

"Markus, my boy. It's good to see you," exclaimed Otto. His thick accent enveloped every word. The two embraced, further greeting one other in German. Turning to Sidney, he asked in English. "And who is your lovely friend? Have I seen her around Alpine?"

"The lovely lady is Doctor Sidney McQueen. She just arrived in Alpine yesterday and is boarding her horse at the stables for a while."

Sidney shot a quick glance at Markus, registering that his vague answer did not fully address Otto's questions. They would need to come up with something better, other than just her name, for future nosy inquiries. However, she would worry about that later. Right now, her mind marveled at what a striking pair this gray-haired German gentleman and his white-haired German Shepherd/wolf dog made. She visualized a portrait of the two, painted by Ruth's expert hand.

"Sidney, this is Otto Webber. He was my father's orderly when they both served in the German army during World War Two. They immigrated to Texas together, staying good friends until my father's death a few years ago."

Sidney offered her hand. "It's a pleasure to meet you,

Mr. Webber. No formalities needed. You can call me Sidney."

Otto took her hand while at the same time kissing both cheeks. "The pleasure is mine. And please, call me Otto."

"Otto, it is."

He nodded his head and turned to Ruth, leaning in as he bussed both cheeks. "You look lovely. As usual."

"Thank you, Otto," Ruth blushed. "I brought extra tickets for the rodeo tonight, if anyone wants to join me. Victor's riding." She turned to Sidney and Markus. "The two of you should come with me, too, if you don't have any plans."

"I don't have any plans," said Markus. "I'd love to. Sidney?"

"A rowdy rodeo, where the atmosphere can get a bit— spirited. And Vincent, the naturally gifted bull rider." Sidney paused for a long moment while Markus and Ruth watched her struggle to come up with an answer. "Uh—all right. Let's go to the rodeo." She forced a smile.

"Are you sure? We don't have to go." Markus shot her a puzzled look.

"I'm sure. Let's go. It might be fun." Sidney waved a hand, dismissing the memory of her Maverick Inn welcoming committee.

"Good," said Ruth, handing Markus a pair of tickets. "I'll see you there. Then we can meet back here for dinner and dancing? Let's make a night of it. I feel like having fun. Otto, can you break away for a couple of hours to join us?"

"I don't know. Saturday nights are busy for the restaurant. I—"

"You should go, Uncle Otto," Dieter spoke up as he refilled the wine glasses. "Heidi and I can manage here for a few hours. Go. Enjoy."

"Well—" Otto shrugged and considered his options.

"Go," Dieter urged.

"All right. If you force me to go, I go." Otto winked at Ruth. "I'll pick you up at the Maverick at five thirty."

Ruth, batting her eyelashes demurely, said, "I'll be

ready."

Turning to Sidney and Markus, Otto said, "Sidney, I hope to see you later. Markus, my boy, *halten sie ohren steif.*"

"*Halten sie ohren steif.*" Markus and Otto hugged and then locked eyes in a shared private moment before Otto hurried away to the kitchen, disappearing behind the split double doors.

"It's such a lovely day," said Ruth. "Let's have our lunch out on the patio."

"I agree." Sidney picked up her wine glass and followed Ruth. She turned to see Markus and the two dogs following close behind.

*****

The covered patio was an oasis of mottled sunlight that filtered onto the graveled yard. Rows of wooden benches and picnic tables crowded together, making for a cozy atmosphere. A large banner hung over the entrance, declaring the patio to be "Otto's Biergarten." Colorful signs and placards in a variety of shapes and sizes advertising German brands of beer were strung on wire and hung around the perimeter walls. Twinkling lights crisscrossing the lattice ceiling made every night a starry night.

"The phrase you and Otto shared, *halten sie*—" started Sidney.

"*Halten sie ohren steif.* Literally, 'hold your ears stiff.' It's a reminder to each other to stay strong..." He stammered, as if losing his train of thought. "...to, to stay strong, no matter what one must endure. I've heard that expression since I was a child. It's what he and my father used to say to one another."

Markus felt a sudden churning in the pit of his stomach accompanied by a dizzying gray-out. Not a blackout where one loses consciousness—he was standing, and, by blinking rapidly, could still see his way through the fog. A word, a phrase, a thought—any of these things—might stir a buried memory.

Halten sie ohren steif. Markus felt the old familiar pull that often accompanied these episodes—that pull toward darkness, toward aloneness, toward that dreaded place in his mind where buried memories threatened to surface.

"Hold your ears stiff," Sidney grinned. "I like that. So, is Otto's dog one of your rescues that you rehomed? He looks like the negative image of Rex."

"Yes. That's Noble, a littermate of Rex." Markus fought to keep his voice and his breathing well-modulated. He sought for a task to focus on—to reframe his mind. He poured a glass of water from the pitcher on the table. His hand trembled; a trickle missed the glass and puddled on the tablecloth. Ice cubes clinked against the tumbler as his hand shook, so he set the glass down. Beads of sweat formed on his forehead. He wiped them away with the embroidered napkin.

The two massive dogs lay side-by-side under the wooden picnic table. Rex thumped his tail at the mention of his name. Noble raised his head, looking at Sidney with the same intelligent, expressive eyes that Rex had.

"That's a great name. He looks noble." Sidney also poured a glass of water, giving each dog a cube of ice.

"I had the honor of naming him," Ruth said. "I'm teaching myself a bit of German, Sidney, and I learned that edelweiss means 'noble white.' Since he's white and looks very noble, well, naming him after the noble white flower of the Alps and after Otto's restaurant seemed the only choice."

"Thank you for not naming him *Flower*." Markus gave Ruth a forced grin. But the grin did not reach his eyes, where a storm quietly brewed.

*****

Sidney watched Markus as he walked around the front of the Jeep. She'd noticed a change in his demeanor during lunch, a darkening of his mood. There'd been nothing outwardly significant other than the trembling of his hands when he'd tried to hold a water glass, plus a few other minor behaviors. But adding them all up, Sidney understood something inwardly significant was occurring.

With Rex loaded in the back, Markus settled into the driver's seat. He fumbled with the keys, dropping them onto the floorboard. Twice he tried to insert the key into the ignition before the third attempt met success. He grabbed the gearshift in a white-knuckled grip, grinding the gears before easing into reverse.

He glanced at Sidney who sat watching him with a penetrating stare that made him shift in his seat. He turned his attention to the road, clenching his jaw, grinding his thoughts like the gears on the Jeep. "I thought you'd like this place called Blue Water Natural Foods. You should be able to get everything you need there. Mostly organic shit—stuff. Sorry."

"You can say 'shit' around me. I won't wilt." She was hoping for a lighthearted reaction but got nothing in return.

She continued to study the man in the driver's seat. Her psychologist's mind kicked in, noting the clenching and unclenching of his jaw, the nervous bouncing of his left leg, and the brutal grip of his fingers on the steering wheel. She combined those behaviors with what she noted at the restaurant —the trembling hands, the sudden loss of appetite, the diminished eye contact, the stilted conversation, the stammering, blinking, perspiring episode. She'd bet her PhD that Markus was in the clutch of a panic attack.

But—what triggered it?

When they pulled into the parking lot of the Blue Water grocery store, Sidney turned to him. "Markus," she said, reaching over and touching his arm as he reached for the key in the ignition. "May I speak frankly?"

He pulled air deep into his lungs, letting the breath seep out through gritted teeth. "Yes. Of course."

"I'm concerned about you and want to know if you're all right—if there's something I can do to help you. I'm making an observational assessment of your physical behaviors, and it appears you might be having a panic attack. Do you want to talk about it?"

Markus stared at her hand still resting on his arm. He drew in another deep breath. Sitting back in his seat, he turned to look at her. Their eyes locked for a long moment before he spoke.

"I don't know if I can afford your professional services, Doctor McQueen." Markus held his eye contact steady, his way of proving, if only to himself, he was back in control.

"I hope I didn't offend you." Sidney removed her hand from his arm.

"You didn't."

"I've had clients with similar issues. I'd be happy to listen."

"It wasn't a panic attack, per se. My post-traumatic stress disorder rears its head on *very* rare occasions. The episodes are so few and far between, I can't recall the last time…. Anyway, I deal with them just fine. But, thanks for your concern."

"How do you deal with them?"

"Mind over matter. Come on, we've got groceries to buy and a rodeo to get ready for." Markus rolled the windows down and gave Rex the 'stay' command.

Sidney knew when to keep her mouth shut, but this conversation was far from over. While she felt concerned about him, she couldn't deny that this situation troubled her. An image flashed through her mind—her running from a menacing figure intent on causing her harm—her needing protection—looking to Markus for help—but Markus, in the dark grip of a PTSD episode, unable to stand guard.

Her present sense of safety revolved around Markus's being in full warrior mode, and the possibility of something weakening his strength distressed her. Images of the morning's incident with the poachers flashed in her mind, and she reminded herself that Markus's quick actions circumvented a dangerous situation. Surely, he'd be able to handle anything, despite his PTSD.

He has post-traumatic stress. He's the one who needs help.

A little ashamed of her selfish feelings, Sidney felt a twinge of guilt for worrying more about her own situation than about this man offering protection. She was the one running from the person she called *the devil*, but Markus, too, was running from his own dark demons.

Fighting off the rising tide of her own panic attack, she grabbed her purse and followed him into the grocery store. As she moved through the electronically controlled entrance, cold air from the overhead vent rushed around her body. The chill stayed with her, long after she'd left.

CHAPTER 13

Fort Worth

Winston Knight stood at the concierge desk in the hotel lobby, far away from the busy front desk where visitors checked in and out. He spoke in a genial, matter-of-fact tone, the kind he used in court when trying to get witnesses to reveal they'd perjured themselves. The person on the receiving end was a tall, lanky fellow whose name badge identified him as Dwight Fincher, the nightshift manager. To Winston, the kid looked like he might be old enough to have just learned to tie his shoes or tell time.

Winston opened a manila envelope and handed the manager two photos. "Do you recognize either of them from your nightshift this past Wednesday night, leading into early Thursday?" Winston studied the manager's eyes as the kid scanned the photos, the picture of Trevor obtained from an Internet search after his cellphone number was traced and the owner identified. The Wounded Warrior Project widely released the photo of the returning veteran and his dog, using the pair as models for publicity.

"Trevor stays here often," offered Fincher. "Everyone knows Trevor and his dog, Gunner." He handed the photos back and shook his head. "Don't recognize the lady."

"Look closely, son." He liked using that word, *son*, when he could work it in. It built comradery. Winston splayed the photos on the top of the desk and waited. He adjusted his

French cuffed shirt, drummed his manicured fingers on the counter, and pulled himself up to his full, artificially enhanced height. "Well?"

Dwight bent over the photos and gave them a perfunctory look. "Nope. Sorry."

"She's been missing since she left this hotel, a hotel known for its superior security. We think she may have left with the man in this photograph." Winston already knew the man's name from performing a background check on the cellphone receiving Sidney's text. He just didn't know if the man was also staying at the hotel when he received the emergency message. Having Dwight confirm Trevor's name would tell Winston whether or not the kid might be hiding the truth.

"Shouldn't the police be the ones asking these questions?" Dwight's Adam's apple worked up and down with each word before finally settling in the middle of his reedy throat.

"They'll be here soon enough, asking their own questions. I got here first." Winston opened an envelope and removed his business card, then slid it over to Dwight, a one-hundred-dollar bill cushioning its move. "She's my wife, son. My wife is missing. She was last seen at *your* hotel. Did you see her leave with the man you've identified as Trevor?"

"Your wife is missing and may have run off with a man you want me to identify, and that information is only worth one-hundred-dollars to you?" The bobbing knob in Dwight's throat vibrated with nervous excitement.

Taken aback, Winston paused, collecting his thoughts. Then, he leaned in close, his words no longer genial, his eyes a narrow slit. "Did you take a look at my business card? Do you know who I am?"

"Yes, sir. You're the man who needs something I have and thinks it's only worth a hundred. It's just business, Mr. Knight."

Winston pulled away from the counter and stroked his chin, tapping his index finger against his pursed lips. He had misjudged the craftiness of this skinny young man. That uneasy, momentary feeling of the world being tipped off its axis was quickly righted as he visualized a plan to put his world back into order.

"All right, son. I'm a businessman. I can respect your position. Name your price."

"A thousand bucks."

"One thousand?"

"A thousand should help me remember something."

Winston reached into his wallet and peeled off twenty one-hundred dollar bills. "Let's make it double-or-nothing. We're both businessmen, but I can see you're also a bit of a risk taker. Am I right?"

"Sometimes." Dwight swallowed, his eyes on the money.

"You give me Trevor's last name, then tell me whether or not you saw them leave together. Answer truthfully—video surveillance footage is easily subpoenaed. We both know this hotel has security cameras in every dark corner. Your truthful answer is worth one thousand dollars. Am I making sense so far?"

Dwight nodded.

"After that, you give me a choice of, say, ten possible room numbers my wife stayed in. If I guess correctly the room number, you lose. If I guess incorrectly, you get another one thousand dollars. Double. Or nothing."

"I give you ten possible room numbers that she may have stayed in, and you get one, *one* guess to get it right. Double-or-nothing on the money."

"That's correct."

"Hand the money over first."

"It's on the counter. Put your hand on it, son. You're in control."

"Nolan. Trevor Nolan. Yeah, I saw them leave together sometime after midnight."

"All right. Fine job. You're up a thousand. Now, give me

ten possible choices which room my wife stayed in."

Dwight entered some data into the computer and studied the monitor, searching for Sidney's reservation. He took a note pad and randomly wrote down nine room numbers, plus the correct one, and handed the paper and pen to Winston.

Pretending to study the paper, Winston trailed the pen over each number before he settled on the one she'd stayed in: the rooftop suite. He circled the correct number, dropped the pen, and slapped his palm onto the counter. The loud noise startled Dwight, who jumped like he'd been poked with an electrical prod. Winston scooped the money up and tucked the bills into his wallet.

"Hey! I didn't even confirm that was the right room before you took your money," Dwight protested. "How'd you guess?"

"It wasn't a guess. I was with her part of the night." Winston's dark eyes gleamed.

Dwight's face turned red, intensifying his freckles' ruddiness. "Well, you're a big fucker, aren't you?"

"You'll have to ask my wife, once I find her. And, I will." Winston smirked. Turning, he strolled out of the hotel, his boot heels echoing in the cavernous, marbled lobby.

*****

The oak paneled walls in Winston's office gleamed from their daily polishing. Heavy, black velvet curtains were drawn back to allow just the right amount of sunlight to stream into the well-appointed high-rise overlooking Sundance Square in downtown Fort Worth. An original Frederic Remington hung on the wall behind his desk, the desk carved from mesquite wood and inlaid with a brass cutout of a Texas longhorn.

An unlit Cuban cigar dangled from the corner of his mouth as Winston punched the speed dial. He waited impatiently for an answer, his booted feet crossed and resting on top of his desk.

"Yes?"

"Next time I have to wait for you to pick up the phone

after twelve, yes, I counted, twelve goddamned rings, Anton, you're fired." Winston almost chomped through the pointed end of his expensive cigar.

"I was busy," Anton replied snidely.

"You're not too busy for me to fire you."

"No one else would do the jobs you pay me to do," said Anton in a thick Spanish accent.

Winston didn't argue, even though he knew the world was full of Antons, their greedy hands out, eager to make the kind of money one could earn working behind the scenes. After a pause, he said, "It's confirmed. Sidney left with Trevor Nolan. You already have his cell number I sent you earlier. Get me his address. I'll be at the club. Don't keep me waiting."

*****

Eli pulled her Range Rover into the driveway of the Mistletoe bungalow, exhausted from the drive to Dallas and back. She used to enjoy an all-day shopping excursion to the Galleria Mall. These days, even the thought made her want to take a nap. But, she'd promised Trevor lunch at The Oceanaire once he returned from San Antonio, and a promise was a promise.

"I'll get your door, Mama." Trevor let Gunner out before opening his mother's door. "We should have stayed home and had tuna sandwiches. You're still too weak to be dealing with traffic on the Tollway."

"I wanted to go. Stop fussing." She pinched his cheek with one hand, while the other hand gingerly grazed the stitches above her brow. "Besides, I'm tired of tuna sandwiches."

They both turned at the sound of a car entering the driveway. A black sedan with dark tinted windows pulled up the length of the drive, stopping bumper-to-bumper against Eli's Range Rover.

Trevor moved next to his mother and asked, "Are you expecting anyone?"

"No. Are you?"

"No." He put a protective arm around his mother's shoulder.

Two men, both wearing dark suits and dark sunglasses, exited the vehicle. The driver, Fredo, remained next to the car's door, his arms crossed in front of his chest. Anton stepped out from the passenger side and approached, a thin smile on his pockmarked face.

"May I help you?" Trevor asked.

"Yes, you may, Mr. Nolan. Or, may I call you Trevor?"

"You can start by identifying yourself and telling me what this is about. If it's about Girl Scout cookies, we've already bought all we need."

Anton raised his right hand in a motion toward the left inside of his suit coat. Before he could produce anything in his hand, Trevor pushed his mother behind him with one hand, and with the other, drew his concealed handgun from its holster.

"Take your hand out of your coat," Trevor demanded. "You're on private property. I'm defending my property."

"Easy. Take it easy. It's a photograph I was reaching for." Anton raised his hands into the air, palms out, shoulder high.

The big man standing next to the car, whose role clearly was more than that of a chauffeur, unfolded his arms. Fredo hovered his hands at his sides, ready for quick action.

Trevor motioned with the end of his Smith and Wesson. "Open your coat."

Anton complied. An envelope protruded from the inside pocket. "See? No weapon. May I take it out and show it to you?"

"Finger and thumb. Nice and slow."

He did as he was told, producing the envelope pinched between his thumb and index finger. He slowly opened the envelope, removed the photograph, and held it out for inspection.

Trevor shrugged. "It's a picture of a pretty lady. Now you can leave."

"Do you know her?"

"Who are you, and who wants to know?"

"She sent you a text message to your cellphone. Her husband wants to know how long you've been dicking his wife."

"You're not answering my questions. This conversation is over."

"Is she here? Are you hiding Sidney in your mother's home? I'm sure you can imagine how risky that is."

"I've heard enough. Leave. Now."

"I'll leave, but let me give you something, first." Anton held out the photograph.

"You can keep it." Trevor's hands remained on his weapon, his eye on his target.

"OK. I'll read it to you." Anton flipped the photograph over and read first the text message that Sidney had sent to Trevor's phone. "But here's the real message. It's from this lady's husband. Did you hear that? Her husband. His message to you. '*You were seen with my wife as the two of you left the Blackstone together on the night she sent you the above message, per an eyewitness from the hotel's management. The hotel's security video surveillance would confirm this if necessary. Keep the hell away from Sidney if you know what's good for you.*'"

Released from Anton's grasp, the photograph floated to the ground as he spun around and retreated to the car. The engine, already purring to life before the passenger door slammed shut, shuddered as it was thrust from park to reverse. The car shot down the drive, screeched to a halt, and then sped away.

Trevor holstered his gun. Grabbing Eli by the hand, he pulled her toward the house. "I'll call the police. And her attorney. Are you all right?"

Eli stopped to scoop up the photograph. "I'm a bit shaken, but it takes more than that to get me stirred."

*****

Aleck Stavros and Officer Hickson from the Fort Worth Police Department arrived simultaneously at the Mistletoe bungalow.

Eli greeted them at the front door and escorted them into the dining room where Trevor had placed the photograph on the table.

"I'm afraid I touched it with my fingers in my haste to pick it up. I should have waited until you arrived, William." Eli called Officer Hickson by his first name. His mother had been her life-long friend and she'd known William since he'd been in diapers.

"The man wore gloves, anyway," offered Trevor. "There may not be any fingerprints to lift. Except for Mama's." He winked and smiled at his mother who appeared distressed despite her protest to the contrary.

"Sometimes we get lucky and find a stray print. These guys aren't always the brightest when it comes to not leaving behind clues." Officer Hickson deposited the photograph in a plastic baggie and sealed it. "Don't worry, Eli. If your name comes up on any felony warrants when they run the prints, I'll give you a heads-up."

"It's nice to have friends in high places." Eli sat down, her legs suddenly feeling as if they might not hold her up any longer. She rubbed a hand across her forehead, the bandage that covered her stitches irritating her skin. "Trevor, pour me some water, please. Or, iced tea. Either would be…"

"Here's some water. Are you all right? You look green around the gills." Trevor handed her a glass.

"I'm just a bit tired. If you're through with me, William, Aleck, I think I'll go lie down for a nap. Catch my second wind before Trevor and I go dance the night away. I think tonight's our night for Hogg Heaven Club. Or is it Cowboy Exchange?"

Polite chuckles were followed by hugs. While Eli disappeared down the hallway to her room, Trevor finished with his statement for the police. Soon thereafter, Officer Hickson left with the photograph of Sidney. Aleck left with a new worry eating at his gut that Sidney wasn't the only one in danger. He'd told Trevor as much.

With the door locked, the window curtains drawn,

Trevor turned to Gunner. "After I send Markus an email telling him about our friendly, black-clad visitors, an afternoon nap's not far off the agenda. Come on boy, let's go." As he passed by his mother's door, he paused and listened. The light snoring sound he heard pulled the corners of his mouth into a smile.

*****

A crashing noise, like that of a window shattering startled Eli from her sleep. She bolted upright, dragging the covers up with her. Was it a dream? Fog in the room made the familiar shapes of her armoire and nightstand seem unreal. But it wasn't fog. Eli began coughing. Sputtering. Choking. Thick smoke seeped in from under the door leading out into the hallway.

That noise!

She covered her ears. As the smoke alarm screeched out its warning, she ran to the bathroom and wet a towel, wrapped it around her nose and mouth, and ran toward the bedroom door with one thought in mind.

I've got to get to Trevor.

She pressed her palm to the door. Scorching heat radiated from the surface. She yanked her hand free—that exit was blocked by fire—she knew better than to open the door only to be eaten alive by flames. Running to the window, she struggled with the old, painted window locks, but they wouldn't budge. In the nightstand—a flashlight. She grabbed it and hammered at the lock. It released. She shoved the window up, threw a leg over the sill, and slid out. Falling onto the lawn, she landed on her hands and knees.

Hands around her waist pulled her up, tugged at her, drug her away from the burning house.

"Trevor!" She screamed. She pounded with her fists and clawed at the hands that held onto her. Trying to pull free, she struggled and kicked. "Let me go. My son is inside—"

He held on tighter so that she wouldn't run back into the house. "Mama. Stop. It's me. I'm here. The hallway was on fire. I jumped out the window, too."

Eli spun around and fisted her hands into his T-shirt. She

stared up at his face, blinking away the smoke stinging her eyes. She had to make sure it was him. When it registered in her mind and in her heart that it was Trevor, with Gunner beside him, she pressed her face to his chest. Her sobs were drowned out by the blaring smoke alarm's high-pitched wail.

Trevor spoke quickly. "Run next door and wait on the porch. I'm moving the car away from the house. Keep Gunner with you."

"Be careful," she called to his back.

Smoke and flames billowed from the roof as Trevor sprinted to the driveway. He opened the car door and shoved the gearshift into neutral. Aided by the natural slope of the drive, he easily pushed the car a safe distance away from the burning building.

"Is your purse in your bedroom?" Trevor shouted, running across the lawn.

"Yes, but it's not important. Don't risk going back inside. Please, Trevor, don't."

"You keep your medicine in your purse." Trevor ran toward the window that smoke now poured from. "Where in your room?"

"On the nightstand," she shouted back. "But I can call the doctor for new prescriptions. Trevor…" Eli's voice cracked. She stood on the neighbor's porch, one hand a worried fist, the other clutching Gunner's collar. She watched her son disappear into the smoky window. The dog stood transfixed. His eyes never strayed from the last spot where he'd seen Trevor disappear.

What seemed like long minutes passed. Curious neighbors gathered on their lawns and porches. Some came over to stand with Eli. A news helicopter appeared and hovered overhead. Fire engines drew closer, their screaming sirens growing louder.

Gunner—anxious and panting—began struggling against Eli's grasp on his collar. He twisted and ducked in his attempt to gain his freedom. The dog's frantic behavior, along with his weight and strength, proved more than Eli could control. He broke free. With his eyes fixed on Trevor's last location, Gunner ran into the smoke and leapt into the window.

CHAPTER 14

Alpine

Sidney stood in front of the full-length mirror and stared at her image. She hardly recognized herself. The stress of the last couple of weeks—months—had taken its toll on her weight, which had plummeted. Seeing her naked body, the protruding hipbones, the washboard ribs she could visibly count, the cheekbones that made her face appear gaunt, brought the harsh reality home.

I'm a skeleton. Not an attractive look for me.

She riffled through her closet, searching for items that might add bulk to her frame. Layers upon layers should do the trick. She piled on the clothes. Panties. Lacy tank top. Ralph Lauren floral mini-dress. A pastel sweater to cover her bony arms. A denim jacket on top of that was even better. Her favorite pair of retro-style cowgirl boots, pink and brown with pointed toes and tooled roses around the shaft to match the pink sweater. A rose-colored scarf? A matching scarf? A contrasting scarf? All of the scarves. Off with the boots. On with some leggings to cover her knobby knees. Back on with the boots.

There. She studied her image in the mirror. *Ten pounds, plus. Much better.*

Five thirty on the dot, and a knock at the door told her Markus had arrived. She checked out the peephole just to make sure.

"Hi. Right on time." She opened the door to allow him inside.

"Didn't want to scare you like I did this morning." Markus eyed her outfit. "You look great. A little overdressed for the Alpine rodeo, but that's okay by me. Are you cold?"

"I… No. Not really. Not with a sweater, jacket, leggings, and three scarves." Sidney forced a laugh. "A bit much, huh?" She unwound the scarves and threw them on the sofa. "If you'll excuse me a minute. Pour yourself a glass of wine, if you'd like."

"Can I pour you one, too?"

"Sure. Be right out."

When Sidney returned to the living room, minus the leggings, the denim jacket, and the sweater, she took the glass of wine Markus offered. "Thanks. So…"

"You're welcome. What was that all about?" Markus sat on a barstool with his back to the breakfast counter, facing Sidney who'd plopped down on the arm of the sofa.

"You mean, all the clothes?"

"Yes."

"It was nothing." She shrugged and sipped her wine. Looked away.

"It was—something."

"I guess I was trying to hide how skeletal I've become. Diet by divorce."

"There's no need to feel self-conscious, Sidney. You're beautiful just the way you are. But if you think you need to pack on some pounds, dinner at Edelweiss after the rodeo will be a positive step in that process." Markus smiled and sipped his wine.

Those dimples and those sad eyes will be my undoing.

"I appreciate the positive reinforcement." The fact that he said she looked beautiful was not lost on her. In fact, it heated her in a place that hadn't felt heat in a long time.

"Well. Are you ready to go?" Markus finished his last sip and set the glass down.

"Might as well." She handed Markus her half-finished wine glass.

"You seem reluctant. I noticed that earlier today. What's up?"

Sidney huffed out a sigh. "I was greeted by some of the rodeo contestants my first day in Alpine. The bunch, more like a pack of wolves, was pretty vulgar and rowdy. Confrontational. Ruth's grandson, Victor, was among them. Please don't say anything to her. It sounds like she dotes on him and I'd hate to ruin that for her. Anyway, it could have gotten ugly, but it didn't. I'll just leave it at that."

"I'll keep an eye on that rowdy bunch. Come here. Please."

"Why?"

"Because I want to tell you something, and I need for you to see that I'm sincere."

"I can hear you from here." But Sidney got up from her perch on the arm of the sofa and walked over to Markus seated on the barstool. "What do you want to tell me?"

Markus took her hands in his. The look in his eyes softened from the earlier darkness Sidney had noticed. Sad still, but softer. She studied them, wanting very much to know what was behind the sadness.

"That I think you're amazing. Kind hearted. Sweet. You're going through a hell of a dark time in your life, you've got the devil on your tail, yet today, you were pleasant and amusing with my friends, you offered to help me with my PTSD, and now, you're concerned for Ruth and how she relates to her grandson. You put others before yourself. Are you always this good?"

"No." Sidney shook her head. She stood in between Markus's spread knees, absorbed the heat from his body, and felt the friction of his thumb as it stroked the back of her hand. And, at that moment, she wanted to scream that all she wanted was to be bad.

"I have a hard time believing you're not always that

good." Markus narrowed his knees until they braced against Sidney's thighs. "You're shaking. I'll buttress you."

Sidney leaned her head back and stared up at him. Tears welled in her eyes. "That's the kindest thing I've heard in a long time. I'll… buttress… you." Her words, breaths, and tears commingled, and she stood frozen in place.

"Do you want me to hold you? Would that be all right?"

"Yes." She nodded. And when he wrapped his arms around her, she melted into him, let him enclose her, and she wept against his chest.

For as long as she needed, he simply held her. Let her cry. Didn't speak. He waited until she pulled away. The moment was over almost before it began. He reached back behind his head where he'd seen a stack of napkins on the kitchen counter and handed her one.

"Now it's my turn to play doctor and assess you." Markus stroked her back, his fingers kneading and massaging along the tense muscles running up and down her spine. "You take care of everyone else. Neglect yourself. You have no one to take care of you. You're stressed to the max with this terrifying divorce from '*the devil*' who has turned you into a fugitive. You barely allow yourself the luxury of a good cry. That was all of what—a minute or two worth of tears? I think you might have a bit of post-traumatic stress, yourself."

"Is that your assessment, doctor?" She blew her nose and wiped her eyes.

"More like mid-traumatic stress, in your case, but I don't think there's a diagnosis for that. We'll just call it a good old-fashioned case of battle fatigue."

Sidney sniffed and blew her nose again. "I *am* in the biggest battle of my life. Fatigued? Yes."

"I've helped lots of Marines and soldiers deal with PTSD. That's how I met Trevor, working with the Wounded Warrior program. You can talk to me, Sid. I'm a good listener. It might help."

"Thank you for the diagnosis, Doctor Markus, and for

offering to help. But, I don't think I can afford your fees." She felt certain she could not, and money had nothing to do with it.

Sidney was aware that he still had her thighs braced between his. She hadn't made a move to pull free from his arms still encircling her waist or from the hands massaging her back. She could have—her hands rested on his forearms. It would have been easy to push away. She saw where her tears left wet stains on his shirt, but he hadn't made a move to pat it dry. In that moment of feeling physically and emotionally connected to this man, to this person who took nothing from her, who asked nothing of her, she—breathed.

"How about a 'trade-for-trade' kind of arrangement?" Markus relaxed his grip and moved Sidney a bit farther back from where she'd been standing. His hands now rested on her shoulders, allowing eye contact.

"Explain 'trade-for-trade, please." She crossed her arms against her chest, a mock-wary expression on her face.

"You have professional and clinical experience. I have professional and battlefield experience. You talk to me. I talk to you. We help each other." His voice was serious. There was nothing playful about the expression in his eyes.

"Trade-for-trade?"

"Yes."

Sidney studied him. It took her a split second to make up her mind. "You give. You support, or buttress, as the case may be. You help. You counsel. You protect. Are you always this good?"

"Not always."

"I was hoping you'd say that."

Sidney stepped into the inner "v" of his thighs. The heat from his body radiated. She ran her hands from his knees to the outside of his upper thighs, feeling his muscles tensing, his entire body tightening and pulling back. She shot him a questioning look, wondering if she'd misread his desire.

"This is what came to mind when I heard you say you'd help me, and I'd help you." Sidney kept her hands firmly on his thighs. "But, I didn't mean to make you uncomfortable. I had the impression you were interested. Am I making a fool of myself?" She gave a self-deprecating half-chuckle.

"Certainly not. I'd be a liar if I said I wasn't interested. It's just that—I don't get involved—not when I'm on a mission. And we both know my mission is to protect and keep you safe. Getting involved goes against my rules."

"Tonight, I don't want to play by the rules." She stared hard into his eyes and added, "And I don't want to get involved either. That's not what this is all about."

"Sid, I get what you're saying. But, I can't. I—"

"Okay. I understand. No harm. No foul." She was fully aware of his hands still on her shoulders. Fully aware that his grip had tightened somewhat.

"Please understand, it's not that I don't want you."

"This is what I want. What I need." She took a tentative step forward, closing the small gap between their bodies.

"Damn it, you're making this hard."

"I hope so." She leaned in and placed her lips against his.

A groan that sounded like an animal released from long captivity rumbled in his throat. Markus lifted Sidney onto his lap, so that her legs straddled his. He cupped her face between his hands, his mouth hovering, his lips brushing against hers. Then, lowering his mouth onto hers, his tongue explored, delving into those hidden places he'd imagined.

Sidney pulled away long enough to catch her breath. She reached to unbutton his shirt, but he caught her hand. He brought her fingers to his mouth and kissed each one. He lingered his mouth on her wrist before placing her palm against his chest. Then, he placed his own palm over her heart.

"I wanted to see if yours was beating like a jackhammer, like mine."

"I can feel they both are."

"Are you sure this is what you want?" Markus kissed her neck, biting along the line between her ear and shoulder blade.

"This is exactly what I want." She threw her head back, savoring the pleasure.

What she wanted was to regain power over her life—to feel again a sense of control over the things that had set her world spinning. And for this moment, she *was* in control. She wanted a man's hands on her body, there because she invited them. Markus did not demand, take, or force. It was not his idea to ask for this. She was asking. She was taking. She knew what she wanted. She wanted Markus.

He stood and scooped her up in his arms and began walking toward the bedroom. Sidney laced her arms around his neck, placing soft kisses on his chest, his ear, his lips, anywhere her mouth could reach.

A noise rattled the silence. Her cellphone vibrated on the nightstand where she'd tossed it next to her purse. Markus lowered her onto the bed. "Do you want your phone?"

"I want you."

"It could be an emergency." Markus picked up the phone and offered it to Sidney as he stretched out on the bed next to her.

"You're right." She reached for the phone.

She played the garbled voicemail on speaker. Sidney recognized Eli's voice, but the message was incomprehensible. They replayed the message several times and still could not determine its meaning, though both agreed it had something to do with Trevor.

Sidney hit the redial button and heard a busy signal. She attempted this several times, each time with the same result. She didn't recognize the number, other than it had a Fort Worth area code. She laid the phone aside and lay back on the bed.

"What do you make of that?" she asked.

"I'm not sure. Maybe Eli was just calling to check on you?"

"I don't know. Why wouldn't it be coming from her home phone? Or, from Trevor's cellphone?"

They lay on their sides, face-to-face. Markus stroked the

length of Sidney's arm and then pulled her body up against his. His mouth sought hers, the kiss tender, deep, and full of questions.

He paused a moment to say, "I can do a reverse search on that phone number to see where it originated. I'd have to get to my computer to do it. Or, I can stay here, pick up where we left off." There, he resumed the kiss.

Sidney pulled her head back and sighed, "Saved by the buzzer." But she pressed her body closer against his, not ready to let go of the moment entirely.

"What do you mean?"

"My cellphone buzzing saved me from my impetuous behavior."

"Impetuous?" Markus's deep laugh rattled against Sidney's chest. "That was passionate. Hot. Like you said, you're a grown woman—you can do what you want. But, we can cool things off, if you've changed your mind."

"I haven't changed my mind, but the situation has changed. I think we need to investigate that number. I don't know why, but I have a feeling something's wrong."

"I agree. I'll run to the lodge and do a quick search. If you still want to go to the rodeo, we can probably make the second half. Be there in time for the bull riding, which is the last event of the night."

"Since Ruth gave us the tickets, I think we should make an appearance. I'll freshen up and be ready when you get back."

"You're not going to pile on all those clothes again, are you? I like you in just this little dress and your cowgirl boots. God, that looks sexy on you." His mouth was on hers again, his hands roaming all over her body.

"Phone... number." Sidney breathed the words out in two separate breaths.

"Right." Markus pushed himself away. "I'll be back in a flash."

*****

The stands of the rodeo arena were packed, shoulder-to-shoulder and hat-to-hat. Fall evenings in Alpine, when cool breezes blew sedately through the valley, and crickets and cicadas serenaded the stars, were the kind of evenings when folks didn't stay indoors. With a rodeo in town, the majority of the population could be found either watching or participating in one form or fashion.

Markus had left word with his contact to research the phone number that continued to offer a busy signal when redialed. He also checked to see if there was a response to his earlier request for a full background check on Rafael and Jessica Cordoba, as well as more information about Winston Knight and his previous divorce settlements and financial status. There was nothing, so far.

No news is good news.

Those words plucked at Markus's mind as he picked Sidney up at the barn. As he drove to the rodeo arena, that same thought continued, interfering with other, more pleasant thoughts—her passionate kisses, her firm, small breasts against his chest. *No news is good news*. He tried hard to believe it.

"There's Ruth and Otto," said Markus, pointing Sidney toward the box seats that were sectioned off and nearest the bucking chutes. "Ruth likes to have the best view to see Victor ride."

"Hi," Ruth waved them over. "I thought y'all changed your minds. You're just in time for the bull riding."

"Hi Ruth. Otto. Sorry we're late." Sidney took a seat next to Ruth. "When does Victor ride?"

"He's tenth out of ten."

"Is that nerve-wracking, him going last?" Sidney asked.

"It is for me. But that's Victor's favorite draw. He likes knowing what score he has to beat."

Markus sat next to Sidney with Rex stretched out across the floor in front of the seats. He checked his cell to see if he'd missed a call. He'd asked his contact to leave a message once they'd found the identity of the mystery number. Hopefully, they'd be able to get through.

Sidney tugged at her wig, flipping the blond ponytail over her shoulder. She scanned the audience, looking for a pair of eyes that might be looking for her. "I wish I'd put on a hat," she whispered to Markus, "or a pair of sunglasses."

"Are you nervous? We can leave if you want."

"No. I'm probably just being paranoid." She massaged away the gnawing beginning of a migraine threatening the base of her skull.

The bull riding event was a blur of dust and dirt, of noisy cowbells and eight-second buzzers. Rodeo clowns, with painted faces and wearing comically baggy overalls, entertained the crowd between intrepid demonstrations of fearlessness. Their job was to save the lives of riders who got a hand hung up in their rigging rope, or who were bucked off after two seconds and then slammed to the ground. Without the clown's intervention, an unlucky cowboy would be a target for a bull dead-set on driving a horn through their back or exacting a swift kick to their head.

Nine riders down. Seven times, the bulls won, the riders earning a score of zero. Two times, the riders won. The judge's marks flashed on the scoreboard. One rider scored a 67, the other an 82. The 82 would be a difficult score to beat, but the crowd knew that Victor was the cowboy to do it. With a maximum score of 50 going to the bull's effort, coupled with a maximum score of 50 going to the cowboy's ride, a possible combined score of 100 was the highest a judge could award. Thus far, it had never happened.

Victor climbed the rails of the chute, his spurs clanking against metal. He straddled the top rung, hovering over the bull's back. The bull snorted and pawed, kicking up dust. Victor worked his gloved hand up and down the rope attached to the rigging wound around the bull's chest—up and down, stroking the rope, creating heat. The motion built friction, which heated the rosin on the rope, providing a tacky surface for his glove to stick to. He eased down onto the back of the Brahmin bull. The animal continued to snort and paw the ground, bumping the sides of the chute, over and over, each time pinning Victor's legs against the metal walls.

Ignoring the bull's behavior, blocking out the crowd's noise and the announcer's jabber, Victor concentrated on his task and on the rope in his rosined left glove. His fingers flexed and maneuvered the rope precisely into his practiced grasp. He screwed his cowboy hat down tight with his right hand, thumped the crown of his hat once with his palm—a superstitious act—and arced his arm up over his head. The chute crew watched intently for a quick nod from the rider. Once given, the two burly men hauled on the ropes attached to the gate, pulling with a vigorous effort, shuffling backward as they did. The gate flew open.

Two thousand pounds of hell-on-hooves burst from the confines of the eight-foot by two-and-a-half-foot chute. Spinning, bucking, and leaping, the bull's single-minded objective was to rid himself of the one-hundred-and-fifty-pound nuisance attached to his back.

"Death Wish," the announcer's voice boomed over the din of the roaring crowd, "has been undefeated four rodeo seasons in a row. This bull has sent more riders to the hospital than any bull in collegiate rodeo history!"

The crowd went wild. On their feet. Stomping. Cheering.

Markus and Sidney stood. Ruth jumped up, clutching both Sidney's and Otto's hands.

Round and round the bull spun in ever constricting circles, a bovine corkscrew, first clockwise, then counter. Leaping in the air, he twisted like a fish on a line. Death Wish slammed to the ground, his front cloven hooves plowing into the dirt, his rear hooves kicking the sky. Snot and saliva were slung through the air with each toss of the bull's head. His performance electrified the audience. It would be nearly impossible for any cowboy to stick for eight seconds. This bull was giving the judges every reason to score him high.

Victor spurred with his outside leg during the spins, his

inside leg gripping tightly. Then, both feet worked like furious pistons, up and down. Victor raked his spur rowels in unison with the forward and backward motion of the bull's explosive bucks. When the bull's front hooves were buried in the dirt, Victor's legs were straight down, too. When the bull tipped back, Victor pulled his knees up, raking the spurs upward. Just like the bull, Victor gave the judges every reason to reward his ride.

The sound of the eight-second buzzer screeched above the noise of the crowd. Victor reached down with his right hand and unwound the rope from his left hand. His goal was to time his leap off the bull's back to coincide with the moment the animal's front hooves hit the dirt. First, he'd be closer to the ground. Hitting the dirt hurt less when he didn't have as far to fall. Second, gravity and the natural motion of the bull's back hooves coming to the earth would give him time to flee to the safety of the arena wall before the bull had time to think about it and give chase.

But Victor mistimed his dismount. He jumped off the bull's back at the moment the bull's front end was rising. The bull twisted up and to the right, throwing his head back. His cone-shaped horn snagged Victor's vest. And, before his boots touched dirt, he was tossed high into the air. End-over-end, he toppled back to earth, landing in a heap under the bull's pounding hooves.

Ruth screamed. Sidney clutched her hand tighter as her other hand clung to Markus's arm. The crowd, still on their feet, gasped and cried out as they watched the young bull rider being trampled and gored.

The rodeo clowns were already in motion. Working as a team, two dashed up to the bull to distract him. One clown waved his yellow handkerchief in the bull's face, darting in and out, getting perilously close to the animal's thrashing horns. Another clown swatted the bull's nose with his feathered cowboy hat, then sped away, inviting a chase. He diverted the bull's attention from the downed rider, and the race was on. The third clown hovered protectively over Victor's limp body until medics arrived.

The bull chased the two clowns to the wall, threatening them with his horns, while the clowns made flying leaps to the fence's top rail. The arena crew threw open the end gates, and the bull spied his freedom. He exited the arena with a grand, majestic trot.

Medics raced to the arena and began ministering to the injured rider lying motionless in the dirt. The announcer, his voice solemn, asked for everyone's prayers for Victor, the first rider to successfully complete eight seconds on Death Wish. The judges turned in their scores. When the scoreboard lit up with an 88, the crowd erupted with sustained applause that became a chant.

"Victor. Victor. Victor."

Ruth remained in the stands, holding her breath— watching the quick hands of the paramedics—waiting for movement from her grandson. Two additional medics ran into the arena carrying a bright orange stretcher. Then, a motorized cart hurried the unconscious rider to a waiting ambulance that sped away, sirens blaring.

Still on their feet, the crowd continued chanting Victor's name.

CHAPTER 15

Alpine

A swarm of friends gathered around Ruth in the Big Bend Regional Medical Center's emergency room. The waiting area was congested with cowboys and cowgirls in dusty denims, and a collective of spur rowels clinked a tune on the linoleum floor. Rodeo clowns in their costumes hovered nearby—bull fighters with sad painted faces. Rescuing riders from under the hooves and horns of an angry animal was all in a day's work. They took it personally if they didn't get to the rider quickly enough. Friends tried to cheer them up with pats on the back and kind words. Medics who'd rushed Victor to the emergency room stayed until another call came in. Older friends who'd known Victor's father crowded around, nodding solemnly to one another, sharing common expressions of disbelief, of "this can't be happening again."

They all knew the history. Some remembered firsthand, while for others, the story was an oft-repeated tale of how Victor's father had been left in a permanent vegetative state in an eerily similar accident. On a cool autumn night, many years ago. In the same arena. Atop a bull with an unridden track record. Victor, a few months old at the time, had been too young to understand.

Victor's mother wasn't able to suffer the thought of being the young, vibrant wife of a paraplegic in a permanent

155

vegetative state. She fled Alpine for Los Vegas, abandoning her husband and her baby boy. She left both to be diapered and cared for by Ruth.

"Can I get you some coffee, Ruth? Water? Anything?" Sidney sat close, holding Ruth's hand.

"No. No, thank you. I'm fine..." Her words trailed away. Ruth squeezed Sidney's hand, but her focus was somewhere off in the far distance.

Sidney spotted Markus who stood with Otto, the two in deep conversation a few feet away. She wondered what the two were speaking about so intently and privately, heads bent together. Maybe she should follow Ruth's lead and learn to speak German.

The double doors separating the waiting room from the surgical suite swooshed open. The surgeon emerged. He was the same surgeon from twenty years earlier who had tried to put the pieces of Ruth's son's skull back together. He strode up to Ruth as an uneasy quiet settled over the waiting room. All ears listened. All eyes watched.

Ruth stood, dragging Sidney up with her. Markus and Otto came up behind them and offered hands on shoulders for support. Dr. Lavine, a weary look in his eyes, removed his signature skull and crossbones doo-rag from his bald head and swiped it over his lined and weathered face.

"Ruth." He laid a hand on her shoulder. "Do you want to talk here, or in a private room?"

"Here. Victor's friends need to know, too."

"As you wish." He cleared his throat. "I set the simple fracture to his left radial bone—the slightly smaller bone in the forearm. The compound fracture to his left ulna—the larger of the two bones in the forearm—was a bit more complicated, but I'm happy with the results. An abdominal ultrasound showed no internal injuries other than a bruised kidney, which we will monitor. Three deep lacerations to his head and face stitched up well. If the scars are bothersome, a consultation with a plastic surgeon can be arranged."

At the mention of the injuries to his head, Ruth began to shake. "Is he…? Will he be…?"

Dr. Lavine paused. "Neurologically, the jury's still out. He was responsive to stimuli before we put him under sedation, which is a good sign. Tomorrow—the next twelve to twenty-four hours—will reveal a lot."

Ruth's skin paled, her voice a whisper. "Here we are, twenty years later. First my son—now my grandson."

"We go way back, Ruth. There's no reason for me to be anything other than blunt, so I'm going to be blunt. Your grandson's injures are severe. I'm not sure yet just *how* severe. But Victor stands a better chance of recovering from his injuries than his father stood. His skull isn't caved in like Lawford's was."

Sidney gasped at the horrific description, her body shuddering at the image of a caved in skull. She wondered why these riders weren't opting for helmets with facemasks, like other athletes of extreme sports seemed to be wearing. At the feel of Markus's arm wrapping around her waist, she leaned into him for support.

"May I see him?" Ruth took a handkerchief from her pocket and dabbed her eyes.

"He's still in recovery. The nurse will come and get you when they've moved him to ICU. Only two visitors. I'm keeping him sedated and in a semicomatose state to allow his brain to rest, and to allow possible swelling to subside. I recommend after you see him, you go home and get some rest yourself."

"Yes. Thank you, Doctor."

"Want I should come with you?" Otto offered.

"Would you? Can you stay away from the restaurant for so long? I hate to ask you to do that."

"You didn't ask—I offered. Anyway, Dieter and Heidi can take care of things."

"Sidney and I'll head to the restaurant and lend a hand there. Is that okay with you, Sid?" Markus asked.

"Yes—yes, of course." Sidney wrapped her arms around Ruth. "And, please let me know if I can help you in any way."

Ruth squeezed Sidney's arm and thanked her just as the ICU nurse stepped into the waiting room and motioned for her to follow. The crowd of Victor's rodeo friends filtered out, leaving behind their well wishes and traces of arena dirt and cow manure. Boot prints trailed out of the exit door and disappeared into the darkness.

*****

It was near midnight when Markus and Sidney pulled into the parking lot of Edelweiss. The number of pickup trucks crowding the space out front indicated Heidi and Dieter would be in desperate need of a helping hand.

Markus let Rex out of the back seat. As he turned toward the building, he noticed a row of a dozen or more motorcycles parked along the building's west wall next to the Biergarten. Custom bikes. Expensive looking. Tough looking. The kind that might belong to tough looking riders. A familiar alarm, soft, not too loud, plucked at his nerves.

Be alert, the alarm cautioned. He took note.

"Whatever happened to Victor's father?" asked Sidney, stopping as they reached the porch of the restaurant. "Is Lawford still alive?"

"No. Otto said he lived for almost five years, if you can call that *living*. Ruth took care of him and Victor, with occasional in-home nursing help when Ruth's husband, Silas, could afford it. But, he contracted pneumonia and never recovered."

"How sad. Ruth's amazing. So cheerful, even after all that."

"Exactly."

"And Ruth's husband?"

"Died last year. He and Otto were fishing pals—really good buds. In fact, when Silas knew he was dying of cancer, he made Otto swear that he'd marry Ruth and look after her. Otto promised he would, so his friend 'could go to his grave with an unburdened heart,' quote-un-quote."

"You're making that up." Sidney placed a palm against his chest, her eyes wide.

"I swear I'm not. Otto is a loyal friend until death. He was to my father, too, after they both emigrated here from Germany. That's just the kind of man he is. Ruth doesn't know about the promise made between friends, though. And, I don't think Otto will marry her. He's an eighty-four-year-old bachelor. But he will look after her, without a doubt."

"Oh, my God! What a loving and romantic gesture on Silas's part, to take care of his wife, even after he's gone. And, Otto. He sounds like a very kindhearted person. I can tell he and Ruth are sweet on each other. I'm loving this story."

"Sweet on each other?" Markus laughed as he opened the screened door. "Aren't *you* the old fashioned, romantic one."

"Sometimes." Sidney smiled and shrugged, stepping inside the door Markus held open.

The lights had been lowered, and the volume of music raised to meet the expectations of the midnight crowd who packed the dining area. Even more people lined the bar and spilled over onto the dance floor. Those who couldn't fit inside the building, or who simply preferred to sit under the stars, gathered on the patio of Otto's Biergarten. The jukebox played the latest country songs while the band took a break, and couples vied for space on the sawdusted dance floor.

Markus caught Heidi's attention and waved her over. "Did you get my message?"

"Ja. Thank you for calling. How is he?" Heidi set a customer's drink on the bar and took another order.

"Out of surgery and in ICU. His prognosis is guarded. He's lucky, though, that it wasn't worse. Ruth and Otto will be on their way shortly. In the meantime, Sidney and I can help here. Put us to work."

Heidi threw Markus a look of relief as she tossed him an order book. "Go to the patio. Please save me from them. An upcoming biker rally in New Mexico, and some on their way there are on our patio tonight."

He caught the order book. "I can do that. Do you need help in the kitchen?" He wanted Sidney out of sight—not out in the public eye.

"Not right now," said Heidi. "Aubrey just got here. I put her to business washing dishes."

"Aubrey?" Sidney asked, the name sounding familiar.

"Victor's girlfriend. The 2012 Women's Barrel Racing Champion." Markus shot her a sly grin. "She's fast all right."

"Ah, yes. I remember. You borrowed her letter jacket that chilly night in the barn." Sidney gave Markus a penetrating look he had a difficult time interpreting. "If not the kitchen, Heidi, where can I be of most use?"

"Could you help Dieter at the bar? Pour wine? Open the beers? Make conversations?" Before Sidney could answer, Heidi rushed away.

Markus clamped a hand around Sidney's arm. "You should be out of sight. Not out front."

"Heidi said she needs me here. I'm bartending. I'll see you later." Sidney pulled away from his tight grip. She smiled over her shoulder and waved behind her head at Markus as she settled in behind the bar.

Resigned, Markus muttered under his breath. "At least you'll be safer there than out on the patio."

Markus considered asking Dieter to trade places and let him work with Sidney. For some reason, he was feeling extra protective. *Nervous?* He shook it off and hurried out to the Biergarten, order pad in hand.

The capacity crowd, a rowdy mix of locals and bikers, was restless. Thirsty. But most of all, impatient and unhappy to see Markus taking their orders instead of Heidi.

"Hey, where's the beer wench?" A mustached man wearing black leathers from head to toe shouted above the music. "I want the beer girl wearing the dirndl serving my order."

Others chimed in, shouting vulgarities. Male and female

alike called out to one another what they wanted from the beer wench. They behaved like a pack, each feeding off the others. As the crudeness escalated, the situation quickly spun out of control.

Markus pocketed the order pad. He whistled loudly, getting everyone's attention. "Sorry to keep you waiting, but there was an emergency. I know Heidi's prettier than me, but she's busy in the dining room. To make it up to you, why don't I just bring out a few icy tubs of the best beer in the house. First round is on me. I'll keep the tubs full of beer, water, and sodas until closing time."

Calm settled over the patio. Friendly chatter picked back up among the bikers. Markus turned and hurried off on his mission, followed by the initial instigator, now offering to help carry the tubs of beer.

"Thanks, man," Markus shook his hand, surprised at its smoothness. Judging by this character's rough appearance—the skull and crossbones doo-rag, the pierced ear, the studded jacket and black leather chaps—Markus expected callouses and sandpaper palms.

"Sure. No problem."

"Can I appoint you to let me know when the tubs need refilling? I'll be in here helping the restaurant crew. What's your name, pal?"

"Everyone calls me Doc."

"Doc, huh? Why 'Doc?'"

"Because I am a doctor." The man smiled, seeming to enjoy the look on Markus's face. "Orthopedic surgeon. Surprised?"

"A bit," Markus admitted, shaking his head. "I was at the hospital earlier. A surgeon wore a doo-rag similar to yours. Is that an insider joke?"

"Doctors are funny individuals, don't you know? Well… Sorry about the ruckus earlier. I didn't mean anything by it, and I sure didn't think it'd turn so ugly. It won't happen again. Thanks for the beer, friend." He clapped Markus on the back and strode out, tub of beers in hand.

"Sure. No worries." Markus made his way to the bar.

Inside, the crowd was beginning to thin. A few clingy couples shuffled around the dance floor while two tables in the dining area were shoved together for a game of cards. The bar was still shoulder-to-shoulder, the boisterous crowd making Markus feel edgy.

One more hour till closing time.

"How's it going, bartender?" He leaned against the far end of the bar and angled his position for the best view to scope out the crowd. Casual. Nonchalant. A man just having a drink.

"Pretty good," smiled Sidney. "Turns out I have a knack for this kind of work."

"Where's Dieter? Why are you here by yourself?" He bristled at the sight of her alone behind the bar.

"He stepped to the kitchen to load up a crate of clean glasses. I offered, but he said the crates were heavy. What can I get you?" Sidney looked sideways at Markus as she handed two beers to each waiting customer.

"A shot of *kirschwasser*. And pour yourself one, too." Markus relaxed—a little.

Sidney set the shot glasses down on the bar, filling them with the crystal-clear cherry water. At the sound of the front door opening, she asked, "Should I pour one for Otto, too?"

Markus looked up expectantly. "I'm sure he'd appreciate that."

"Thank you," said Otto when he reached the bar, his "thank" sounding like "tank." He took the shot glass from Sidney. "And thank you for helping out. Poor Ruth. She wanted to stay at the hospital, but the nurses told her 'go home.' Here's to Victor's quick recovery. I don't see that Ruth could handle another death."

They toasted to Victor, clinking their glasses together. At the sound of Otto's voice, Noble came around from where he'd been lying behind the bar, Rex following. The big white dog leaned against Otto's leg, the bond and affection evident. Rex lay down at Markus's feet, heaving a sigh.

"Well, look at that," the male customer, on his way to his well-earned hangover leaned out from his perch midway down the bar. He pointed to the two dogs. "Them look like wolves. How did ya' hide them stinking animals back there all this time and I didn't see 'em?"

"They're not wolves and they don't stink. But it's dark in here. I'm sure that's why you didn't notice them. How about a glass of water, or a cup of coffee?" Sidney walked over and reached for the coffee pot. "Black? Cream and sugar?"

"How about I decide what I wanna drink? Make it another whiskey and coke." His slurred voice was loud and could be heard across the room, turning the heads of Heidi and the customers she waited on.

"I'm sorry, sir, but I can't. I remember hearing Dieter say that last one would be your final round." Sidney saw in her peripheral vision that Markus had stepped closer to where the troublemaker sat.

"Well, he ain't here. You can get me a whiskey, then you can get me what I really want." He elbowed the stranger sitting to his right, speaking companionably to the unfamiliar person, as drunks will do. "What I really want is some of her tight blond pussy."

"All right, pal, that's enough." Markus lifted the man by his shirt collar and dragged him backward off his barstool.

Despite the man's inebriated state, his fight-or-flight reflex instinctively kicked in. He scrambled to his feet and came up swinging. Markus dodged the sloppy punches and tried to grab hold of the man's jacket, wanting to pull him off balance.

The man dashed a hand into his jacket pocket and came out with a knife. With a flick of his thumb on the spring-loaded button, the switchblade jumped to life. "Aw' right. Come on." His hands made a welcoming motion, inviting a fight.

Faster than anyone thought possible, Otto ducked behind the bar where he kept his shotgun, and then ducked back out. The loud slam of the butt-end of the gun striking the top of the bar where Otto stood caught everyone's attention, including the man with the knife.

"I don't allow fighting in Edelweiss," he shouted, the meaning of his words not hampered by his thick German accent.

Seeing his opportunity, Markus karate chopped the knife out of the man's hands, and followed up with a punch to the gut. The man dropped to his knees, gasping for air.

Otto turned to Sidney. "Go trade places in the kitchen with Dieter. Have him phone the sheriff."

"Yes, sir." Sidney slid from behind the bar, easing past Otto. She aimed for the double doors, glancing over her shoulder to see Markus give orders for the man to stay on the floor, flat on his belly.

Markus felt the weight of Sidney's eyes on him. He realized it was the second time in less than twenty-four hours that he'd let this woman hear him give that order to someone— that she'd seen him unleash violence against another person.

But it was necessary. Both instances, they were the perpetrators.

He felt it coming on, the gray-out that proceeded the dark episodes. Hazing his vision. Pushing in. Pricking at the corners of his eyes. Markus tightened his jaw and ground his teeth as he blinked the fog away. With great effort and determination, he willed it not to intrude. He knew he must focus on his prisoner. On his mission. Focus.

CHAPTER 16

Alpine

Sidney stayed in the kitchen until the sheriff left with the handcuffed, drunken troublemaker. She'd overheard the statement given, and again, Markus managed to leave her name out of the police report. His terse account conveyed the event to the sheriff: The drunken patron requested another drink; the bartender refused his request and asked him to leave; he pulled a knife and Markus disarmed and disabled him. No one sitting at the bar offered his or her opinion to contradict Markus's version. With so much alcohol addling his brain, chances were good the drunken customer wouldn't remember the blond behind the bar he was harassing, or his crude comment that started the scuffle.

At least, Sidney hoped that would be the case.

"I overheard what you told the sheriff." She took a seat at the end of the bar next to Markus. "Thanks for keeping my name out of it. That's twice today. Should we go for a trifecta?"

"I'm okay with not. Glass of wine before we head back to the ranch?"

"Sure."

Markus stepped behind the bar, seeing that Dieter was busy at the other end. He handed Sidney a glass and they sipped their wine and watched the few remaining guests spin around the dance floor as the band cranked out the final song of the night, a country-and-western classic.

Sidney hummed along, singing a few phrases and thinking to herself that being in Amarillo by morning, as the lyrics suggested, might not be a bad idea. She stole a glance at the man sitting next to her and thought Alpine in the morning might be just fine, too.

"I like this song." Markus eased off the barstool and pulled Sidney along with him. "Come on, I'd say we're due a little fun."

Before she could resist, Markus led her to the dance floor. She tried to think of the last time she'd been held in a man's arms, bending and swaying belly to belly around a neon lit room with other dancers lost in their own private moments. The singer's nostalgic voice and the sound of boots scratching out a rhythm mingled in a languid, four-beat progression around the floor. The neon glow from the beer logos lining the walls and the soft glare of the television behind the bar induced a sense of calm, allowing Sidney to block out the worries that had dogged her since before she had left Fort Worth. Here, she felt safe. Insulated. Protected.

"You're a good dancer." Markus twirled her under his arm, and then pulled her close.

"You're not too shabby yourself." She felt his breath on her skin and smiled up at him, enjoying this version of Markus, this relaxed, worry-free side. Yet, there was something about the tense set of his jaw that told her it didn't come without effort. Of course, it would take determination, she told herself, given the events of the last twenty-four hours. Still, she found it remarkable that he could seemingly shift with ease between full throttle and cruise control.

As Markus spun her under his arm one more time, she caught a glimpse of the television above the bar. A late edition of the news was airing, with the running message scrolling across the bottom of the screen.

"Stop." Sidney pulled away from Markus. "Oh my God." A hand flew to cover her mouth.

"What? Did I step on your toes?"

She didn't answer. Her face went ashen as she slowly walked closer to the bar, straining to hear the reporter and to see the scrolling text. "It's Aleck." She shot a frightened look at Markus. "Aleck Stavros, my attorney."

Markus walked up behind her, gripping her shoulders with both hands. Sidney shivered. The shiver escalated into a full-body tremor. Standing in front of Markus, she leaned her weight against his body to steady herself. Nausea washed over her in waves of prickly heat.

The reporter, a thin woman wearing her hair in a trendy blond bob, stood in front of a building on Weatherford's historic downtown square. Sidney immediately recognized the building behind the reporter—the building Aleck Stavros shared with his two partners. Yellow crime scene tape cordoned off the front of the building while police, some in uniform, some plain clothed, threaded in and out the door.

A press release photograph of Aleck taken weeks earlier was displayed in the upper left corner of the screen. He'd spoken at a symposium sponsored by a local women's shelter. The fundraising event's goal was to spread awareness about the alarming rise in human trafficking.

"Dieter, turn the volume up." Markus pressed his body closer to Sidney's as the band's final song wound to a close. "Louder. Please."

The reporter spoke into the microphone, her head pivoting from the camera to the crime scene and back. "Mr. Stavros's body was found seated at his desk in his office. Police are trying to determine if the file found next to the deceased victim is in any way related to his slaying. Official cause of death has not been released, but our inside source claims Mr. Stavros was strangled, the wire used as a garrote wrapped around his neck tightly enough to cause near-decapitation. The source also said investigators believe this appears to be a gangland style murder. Mr. Stavros's hands were bound behind his back and a rag was stuffed in his mouth—an obvious message of silencing the victim."

As the reporter attempted to corner a detective for an official statement, Sidney felt Markus pushing her toward the door. She heard his voice call out to Dieter that they were headed to the ranch and heard him apologize for not helping close up the restaurant. He called for Rex to come. His words settled on her ears as if through thick cotton, sounding strangely muffled.

The night's cool breeze felt unnerving against her clammy skin as they hurried toward the Jeep. The car door shut with a bang, and she jumped. The sound of the engine whirring to life, gears grinding, gravel crunching under tires, barely registered in her mind.

Her world came crashing down—spiraling out of control —freefalling in a terrifying descent into a hell she had not envisioned possible.

"Sidney, look at me," Markus demanded in a loud voice, trying to break into her stupor. His left hand gripped the steering wheel, his right hand a vice on her arm. "Sid. Look at me. Talk to me."

Slowly, as if coming out of a trance, she gazed over at the driver's side window, not focusing on any one thing, but staring off into the distance. She blinked away her glassy-eyed stare, bringing the moment into sharp focus. The clarity of what she knew, of what she feared, filled her with dread. "I think my husband murdered Aleck."

"Sid, give me all the specifics—why you think this is possible. Not a sanitized version. Fill in the blanks of Trevor's email. I need to know everything, every detail." He squeezed her arm, and then relaxed his grip.

For the remaining drive to the ranch, she kept her eyes straight ahead, speaking in a detached, rapid-fire manner, summarizing her past. The courtship, the wedding, the marriage, the filing for divorce. Winston's abusive behavior, his intimidations, his threats. Her fears. Meeting Trevor. The video. The S. A. D. file. Rattling off all the ugly details, it was as if the events she described had happened to another person, she the narrator, telling the story of someone else's life.

She hadn't registered the fact that they'd driven through the gate, gone past the arena, and were now parked in front of the barn. It stunned her to feel him staring directly at her with such intensity, and she felt a moment of panic that he wasn't watching the road. Then, realizing the situation and where they were, she let out a relieved sigh that sounded more like all the air in a balloon whooshing out in one single rush.

"And that's why my gut says it must have been Winston. He may not have been the one who physically committed the murder, but he, *undoubtedly*, had it arranged." She turned in her seat to face Markus.

"I'd like to know what file they found on the desk next to Aleck's body. I don't have any contacts in the Weatherford PD." Markus chewed on the inside of his cheek. "Do you?"

"No. But I might in Fort Worth. An Officer Hickson. Aleck brought him to Trevor's house to give me a quick personal safety lesson. Maybe he could help? He and Aleck were close, and he is also a family friend of Eli's."

"I'll check on Officer Hickson and see what I can come up with. But right now, I want you to get your suitcases packed. You're not staying here by yourself. I'm moving you into the lodge. And bring your old cellphone and the file. I'll put them in my safe."

Sidney didn't protest.

*****

Feeling numb, Sidney stood in the cozy suite next to Markus's room. The king-sized bed faced a fireplace that roared to life at the push of a button. Hanging above the fireplace was an oil painting of a spotted fawn almost hidden in a pile of autumn colored leaves. With one glance, Sidney discerned Ruth's masterful brush strokes. She quickly unpacked her suitcase, gathered the file and her old phone, and stepped out into the hallway. She tapped lightly on Markus's door.

"Come on in," he shouted behind the door.

169

Markus was seated in one of the two overstuffed chairs next to the fireplace. Another of Ruth's paintings adorned the wall above the mantle. Lying at Markus's feet, Rex thumped his tail on the floor when Sidney entered.

"Do all the rooms have fireplaces and Youngblood paintings?" She stepped over to admire the portrait of a wolf stalking invisible prey. Whatever he was pursuing, Sidney was left with the impression that he would make the kill.

"They do. Is your room satisfactory?" His hand stroked Rex's head while he watched Sidney's profile studying the painting.

"Yes, very comfortable." Turning, she held out the S. A. D. file she'd retrieved from the locked tack compartment of her horse trailer, along with her old cellphone. "I appreciate your offering to put them in your safe."

"May I look through the file first? And I'd like to see the video and listen to the audio recording."

"Sure. I figured you would, but I'd rather not be in the room when you play the audio. I don't want *that* voice in my head."

"Understandable—I'll play it later. I'm having a brandy. I poured you one, too." He nodded toward the snifter sitting on the table between the two chairs. "Have a seat."

While Markus watched the video, and perused the contents of the Sidney Alexis Dollar file, she checked her email on her new cellphone, hoping to hear from Trevor. There was mail, but it was from Eli.

Sidney said aloud, "I have a message from Eli."

Markus set the file aside. "What does it say?"

She read aloud. *"Dear Sid, please forgive the earlier urgent message I left on your phone. I wasn't sure yet how bad Trevor's injuries were. Smoke inhalation, and minor burns on his hands. The doctor says he can probably go home Monday. But home is a relative term. The house was a total loss—the fire completely destroyed everything. I'm staying at a hotel until I can figure out a plan. I have Trevor's cellphone with me. Please call when you get this message. Love, Eli.*" Sidney's voice was shaking by the time she finished reading.

"My God. Unbelievable." Markus poured another inch of brandy into his glass. "Possibly a message from Winston that he's trying to silence someone else?"

"What's your guess?"

"It appears to be an in-your-face message and not a coincidence. But we need to talk to Eli. She didn't say if the fire was an accident or arson."

"It's almost one o'clock. She's probably sound asleep. I'll call her first thing in the morning. She didn't mention Gunner—I hope Trevor's dog is all right."

"Me too." Markus reached for Sidney's phone. "May I read the email again?"

"Of course." She handed him her cellphone and then pressed her fingers against the back of her neck, rubbing at the migraine that had threatened her all day but had yet to materialize. "I can't stop thinking about Aleck…"

"I know—and I'm sorry." After reading the email twice to look for clues or something he'd missed, Markus got up and walked around behind Sidney. He began massaging her shoulders, his thumbs expertly pressing the spot on her neck where pain radiated upward over her skull.

"Sip your brandy," he directed. "That and a good old-fashioned massage should get the kinks out."

Leaning into the pressure from his strong hands, she let his fingers knead away the tension. *God, that feels good.* She downed the brandy as if it were medicine and then set the empty snifter on the table. Closing her eyes, she tried to clear her mind as Markus worked his magic on her tight muscles. The low, moaning sounds she made could have been interpreted as a woman experiencing any sort of immense pleasure.

"Are you feeling better?" For several minutes, he kept massaging her shoulders and neck, waiting for a reply. "Sid? Hello?"

She'd fallen fast asleep. Lifting her out of the chair, he

carried her to his bed and laid her on top of the comforter. After removing her boots, he covered her with the blanket folded across the foot of the bed.

*****

Markus picked up the S. A. D. file and examined the contents once again. He gave a cursory glance to the nude photos he'd bypassed earlier. He wondered what kind of husband stalks his own wife and takes these kinds of pictures. *The sickening psychopath kind. Dangerous—in an evil way.* It's no wonder Trevor's email contained the caution for me to watch my back, he thought. He'd watch his back, front, and both sides.

Closing the file, he quietly made his way to the wall that concealed his safe-room. He peeked over his shoulder at Sidney, making sure she was still asleep. The form under the blanket hadn't stirred. After going through the procedure to gain entry, he stepped into the room behind the tapestry.

He booted up his computer and saw an email responding to his earlier inquiry. The phone number Eli had called from traced back to the emergency room at Harris Hospital in Fort Worth. Replying to this new email, Markus asked for information about an arson investigation at the Nolan residence in Fort Worth's Mistletoe Heights neighborhood, as well as information about the murder of Aleck Stavros. He suggested to his contact that the fire and the murder might be connected, recommending that the appropriate agencies be notified to look closely at Winston Knight as a suspect.

He quickly fed the pages from the S. A. D. folder into the scanner, saving them in an encrypted file. From Sidney's old cellphone, he downloaded the video of Winston and the audio recording of his verbal threats, saving them to the same file. Attaching the file to his email, he went on to describe Sidney's situation, how Trevor Nolan had become involved, and that Stavros was Sidney's attorney. In his gut, he felt certain the two incidents were at the hand of the bastard she was divorcing.

Before sending the email, Markus sat back in his chair and considered the situation in its entirety. Given the damning content of the video, he felt compelled to make an additional request. He wanted a team standing by, ready to descend on Alpine if needed. If Winston was involved in any way with the *Río Negro* cartel, having well-armed, well-trained backup was imperative. Markus named Moose Erikson to be in charge of the team, with Moose handpicking his desired team members.

After placing the blue-tabbed folder and the cellphone into the bottom drawer of his desk, he locked the drawer, returning the key into its hidden compartment.

When Markus stepped out of the room, prepared to retrace his maneuvers to re-secure the door, he felt he was being watched. Pushing the tapestry farther aside, he looked directly into the wide and questioning eyes of Sidney who was sitting up in the bed.

"I heard a noise. I'm a light sleeper."

"Sorry. I didn't mean to wake you."

"What's behind the curtain, or door number one?"

"It's a walk-in closet, basically. Reinforced as a safe-room."

"A safe-room? Safe from what?"

"From things that don't concern you."

"Everything concerns me."

"Some things you don't need to know."

"Who are you, and what do you really do?"

"I'm Markus Yeager. I keep people safe. Now, enough with the questions for tonight, okay?" He offered a tight smile but didn't wait for her reply.

Sidney watched as he pulled the tapestry across his back in an effort to conceal his movements. She heard a few sounds like someone tapping a hand on a wood panel. A soft swishing like that of someone heaving a deep sigh was the final sound before Markus stepped out from behind the tapestry.

"The same red dragon as what hangs above your entry gate," observed Sidney.

"The same."

"What does the writing say? Is that Japanese?"

"Japanese Kanji. It reads, 'A warrior is worthless unless he rises above others and stands strong in the midst of a storm.'"

"You're that warrior."

"I am." Markus stood rooted in place in front of the tapestry. He wondered how many other questions he'd have to give vague half-answers to. As it turned out, there was only one more.

"I don't want to be alone. May I sleep in your room tonight?"

"Yes." No need for a vague, half-answer—this was a no-brainer.

Throughout the remaining hours before dawn, Markus lay in his bed, eyes open, mind racing, watching Sidney flip-flop back and forth before curling up into a tight ball. She murmured in her sleep, unintelligible sounds and mixed up words. When he laid a hand on her shoulder or stroked her hair offering comfort, she jumped as if slapped and jerked away from him. Afraid to be touched. Fearful of what haunted her dreams.

Even in sleep, she's terrified.

CHAPTER 17

Fort Worth

Still dressed in sooty clothes that smelled of smoke, Trevor sat on the side of his hospital bed. He tapped his foot and pushed the buzzer again to call for a nurse. He had requested to be discharged, his request sounding more like a demand. As he waited, he flexed the fingers of both hands, ignoring the pain. Gritting his teeth, he stretched and contracted them repeatedly, trying to gain a degree of mobility despite the gauze dressings winding around both wrists, covering his blistered palms like fingerless gloves.

As he waited, he ran through in his mind, for what felt like the millionth time, the details he could recall from the fire.

What he remembered from the previous day was climbing into the burning house through a window in his mother's bedroom. He recalled groping for her purse on the nightstand. Upon locating it, he remembered turning back toward the window just in time to get a fleeting glimpse of Gunner bounding through the opening and disappearing into the sooty grayness that filled the room. Coughing and gagging on the acrid smoke, he had tried calling Gunner's name, but his words were choked off.

Leaning out the window, he threw the purse as far away from the house as he could manage. He took a deep breath and filled his lungs before dashing into the hallway where flames surged from the ceiling. He knew Gunner was searching for him and would have gone straight to his bedroom.

He crawled on his knees, keeping his body close to the floor. A few feet into his bedroom's doorway lay his dog's limp body. Without stopping, he clamped one hand onto the dog's harness, dragging Gunner to the window.

The panes had been blistering hot. Moving his hands over the scorching glass, he was frantic to locate the lock, but the thick smoke made it impossible to see. His hand found the metal latch, but the old window wouldn't budge. He removed his T-shirt, wrapped it around his fist, and busted out the glass, punching it over and over to create enough space to escape.

This last scene played again and again in his mind—lifting Gunner's body and thinking how heavy the dog felt, thinking he couldn't hold his breath any longer—turning to the window and trying to crawl through while shielding his dog's body against the shards of glass.

And there his memory went blank.

A nurse too bright and too jaunty for Trevor's mood poked her head into his room. "Your mother just called the nurse's station. She said to tell you she's on her way. And, I've relayed your request for discharge to your doctor, but it may be a while before he answers his pager, it being Sunday morning and all. Then again, he may not approve your discharge—it's awful soon." She offered this information with a sunny smile.

"Then I'll discharge myself."

"Against doctor's orders, you might have a fight with your insurance company on your hands."

"I have bigger problems on my hands than worrying about my insurance company."

Still smiling, she asked, "Can I bring you a breakfast tray? Gray mush they claim is oatmeal? Cold scrambled eggs, burnt toast, and bitter coffee sound good?"

Trevor grinned, despite his gloomy disposition. "I'll hold out for a Starbucks, thanks."

"Suit yourself." The nurse's shoes squeaked her

departure.

These fluorescent lights are killing me.

Sensing an imminent headache, his right eye still stinging from the smoke, he reached for his dark shades and slid them into place. Then, a familiar clip-clop of heels lightly striking the floor grew louder. Despite his partial hearing loss, some sounds he always recognized; it was his mother. But, something seemed off. Different. He stood and moved closer to the door, trying to get a better feel for what he was hearing.

Disbelief, followed by immense relief, washed over him as he stepped out into the hallway. "Gunner! Come here, boy."

Eli released the leash, allowing him to run. The big dog jumped against Trevor, paws on his chest, and the pair fell to the floor. The clanking of metal on tile echoed in the hallway as Trevor's prosthetic leg banged down noisily against the marble surface.

He buried his face in the soft yellow scruff, letting the tears flow.

"You all right, sir?" The squeaky-shoed nurse reappeared. "Do you need help getting up?"

"I'm fine—I'm fine. Thank you." Composing himself, he wiped his face with the bottom of his sooty T-shirt that was cut in several places from breaking out his window. Rolling onto his hands and knees, he cued Gunner to move close alongside. Trevor used the dog's broad back for balance, then pushed himself up and stood.

Eli embraced her son for a long moment. "I could barely keep him from pacing the hotel room last night. He was so eager to be with you."

"I thought he was dead. I remember lifting him out the window, but I don't know what happened after that."

"Sweetie, I told you last night before I left for the hotel that he was fine. You were out of it, though, so it's no wonder you don't remember. They gave you some good pain meds so you'd rest."

"I'm rested enough. I've already requested to be

discharged. Just waiting on the doc to approve it." He sniffed the air. "Am I smelling what I think I'm smelling?"

"If you think you're smelling pumpkin spice latte, then yes." Eli smiled and led her son back into his room. "I set it on your food cart while you and Gunner were wallowing on the floor."

"Thanks, Mama." Trevor gave her a kiss on the cheek. "You bring me my dog *and* a Starbucks. What did I ever do to deserve you?"

Eli plopped down on the visitor's chair by the window. "I remember the good old days when my stomach would let me drink coffee... I still love the smell."

Trevor reached for the coffee on his tray. After removing the lid from his cup, he took a gulp, the creamy foam leaving a small mustache on his lip. "So, fill me in, now that I'm awake and drug free. What happened after I climbed out the window?"

"You never actually made it out of the window. The fire trucks had just arrived, and one of the firemen happened to see you trying to escape. By the time he and another got to you, you had fallen back inside, with Gunner landing across your chest. One fireman crawled in, hefted Gunner out the window, then hauled you out, too."

"I don't remember any of that."

"Trevor," Eli leaned forward in her chair. "I overheard the fireman who lifted you out tell the police he saw several gas cans on the back porch. The fire marshal and a police detective asked me if they belonged to us. When I told them no, those were not our gas cans, it went from a house fire to an arson investigation." Her eyebrows knitted together in worry.

"Arson? That's crazy... It's amazing we got out alive."

"Yes." She sighed heavily. "It is amazing you weren't killed. And what else is amazing is the contraption they strapped on Gunner's head. While some were giving you oxygen and checking your vitals, another fireman placed what appeared to be a diver's helmet on your dog. It forced oxygen into his lungs. Then they gave him IV fluids, just like they did you. Those firemen seemed just as jubilant when Gunner came to as when you did."

"I need to stop by the station later and thank them."

"On our way to get both of us some new clothes, we'll do that." Eli's attention was drawn to the buzzing sound coming from inside her purse. "It must be your new phone—I don't recognize the ring tone." She dug around and pulled it out, handing it to Trevor.

"Yes?" He asked sharply as a greeting, not recognizing the number.

"Trevor, thank God. It's Sidney. After Eli's email last night, we were worried sick. How are you? What happened? What fire?"

"Easy—slow down. I'm going to be fine. Nothing major —"

"Sorry to interrupt. Markus is here with me. I've got you on speaker phone."

"Perfect. Hey, Markus."

"Trevor, how are you, buddy?" Markus's voice sounded pleasant, but strained.

"I've been better. But considering the circumstances, I'm not too bad. Hold on, I'll put you on speaker, too. Mama's here."

Hellos and greetings were passed among the four of them until Markus and Trevor took over the conversation, with Eli and Sidney making an occasional comment.

"I have to ask you, Trevor. Was the fire accidental? Or, do they suspect arson?" Markus got right to the point.

"Interesting you'd ask. The Fire Marshall hasn't contacted us yet with an official ruling, but Mama overheard a fireman tell the police that he'd seen several cans of accelerant at the scene. It was no accident."

"Thank God both of you got out. And Gunner—is he…?"

"Hold on." Trevor gave the command to speak and Gunner responded with a loud bark. "I thought I'd lost him, but thanks to the Fort Worth Fire Department, he's fine. Just a little smoke inhalation..." His voice broke with those words.

Eli chimed in, asking, "Markus, is there a reason you asked if it was arson?"

"There is a reason," Markus said, his tone somber. "Did you have the television on last night or this morning? Seen any news?"

"No," responded Trevor as Eli shook her head. "Why?"

"It's been on all the channels, both local and national, and it is the headline of this morning's paper. Aleck Stavros was murdered last night in his office, gangland style."

"Oh—my—God." Trevor shot an incredulous look at his mother who sat with one hand covering her mouth, the other in a white-knuckle grip on the arm of her chair.

"I don't think it's a coincidence that Sidney's divorce attorney was brutally murdered on the same day that the person who facilitated her disappearing act and whose text message was intercepted had his house torched. Do you?"

"No, I don't. And we can give the police a description of possible suspects." Trevor filled them in on the thugs in the black sedan who'd paid a call yesterday, and he described the photograph of Sidney he'd been handed. "The emergency text message from her phone to mine was written on the back of an eight by ten glossy of Sidney, along with a personal message from, quote-unquote, her husband. It was a direct threat for me to stay away from her, if I knew what was good for me. I gathered he was acting on the assumption that Sid and I were having an affair."

"Did Aleck know about that incident?" Markus asked, his voice edgy.

"Yes. I called him after I called the police. He came over right away. In fact, he warned me as he was leaving that his concern was not just about Sidney's safety. He felt ours was in jeopardy, too. I shot you a quick email before I lay down for a nap. Both Mama and I were exhausted."

"Fuck. I never got the email," said Markus. "Sorry, Eli.

Pardon the language."

"No apology necessary," said Eli. "Go on, Trevor. Tell the rest."

"I woke up with the house on fire. All I had time to do was grab my cellphone and my wallet, and Gunner, of course. I tried getting to Mama's room, but the smoke was too intense. So, Gunner and I went out through a window in the next bedroom. Mama was already outside, thank God."

"I'm so sorry," said Sidney. "This makes me sick."

"And then, Trevor went back inside to get my purse," offered Eli. "Gunner followed him in. I almost lost both of them." With that, Eli broke down, sobbing.

Trevor moved next to his mother and put a comforting arm around her shoulders. "But you didn't lose us. We're here. And, we'll be fine." He handed her a tissue from the box next to his bed.

"Yes, and I'm grateful," she sniffed, dabbing at her eyes. "Sid, how're you holding up through all this?"

"Holding up—just—I guess, in shock. I'm so sorry about your house."

"Like you, I'm in shock. I cried myself to sleep last night, thinking about all that was lost in the fire. All the memories. The photographs. My sons' baby clothes I'd been saving to some day pass down to grandchildren. The chair I rocked my babies in. I still have the memories, and I'll get over it. It'll just take time. It'd be a different story had Trevor and Gunner not made it out. I don't know what I'd do if…" Eli's voice trailed away.

"I'm so sorry, Eli. I wish there were something I could do," Sidney consoled. "And your wigs! I should send you the one you loaned me."

"Oh honey, I think you need that one more than I do. Besides, I've been thinking about changing my hair color, anyway. Maybe I'll rise from the ashes and come up a mysterious brunette, or a fiery redhead."

"That's Mama," said Trevor. "She takes things in stride

and comes out smiling."

"Eli, I admire your spirit, and I'm sorry for your loss. If I can help in any way, just let me know," said Markus.

"Thank you. I've already contacted my insurance agent. Everything will be fine."

"Trevor, how long will you stay in the hospital?" asked Markus.

"Doc wants me to stay until tomorrow, but I'm leaving today, with or without his blessing."

"Are you sure you're okay to leave? What's one more day?"

"One more day that could be better spent putting a plan in place. My first thought is to get Mama out of the country. Her passport, which she can get tomorrow, is in the safety deposit box at the bank. Today, however, we need to buy some clothes and essentials. There's a lot to do. I can't sit around here."

"All right. I agree. Let's discuss a comprehensive plan for both of you. Are you up for coming to Alpine, once Eli is safely on her way to…where are you sending her?"

"My brothers are in England at a soccer symposium in York. Mama is giving me a thumbs up and a smile of approval."

"Perfect. I could use another set of eyes and ears here to help me, if you're willing. You need to get the hell out of Fort Worth, anyway, but with extreme caution. Covertness is essential."

Trevor chuckled and said sarcastically, "My hearing and my left eye might not be much use to you, but I'll gladly offer the service of my right."

"Sorry, buddy. I forgot."

"I forget sometimes, too. Anyway, I agree on coming to Alpine. What're your thoughts on a plan of execution?"

Markus laid out his strategy, thinking aloud, and taking notes as he went. When Trevor brought up the subject of stopping at the Fire Department to show his appreciation, Markus advised to forgo that social call. The fewer the stops made, the greater their chance of disappearing successfully.

Trevor and Eli followed his instructions precisely, including rescinding his request for the doctor's discharge orders. To anyone who might call the hospital seeking information, it would be preferable for it to appear that the patient was still there.

As soon as the call ended, Eli went to the hospital's gift shop and purchased two Dallas Cowboy's ball caps she'd spied in the display window earlier. She donned the cap, Trevor his, along with T-shirts she'd purchased announcing the wearer was the proud parent of a new baby daughter. They exited the hospital through the emergency room door where there'd likely be more people coming in and going out, making it easier to blend in with a crowd.

Having left Eli's Range Rover in the hospital's parking garage, they took a taxi to a car rental facility where Eli rented a small compact. With one stop at Target where they picked up suitcases, clothes, and other necessary supplies, and then another stop at a veterinary clinic to have Gunner checked over, their errands were complete.

They drove to the Hyatt Regency Hotel located within the gates of the Dallas Fort Worth International Airport, all the while keeping an eye on the rearview mirror, making sure they hadn't been followed. There they would wait for the delivery of a boarding pass for Eli on a nonstop flight to London's Heathrow airport. Included in the delivery would be a train ticket from London north to York. Markus's contact would purchase them in Eli's name but would pay using an untraceable credit card issued under an assumed name. He promised a courier would have it to her no later than 10:00 A.M., and told Trevor to look for an email with further instructions for him.

The following morning, after obtaining Eli's passport her boarding pass, they dropped off the rental car and took a shuttle bus to the terminal. Waiting for the three o'clock departure time would be an excruciating test of nerves. As she and Trevor hugged goodbye, he encouraged her to have a Bloody Mary to relax. She followed his advice. Then had a second.

Trevor had received Markus's email earlier on his cellphone. As instructed, he hailed a taxi, and he and Gunner made their way to Fort Worth's Meacham Field Airport where Markus had arranged for a private flight to Alpine. The pilot, a retired Marine who went by the nickname "Vader" because of his raspy voice, ran a small air taxi service. He owed Markus a favor and was happy to help—anything for a fellow Marine—and, anything to get more flight time.

According to Federal Aviation Administration regulations for flights leaving out of Meacham Field, a flight plan had to be filed for departures using instrument flight rules. Vader filed it as required; however, it was filed showing Taos, New Mexico as the destination. Once out of the terminal controlled airspace, the plan called for Vader to cancel his IFR route and continue on via visual flight rules. Doing so would make it easier to keep his plane's movements from being tracked to Alpine. When asked if he wanted to receive flight following service from the air traffic controller, Vader politely declined.

Soon after the twin engine Beech Baron's wheels cleared the runway and they were safely airborne, Trevor breathed a sigh of relief. He gave Gunner a new chew toy and then closed his eyes, leaning back in his seat. For the first time since waking up in the hospital almost thirty-eight hours earlier, he let his mind and body relax.

*****

After the plane cleared the end of the runway and banked left, Anton held binoculars to his eyes and read aloud the plane's tail number. He stood next to a black sedan parked near the tarmac, the same black sedan that had followed Eli and Trevor when they'd left the hospital. The same black sedan that had shadowed their every move, unobserved. The person sitting in the back seat nodded as he scribbled the numbers down on a pad of personalized stationary. The embossed letterhead showed a knight wearing armor and sitting astride a black warhorse, the initials C. W. K., III written in dark red script.

CHAPTER 18

Alpine

Sidney powered off her cellphone, watching Markus intently as he finished scrawling a few notes, at times chewing on the eraser end of his pencil or tapping it against his palm. It would be good to see Trevor tomorrow, she thought. And, she was filled with relief that Eli soon would be safely out of the country.

Sitting with her back against the headboard of Markus's bed, different thoughts played out in her mind. She thought about the Mistletoe bungalow, the home Eli had loved dearly and where her family had forged a lifetime of happy memories. Their home being burned to the ground devastated Sidney. She felt responsible that it was her text message to Trevor that had led the arsonist there.

Stranger therapy wasn't very therapeutic, at least not for Trevor.

She wished she'd kept her mouth shut and her personal misery to herself. If she'd turned down Trevor's invitation of unburdening her worries on him, he and Eli would have been spared this catastrophe.

Would Aleck still be alive?

"Hey, where'd you go? You're a million miles away." Markus placed a hand on her arm as he turned to face her, setting his pencil and notebook aside.

187

"Not that far, only about four hundred miles, give or take. My mind was back in Fort Worth, wondering if Aleck might still be alive and Eli's house still standing had I not entangled Trevor in my disastrous life. I feel responsible for—"

"Don't, Sidney. You're not responsible. It was a tragedy, no doubt, Aleck's murder, Eli's house. But you can't take the blame for the actions of a deranged maniac."

"I understand where you're coming from. I get it. But still, look at the chaos that trailed behind in my wake when I left Fort Worth."

"But still, nothing. You fled a dangerous situation, running from that evil bastard of a husband. He'll be held accountable. Trust me." The severe look he leveled on her conveyed as much.

"Whether I trust you or not is irrelevant." Sidney drew her knees up to her chest and wrapped her arms around her legs. Her shoulders rose and fell as she filled her lungs, then expelled the air forcefully. "Some evil bastards, to borrow your phrase, have ways of circumventing laws, especially when they know the laws inside and out."

"I don't blame you for being cynical. But it would be nice to hear you say you trust me—not for my sake—but for yours. Giving your trust to someone and having them prove you right by honoring that trust validates you."

"Before your so-called plan of validating me occurs, I need to get back to the point of trusting myself. Of listening to my gut." Sidney fought back tears. "That's the only validation I need right now."

Markus stood, picking up his notebook. "You listened to your gut and followed Trevor's advice to come here. That was exactly the right move. Now if you'll excuse me, I need to get on the computer for a bit. I have some coordinating to do with Eli's plane ticket and getting Trevor here."

"Back to the bat cave?"

Markus chuckled. "Yes, to the bat cave."

"I need to get a message to my cousin, to let her know

what's going on. I've been afraid to call her, afraid that Winston somehow has eyes and ears on her, too. Is it possible that you could contact her safely?"

"I can make that happen. She can only be told you're okay. Not where you are."

"I understand. Do you need her email, physical address, or phone number?"

"I already have her info. I'll request an agent contact her in person to deliver your message. It'll be done discretely. They know what they're doing."

"You already have Jessi's information?"

"Yes." Markus gave a slow nod.

"How did you come by that?" Sidney peered up at him with a puzzled expression.

"Through my contact in the Company. A background check was in order for anyone who might be under pressure from Winston. His involvement with the *Río Negro* cartel leaves everyone subject to scrutiny. Even family."

"Jessi's like a sister. She would *never* have anything to do with Winston or his shady business ventures."

"Shady? They're much darker than shady. They're downright black."

"All right. I agree. But I can assure you, Jessi is as innocent as a lamb."

"A lamb in distress might bleat what they know to the person applying pressure. It happens all the time."

Sidney considered this. Yet, she couldn't fathom her cousin not having her back. They'd grown up together like sisters, and were still each other's best friend. No, she decided, Jessi would never betray her, no matter what type of strain she was under. Besides, who would put pressure on her in the first place? And, why? If Winston did have someone watching Jessi, then he would know that the two were no longer in communication.

Sidney took the notepad from Markus and jotted a quick message, signing it: L & L from the M. P. Handing it to him, she said, "This is what I want to tell Jessi. It's okay if you read it. Nothing classified or top secret."

He scanned the note, and then raised his eyebrows. "I'll make sure she gets it. L and L from the M. P.?"

"Love and laughter from the Mountain Princess. Signing it this way, she'll know it's legitimate and from me."

"Is that a super top-secret code name?" Markus asked, half in jest.

"When I was a young girl, my grandfather started calling me his little mountain princess. We were vacationing in Alaska, flying over Mount Denali, and my father had a heart attack at the controls of the Piper Super Cub he'd rented for the day. We crashed on the side of the mountain. It killed my mother, too. Grandfather used to make up stories and draw fantastical, fanciful pictures of a mountain princess who floated on snowflakes far above all the scary things below."

"That must have been awful. I'm sorry that happened to you."

"I bet you already knew all about it, though. I'm sure you did a background check on me, as well. Why wouldn't you?"

Markus's expression didn't convey affirmation or denial. He held her eye contact for a long moment before offering only a few carefully chosen words, "I didn't know about your being nicknamed The Mountain Princess."

"But you know everything else about me. Thank you for confirming my suspicion." She didn't feel shocked or perturbed that he'd done a background check on her. If the tables were turned, she'd have done the same thing.

"I'd be a fool to think I know everything about you. I have a feeling that's a complicated subject requiring further exploration," he said with a teasing tone to his voice.

The way his slow drawl melted over the words "further exploration," caused all sorts of images to flash through her mind. She fought to refocus on the conversation and tried not to stammer.

"And, Grandfather shortened it—he shortened it to just 'Princess.' From the time I was a little girl until the day he died, that's what he called me."

"Well, Princess, if you'll excuse me, I need to take care of business now. I won't be long."

"While you're doing that, I think I'll go to my room and shower." Sidney stood to leave, wishing he'd say more about what he found out about her background, yet knowing he would not.

"Are you okay being alone? You can use my shower if you want."

She put on a brave smile. "Thanks for offering. I'm fine now, in the light of day. It was just last night that I was afraid to be alone."

"It's okay to be afraid. Only sociopaths don't feel fear. I'm glad you're not a sociopath," Markus teased.

"I've experienced more fear than I care to admit, which must indicate that you're safe with me."

"Likewise." He gave her a momentary flash of a grin.

Sidney picked up her boots off the floor, and as she made her way across the room, she paused. "What's the saying on that John Wayne poster hanging in the barn apartment? The poster in the bedroom?"

"Ah, yes. Words to live by. It reads, '*Courage is being afraid but saddling up anyway.*'"

"Yes, that's the one. I'm adopting that as my motto." She jutted her chin in defiant affirmation. "Um, is it okay if I leave the bedroom doors open while I shower? Just in case…"

"Sure. Leave all the doors open, if you want."

*****

Fog covered the upper half of the mirror hanging above the vanity sink. Because the door was wide open into her bedroom, steam escaped the cozy bathroom before leaving its full mark on the glassy surface.

Sidney rushed through the tasks of hair washing, body scrubbing, and leg shaving before hurriedly turning the faucets off. She'd left the shower's glass doors cracked open to have a better view of what lay beyond. The custom doors were etched with a landscape scene of pine trees and mountains. The scene soothed her, and she imagined what those pine trees might smell like after a soft rain. With the doors open, the spray from the shower soaked the towels she had spread on the floor.

She stood at the sink, one towel wrapped around her body and another wound around her head. Swiping a hand across the foggy mirror, she peered at her wet, distorted image. "I'm courageous—afraid—but saddling up anyway." She solemnly spoke the words to the woman in the mirror staring back at her.

Glass shattered from somewhere outside her room. She jerked around, the unnerving sound ripping her from the image in the mirror. Her breath caught in her throat. *Where did that come from?* She gripped the doorframe with both hands and eased cautiously into her bedroom—listening—waiting—her pulse pounding in her ears.

She thought about closing and locking her bedroom door. But then what? Why didn't she have the Taser with her? Or any weapon, for that matter. Standing frozen in place, trying to figure out what to do, she stared at the window and considered crawling out. It would be a long two-story drop to the ground below, and then a short sprint to the truck and her Taser. She weighed the odds, realizing that the likely possibility of a broken ankle would make escaping difficult.

A voice, followed by a familiar noise broke through her fear. She heard Markus shouting a few choice curse words, and then the sound of what she gathered to be a vacuum cleaner. Releasing the breath she'd been holding, Sidney eased out into the hallway and peeked into Markus's room. He was on his knees, half in and half out of the bathroom, using a cordless vacuum to suck up shards of broken glass scattered across the slate tile floor.

"I may be a bit jumpy, but that scared the crap out of me." She walked into the room, her hand clutching at the towel around her body. "What happened?"

"Sorry to scare you. I guess my shaving mirror wasn't attached to the wall securely enough. Careful, don't walk any closer. I wouldn't want you to cut your feet." He stood and turned, his body bare except for the jeans hanging loose and low on his hips.

"I hope that doesn't mean seven years of bad luck." Sidney was acutely aware of her own lack of clothing as she felt his eyes sweep up and down her towel-cloaked body.

"I'm not superstitious, but I *am* a believer in luck, both bad, and good."

"I concur. Need some help?"

"No thanks. I've got it." His eyes lingered for a long moment before he turned his attention back to the mess on the bathroom floor.

Sidney stood transfixed, disturbed at the sight—not at the broken glass—disturbed at the sight of this man's broken and battered body. Markus bore numerous scars across his muscular back, some deep and telling of what must have been unbearable pain, some superficial and appearing to be the result of systematic torture. A curious pattern of wounds wound around both shoulders, and a zigzag of slash marks still reddened the flesh across his abdomen.

"Markus…" Sidney moved farther into the room. "Please tell me. What happened?"

"I knocked my shaving mirror off the wall." His voice was modulated, but his words were clipped.

"Don't be obtuse. I meant…"

He stood and turned, meeting her gaze. "I know what you meant. You don't want to go there."

"What if I do?" She stepped closer, placing her hand softly against his chest and trailing it lower across the scars crisscrossing his stomach. "What if I do want to go there? What if I want to know everything?"

His stomach sucked in at the coolness of her touch. Markus grabbed hold of Sidney's wrist and pulled her to him.

With the other hand, he removed the towel from her head and wound his fingers into her damp hair, tilting her face up to his. "What if I can't tell you?"

"Can't, or won't?"

"Both." With his hands now firmly planted on either side of her waist, he lifted Sidney up to eye level. She wound her legs around his middle, her arms around his neck. His mouth on hers decisively ended any further discussion of the matter.

The towel covering Sidney loosened. She wriggled free of it and allowed it to fall away. The primal noise she heard coming from Markus resonated from his throat—or deeper. His kisses matched the need and desire she no longer could contain. She wanted to touch, to feel, to breathe, to taste. All at once. Now.

Markus stood rooted in place, holding Sidney, devouring her mouth, filling his senses with her naked body pressed against his bare torso. With caution, he moved gingerly away from the bathroom. A stray shard he didn't see bore into his heel, causing him to curse and hop on one foot. This sent them toppling onto the bed in a twisted heap.

"Ouch. Damn it." Markus caught himself with one arm braced against the fall, while clutching Sidney to him with the other.

She landed on her back, with Markus splayed halfway on top of her. Attempting to stifle her giggles proved useless, so she gave in to them. The giggles deepened into a wholehearted laugh that began with a snort through her nose.

"Well, that was suave." Markus joined in with the laughter. "One of my better moves, I must say."

"Not exactly romantic, but now that you've got me where you want me, what are you going to do about it?"

"I'm going to make amends and show you how romantic I can be."

She took a deep breath, letting it out slowly. "All right. Show me."

He dropped to the floor on his knees. Pulling her body to

the edge of the bed, he spread her knees with his broad shoulders. What he began to do was, in her way of thinking, more carnal than romantic. But then her mind spun away to another realm where words had no purpose. Her body melted into that place where urges and passion and desire were all that mattered.

*****

Markus lay on his side with Sidney spooning against him, and he listened to the sound of her deep breathing as she drifted off to sleep. Her buttocks pressed against his crotch and he resisted the urge to wake her up.

He still wanted to show her that he could be romantic. However, if he were honest with himself, neither of them had any notion that romance was necessary. And it was a good thing, because there had been nothing sweet and tender about what they just did. Theirs was an act of primal, scorching, need-you-now sex, with each as needy as the other.

At the same time, though, it had been freeing. Or, at least for him, more like an awakening. The last time he'd had sex was in Sarajevo with Sonja. *Jesus Christ, had it really been over four years?* He shook his head, wanting to put those thoughts of her back into the safe place in his mind where he'd shelved all remembrances of that place and that woman—of what those bastards did to her—of everything about their last day.

Sidney stirred, her body pressing closer, and heat shot through Markus's groin. Ignoring his aroused state, he closed his eyes, willing himself to clear his mind, to think neutral thoughts, to ignore the naked woman lying in his arms. Yet, the way her hair smelled and felt when it brushed his face, and the feel of the small curve of her breast in his hand caused him to think many other thoughts that had everything to do with wanting to stay awake.

Jeez. Stop it. Go to sleep.

On the verge of drifting off, the sound of Rex whining to be let out brought him back to the present. He pulled on a pair of boxer shorts and a T-shirt and quietly made his way down the stairs, hobbling on his wounded foot. Waiting for the dog to do his business, he tweezed the piece of glass from his heel, and his mind started racing, thinking about the things he needed to accomplish this day. But mostly, thinking about Sidney. He decided to stay up and not go back to bed. Make some coffee. Waffles sounded good. And bacon.

He carried a tray upstairs, the tray laden with a plate stacked with waffles covered in maple syrup along with strips of crispy peppered bacon, two cups of coffee, and two glasses of mimosas. Walking on the ball of his right foot, he tried not to anger the open wound on his heel, while at the same time, trying not to spill the drinks.

When he reached the top of the stairs, Sidney, wearing one of his shirts, opened the bedroom door. Sunlight streamed in from the window to her back, creating a soft halo around her. He stopped midstride, capturing the moment in his mind.

"You look gorgeous." He moved forward, not taking his eyes off her.

"I'm sure I look a mess, but thank you. You've been busy."

"Are you hungry?"

"Starved. I thought I smelled coffee. And bacon."

"Get back in bed. I'm going to feed you. I haven't forgotten about showing you my romantic side."

She turned around, slid out of his shirt, and slipped back into bed.

*****

Sidney sat upright and propped against the headboard. The dark burgundy sheet tucked under her arms provided a modest cover. She patted the corners of her mouth with a linen napkin, a satiated smile easing across her face.

"That was delicious," she said, feeling a bit tipsy from the champagne.

"I'm glad you enjoyed it." Markus refilled their coffee cups. "But, was it romantic? Did I prove to you I'm not a bumbling, stumbling oaf?"

She laughed. "Yes, it was romantic. I didn't realize how much I loved maple syrup." Markus had dipped his finger into the syrup and she licked it off. Actually, as she corrected her thought, she sucked it off. Then, at one point, she started to wipe a dribble of syrup off his mouth but elected to kiss it away instead, which led to some playful tongue gymnastics.

"There's more downstairs in the kitchen," he said with a lascivious grin. "A whole bottle."

She couldn't tell if he was sincere or joking, but the thought of licking a whole bottle's worth of maple goodness off his entire body appealed to her. Or, vice versa. "Later, perhaps. Right now, can we be serious for a moment? I want to say something to you that I've been thinking about."

"Of course, Sid. Is something wrong?" He sat back, giving her his full attention.

"No, not wrong. I just wanted to clarify something. Romance, or your being romantic, is not what I need or want. Please don't get me wrong, I appreciate the effort, and I, well, I don't really know what I'm trying to say. Everything about this morning felt so natural, so easy. So— right. The sex was great. More than great. But, that's all I want, or expect at this point."

Markus lay on his side, his head propped in the palm of his hand. The more he studied her, the more fidgety she became. With sheer determination, she forced her feet to stop swishing under the covers. Had she been too blunt? She didn't think so— she honestly spoke what was on her mind.

I only want your body. It's all about the sex.

Not quite—it's all about my feeling in control. And, the sex.

Jeez, what's he going to think about me?

Her feet began swishing back and forth again under the covers.

"I've been thinking the same thing. And I agree with you. When I said I wanted to show you I could be romantic, it was just a throw away expression and my attempt at humor. I do that a lot. Use humor to—"

"To diffuse tense situations. Yes, I've noticed."

"Or embarrassing situations, like my dropping you on the bed and falling on top of you."

"And I thought that was just you performing your caveman act."

"Hardly. Although, being a caveman has a certain charm."

"Well, I'm relieved to hear you're on board with 'no romance required.' Thanks for understanding." She reached out a hand and stroked his face, running her fingertips against the roughness of his whiskers still needing a shave. "Truly. Thank you."

"You're welcome. So, we'll be friends with benefits. Isn't that the popular slang?"

"Yes, I believe that's what it's called. And, I'm okay with that. More than okay."

"Please hold that thought." Markus picked up the tray and empty glasses. "I'll be right back."

She held that thought, along with dozens of others vying for attention. She wanted to encourage him to open up and tell her what had caused such horrific scaring on his body. Or, to share with her what tormented his mind. She wanted to ask him about the significance of the red dragon hanging over his entry gate and painted on the tapestry concealing his safe-room. That same image of the menacing serpent he also had tattooed on his right hip.

On the one hand, she felt cautious about opening herself up to the intimacies involved when one knows too much about the other. She didn't want to get too close. Yet, how was she going to help him with his PTSD if she shut him off?

It would take a delicate balancing act, protecting her emotions while gaining his trust, enough so that he'd answer her questions. However, she knew better than to broach those subjects now. In time, he might allow her a glimpse into his past. But, she understood today was not going to be that day.

When he returned, he took Sidney by the hand, giving it a playful come-with-me tug. With a complicit grin, she slid out of bed and allowed him to lead her to the bathroom and into the luxurious shower, spacious enough to rival any five-star spa. She figured this was an ideal way to whittle away the hours until tomorrow when Trevor would arrive. All the while, she pretended not to notice the bottle of maple syrup clutched in Markus's other hand.

CHAPTER 19

Fort Worth

Winston sat at his desk, the office lights dimmed to a faint glow. Leaning back in his chair, he propped his booted feet cross-ankled on his desk. He stared at the cigar stub he'd just ground out in the Texas-shaped turquoise and silver ashtray. His attempt to only chew the cigars, and not smoke them, had been short-lived. He drummed his fingers against the chair's armrests and glared out the window at contrails crisscrossing the clear blue sky.

Where the hell are you, Sidney? He picked up the stubby cigar and considered relighting it before crushing it completely in the ashtray. *Wherever Trevor has flown, that's where I'll find you.*

His cellphone's jarring ringtone, the repetitive sound of a trumpet blaring, jolted him from his reverie. "Yes? What'd you find?"

Anton replied, "After departing Meacham, the plane cancelled its IFR flight plan to Taos. It never landed there."

"It didn't just disappear, Anton. It landed somewhere, goddammit."

"I was getting to that. Our pal Bruno with the DEA tracked the tail number for us. He located the plane. It landed in Alpine."

"Alpine? In west Texas?"

"That's the place."

"Take Fredo and Juan with you and get out there ASAP. I'll call the hangar and have the Citation jet ready. I want you there before the sun goes down."

"And then what, Boss?"

"Find my goddamned wife and bring her home. And I want that file she took from my briefcase. It contains—sensitive information. You know what to do about that bastard, Trevor."

"I know what to do. We'll take care of it, Boss."

Winston disconnected the call. *Even this Boss answers to a bigger Boss.*

His thumb hovered over the speed dial. He vacillated, drawing in deep breaths in an effort to alleviate rattled nerves that had soured his stomach and loosened his bowels. Dropping the phone onto his desk, he grabbed a magazine and hurried to his private restroom. That call would have to wait.

Thirty minutes later, Winston emerged, knowing he couldn't put off the phone call any longer. Feeling pale and unsteady, he decided a cigar and a scotch would ease those symptoms. Before he could cross the room, his phone vibrating against the surface of his desk and the incessant trumpeting demanded his attention. Glancing down, he saw that the caller ID was blocked, but in his roiling gut, he knew who was calling.

Answering was the last thing he wanted to do.

But what he wanted or didn't want was of no concern to the person calling, and he knew it. He snatched up the phone and barked into the mouthpiece, "Yes?"

The voice on the other end also ignored any greeting or pleasantry but got straight to the point. He spoke with a cultured European accent. The man known as *El Cuchillo*, The Knife, calmly informed Winston of a change in plans.

Winston's jaw tightened as he listened. "Now, hold on a minute. That's not what we agreed on. I instructed Anton to take care of Trevor but to bring Sidney home," he argued emphatically.

"Anton doesn't answer to you anymore. I've removed

you from the equation. From here on out, Anton will answer directly to me. He called me as he was departing Meacham Field for Alpine. Apparently, he's lost confidence in you and your decisions. As have I."

Winston reached into his desk, and grabbing a bottle of antacid tablets, popped several into his mouth. "Ordering Anton and his crew to torch that house was a good decision. It sent a clear message."

"Ordering a daytime arson hit was imprudent. It should have been carried out at night. You took too big a risk and the crew almost came face-to-face with curious neighbors. Anton reported that if not for a high privacy fence they were able to scale and hide behind in the alleyway, they would have been caught red-handed."

"If they had been caught, it would have been because of their own stupid carelessness."

"Similar to your own carelessness? You allowed your wife to walk away with—how did you say it?—*sensitive* information. The DEA, the FBI, and the ATF all would piss themselves to get their hands on your *sensitive* documents. If it weren't for Anton's sharp eye and his turning that file over to me after he removed it from that attorney's office, I'd have never known exactly how damning all of that information was. You kept meticulous notes."

"Anton is a disloyal back-stabber." Winston's voice shook with anger at the thought of his protégé turning against him. "If it weren't for me, he'd still be a falcon, an information gatherer. I plucked him off the streets, and it was I who promoted him to hitman."

"His loyalty now belongs to me. He will make sure both Trevor *and* Sidney keep quiet. Permanently." His voice sounded impatient.

"Trevor must be taken out. I agree. But once I have Sidney back home, I know I can persuade her to keep her mouth shut." Winston's stomach churned. Painful and violent spasms knotted his gut. He wondered if he'd have to make another dash to the toilet.

"She's a liability. She won't be coming home. This matter no longer concerns you."

"Everything about my wife concerns me." Winston gripped the phone tightly. Despite cool air blowing from the vent, perspiration soaked the back of his tailored French shirt.

"Then concerning your wife, I'll allow you to give one final order as a quasi-lieutenant, a lieutenant who failed his probation period miserably. I have many customers worldwide who'd pay a handsome price for—how should I say this—use your wife for their pleasure. Or, she can be dead. You choose."

"You son of a bitch," he hissed through gritted teeth.

"Careful. You're on shaky ground."

Winston froze, the moment dragging out for what seemed like an eternity.

"Well?" *El Cuchillo* asked, his voice devoid of emotion. "What is your decision, ex-lieutenant?"

Winston's chest heaved out and in with each deep, ragged breath. He held the phone in a vice-like grip, pressing it hard against his ear and grinding his teeth until his jaws ached. Dropping his chin to his chest, he said in a resigned voice, "Sidney won't be anyone's fucking sex slave."

El Cuchillo abruptly ended the call.

Winston threw his cellphone against the wall, the impact gouging a dent in the plaster. Pacing the room, he stomped to the liquor cabinet. His hands shook as he lit a fresh cigar and poured a double scotch, downing half in one gulp. "Goddammit," he shouted to no one. "Only Trevor was supposed to die."

Fuck you, Rafael.

From the moment he had first met Rafael Cordoba, known as *El Cuchillo* throughout the organization, Winston was given a rare glimpse into the world of the *Río Negro* cartel. After all, it was a family business. When he and Sidney married, he was immediately considered family, and family loyalty was not only implied within the ranks of the organization, it was expected.

Winston knew an opportunity when he saw one, and he'd seized it with both fists. He was certain his star would rise and he'd gain promotion to more than simply the attorney, business adviser, and money launderer. Being invited to act as a lieutenant in the Texas arm of the organization meant more power, more money, and more freedom. As a lieutenant, he would have the clearance to order any of the cartel's jets based at Meacham Field to fly wherever the hell he wanted. And, it cleared the way for him to make himself indispensable to a man he considered his cousin, not by blood, but by marriage.

Dammit—it's not supposed to end like this.

Winston downed the remainder of his scotch. Pouring another double, he tossed it back, ignoring the burning sensation in his throat. For several long moments, he stared at the empty tumbler in his hand. Then, he slammed it onto the wet-bar's marbled surface, sending a spider's web of cracks throughout the glass.

*****

The Beech Baron touched down on runway one nine and taxied to Alpine's Fixed Base Operations building. Markus and Sidney waited in his Jeep parked adjacent to the FBO. As soon as the plane parked, the pair strolled out to the tarmac. Markus waved at Vader who was already out of the plane and speaking with the avgas fuel truck driver. Gunner was next to disembark, yipping a greeting before coming nose-to-nose with Rex. Both dogs' tails waved in friendly recognition of the other.

It wasn't that long ago, thought Markus, when Rex would have acted aggressively toward another male dog, and even more so, toward strange people. Working with him and building his trust had taken months. At one point, he'd considered the very real possibility that Rex would always be unpredictable and aggressive, thus requiring euthanasia.

Thank God you proved me wrong. He scratched the big dog's ears, and Rex leaned into him for a moment before moving to Sidney's side. *Traitor.* Markus smiled to himself, yet he was pleased that Rex had assumed the role of her protector.

Trevor stuck his head out of the plane's wide double doors and gave Markus a salute. "Hey captain, good to see you. Coming your way!" He threw his backpack, which Markus caught with one hand. "Nice catch. Gunner, come."

The dog trotted over and stood quietly as Trevor used him to steady his balance while he stepped out from the cargo end of the plane. Engulfing Sidney in a tight bear hug, he said, "Am I ever glad to see you, lady."

"I'm glad to see you, too." She started to pull away.

"Not so fast. That hug was from me. This one's from Mama." He hugged her again, tighter.

"I wish I could return it to her in person. Tell Eli 'thank you' next time you talk to her."

"Careful there, buddy, you'll crack her ribs," teased Markus. "How are you, man? Good to see you." He slapped Trevor on the back.

"Good to see you. I'd shake, but my paws are still bandaged." Trevor held up both hands and shrugged. "A few more days, or at least until the blisters heal."

Vader joined the group, shaking hands with Markus and tipping his ball cap when introduced to Sidney. Turning down Markus's invitation to join them at the lodge for dinner, he said, "Thanks anyway, but as soon as I've visited the head and my plane's refueled, I'll be getting back to Fort Worth. Denise will have the kids put to bed by the time I get home, and she and I can have a romantic dinner. It's our anniversary."

"Ah. Well, happy anniversary. Please give my best to Denise, and to Molly and Jake."

"Thanks, Markus, will do. Trevor, I'll see you later, I'm sure. Sidney, it was nice to meet you." Vader waved goodbye and sprinted to the operations building as the avgas truck pulled away from the plane.

"Let's head to the ranch—the sooner, the better. I hope you're okay for now with what you brought in your backpack. I don't want to risk going into town," said Markus.

"If it's not in my backpack, then I don't need it."

"You know where my closet is, if you decide otherwise. Come on." Markus steered them in the direction of the parking lot. "I emailed Otto earlier, and he sent Heidi over with food and a few groceries. Anything else we need, Otto will take care of."

"Sounds good."

"I hope you don't mind being wedged in the back seat between two dogs. My jeep is not the roomiest of vehicles."

"I've been in worse tight spots," Trevor said, smiling.

"I'll sit in the back seat with the dogs," offered Sidney. "It'd be more comfortable for you in the front, Trevor."

"Thanks, Sid. Either way, let's get the hell out of here."

They made their way to the parking lot in the early evening's sparse light. As the overhead streetlights flicked on, Markus turned and looked over his shoulder. A feeling of being watched, or that something was not quite right, ramped up his persistent wariness. The hairs on the back of his neck stood on end. He scanned the area in front of the operations building. It was empty of planes except for the Beech Baron. The only people he saw were Vader striding across the tarmac to his plane, coffee mug in hand, and the driver of the fuel truck disappearing into the far distance.

There's no one. It was nothing. Yet, the hair on the back of his neck remained bristled.

*****

Sidney sat in the back seat between Rex and Gunner, and as she listened to Markus and Trevor's easy banter, she decided theirs was a language she didn't understand. It must be the common language spoken by those who'd served in the military, and most likely, specifically in the Marine Corps. She guessed each branch of the military probably had its own unique form of communication with specific words and acronyms, but she imagined that any soldier, sailor, airman, or Marine would be able to interpret another branch's language easily enough. She, herself, would need a decipher code.

The short drive from the airport to the lodge gave Markus and Trevor a chance to catch up on other Marines and friends who had served with them or had participated in the Wounded Warrior Project. She was keenly aware that Markus's voice sounded much more animated than she'd heard him speak before. This was a conversation he was enjoying. Yet, as she looked at his eyes in the rearview mirror, they seemed uneasy, much like her own, she felt certain, even without a peek at herself in the mirror.

As they passed the barn, Sidney asked if they could stop for a moment to check on the horses. She wanted to see and touch Mocha. And smell her—that woodsy smell unique to mares. Simply being in the barn and in the presence of horses acted as a balm for her soul.

"Sure. It's feeding time, anyway. The three of us can knock it out quickly." Markus pulled into the parking lot, and as soon as they stepped into the barn, all the horses began to nicker their greetings.

"Did I tell you I learned how to ride a horse out here at one of Markus's Warrior camps last summer?" asked Trevor as he gingerly gripped a feed scoop with his fingertips and thumb, the only uninjured parts of his hands.

"That's excellent. How'd you like it?" Sidney held the bucket of oats as Trevor scooped, while Markus busied himself with the hay cart, delivering fresh alfalfa to each stall.

"I loved it. I'll never be a John Wayne, but I think I did pretty well."

"Pretty well? The kid's a natural," shouted Markus from the other end of the barn.

"He's being generous. But I have to admit, galloping cross country was a blast." Trevor gave Mocha a scoop and a half at Sidney's instruction. "How's your girl here settling in?"

"She's settling in just fine. We both are, despite the circumstances." Sidney walked into Mocha's stall and wrapped her arms around the mare's neck, breathing in the smell that, for her, was far superior to any expensive aromatherapy.

Trevor followed her into the stall and buried his nose into Mocha's mane. "Yep. Better than perfume. Sure wish someone would bottle that smell."

Sidney breathed in again. "I couldn't agree more."

"If you two are through scratching and sniffing on that horse, then let's close up the barn for the night. I'm hungry, and Otto promised Wienerschnitzel and Spaetzle for dinner, compliments of Heidi."

Walking back to the Jeep, Sidney noticed that Markus had shed his denim jacket, so his normally concealed shoulder holster was now in full sight. She heard him tell Trevor not to worry about losing his weapon in the fire, that he'd make sure Trevor was armed at all times once they reached the lodge. Being protected by these two bodyguards who were armed and dangerous made her feel ill prepared. At the very least, she would remember to start carrying her Taser.

*****

Markus steered onto the driveway, the lights glowing warmly in the lodge's windows a welcoming sight, he thought. Once they were behind locked doors and under the electronic protection of his high-tech security system, he could relax—a bit.

As they walked through the side door leading into the kitchen, he heard the telephone ringing. Not many people called him on the landline, other than Otto, Ruth, and a handful of clients who preferred talking rather than texting or emailing.

Lifting the receiver, he said, "Hello. Yeager Stables and Lodge."

"Markus, it's Ruth here. I was wondering if you knew how I could get hold of Sidney. I've tried her cellphone with no luck."

"You're in luck now. She's right here. Oh, how's Victor?"

"He's doing much better. The doctor says he's releasing him tomorrow morning. That's why I'm calling—I wanted to share the good news with Sidney."

"He must be doing a *lot* better. That's awfully quick,

isn't it, for him to be released?"

"You know how insurance is. As soon as it's demonstrated that a patient can walk to the bathroom without assistance and pee in a cup, they want 'em shoved out the door. Victor was up and around this morning, begging for some home cooking."

Markus chuckled. "Well, I'm relieved to hear it. Hold on, here's Sid."

Sidney took the phone from Markus. "I overheard. I'm so happy for you. And for Victor. What wonderful news."

"Thank you. The stitches and staples come out in a few weeks. The broken bones will heal in time. His kidney is no longer producing bloody urine. Sorry if that's too graphic. And, the best part is Doctor Lavine says there are no neurological issues."

"What a relief."

"Indeed. Victor said his head's too hard to crack and insists he gets that trait from me. Honestly, can't dispute that."

"You have much to be thankful for this Thanksgiving week."

"Yes, I do. And we should celebrate with an early Thanksgiving feast. I don't want to wait till Thursday. I've already picked up a smoked turkey from the grocery, and my pumpkin pies are in the oven."

"That sounds delicious. I love pumpkin pie."

"You and Markus are invited. Of course, Otto is coming, too. Tomorrow, around one o'clock in the afternoon. Can y'all come?"

"I'll check with Markus. And, would it be all right to bring a guest? Markus's friend, Trevor Nolan, is visiting."

"Of course. I remember Trevor. He's been to Alpine a few times."

"Great. I'll call you back soon."

Markus handed Sidney a glass of wine, asking, "So, what will you have to check with me?"

"Ruth wants us over tomorrow for an early

Thanksgiving to celebrate Victor's coming home from the hospital." She swirled the dark red wine around in the long-stemmed glass. "I didn't want to commit to anything before checking with you."

"As much as I'd like for us to go, I'm afraid it's impossible." He couldn't shake off the uneasy feeling he'd had earlier when they'd left the airport. "Your being seen any more in public is too dangerous, even with you in disguise. I'm confident you're safe here, but outside these gates, that's a different story. I need to get a better assessment of the situation."

"I understand. What reason for our not coming shall I give Ruth?"

Markus saw the look of disappointment on Sidney's face, and he wished there were a way to bring some joy into her life. If only for a day, it would be nice to pretend that everything was normal, and good, and there wasn't a monster out there who wanted her dead.

"I have an idea," Markus said, a small grin wrinkling the corners of his mouth. "If you'll help Trevor get dinner heated up, I'll call Ruth back."

"Sure thing." Sidney took her glass of wine and moved to the stove where Trevor was already at work.

As she walked away, Markus resisted the urge to take her in his arms and hold her. And then take her upstairs to his bedroom. He was hungrier for her than he was for dinner. They had spent the better part of Sunday as well as this morning either in bed, in the shower, or riding horses, and the more he had of her, the more he wanted her. And he knew it was mutual. Even today while out on horseback when they'd stopped near the upper creek to admire the view, they couldn't keep their hands off each other. Spontaneous sex outside, he decided, should be on everyone's bucket list.

He picked up the phone and redialed Ruth's number. If she were agreeable, he'd move the Thanksgiving feast to the lodge. Perhaps he could talk Otto into closing the restaurant, just during lunch, so Heidi and Dieter could join them. He would explain to Ruth that there was much more room at the lodge for a large party than at her small cottage.

"That sounds fine, Markus. Thank you for offering your place. I'll bring my food over in the morning before I drive to the hospital to pick up Victor." Ruth sounded relieved to change plans. "I've always admired your big dining room, and it will certainly accommodate this party that's growing in size. And, Victor loves being at your ranch. It sounds perfect."

"Excellent. See you in the morning." Markus breathed a sigh of relief. The compromise, he hoped, would put a smile on Sidney's face.

"And, one favor?" Ruth asked. "Since we're moving the meal to your place, may I invite my good friend Bonnie Kirkpatrick to join us? You know Bonnie—from the airport. She lives alone, and I think it would be nice for her to come."

"I know Bonnie. She's a good lady. She's more than welcome."

"And Aubrey, Victor's girlfriend."

"I expected she'd come, too."

"This will be fun," said Ruth. "See you in the morning."

Fun? Yes—we'll eat, drink, and be merry, for tomorrow.... Markus left the quote unfinished, the thought dangling midair as he dialed Otto. After making arrangements with him for the event, he strode into the dining room where plates of steaming Schnitzel and Spaetzle were set on the table. Joining Trevor and Sidney, he lifted his glass of wine and made a toast to tomorrow.

"You're looking rather pleased," said Sidney. "What did you and Ruth come up with?"

"A fine compromise. We're hosting the meal here tomorrow at noon. There'll be a full house. Ruth's bringing turkey and dressing, and her famous pumpkin pies. She'll drop them off tomorrow morning on her way to the hospital to get Victor." Markus grinned at the smile warming Sidney's face. It was exactly what he wished to see.

"Who else is coming?" asked Trevor, sharing a look of mutual concern. Each knew what the other was thinking.

"Only people I know well and trust completely. Besides Ruth and Victor, there'll be Aubrey, Victor's girlfriend. Otto's agreed to close Edelweiss for lunch so he, Dieter, and Heidi can come. And Ruth's longtime friend, a lady named Bonnie Kirkpatrick. Bonnie works at the FBO out at the airport. She's a no-nonsense, anti-gossiper, tell-it-like-it-is kind of lady—just like Ruth."

"Ten of us, all together. This will be great." Sidney beamed at Markus. "I've always loved Thanksgiving and the holidays. May I raid your pantry and see what there is for me to cook or bake to add to the menu?"

"Make yourself at home. Otto's bringing potatoes. Heidi's bringing red cabbage. It will be a feast."

"I'll make deviled eggs, then. And, cookies. Something to eat before and after the meal."

"If you want my help, I'm the champion cookie dough taste tester and bowl licker," offered Trevor.

"What kind of cookies?" Markus asked.

"Oatmeal-walnut-maple." Sidney gave him a sly wink. "If there's enough maple syrup in the pantry."

"I think you'll find everything you need." Markus locked eyes with hers for a long, intense moment before turning to Trevor. "So, champion cookie dough taster, while the two of you are doing the baking thing, I need to spend some time at the computer. It won't take long. When I come back down, I might have to challenge you for bragging rights."

Despite finishing the meal in companionable silence, Markus couldn't ignore the prevailing reason that had brought them here together, and apparently, neither could the others. Sidney's mood seemed to shift between enthusiasm and lethargy. He watched her pick at her food and push it around her plate. The excitement she'd shown about tomorrow's Thanksgiving celebration notwithstanding, her tense smile and genial conversation required obvious effort. Even Trevor, whose normally affable personality was now subdued, showed signs of extreme tension in the expression he wore. Markus understood their wide-ranging clash of emotions. They matched his own.

CHAPTER 20

Alpine

As midnight neared, the Citation X jet taxied off the runway and made its way to the fixed base operations building. The thin, middle-aged woman seated behind the desk looked up from her book as three men walked through the door. Two headed to the restroom while one approached the counter.

"May I help you, sir?" Bonnie Kirkpatrick laid her book aside and walked to the counter, hoping this would be quick. The new romance she had just started reading was already getting steamy, unusual for this particular publisher. Normally, she had to get at least half way through before the first kiss occurred, let alone anything hands-on or skin-to-skin.

"Yes ma'am, you sure can." Anton slid a photograph of Sidney across the desk. "Have you seen this lady? She's a friend of mine. Her mother is sick and needs to get in touch with her."

She studied the picture, adjusting her jeweled, cat-eye reading glasses for a better look. "Pretty lady. Mine used to be red, too, thanks to Sandra's Hair Faire." She shoved the photograph back across the counter. "If she flew in today before four o'clock, I wouldn't have seen her. I work the swing shift— four to midnight."

"She's been in Alpine a few days now. I just thought maybe you'd seen her around town, or something." Anton gave her the friendly smile he used when trying to establish comradery as he pointed to her name badge. "Bonnie Kirkpatrick. That's a nice name. Are you Irish?"

"The clan Kirkpatrick is Scottish," she replied with a proud air, pulling herself up to her five feet nine-and-a-half-inch height. "Sorry, I don't recognize your friend." Friend, my ass, she thought to herself, wondering what shenanigans these three were up to, especially this one with the creepy grin.

"She may have met a man who flew in on a Beech Baron earlier this evening. Red with black markings. Tail number November Seven Three Three Romeo Bravo. Do you remember if that plane landed here?"

"I remember every plane that lands on my shift. Three Romeo Bravo landed, refueled, and then took off again at eighteen hundred hours, on the dot." Her short reply and suspicious eyes did not match the pleasant smile she wore. The words, "*she may have met a man here earlier*" told her everything she needed to know. This man asking nosy questions was probably a jilted lover stalking his ex. Or, maybe he was a hired private eye working *for* the ex. Either way, she wanted nothing to do with this.

"Did you see the passenger or notice who picked him up?" Anton asked as Juan and Fredo joined him at the counter. "Anything you could tell me would be helpful."

"The pilot came in briefly. No one else was with him." She wouldn't lose sleep from telling a little white lie; the pilot *was* alone when he came in. What business of theirs was it that even from a distance, she could plainly see Rex, the big black dog that belonged to the man she recognized as Markus Yeager, who was with some lady she *didn't* recognize. They greeted a male passenger and his service dog. If she'd learned one thing in her sixty-three and a half years, it was to keep her nose out of other people's business. Keeping her eyes and ears open, well, that was another matter.

"Did he file a flight plan or mention where he was headed?"

"No. He used the facilities, filled his coffee mug, and

departed VFR as soon as his plane was refueled. Sorry I can't help you." She offered another pleasant smile as she pointed toward the pilot's lounge. "I just brewed a fresh pot. Help yourselves."

"Thank you." Anton motioned for the other two to follow him to the lounge.

"You think she's lying?" asked Juan as he poured coffee into three Styrofoam cups.

"Keep your voice down." Anton blew away the steam rising from the cup before sipping. "Maybe, but why? Could be that the passenger stayed on the plane. Could be that the lady didn't see him get off the plane and he left without her noticing. Her nose was stuck in a book when we came into the building."

Fredo, leafing through a magazine he'd picked up from the coffee table, said, "I think we should have our buddy Bruno run another check on that tail number and see if it's landed somewhere, or if the pilot filed an in-route flight plan."

"I'll do the thinking, Fredo," snapped Anton. "But that's a good idea. I'll call Boss and see if that's what he wants us to do. Push that door closed, Juan."

The phone conversation with *El Cuchillo* was mostly one sided, with Anton listening, nodding, and replying "yes sir" numerous times. While he was put on hold for several long minutes, he refilled his coffee cup and paced the room before stopping at the picture window looking out onto the runway. As he often did to engage his mind, he searched for something to count. Counting things, like the number of floor tiles in a toilet stall, or the number of beads on a Rosary helped him focus. He decided to count the number of times the green and white lights of the airport's rotating beacon flashed across the night sky. Keeping the phone pressed to his ear, he waited for information on the Beech Baron. Eventually, he gave a final "yes sir" before clicking off his cellphone.

"Okay, Three Romeo Bravo landed back at Meacham Field two hours ago. It returned without a passenger, according to a contact Bruno has at the hangar where that plane parks.

Boss is ordering the Citation to return to Meacham Field, but we'll stay here as long as it takes, looking around, asking questions, seeing what we can find out. He's convinced Trevor and Sidney are here. We just have to find them."

"Once the mission is complete, what'll we do?" asked Fredo.

"We'll go to Disney Land, dumb ass." Anton flashed his favorite grin.

*****

Bonnie Kirkpatrick's final chore of her swing shift was to call a taxi for the three men and to give them information about hotels in Alpine. She recommended the Best Western or the Hampton Inn because the popular boutique hotels were booked for the upcoming holiday. She knew this, she explained to them, because she'd made similar inquiries for numerous other travelers flying in for Thanksgiving or for the opening of deer hunting season. She shivered, thinking about hunting season and what these three men might be pursuing. She didn't like the feel of this, one bit.

*****

The next morning, Anton awoke with a start and sat bolt upright in his bed. He wasn't sure if it was a subconscious thought or a dream, but in his mind, he heard the lady at the FBO counter speaking to him, whispering in his ear the sequence of events from the previous evening. He visualized Three Romeo Bravo landing and taxiing to the FBO, the pilot getting out and going inside to take a piss, filling his coffee mug, coming back out and departing again—*after refueling.*

Anton threw his pillow across the room at the other bed, hitting Juan in the face. "Wake up, dummy. Give Fredo a jab in the ribs and wake him up too." Anton was already out of bed and pulling on his jeans.

Juan stuffed the extra pillow under his head and yanked the blanket off Fredo who'd been hogging it all night. "What's up?"

"Not you. Get your lazy ass out of bed. We're going

back to the airport."

"We're leaving? I thought Boss said to stay until we found those two." Juan looked perplexed.

Anton ignored the remark and continued dressing. Explaining higher order thinking to Juan and Fredo was becoming tiresome. If it were up to him, he'd be doing this job solo. Then, it wouldn't be long before *El Cuchillo* promoted him. He'd rise through the ranks from falcon, to hitman, to lieutenant in record time. These two boneheads would forever be falcons—capable only of street work.

"I'm leaving without you two if you're not ready in five minutes," Anton said over his shoulder. He checked the polish on the toes of his boots and frowned, rubbing away a smudge before pulling them on. A black leather blazer matched his black belt and boots. Assessing his image in the full-length mirror, he was pleased with the reflection smirking back at him.

Turning quickly, he left without another word. Say something once, why say it again? Those two better wise up and understand that he meant business. Once outside the room, he paused and pressed his ear to the closed door, smiling when he heard them jumping and fumbling around for their clothes, cursing at each other to get out of the way. He strolled down the hallway and out to the parking lot, his thumbs hooked in the pockets of his well-starched jeans.

The rental car would have to do—it was a subcompact, the only thing available in this one-horse-town. He'd have preferred a long black Cadillac like the one Winston let him drive. On a bright note, at least this miniature roller had dark tinted windows.

By the time he'd started the engine, adjusted the seat, and checked his hair in the visor mirror, Juan and Fredo were running to the car, fighting over who'd have to ride in the back. Juan, the shorter of the two, lost the argument.

"So, why're we going back to the airport?" asked Fredo, squeezing into the front seat.

"Both of you buckle up. I don't want to be stopped by a

cop for a lousy seatbelt violation." Anton knew the rules—always comply with even the most minor motor vehicle laws. Never give the police an opportunity to stop you and ask nosy questions. "And if you must know, I want to talk to whoever refueled Three Romeo Bravo last night. Maybe he saw something."

"Yeah. Good thinking, Boss." Fredo nodded in agreement.

Anton started to correct him. Only a lieutenant should be called "Boss." However, he let it slide, liking the sound of the word and all it implied. He might as well get used to hearing it. Driving to the airport in silent contemplation, he counted the number of road signs and mile markers along the way.

*****

As he pulled into the parking lot adjacent to the avgas building, Anton scanned the tarmac and the taxiways, looking for a fuel truck, or for any movement at all. By its appearance, the airport seemed shut down, with no one in sight. Overhead, not a single plane circled in the published "left turn to base leg" landing pattern. No propellers whirred to life doing run-ups on the tarmac. A few vehicles sat empty in both the FBO and the avgas parking lots. He looked at his watch and cursed this sleepy little town and the two people who were the cause of him being here. He'd rather be back in Fort Worth with his Lola. Or, Ramona. Even Benita would do.

"It's eight forty-five already. What time does this shithole come alive?" He got out of the car and started toward the building, Juan and Fredo on his heels.

The slight, bald man behind the counter set his newspaper aside as the three men strolled in. "*Buenos dias*. Can I help you?"

Anton gave him a friendly smile. "*Si, Señor*. Good morning. I believe you can. I'm looking for whoever was on duty yesterday evening around six. He might have refueled a Beech Baron."

Putting his paper down, the man, whose nametag read

Carlos Ortiz, Service Manager, asked in a concerned voice, "Was there a problem? Something happen to that plane?"

"There was no problem, Mr. Ortiz. It's just that my friend flew in yesterday on that Baron, and when he got off the plane, he dropped his watch. He said it happened about the time the plane was being refueled. It's a pretty expensive watch. He's hoping that your guy might have seen it and picked it up. For safekeeping, of course."

"That would have been Wesley on duty then. He's over picking up a truck from the mechanic's shop. He didn't mention anything to me about a watch." Ortiz thumbed over his shoulder, indicating the hangar behind the avgas building.

"Do you mind if we go talk to him?"

"He should be back any minute. Make yourself at home. There's plenty of coffee."

"*Muchas gracias*, but we're kind of in a hurry. My friend's nervous about finding his watch. I'm sure you understand." Anton headed for the door.

"*De nada*. I understand." Ortiz sat down and picked up the sports section of the newspaper. "Tell Wesley I better not find out he pocketed your *amigo's* watch. Of course, if he's like his *padre*, he's already visited the pawn shop." He snorted a short burst of air through his nose before raising the paper, not seeing the dismissive look Anton shot his way.

Strolling to the south side of the building and toward the mechanic's hangar, Anton played out in his mind a few scenarios of what to say to this Wesley character, but he had to think quickly. The avgas truck was pulling out of the hangar and headed their way. As the truck approached, Anton held up his hand and stepped in front of the vehicle.

A stout, dark haired young man stuck his head out of the window. "It's a good thing my foot didn't miss the brake pedal." He wore sunglasses, despite the gray, overcast sky.

Anton stepped to the side of the truck. "You must be Wesley. Your boss said you'd be coming from the mechanic's. How you doing?" He stuck out his hand in a friendly gesture.

After giving the proffered hand a long stare, Wesley shook it. His grip tightened in an unspoken challenge. Releasing the man's hand in a dramatic fashion, he propped his elbow on the open window frame and said with a thick drawl, "I'm Wesley. What of it?"

The vibe this guy was giving off—his confrontational posturing—didn't sit well with Anton. He drew in a deep breath and let it out slowly, grasping that this might be an expensive morning. Guys like Wesley didn't give anything away for free. They always expected a tip or some reward, even if they were returning a lost dog to its rightful owner, a dog they probably stole in the first place. He'd bet this guy had a bumper sticker that read, *"Either gas, cash, or ass – no free rides."*

Friendliness and flattery wouldn't work on this turd. Anton decided to cut through the bullshit and get right to the point, but he wouldn't play all his cards at once by offering money up front. He'd make the kid ask for it.

"You refueled a red and black Beech Baron yesterday evening around six o'clock. I'm after some information about the male passenger who came in on that flight. You got anything you can tell me about who got off that plane?"

"A red Beech Baron with black Maltese crosses both sides of the tail, black and gold stripes down the fuselage? November something Romeo Bravo, the Romeo Bravo most likely standing for 'Red Baron?'"

"That would be the one."

"Never saw it." Wesley smirked. He put the truck in gear and slowly pulled away, rolling a few feet before Anton slapped the side of the door with his palm.

"All right, smartass. Stop the fucking truck. Let's talk." Anton kept pace alongside as it continued to roll.

After letting the truck coast along a few yards, Wesley braked to a halt, shoving the gearshift into park. "If I tell you what I saw, it'll cost you."

"I expected you wouldn't give it away. What's your price?"

"I don't believe that's how it works." Wesley took off his sunglasses and tossed them onto the dashboard. "I reckon you ought to tell me what it's worth to you."

Anton gritted his teeth and pulled out his wallet. He hated dealing with jerk-wads like this one. He held up three one hundred dollar bills. "Tell me who, if anyone, got off that plane, and these Ben Franklins go home with you."

"Not enough." Wesley shook his head, unflinching under the man's cold stare.

Anton added two more. "Five's it, buddy. Take it or leave it. Maybe someone else saw something who'd like to talk to me for free."

Wesley held out his hand and then stuffed the money into his jacket pocket. "A dude with only one leg—well, he had one of those fake, metal things on the other—got off the plane. He had a yellow lab guide dog with him."

Trevor. Anton experienced a familiar surge of adrenaline, like he always felt when closing in on a target. "Did you see where he went, or maybe who picked him up?"

"That first five hundred covered your first request for information, which was who got off that plane? Remember?"

"I remember." *What a fool, to test me.* He pulled out five more bills. "Tell me what else you saw, and I mean everything you saw, or I'll take my money back, after I've slit your *gringo* throat." His eyes hardened, his smile slowly stretching from ear to ear, exposing gleaming, gold-capped molars.

Wesley hesitated a moment before shoving the other five hundred in his pocket. "No need for the threats, man. I'll tell you. Two people walked out to the plane as I was refueling it. The dude is a guy I know. My ex-girlfriend keeps her horse out at his stables. His name's Markus Yeager. He doesn't go anywhere without this big black wolf-looking dog tagging along. Yeager was with a chick I didn't recognize."

Anton pulled a photograph from his breast pocket. "Did she look like this?"

Wesley studied the photo for a moment. "I don't think

so. It was getting dark, so I didn't get a good look at her. But the chick last night had long blond hair, not red like this woman here. That much I saw. That's all I got, man. I need to get back to work."

"Not so fast. This Yeager character—is his place close by?"

Wesley paused, as if calculating whether or not he should ask for more money for this third piece of information. He opted for *not*. "It's maybe ten miles or so from here, but I don't know the exact address. It's called Yeager Stables and Hunting Lodge."

"Can you draw me a map?"

"I reckon."

Anton handed him the photograph of Sidney. "Just draw it on the back of this."

Wesley did his best at scratching out a map, his tongue working in his cheek as he drew. Handing it back, he pointed to the road that ran in front of the stables. "This road's not marked, and I don't think it even has a name. But if you go a little farther, this road here turns into an old cattle trail that'll take you to the back of his property. My old man and my uncle discovered this hidden trail, and they use it to hunt back in there —unobserved, if you know what I mean. I'm talking trophy antlers." He held his hands out in a wide span, his eyes twinkling.

"Very good, Wesley. You did very good. And for that, I'm rewarding you. Here's another five hundred dollars for doing one more thing. And I expect you to do this one more thing very good, too." He counted off five more bills and held them out.

Wesley grasped onto the money but Anton kept a tight hold, not releasing the bills. "What else? I don't know anything more to tell you."

"It's not what you'll tell me, it's what you'll tell everyone else, which is nothing. Not even your boss, who's watching out the window as we speak. Don't ask me why, but just tell Mr. Ortiz that you never saw a watch that my friend supposedly lost on the tarmac."

"What do you mean, I never saw—"

"I said don't ask."

"Okay. Got it. I never saw a watch." Wesley tugged on the bills, a relieved expression washing across his face when Anton released the money. He had pocketed more in five minutes than he made in a month working part-time at the avgas hangar.

Snapping his fingers, Anton motioned for Juan and Fredo to join him as he turned and hurried to the rental car. If Trevor was here, surely the bitch was, too. The initial rush of adrenaline he'd felt when it was confirmed his target had gotten off the plane was soon replaced by a calming sensation. He expected the calmness. Moving into that realm was an accomplished practice. He would not allow nerves to interfere. He never let that first surge of excitement get in the way of completing a job. He reached into his pocket and fondled the cool, soothing beads on his Rosary.

CHAPTER 21

Alpine

In the early hours before dawn, Markus quietly slipped out of bed, trying not to wake Sidney. He blindly went through the procedures to allow access into his safe-room. Wishing he had a cup of coffee, he sat staring at his computer as it booted up and came to life. He picked up a pencil and doodled stick figures on his notepad before writing in bold letters: ***WHAT AM I MISSING?***

Pushing the pad aside, he read the email confirming Moose had put a five-man team together. In addition to himself, Moose would be joined by Bradley "Cooper" McClung, Andrew "Cannibal" Donner, Sam "Rocky" Rhodes, and Elwood "Master" Bates. On Markus's command, Moose and his crew would fly from Virginia to Fort Bliss in El Paso and would be standing by, awaiting further instructions. Once given the command, a Black Hawk helicopter could be setting down at his ranch in a little over an hour.

Good choices, Moose. Markus smiled as he read the code names of the handpicked team. He knew them well, had worked with each of them on different covert operations, and each of them brought something special to the team.

Leaning back in his chair, he crossed his arms behind his head, chewing on the inside of his cheek. Should he go ahead and make the call to bring Moose and his team to El Paso?

Doing so would put them four hours closer, and if the situation escalated, four hours could mean the difference between the mission's success and failure. But, he hated to uproot those men from their families at Thanksgiving if it weren't necessary. Easing forward, he wrote a reply:

> *Tell Moose and his men to standby in place. I'll notify you when it's necessary to transition them to El Paso. What's the status of the background check on Jessica and Rafael Cordoba? Any progress there, or on Winston Knight's previous divorce settlements and financial situation? Also, what's the status of the message Sidney wrote to her cousin? Was it delivered—any response? Do you have any information on the Nolan arson or on the murder of Aleck Stavros? Don't mean to sound impatient, but I'm impatient. Time is of the essence.*

As soon as he clicked the mouse to send the reply, he shot off a follow-up email, suggesting that Jessica and Rafael might be in danger, as well. If Winston were responsible for the arson and/or the hit on Sidney's attorney, her cousin might be the next target. As a precaution, it would be prudent to assign someone to the Cordobas for their protection.

Markus shut down the computer, then exited and secured the room. As he stood quietly facing the tapestry, he heard Trevor in the kitchen below talking to Gunner, the microwave beeping, and the gurgling coffee pot brewing. The smell of cookies wafted up the stairwell, and he imagined Trevor heating them up in the microwave. The aroma reminded him of growing up in Boerne, Texas, when his grandmother's house always smelled of freshly baked cookies, and like Trevor, he would eat them for breakfast.

Images of his childhood flashed through his mind, the images of home and of family. His mother's image was indistinct, a filament hardly glowing. She'd died when he was six. The image of his father, Wernher Yeager, glowed brighter. Markus remembered camping and horseback riding with his father, and, learning everything his young mind could soak up about archery, firearms, and other weapons. Although German and English were spoken at home, Wernher encouraged Markus to study Russian and Japanese at school.

Yet for Markus, as much as he loved and respected his father, it was Otto whom he thought of when he reminisced about home. Otto had always been a part of the family, part of their lives, ever since he and Wernher immigrated to the U.S. from Germany after the second world war.

Though Markus learned a lot from his father, Otto taught him other life lessons. Rudimentary hand-to-hand combat. How to curse in French and Spanish. The proper way to train the German Shepard dogs his father imported for protection work, speaking the Schutzhund commands in German. The difference between a fine scotch and one that would strip paint.

It was from that last lesson that Markus ultimately chose his undercover name, Johnny Walker, later shortened to John. No one would suspect he'd go by *that* name—the least favorite of his favorite scotches. Originally preferring the name Glen Morangie, it was quickly discarded, as anyone who really knew him would suspect it was his undercover ID.

There had been times when he drank Glenmorangie scotch like some drank tea. After Adina divorced him and moved back to Japan with their infant daughter. After his father died. After Sonja was murdered.

Don't go there, he told himself. Yet, his mind was already back in Sarajevo.

The morning he'd told Sonja he was leaving for an assignment in Dubrovnik and would not be coming back, they'd lingered in bed for hours. Each knew they were making love for the last time. She was lying in his arms, weeping quietly, when Russian hit men stormed his flat.

Four men overpowered him, while two others held Sonja. He was brutally attacked, yet stuck to his story that he was Jürgen Hoffer, a German government aid worker. Insisting he was the American spy, John Walker, they cut and burned him with knives and cigarettes, slashing and scorching his stomach, back, and genitals. They gagged and then bound him to the bedpost with strands of barbed wire around each shoulder, around his neck, the wire's barbs puncturing his flesh despite his attempts to not struggle against it. He listened as one man ransacked his kitchen, and then screamed in agony as vinegar was doused on his wounds.

He was forced to watch as the six men took turns raping Sonja, each man more brutal than the previous. With the gag in his mouth and unable to speak, Markus pleaded with his eyes for Sonja to give them the answers they demanded in order to end the torture, but she turned her face away from his. The "whore traitor," as the Russians called her, screamed in pain but never begged for them to spare her. Either way, she knew she was dead.

Then—the sound of a gun's repeated firing. The feel of his knee and shoulder shattering, his torso ripping. The smell of blood. The taste of death. The sight of Sonja. And there—his memories always faded to nothing, nothing, nothing.

How did I go from reminiscing about the aroma of my grandmother's holiday cookies to remembering this?

Markus drew himself up and filled his lungs with as much air as they could hold. The mental struggle to expunge from his mind thoughts about his past took enormous effort. The physical aftermath of his internal reckoning left him sweating, his hands shaking.

Dwelling on Sonja, on what happened in Sarajevo, always took him to the brink of that dark place in his mind where he felt on the verge of tumbling into a gray abyss and losing control. Yet, throughout his career, the times when he felt most *in* control were the times when he was doing what an assassin was hired to do—kill bad people.

He never lost sleep over those justified kills. But he took personally the responsibility to keep his assets safe. He'd failed

Sonja. It was her death that haunted him.

And what the hell am I doing, getting involved with Sidney?

"Hey, good morning." Sidney sat up in bed, the covers tucked under her chin. "How long are you going to stand there staring at the wall?"

Markus jerked around at the sound of her voice. "Good morning. Sorry if I woke you." He stood rooted in front of the tapestry, his sweaty hands clasped behind his back. He drew in a deep, calming breath. Let it seep out through gritted teeth. Forcefully ignored the darkness encroaching on his vision.

"You look like you've seen a ghost. I didn't mean to startle you. Everything okay?"

He took another slow, deep breath. "Everything's—fine. Just taking a trip down memory lane."

"By your expression, I gather "memory lane" wasn't a pleasant trip."

"Not as pleasant as the present road I'm on." He forced a smile that quickly dissolved into something akin to a scowl. "I'll bring up coffee. And it smells like Trevor's heated up some of your maple oatmeal cookies. The breakfast of champions."

"Sounds perfect." Sidney snuggled back under the covers. "I'll keep the bed warm."

As he stopped in the doorway, he turned to look at Sidney, to say something, but the thought darted from his mind as his eyes were drawn to the tapestry. He read again the words of the quote seared in his memory. *A warrior is worthless unless he rises above others and stands strong in the midst of a storm.* He knew in his gut a raging storm loomed ahead.

*****

The door to Trevor's room was slightly ajar, and as Sidney walked past, she saw Gunner lying at the foot of the bed. The dog's nose rested between his paws as he watched Trevor on the floor doing pushups.

"Knock, knock. May I come in?" She poked her head in the room. "You're up early."

"So are you." He spoke without losing his smooth rhythm of fast dips and slow rises, his elbows close to his sides in the military style of the exercise. "What's going on?"

"I want to go for a run before everyone gets here, but Markus needs computer time this morning. Apparently, I'm not allowed to leave the house without an armed bodyguard. He said I could go if you went with me." She scrunched her face, seeing his unbandaged hands pressing against the tile floor. "Doesn't that hurt?"

Trevor sat up and wiped the sweat from his brow. "My right palm is nearly pain free. See, no need for a bandage this morning." He held up his hand for proof. "The left is still a bit sore, but not too bad. As the saying goes, 'Pain is weakness leaving the body.'"

"I saw that on a T-shirt somewhere." She smiled, thinking there was so much to admire about this man. "So, you up for a run? Three or four miles?"

"Only three or four? What a slacker." He tossed his sweat rag at her. "Give me a minute to put on my running shoes, the only shoes I happen to own. Gunner—here." The dog jumped to the floor, allowing Trevor to brace against him as he stood.

"Great. I'll meet you downstairs." She threw the rag back at him. "While we're out, I need to get something from my truck. It's parked at the barn."

"Sure. Not a problem," he said as he finished tying the running shoe onto his prosthetic foot. Strapping the leather shoulder holster on over his T-shirt, he checked the safety and the load in the chamber before holstering the weapon.

"I'm getting my Taser from the truck. That's why I want to stop at the barn," Sidney offered as she watched Trevor arm himself. "I need to make it a habit, I guess, carrying a form of protection. This is such a new mindset for me. I'm not used to thinking in these terms."

"If it'll make you feel better, then by all means, we'll get the Taser. But as long as you're with either me or Markus, you'll be protected." Trevor stood with his hands on his hips, his serious expression no longer playful.

"It will make me feel better, if for no other reason than to think I'm actively participating in my own safety." I may never use it, she thought, but I'll know it's there.

"I understand. Let's go." Gunner bounded ahead of them as Trevor closed his bedroom door.

Markus opened his bedroom door to let Rex out. "He heard y'all out here in the hallway and started whining like a puppy, wanting to be included. It'd be a good idea if he went with you, Sidney. Have you got the GPS wrist band on?"

"Got it." Sidney held up her arm. "After stopping at the barn, I'm taking the upper creek path that we rode the other day, then straight back here. We won't be gone long."

"Be safe. Please." Markus wrapped an arm around Sidney's waist, pulling her to him. "And hurry back. Run that Marine's ass into the ground, if you have to."

"Run *my* ass into the ground? Guaranteed, I'll keep up," said Trevor, an amused smile spreading across his face as he looked back and forth between Sidney and Markus.

"Stay away from the perimeter fence line. Keep to the interior of the property. The upper creek path is a good choice." He held Sidney close a moment longer, stroking her cheek with his finger before releasing her.

*****

As they jogged toward the deer trail leading to the stables, Sidney looked over her shoulder and saw Markus standing in the window watching them. She waved and smiled, but a tightening in her stomach couldn't be ignored.

What was so important on the computer that he couldn't join them? Had he heard from the contact who was supposed to get a message to Jessi? She'd have to ask him when they got back. Right now, she just wanted to get to the barn, to her truck, and to her Taser. She felt silly for making it such an important issue, even in her own mind, but thinking about her own safety and being able to protect herself made sense. She stepped up her pace, anxious to catch up with Trevor.

CHAPTER 22

Alpine

Fallen leaves covered the upper creek trail. Cottonwoods and post oaks were bare except for a few yellow, orange, and gold hangers-on that refused to yield to autumn's will. Gunner plunged into a pile the wind had heaped against the trunk of one large oak, sending a squirrel scampering up the tree. In a tag team effort, Rex planted both paws on the trunk and barked furiously at the frightened animal.

"Goofy dogs. Come on, we can't stop to chase squirrels." Trevor maintained a steady stride, following Sidney who'd taken the lead. They'd been running side by side since leaving the barn, but on these narrower trails, he preferred her in front. With his limited vision, following her made it easier to navigate around potential obstructions.

"No—no stopping. I don't want this GPS to set off the stop-movement alarm." Sidney kept a cautious eye on the trail as it wound around the left bank of the creek before descending into a ravine. The wooded path widened as it led back to the lodge.

That was the most they'd conversed since leaving the barn and stopping to get her Taser. Trevor guessed that Sidney shared a similar habit, using her running time as thinking time. While he didn't want to intrude upon her private thoughts, he *was* curious about the relationship blossoming between Markus and her. It wasn't any of his business, so he decided not to inquire about it. However, he wasn't at all surprised. The more he learned about Sidney, the more he could see she was perfect for Markus. Under different circumstances, it would be a match made in heaven—not that he cared anything about playing Cupid.

As they rounded the final bend, Trevor jogged up next to Sidney, Gunner on his left, and Rex on Sidney's right. Sunlight filtered through the bare branches of the trees lining the flat, straight pathway. The spotty shadows fooled his eye, making foot placement difficult. He remained in a state of heightened vigilance to keep from falling.

"Let's slow down a bit," Sidney said. "We're almost back at the lodge, and I wanted to talk to you about something —about Markus and me."

"You must have been reading my mind." He shot her a surprised look. "It's none of my business, but I'll admit I'm curious. Are y'all officially a couple?"

"A couple of needy individuals wanting the same thing? Yes. But we're just friends. Nothing serious. Neither of us wants anything more than a physical relationship. I hope that doesn't make me sound whorish."

Trevor threw back his head and laughed out loud. "Whorish? Hardly. It makes you sound human-ish."

"Thanks for being nonjudgmental-ish. I feel like you and I have been friends longer than just for a week."

"I agree. And I have to be frank. I detect more than a physical relationship going on between you two. I'm seeing a deep caring—I don't know—a tenderness that says it's more involved than sex alone. I'm just saying…"

"It's impossible for me *not* to care about him as a person. He's the kind of man who could make me want more than just a friendship with physical benefits. But at this point in my life, I'm not in a position to…"

Sidney stopped and turned around, her hand on Trevor's arm. "What was that? Did you hear that?"

"I didn't hear anything." He shrugged his shoulders. "Then again, my ears aren't as good as yours."

"Shh. Listen. I hear voices coming from over there." She pointed in the direction of the back fence line. "The last time I heard voices, I stumbled upon a couple of poachers who'd killed a deer."

"Rex heard something, too. Look at him. He's all bristled up."

"This makes me nervous. Here boy, come." She spoke in a loud whisper, motioning for the dog, but he ignored her. Crouching lower to the ground as if stalking prey, he moved slowly in the direction of the voices, a low growl rumbling in his throat.

"Rex, come," Trevor commanded as quietly as possible. He took Sidney by the arm, urging her to start walking. Rex paused for a moment before disappearing into the woods.

"Shit," Sidney hissed through gritted teeth. "Should we go after him?"

"No." Trevor quickened his steps, hurrying her along. "We need to get to the lodge and tell Markus. We'll take the Jeep to look for him."

They sprinted a quarter of a mile to the juncture where the upper creek trail joined the upper ridge road. Sidney tugged on Trevor's arm, stopping short. Pointing down the long slope of the gravel road, she asked, "Do you see what I see?"

"It's blurry, but I can make out the lodge. Barely."

"Markus and Ruth are standing next to her car in the driveway. It wouldn't be wise for her to see me without my wig on. We have to keep moving, but walk slowly."

Trevor cursed under his breath. He wanted off the ridge where he felt vulnerable to attack. The image of being in a sniper's crosshairs flashed through his mind, and he shuddered at the thought. Getting Sidney safely back to the lodge was more important than Ruth's surprise at seeing her with red hair. They could explain away the change by claiming a box of drugstore dye and a pair of scissors did the trick. It was going to be difficult enough explaining to Markus in front of Ruth why his dog took off and why they came back without him.

"I say we walk a little faster," he urged, his long strides clearing ground.

"I say we run. Ruth is leaving—I see her waving out of the window as she's pulling away. Markus is carrying something inside."

They took off at a fast clip, but the gravel slope made running a difficult proposition. Trevor held onto Gunner's harness for balance. He felt his tension easing the nearer they got to the lodge. As the slope flattened out and the gravel gave way to firmer footing, he let go of the harness, his short, halting gait gliding into a free-flowing sprint.

*****

Huddled underneath the low branches of a cedar, Anton pressed a pair of binoculars to his eyes. He heard voices in the distance —both male and female. Now, it would be only a matter of patient surveillance before he located his kill. Scanning the pathway winding below his rocky perch, he paused when his binoculars settled on the redheaded woman running alongside the tall, blond male with the prosthetic leg, accompanied by two hounds.

"Targets confirmed," he said to himself, smiling briefly before realizing the pair was acting as if they'd grown suspicious. They were looking in his direction and backing away, the big black dog he'd just seen with them now nowhere in sight.

A commotion coming from behind drew his attention away from his targets. He lowered the binoculars and stomped over to where Juan and Fredo were in an animated discussion about the headless deer carcass they'd stumbled upon.

"How many times do I have to tell you to keep your goddamned voices down," he growled. "I think they've heard us."

"You saw them?" Fredo stepped closer and reached for the binoculars while Juan stood over the grotesque, maggot riddled carcass, seemingly mesmerized at the sight.

"I said keep quiet." Anton held the glasses firmly in his grasp, leveling a cold stare on his associate. In a lowered voice, he said, "I've confirmed the targets. Let's get the fuck out of here before that dog sniffs out our location, thanks to you two mouthy idiots."

Anton stomped off toward where he'd parked the rental car just on the other side of the perimeter fence line. For once, he felt grateful for this tiny car that fit through the narrow passages of the rutted cattle trail. He would come up with a "Plan B" for dealing with the targets once he checked in with the Boss to let him know they'd been located. First, he had to make sure he wasn't being followed, or being tracked by that big, black beast of a dog. Looking over his shoulder, his finger rested on the trigger of his AK-47.

*****

Markus stood on the stoop leading into the kitchen, a pumpkin pie in each hand. Out of the corner of his eye, his attention was drawn to movement in the near distance. Pushing the door open with his foot, he placed the pies on the counter and then stepped back out onto the porch.

There's Trevor, Gunner and Sidney. But where the hell is Rex?

He hurried down the steps and met them at the end of the driveway. "Where's Rex? Everything okay?"

"About three-quarters of the way along the trail, I heard voices. We tried to call him back, but Rex took off." Sidney placed her hand on Markus's arm. "I'm sorry. Both Trevor and I tried to get him to come with us, but—"

"It's not your fault. I'm the one who insisted you take him along. I thought he'd obey you. Where exactly on the trail were the voices coming from?"

"From the direction of the south fence line, near where the creek drops down into the ravine."

"I thought it'd be best to come get you and we'd take the Jeep to look for him," said Trevor.

"That back fence line is a hot-spot for poachers. Maybe that's who the voices were. But, maybe not." Markus shoved his hands in his pockets and stared off into the distance for a short moment. "Trevor, I want you to take Sidney inside. You know the combo to activate the security alarm. I'll drive the jeep up there and see what I can see. Maybe I'll find a lost dog in the process."

"Don't you want me to go with you?" asked Trevor.

"I don't want Sid going, and I don't want her left here alone, either." Markus hurried into the kitchen to retrieve the keys to his Jeep.

Sidney stepped through the door behind him. "I'd feel much better if Trevor went with you. I'll be fine here behind locked doors."

"And I'd feel better if Trevor, who knows how to shoot to kill, stayed with you."

"I have my Taser with me."

"I'm glad. That's a step in the right direction." He reached for her hand and pulled her close. "Soon, I'll teach you to shoot to kill."

"Hmm—I don't know. I'll think about it. Please, be safe out there." Sidney squeezed his hand before pulling away. "Please."

From the porch, Trevor called out, "You can put your keys back. The prodigal dog returneth."

Markus and Sidney ran outside to see Rex trotting up the driveway, his tail waving from side to side. Briars tangled his coat, and his tongue lolled out of his panting mouth. His sides heaved with the effort of breathing.

"Here, Rex." Kneeling down, Markus plucked the thorny briars from his ruff. "Whoever, or whatever you chased, I hope it was worth it because it's back to boot camp for you, buddy."

Rex sat, leaning his weight against Sidney's leg. He looked at Markus and cocked his head in a comical manner as if apologizing, eliciting laughter all around.

"All right, you're forgiven." Markus scratched the dog's head. "But don't think I'm letting you off the hook. Boot camp begins now."

"Doggie boot camp?" asked Sidney, stroking Rex's back and ears. "Sounds hardcore."

"Not really. He just needs a refresher course in manners."

"Well, I hope he's not in boot camp very long. I enjoyed running with him, before he took off, that is."

"I'm still making a sweep of the upper fence line. I need to see if there are signs of poachers, or, something else. When I get back, we'll have a couple of hours before everyone arrives for our little Thanksgiving feast. If you want, I can show you how to give Rex commands he'll respect. At some point, he'll be able to go running with you again."

"Sounds good. I don't want to worry about your dog running off on my watch."

Markus watched Rex leaning against Sidney, and he remembered that first encounter with her, when Rex jumped out of the woods, frightening her. Then, as now, he suspected his dog had chosen someone else to attach his affections to.

Can't say I blame you, boy.

CHAPTER 23

Alpine

The lodge filled with the sumptuous smells of Thanksgiving, the variety of aromas blending into a singular aroma that smelled of holidays past, of home. Animated chatter and laughter rose and fell as each person arrived, greeting the others.

Sidney stood in front of her bathroom mirror, adjusting her wig. She heard Markus and Trevor's voices. Recognized Ruth's, Victor's, and Aubrey's. The female voice she didn't recognize must belong to Ruth's friend, Bonnie. Soon, she heard the familiar voices of Otto, Heidi, and Dieter as they arrived, bringing in other marvelous aromas with the food they'd brought.

Why am I nervous?

She smoothed her hands down the front of her dress and rechecked her makeup, thinking she should put on more lipstick before wiping it off and applying a sheer coat of lip balm. Making a closer inspection, she spied a stray red hair and tucked it back into place under the wig.

"It's Victor, isn't it?" she asked herself in the mirror. "You're worried about how to handle Victor. Well, don't be. It's he who should be worried when he recognizes *you*." Turning away from the mirror, she made her way down the hallway and down the stairs, putting on her bravest smile, shoulders back, chin high.

"I was just coming up to check on you." Markus stood at the bottom of the stairs, waiting for Sidney to descend. "You look beautiful."

"Thank you. You clean up pretty well, too."

"You seem deep in thought. What's on your mind?"

"I was thinking about how incongruous it is feeling relieved that you only saw signs of poachers earlier and not someone, or something else. *Only* poachers."

"That's not to say the voices you heard were definitely the poachers, but a headless deer carcass is a sure sign someone up there wasn't hunting for meat, they were hunting for the sole purpose of a trophy mount."

"That makes me sick. What a waste."

"The game warden has his hands full. He said mine was the second call today. Well, everyone's in the den. Are you ready?" He took her by the hand, leading her toward the noisy crowd.

"Yes, and they seem to be enjoying themselves. What a good idea this is. Thank you again for today."

Markus raised her hand to his mouth and kissed it. His intense stare held on to her. "It's my pleasure."

As they entered the room, Markus called for everyone's attention. "I think you've all met Sidney, except for Bonnie. Bonnie, this is Sidney."

Sidney extended her hand. "It's nice to meet you, Bonnie. Markus said some flattering things about you."

"It's nice to meet you too." Bonnie shook her hand, studying her face. "You look familiar. Have we met before?"

"No. I've only been in town about a week."

At that moment, Victor, who was sitting in a recliner and facing the fireplace, spun his chair around. The water he'd just taken a sip of came spewing out his mouth. "Holy shit—I mean —sorry—uh—nice to meet, I mean, nice to see you again. Ma'am."

Sidney laughed at the sight of Victor blushing, water dribbling down his chin. "It's nice to see you again, too."

"Y'all have met?" asked Ruth, walking over to give Sidney a hug.

"Briefly. He was part of a group of rodeo team members who gave me a raucous welcome my first day in Alpine. Victor impressed me by showing me his enormous championship belt buckle." Sidney offered him an innocent smile.

Blushing a deeper shade of crimson, Victor squirmed in his chair. "Is anybody besides me ready to eat some turkey? I'm starved. Hospital food sucks."

"I think that's as good as a dinner bell. Let's eat." Markus escorted Ruth and Bonnie to the dining hall, and the rest of the group followed.

Victor took Sidney by the arm and pulled her aside. "Ma'am, I'm so sorry about that first day. I don't know why I did that. It was stupid, and I shouldn't have embarrassed you like I did."

"I think you're more embarrassed now than I was then."

"I'm—most definitely embarrassed," Victor nodded, looking contrite. "Thanks for what *you* did by not saying anything. My grandmother would have freaked out."

"And rightly so. But, apology accepted. It's forgotten. Now, would you like to escort me to the table?"

"Yes ma'am, I would." Victor offered her his right arm. His left, encased in a wrist-to-shoulder plaster cast, was carried in a sling tied around his neck.

*****

After the meal, Heidi, Aubrey, and Sidney cleared the table while Ruth and Bonnie served the pumpkin pie. Markus poured brandies and served coffee. The conversation ran the gamut from how to make the perfect piecrust to what constitutes a memorable Christmas parade.

"Sidney, to give you a little background, Alpine prides itself on its Holiday of Lights parade. The first Friday in December, you'll see the whole town turn out, vying for the best parade float," Bonnie said before forking a bite full of pie loaded with whipped cream into her mouth.

"What was the best float last year?" Trevor sipped his brandy and picked at the crumbs on his pie plate.

"Ah, last year," said Otto, his eyes twinkling. "Last year a few restaurants got together and made a float depicting a dining table full of food, with mannequins sitting in the chairs. It would have won the grand prize had the wind not blown the mannequins over. They all looked drunk, some face down in their plates. That was my favorite."

"Mine was the homecoming queen's car." Victor laughed at the memory, ignoring his grandmother's stern look.

"So, tell us," said Dieter, already on his second piece of pie. "The homecoming queen's car, why was it such a favorite of yours?"

"It was a favorite of everyone's except maybe the queen and her parents." Victor blew on his steaming cup of coffee. "The queen rides at the head of the parade in a brand-new convertible. Sitting on the back, waving to the crowd, wearing a red Christmas crown of poinsettias. At the last minute, someone, and I'm not telling who, placed a big sign on the back of the queen's convertible. The sign read, 'One whores open sleigh.'"

"Victor," Ruth frowned at him. "Whoever did that should've been reprimanded. What a horrible thing to say about a young lady."

"It was truth in advertising, Grandmother, and everyone knew it. Right Aubrey?"

"Everyone but her parents, who were horrified," Aubrey confirmed. "But even so, it wasn't funny. I felt sorry for her."

"I feel sorry for her and I don't even know this queen of the parade," said Heidi as she wiped a crumb of crust from Dieter's chin.

"Not to change the subject," said Markus, "but what are your plans, Victor, now that you're on the injured list and can't rodeo for a while?"

Victor leaned back in his chair and shared a private look with Ruth, locking eyes for a long moment. "Well, sir, I'm glad you asked. Grandmother and I have been talking about it, with

Aubrey, too. I've decided to hang up my bull rope. I'm not rodeoing anymore. I can't afford to end up like my dad."

"I'm sure that was a tough decision," said Markus.

"Yes sir. It was. I love riding bulls, but there're other things I love more, like my grandmother, and this girl sitting next to me. After we graduate the end of next semester, we're getting married."

Aubrey held up her left hand, showing off the diamond engagement ring on her finger. "It belonged to Ruth. She's giving us her wedding set."

"How wonderful. Congratulations, both of you." Markus raised his glass in a toast, and everyone around the table joined in. "Best wishes for a happy future."

"Thank you." Victor raised his coffee cup, clinking it with the other raised cups and glasses. "And speaking about the future, I wanted to talk to you about your barn manager's position. It's been vacant for a while. Are you looking to fill it?"

"I am. When can you start?"

"Tomorrow."

"You're hired. But make it next Monday. A little recuperation under your grandmother's care will do you good." Markus winked at Ruth who gave him a relieved, grateful smile.

Without warning, Bonnie snapped her fingers, startling everyone. "I know why I thought we'd met before," she said, turning to Sidney. "There was a man at the FBO last night looking for a woman he claimed was his friend. He showed me a photo of her. Y'all look alike, except she had red hair."

Sidney gasped, then immediately realized she shouldn't reveal her alarm. She covered by finishing the gasp with a small cough. "Excuse me." She patted her mouth with her napkin. "A man looking for a woman at the airport and showing her photo around? That's rather odd." She glanced at Markus and then at Trevor, who both seemed as stunned as she was.

Bonnie nodded in agreement. "I thought so. Besides the one showing the photo, there were two others. They flew in on one of those expensive Citation X jets."

"Have they flown in before? Anybody you recognized?" asked Markus. His smile and casual voice contradicted the hardening expression in his eyes and the tightening of his jaw.

"I've never seen them around before. And strangely enough, he also asked about a Beech Baron that landed on my shift." Bonnie cast a glance at Trevor and his dog lying beside his chair. "It wasn't any of their business, so I didn't tell them anything I saw."

"I'm sure it was just a coincidence, them asking about the plane Trevor happened to fly in on. But thanks for mentioning it. Now, please pass some more of that delicious cranberry sauce." Markus forced a thin smile.

Sidney sat back in her chair and sipped her brandy. She listened to the easy flow of conversation and watched the newly-engaged couple flirt and share coy smiles. This happy, everyday-life scene felt crazily out of place. Life went on about her in a normal, blissfully naïve way, while she, Markus, and Trevor knew evil waited beyond the gates of this ranch. Silently giving thanks, she felt grateful for this moment of quiet peace, however fleeting it might last.

*****

After the guests departed, the house was quiet. Trevor stretched out on his bed, thinking a nap was in order. Gunner lay on the foot of the bed, already asleep, paws twitching in a dream of chase or catching a ball.

Unable to turn off his mind, he reached for his cellphone, checking for an email from his mother. It was there, confirming she'd arrived safely in York, the twins surprised, yet delighted to see her.

A soft tapping at his door diverted his attention away from reading of his brothers' soccer exploits. "Come in," he said, setting the phone aside.

Sidney poked her head into the room. "Markus is through with what he needed to handle on the computer. He and I are taking a little jog to the barn to check on the horses. Mostly, to work off some calories from all that food we ate."

She rubbed her belly and puffed out her cheeks. "Want to join us?"

"Sure. I was thinking I'd nap, but my mind's too busy. I'll meet you downstairs in a minute."

"Great."

Trevor strapped on his prosthetic leg, followed by his shoulder holster. Out of habit, he checked the gun's safety and made sure a round was chambered. After holstering his weapon, he grabbed Gunner's harness, the dog now sitting expectantly at his feet.

"Sorry. No more chasing rabbits in your sleep. Let's go."

In the kitchen, Sidney leaned against the counter, Rex at her side. She looked up when Trevor entered the room. "Markus had an emergency call come in. He said for us to get a head start and he'd catch up with us in a minute."

"Sounds good." Trevor held the door open, and Rex tried to follow Gunner out.

"No, Rex. You have to stay." Sidney shoved her foot across the opening, barring the dog from leaving. "Sorry, but Markus said you couldn't go anywhere without him. The doggie boot camp thing, remember?" She slid out the door, with Trevor close behind.

The western sun glowed faintly on the horizon as they jogged toward the deer trail leading to the barn. "Markus stayed in his safe-room all afternoon on the computer," Sidney offered. "He said he'd brief us later on what he called a 'plan to secure the perimeter.' Apparently, he's put the wheels in motion to get a team in place to secure the ranch until he can get me out of Alpine."

"He'd told me as much. I think it's a wise move, now that we know someone's snooping around town and asking questions."

They jogged the rest of the way to the barn in silence. All the while, Trevor ran over in his mind the actual words Markus had said to him. The plan involved a Black Hawk helicopter flying in from El Paso's Fort Bliss sometime after midnight, bringing in a team of Special Ops experts. How in the hell, Trevor had asked him, did he have the authority to commandeer a Black Hawk? On top of that, on whose authority was he ordering in a Special Ops team? Markus's response had been ambiguous at best—something about having friends in high places.

Must be God, or Generals, or someone higher.

Sidney threw on the light switch as they entered the barn. "I'm surprised Markus hasn't caught up with us yet. That phone call must be *very* important."

"No doubt." Trevor grabbed the cart with the feed buckets, remembering the routine. "I'll wheel the cart—you scoop."

"How are your hands feeling? If you'd rather, I'll push the cart while you scoop the feed."

"I'm good. My hands are almost back to normal," Trevor exaggerated.

They made the rounds, going up and down the aisles of the barn, scooping oats and throwing hay for the nickering horses eager for dinner. When they'd finished, Trevor parked the cart, leaving the buckets ready to be filled for tomorrow morning's feeding.

"Gunner is whimpering like he needs to go out," said Sidney. "I'll turn the lights off and close up the barn while you take him outside."

"No," said Trevor. "Gunner can wait. I'm not leaving you by yourself for—"

The explosive sound of gunfire rang out. Trevor grabbed Sidney by the arm and pulled her to the ground. Unholstering his pistol, he rolled in front of Sidney, shielding her with his body. Another shot rang out. The bullet ricocheted off the cement floor and struck the wall behind them.

Sidney screamed. Terrified, she scooted backward toward the feed room. "In here, Trevor."

"Get inside. Lock the door. Now. Take Gunner."

"Not without you."

"Go. Now."

Sidney crawled toward the door of the feed room, yanking on Gunner's harness. "Come with me. Damn it, Gunner, cooperate." The dog's nails scratched uselessly on the cement floor in his attempt to gain traction. He struggled against Sidney's grip, barking frantically as he tried to get to Trevor. She managed to drag the dog inside before slamming the door behind her.

Three silhouetted figures moved toward him, their pistols raised. Trevor rolled to his side and then belly-crawled to the bales of hay stacked on a pallet next to the feed room. He crouched in the shadows. Waiting. Letting them get close enough for his eye to identify his targets.

The men crept nearer. Trevor fired off three rounds before a bullet ripped through his left arm. The impact sent him sprawling backward onto the floor. He fired another round at the figure looming over him and watched the man's face disintegrate in a wet spray of blood, tissue, and bone.

Anton kicked the gun from Trevor's hand as he shouted to Fredo, "Get the girl. She's behind that door."

Fredo jiggled the doorknob. "It's locked." Backing away a few paces, he fired three rounds into the door, shattering the lock.

Gunfire echoed throughout the barn, sending the horses into a panic. The frenzied animals called to one another in shrill, high-pitched whinnies that mingled with the sound of Sidney shrieking in pain as her Taser was ripped from her hands and used against her.

Trevor tried to stand—tried to get to Sidney—tried to block the boot as it came down hard against his temple. Then, everything went black.

CHAPTER 24

Alpine

Markus emerged from the safe-room, satisfied his plan was coming together. Moose and his team should depart Langley soon, be in El Paso by twenty-two hundred hours, and then board a Black Hawk at Fort Bliss to land in his arena by midnight. Even though his plan called for him to collect on a debt from his former boss, who was now a Deputy Director in the CIA, it was still the most expeditious way to ensure Sidney's safety until the CIA could turn the case over to the FBI.

Deputy Director O'Connor, Colonel James J. O'Connor, USMC (Retired), had been Markus's commander during his days in Force Recon. Later, Markus worked indirectly for Colonel O'Connor during a stint with Special Forces Command. After O'Connor's unexpected retirement from the Corps and his entry into the CIA, he was instrumental in convincing Markus to join the CIA's special covert Black Ops unit.

Collecting on a debt was more of a euphemism than anything. In the Corps, as well as in the CIA, whether active duty, retired, or undercover, the band of brothers was just that— a band. They stuck together. When one needed help, the others came running.

After arming the security system, Markus set out at a jog along the deer trail, Rex obediently heeling at his side. He ran through in his mind the rest of the plan to make sure he'd not forgotten anything. Moose and his men would set up a perimeter around the lodge, keeping it under 24/7 surveillance. The FBI would send in a team to brief Sidney on the witness protection program. After they had evaluated potential locations, they'd evacuate her to an undisclosed safe house. Then, she would disappear for a while.

That last part tightened his gut, but he'd not dwell on it, he told himself.

In the near distance, Markus saw the barn's lights glowing in the stall windows, the shadowy shapes of Trevor and Sidney moving about as they fed the horses. He picked up his pace, wanting to be a part of the evening's feeding chores.

As he neared the barn, Rex began growling and running ahead, refusing to obey commands. Markus yelled for the dog to come back, but his words were drowned out by a sudden blast of gunfire. Another shot split the night. Markus unholstered his Glock, his tactical mode automatically switching into high gear. Now at a dead run, he reached the barn to hear four shots fired in quick succession. Another soon followed.

Three more shots pinged off metal, followed by the gut-wrenching sound of Sidney shrieking. Images flashed through his mind of what that shriek foretold. Crouching low to the ground, pressing his body against the barn, he crept inside, staying to the shadows.

Move toward the sound of the guns.

As his eyes adjusted to the light, he crawled along the main aisle of the barn. Muffled noise coming from the area of the feed room told him where to look. Rolling over and maneuvering into a crouching position, he took aim at the man in black dragging Sidney by her hair.

He raised his weapon. He took a deep breath. Expelled it halfway. Held the remaining air in his lungs. Steadied his body. Saw his target. Saw what lay beyond his target. Saw a clear shot. His finger rested on the trigger, ready to squeeze.

Before Markus could fire, Rex hurtled from the shadows and knocked the man sideways. Sidney collapsed onto her hands and knees. In a fluid bound, Rex leapt again, this time latching onto the assailant's throat. The dog's momentum sent the man stumbling, and they fell to the ground in a heap. Maintaining his death hold on the attacker's neck, the maddened animal jerked his head left and right while pulling backward, dragging his victim across the cement floor. With a relentless crush of powerful jaws and teeth, Rex ripped out the man's esophagus.

Seeing movement, Markus spun to his right. Another dark-clad figure straddled Trevor, a knife gripped in his hands and raised over Trevor's chest. The man's eyes widened in surprise as he stared at the sight of Rex mauling his associate to death. His stunned pause allowed Markus time to aim and shoot the knife out of his hands, the bullet ripping off fingers in the process. The man roared in pain as he scrambled to his feet. But the tackling force of Markus's body crashing against his propelled him to the ground.

"Make a move, and I'll splatter your fucking brains," growled Markus, his Glock pressed against the base of the man's skull. He put all of his weight onto his knee and bore down on the attacker's back, producing unbearable pain.

"Okay, okay." His harsh, raspy voice was hardly audible with his mouth crushed against the floor.

"How many of you?" Markus ground down harder with his knee.

"Three" His body writhed in pain.

Markus looked around for the third person and spotted a body lying near Trevor, the body missing most of his face. "Who are you and who sent you here?"

"Anton. Nobody sent me. I don't work for nobody."

"I don't believe you." Markus swung the butt end of his pistol, striking Anton in the temple and knocking him unconscious. Grabbing a lead rope hanging nearby, he hogtied Anton's hands to his feet behind his back. Pushing away from the motionless body, he turned to Sidney who was on her knees, struggling to stand.

Rex crouched in front of Sidney, blocking her from anything he perceived as a threat. The hair along his spine stood on end. His rigid tail extended straight out, ears pulled flat against his skull. Growling. Teeth bared. Blood and saliva dripped from his muzzle.

As Markus approached, Rex's growl intensified. The dog crouched lower in a defensive stance, prepared to attack. Markus stopped and relaxed his posture. He held out one hand for Rex to sniff. In the other hand, he kept his finger on the trigger of his pistol. "Easy, boy. It's just me. Easy."

"Rex, it's okay," Sidney soothed. Now standing, she reached out and rubbed her fingers down the dog's back. No longer growling, his carriage softened. He looked from Sidney to Markus, a confused, though still wary expression in his eyes.

"Give him a command, Sid. Anything I taught you earlier. Make him obey you." If Rex didn't recognize Sidney or him as an alpha pack leader, he'd likely attack again. *And it'll probably be me.*

Sidney eased closer to Rex, her shaky voice as forceful as she could manage. "Rex, *platz.*" She gave the German command for him to drop to the ground in place. He obeyed, lowering to the floor in a sphinxlike pose.

"Good job, Sid." Getting the dog's attention, Markus called to him. "Rex. *Achtung. Hier.*" Rex seemed to waver a moment before rising and walking to Markus. He sat at attention, waiting for another command, allowing Markus's hand to stroke his head. "Good boy, Rex. That's a good boy."

From across the floor, Trevor stirred and tried to sit up. But he collapsed, moaning and cradling his arm against his chest. Markus rushed over and dropped down next to him. He felt for the strength of his pulse and assessed the gravity of his wounds. Ripping off his T-shirt, he wound it around Trevor's arm, securing it firmly over the bullet wound.

"He's got a strong pulse. No great blood loss yet." Turning to Sidney, he said, "Come and put pressure on his arm, firm and steady, while I attend to Rex."

Sidney limped over to Trevor who slipped in and out of consciousness. She knelt beside him, placing her hands over the wound and pressing down. Blood soon soaked through the shirt and covered her hands. "He's bleeding through," she shouted over her shoulder.

"Keep pressing down. I'll be right there." Markus knew that in Rex's current state of confusion and agitation, he was as lethal as a loaded weapon. Calming him with soothing words, he hosed the blood off of his coat, encouraging the dog to drink water. He rubbed disinfectant into Rex's fur, leaving it on to mask the smell of death.

With that done, Markus hurried over to Sidney and knelt next to her. Placing a hand on the back of her neck, he asked, "Are you hurt?"

"My thigh is on fire from being tasered, but I'm okay." Tears welled in her eyes, but she fought them back.

"Are you sure you're okay?" He took over the task of keeping pressure on Trevor's wound.

"I'm sure." Rocking back on her heels, she stared at the blood on her hands, at Trevor lying unconscious on the ground. She began to shake.

"Get one of the horse's leg-wraps from the tack room and wind it around Trevor's arm. Don't remove the T-shirt, just add another layer. Continue applying pressure. I need to secure that asshole." He nodded toward Anton.

Markus noted her trembling body and her pale, shocked expression. Giving her a task was critical in helping her to focus on the present—to not dwell on the horror she'd just witnessed. He didn't want her going into shock.

She hobbled as best she could to the tack room and came out with white, quilted wraps used for protecting a horse's legs during shipping. She wound one around Trevor's bloody arm, holding it in place with steady pressure.

Markus moved to where Anton lay unconscious and dragged him inside the nearest empty horse stall. With another lead rope, he lashed the limp body to the stall's metal frame and tied a gag in his mouth. After he removed the padlock from his personal locker in the tack room, he bolted the stall door and secured the lock.

Rex followed on his heels, as if seeking nearness to the one he considered his pack leader. Understanding how close he'd come tonight to shooting his dog sickened Markus. But if Rex *had* lunged at him, he would have had no option but to shoot.

"He's coming around," Sidney said to Markus when he returned.

Trevor moaned and blinked his eyes. He rolled his head from side to side in a struggle to wake up as he slipped in and out of consciousness. Gunner lay at his side, whimpering softly and resting his head on Trevor's stomach.

"All right. Let's take a look here." Markus removed the bandage and T-shirt from Trevor's arm so he could evaluate the damage. "The bleeding has stopped. That's a positive."

He saw that the bullet had gone straight through the bicep, a clean shot just above the elbow joint that still operated freely. The cut on his temple would require a few stitches, and the apparent concussion, as evidenced by the dilation of his pupils, would take time to resolve.

Markus retrieved a first aid kit from the veterinarian's supply cabinet and began cleaning the entrance and exit wounds with the same Betadine disinfectant he'd used on Rex. Then he flushed the open wounds with saline solution, rewrapped the arm in clean bandages, and secured it with a sling wrap. By the time he had disinfected and stitched the head wound, Trevor, though dazed, had awakened.

"Where's Sidney?" Trevor asked, his eyes darting around. "Is she okay?"

"I'm fine. I'm here behind you, holding your head in my lap."

Trevor sucked in deep breaths, his voice unsteady. "How bad are my injuries?

"You took a bullet to the left upper arm, clean through

the muscle. No broken bones, and the elbow joint doesn't appear damaged," said Markus. "Looks like a blow to the temple knocked you out, though with your hard head, you'll be all right."

Trevor managed a weak smile and tried to move the arm secured in the sling. "There were three—I remember seeing three. Did we get them all?"

"You got one. Rex took one down. I've got the other secured. A dead man can't talk. I want to hear what the live one has to say." Markus's skill at interrogating prisoners was still lauded among those at the Company, those who knew him as John Walker. Getting a prisoner to talk was sometimes challenging, sometimes bloody, but their *not* talking was never an option.

"Help me up." Trevor tried to roll onto his right side, but searing pain ripped through his head, forcing him onto his back.

"Hang tight, buddy. You don't need to get up yet. I'll be just a minute." Markus ran to his office across from the tack room, rifling through the keys on the ring hanging inside the door. Locating the correct key, he hurried out to the parking lot to his pickup. He backed the truck into the barn as close to Trevor as he could maneuver.

"What can I do to help?" Sidney placed Trevor's head on the stack of unused bandages and began gathering the bloody gauze and discarded needle and thread.

"When you're done, help me get Trevor loaded. Then, I'll need you to drive this truck to the lodge. I'll be riding in the back with my prisoner. Are you up to that?"

"What about Rex? Is he going to be all right? Has this—changed him?"

"Time will tell. He's subdued and wanting human contact. That's a good sign. But, we'll need to keep a close eye on him. Now, can you drive?"

"I can drive, yes," she said, walking closer to where Markus stood. "But, shouldn't we call the police?"

"Some things aren't handled by the police. Some things

never make the headlines or the ten o'clock news."

"I don't understand—"

"The right people are handling this. I know who I can trust, but I don't know who I *can't* trust. These street thugs didn't figure out where you were hiding on their own."

"But what about getting Trevor to the hospital? He should see a doctor—"

"I'm the only doctor Trevor's going to see for now," Markus snapped. "The cartel has infiltrated Alpine. We're not leaving this property until I have reinforcements in place—not even for a hospital. Do you understand?" His austere expression matched the severity of his words.

"I—I understand." Sidney backed away, visibly shaken by his sudden harsh coldness.

"I've tended to far worse wounds on the battlefield than his," said Markus, his voice still severe. Seeing her recoil, he took a few deep breaths to regain his composure. "Sorry, Sid. I didn't mean to snap at you. Trevor will get more care later. He's going to be fine. Trust me."

Sidney dropped her gaze to the floor, averting his eyes. She ran clammy hands down her shirt, then rubbed them together. Clearly in turmoil, she hesitantly questioned the word, "Trust?"

"Yes. I need you to trust me." If she can't trust me by now, then what the hell am I doing here, he thought, as he waited for her response.

Guardedly, her voice scarcely a whisper, she said, "I chose—to trust you."

Markus heaved a sigh of relief. "Good. Thank you. I'm going to need even more trust, not only about this situation, but about a lot more I can't go into right now. Will you do that for me, trust me like I need you to do?"

She nodded. "Yes. I will."

Besides her verbal declaration, it was the set of her jaw and the resolve in her eyes that told him she'd truly made the decision to trust him. He understood what a monumental leap she'd just taken. Knowing Sidney's past, of her trusting a man who didn't deserve it, but who in fact had used that trust against her, made him feel more than relieved. He felt humbled—and determined to not let her down.

They helped Trevor into the back seat where he could stretch out, Trevor's muffled grunts and groans mingling with his dog's whimpers. After they eased Trevor inside, Gunner hopped in and sat on the floorboard, his head resting on the seat.

Sidney opened the front passenger door, allowing Rex to jump in. She grabbed him by the scruff of his neck and buried her face in his fur. "You saved my life," she murmured, her tears adding to the wetness of his coat. Wiping her eyes on her shirtsleeve, she moved around to the other side of the truck, settled into the driver's seat, and waited.

Markus unlashed Anton from the horse stall, loosening the rope around his ankles so he could walk. With his Glock pressed against Anton's back, Markus instructed him to climb into the empty cargo box in the bed of the pickup and lie down. Anton put up a brief struggle, but Markus forced the lid down, then locked it and pocketed the key. He tapped on the rear window, signaling Sidney to drive.

CHAPTER 25

Alpine

Sidney paced the floor, massaging the back of her neck while Markus reloaded Trevor's pistol. Trevor assured them he was fit to fight, should the need arise. Markus gave him a quick test of his reflexes and checked the dilation of his pupils, pronouncing him as fit as could be expected. Thankfully, Trevor was right handed, and despite his burns, could still aim straight if need be.

With Sidney and Trevor safely sequestered behind locked and secured doors, Markus could now focus on his mission. What to do with his prisoner. How to get him to talk. He eased into the driver's seat, ignoring the furious kicking coming from the cargo box.

He steered the truck onto the gravel lane that wound past the lodge and snaked behind the long row of garages meant for customers' expensive sport utility vehicles. Beyond the garages, the lane continued past a small cluster of storage sheds. Pointing the truck toward the end of the row, he braked to a halt in front of a stone building that housed the meat locker and processing room.

Markus slammed his door shut, and then moved to the bed of his truck. After unlocking the cargo lid, he pulled Anton up by his shoulders and dragged him out of the box. Anton struggled against Markus's grasp, making the short walk to the building's door a difficult task.

Once inside, Markus flipped a switch, flooding the stark room with fluorescent light. The butcher's table stood against the far wall, the instruments of bleeding, skinning, and dismembering a carcass displayed in plain view. To the side of the table and centered over a gaping drain in the floor, a meat hook dangled from an overhead hoist used to lift deer carcasses ready for gutting and bleeding.

Markus shoved Anton onto his knees and removed the gag from his mouth. "You can cooperate, and I'll let you live. Or, you can *not* cooperate, and I'll inflict such unbearable pain on you that you'll wish you were dead."

"Fuck you, you goddamned prick." Spit flew from Anton's mouth with his raging response.

"Wrong answer." Markus grabbed Anton by his collar and dragged him to the hoist. Lifting him to a standing position, he attached the hook to the rope binding Anton's wrists behind his back.

Anton looked on in horror, his eyes wide with fright as he watched Markus reach for a remote control. Markus pushed the button controlling the hoist. The mechanism lifted Anton off the floor, leaving his boots hovering inches above the drain.

Anton's inhuman scream filled the room. His high-pitched shrieks sounded like those of an animal caught in a trap. He glared at Markus with panicked eyes. His rasping pants increased, yet he still refused to talk. Soon, Anton lost control of his bladder, and a wet stain spread across the front of his jeans.

"I don't have all night. Things are only going to get worse. Who sent you here?"

He spat at Markus. "I don't talk to no *gringo* mother fucker."

"Have it your way. But I won't just stand around waiting for you to decide you've had enough."

Leaving him dangling from the hoist, Markus hurried out of the building, soon returning with the jumper cables from his truck. After binding Anton's ankles and unbuckling his belt, he yanked down the man's jeans, exposing his genitals. He fastened one clamp of the jumper cables onto Anton's nipple, the other clamp to his scrotum.

Anton's body bucked and twisted as he spewed a volley of Spanish curses. *"Tienes un pene pequeno, pinche cara de mecos."*

"No woman has ever complained about the size of my cock," Markus countered as he calmly walked away, choosing to ignore the "sperm face" part of the insult.

Using his pocketknife, he removed the plate from a wall socket and pulled out the wires. He uncoiled the remaining length of the jumper cables and attached the black clamp to the negative wire, while his hand holding the red clamp hovered near the positive wire.

"Talk, or shock—you choose," Markus said, matter-of-factly.

"Yo cago en la leche de tu puta madre," Anton spat.

"That would be difficult. My mother's dead." Markus touched the metal tip of the jumper cable to the wire, sending a current of electricity coursing through Anton's body.

Anton's back arched in a violent spasm. Despite jaws clamped shut, a primordial grunt escaped. Several seconds passed before Markus removed the metal tip of the clamp from the exposed wire and broke the circuit. As Anton's body went limp, his bowels released and he defecated himself.

"So much for shitting in the milk of my mother, who, by the way, was *not* a whore. Looks like you've shit yourself." Markus remained squatted down by the wall. Making a dramatic movement as if to reconnect the cable to the wire, he asked again, "Talk or shock. Same choice as before."

"Parada. Stop." Anton begged. "I'll talk."

"That's what I thought you'd say."

Markus unclamped the jumper cable from the wire, letting the end he was holding drop to the floor. Stepping over to the hoist, he lowered Anton a few inches until he could support his weight on the balls of his feet. Anton let out an agonized shriek as pressure was taken off his shoulders. With the slight movement, severe pain shot through each arm.

His voice even and measured, his eyes cold, hard slits, Markus said, "So, let's try this again. Who sent you?"

Gulping mouthfuls of air, Anton hissed, "His name is Winston. Winston Knight."

"Have you been in recent contact with him?"

"*Si*. Always in contact."

"Is he here in Alpine, too?"

Anton shook his head. His clammy skin had turned pale, and perspiration soaked his clothes.

"Is Knight responsible for ordering the arson on your male target's home, or ordering the murder of your female target's attorney?"

"Yes. *Si*. It was him."

"Does he traffic drugs and weapons? Is that how he's made his fortune?"

"We…" Anton struggled to maintain even breaths and to keep his body from swaying. Every small movement inflicted more pain to his shoulders. "*Si*. We run things for him."

"And who is the big boss? Who does Winston answer to?"

"Nobody. Knight—gives—all the orders." Anton's head lolled forward and back. Drool trailed from his mouth onto his shirt. His eyes rolled to the back of his head as he fell unconscious.

"Sure. Winston Knight gives all the orders." Markus doubted Winston was at the top of the pyramid, but he'd heard enough. Stopping his cellphone's voice recorder, he thought twice about unclamping his jumper cables. The one attached to Anton's nipple wouldn't be a problem, but without a protective glove, he wasn't going near the one clamped to the man's scrotum, not after it had been pissed and shit upon. He decided to leave the clamps attached.

*****

Markus drove his pickup to the edge of his outdoor arena and parked against the fence. Glancing again at his watch as he strode over to the power pole, he figured it would be at least an hour before Moose and his team arrived. However, just in case the Black Hawk came sooner than expected, he flipped on the switch, bringing the arena's glaring lights to life.

Forty-five minutes later, the whop-whop-whop of a helicopter's rotor blades whirred in the distance. Looking to his left, he saw the approaching Black Hawk flying just above the tree line. As it neared the arena, gritty sand blew into the air, creating a sepia-colored dust cloud. Markus shielded his eyes with his arm as he jogged to meet the crew.

This reminds me of Afghanistan. Except now, the enemy is in my own backyard.

The chopper landed in the middle of the arena amidst a whirlwind of blowing sand. The doors slid open and Moose jumped to the ground, followed by Master, Cannibal, Cooper, and Rocky. The pilot killed the engine and the rotors slowed to a stop.

After greeting the team, Markus pulled Moose aside. "The situation has changed since I arranged for you and your team to come and secure a perimeter around the lodge. The perimeter has been breached. I had a messy situation on my hands earlier."

"Give me the abridged version. What the hell happened?"

"A team of three cartel thugs infiltrated the premises and ambushed Sidney and Trevor, the "witnesses," if you will. Two of the thugs are in the barn—dead. I captured the third for interrogation purposes. He's hanging in the meat locker, probably still alive."

"Probably?"

Markus shrugged and nodded. "Most likely."

"Your witnesses—are they injured, or…?"

"Trevor—walking wounded. Gunshot through the left bicep. Possible concussion. I doctored him up as best I could, but he should be medevac'd when possible. Sidney was tasered, but no serious damage. If these goons got word back to whomever they work for, supposedly Winston Knight who is Sid's estranged husband, then Sidney's not safe here. They're both in danger the longer they're here."

"No doubt. So, what's the new plan?" Moose listened intently, crossing his arms over his broad chest.

"Exfiltration, ASAP. Use code names in all communications. Sidney's code will be—Princess. Trevor—Iron Man."

Moose nodded. "Got it."

"Get them to a safe location—I'm thinking the Farm." Markus noted Moose flinching at that. "Send another helicopter to remove the dead and to secure the prisoner. Turn him over to the FBI. Let them handle it."

Moose paused before answering. "Dragon, you know what you're suggesting is beyond my capacity to approve."

"Then get your boss on the phone. He can approve it."

"And then what? Should I tell him we've got a twisted fairytale on our hands, where Dragon is trying to rescue the Princess from the dangerous Knight?"

"Nice play on words, Moose. Just make the call."

"It's late in Langley. A middle of the night call never goes over well." Moose retrieved his phone and pressed the speed dial. After a brief pause, he said, "Sorry to wake you, sir. We've arrived at Disneyland and I'm here with Dragon. The situation has escalated, prompting the need for a Plan B. I think you better handle this."

Markus reached for the phone. "How are you, sir?"

"Doing well, Dragon. I gather you're not. Let's cut through the minutiae. What's changed?"

"Two dead Rio Negro cartel members in my barn. One thoroughly interrogated cartel member hanging in my meat locker. Two frightened witnesses sheltering in my lodge, one with a bullet wound to his arm. That's what's changed."

"Jesus Christ, Dragon." A pause. "I'm afraid to ask, but what is it that you want me to provide you now?"

Without hesitation, Markus issued his requirements.

"Get the witnesses, coded Princess and Iron Man, out of here—tonight—on this chopper. Have a jet waiting at Fort Bliss to evacuate them to the Farm. Send another chopper back here to pick up the cartel members, both dead and alive. Turn the one calling himself Anton over to the FBI, and tell them I've got a recorded message from him they'd be interested in listening to. It implicates the female witness's estranged husband as being involved with the cartel's criminal activity. Review the S.A.D. file I sent in an email to my former Ops officer."

"And then what, Dragon? You know this is highly unorthodox. You're not on the payroll anymore, and your request is out of line. I've already stuck my neck out for you, getting Moose and his team there. Evacuating potential witnesses to a federal crime falls under the jurisdiction of the FBI. This is not the CIA's problem."

"Come on, Jim. I'm not just talking about arson, murder, and attempted murder. Knight, is also involved in international arms and drug trafficking, something the CIA's been dirtying their hands with for a long time. These are witnesses that should be protected. And I'm going to protect them whether I'm on anyone's goddamned payroll, or not." Markus sucked in a deep breath, knowing he may have crossed the line.

After an extended moment of silence, the Deputy Director responded. "You and I have a long history, Dragon, a history of trust and respect. It goes way back—"

"Way back to when you and I started the Company's 'Code Red Dragon' program. Even farther back to when you were my Special Ops commander. You trusted and respected my instincts then. I'm asking for you to do so now. Sir."

Pausing, a deep breath rattling over the connection, he said, "All right. Proceed as requested. But remember this. You've been officially retired for three years now. Your *unofficial* ID has been dead longer than that. You're flying solo on this mission. Whatever happens from this point forward will never be recognized as a legitimate operation. Do you understand the implications?"

"Yes, sir, I do. Thank you, sir."

"I'll have a company jet waiting for you tomorrow morning at Fort Bliss to fly you and the others to Langley. There, I'll have a helicopter waiting to bring you to the Farm. Then, you and I will have a face-to-face sometime later, depending on my schedule. At that point, everything will be turned over to the FBI and I can wash my hands of this."

"That's a fine plan, sir. But, I'm not coming. I'm putting Moose in charge of getting the witnesses to El Paso and points beyond. I have to take care of some business in Fort Worth."

"Business in Fort Worth? What the hell is this about?"

"It's personal, sir. You don't want to know."

"Call me when you get to Virginia, for Pete's sake, whenever that may be." O'Connor hung up the phone.

*****

Under Markus's direction, Master and Rocky were dispatched to guard Anton and to clean him up sufficiently enough to ride in the helicopter without sickening the crew. Cooper and Cannibal were sent to clean up the mess in the barn and to prepare the bodies for transport. Moose was appointed to supervise both exercises.

And Markus was left to figure out how in the hell he was going to explain to Sidney why he wouldn't be flying out of Alpine with her.

CHAPTER 26

Alpine

Sidney curled up on the sofa with Rex at her feet, waiting for Markus to return. Her hair, damp from her shower, felt cool against her neck while the skin on her hands and fingers felt raw from scrubbing away the blood. She had tossed Trevor's and her stained clothes into a trash bag that she'd left by the back door, ready to be taken to the dumpster. As soon as it was safe to go outside, she told herself, she would.

As soon as it's safe… How many times these past months have I thought those words?

Across the room, Trevor paced in front of the fireplace, his pistol in a waistband holster at the small of his back. After he'd showered, he'd taken Markus up on his earlier offer and raided his closet, finding jeans and a T-shirt to wear. Gunner watched him intently as he paced, his eyes following every movement.

"I'm getting more coffee. You want anything?" Sidney stood and stretched, pressing her fists against her back.

"Yeah, I'll take a quadruple bourbon, straight."

"I didn't think you took anything straight."

They both cracked up laughing. "Very funny, sister. Actually, I'll take another black coffee, thanks."

"That felt good—to laugh." Sidney paused in the doorway. "Besides just now, when was the last time you had a good belly laugh?"

"I can't remember." Trevor shrugged, shaking his head.

"I can't either."

Returning with two cups of steaming coffee, she handed one to Trevor. "When interrogating a prisoner, I wonder how long it takes to get to the truth?" Her question reminded her of the old television commercial that asked how many licks did it take to get to the center of a Tootsie Pop, and she felt strangely saddened by the comparison.

Trevor strode to the window and drew back the curtain. "Apparently it takes this long. He's pulling in now."

They hurried to the kitchen to meet Markus as he came through the door. He stood in the entryway and kicked off his shoes, a dark, unreadable expression on his face. He smiled and said "Hello," but his expression remained aloof.

"Are you okay?" Sidney asked, pressing a hand to his cheek.

"I am. Come here." He took her by the wrist and pulled her close, enfolding her in a tight embrace. He pressed his lips against the top of her head.

Sidney wound her arms around his waist and rested all her weight against his body. She moved in rhythm with his chest as it rose and fell with each breath. Speaking softly, she asked, "Do you want to talk about it?"

"No."

"I'm here if you do."

"Everything's good." Markus glanced at Trevor who stood at the sink. "It figures you'd take one of my favorite T-shirts."

The black shirt had the U.S. Marine Corps logo on the front, and on the back, a slogan that read, *Nobody ever drowned in sweat.* A size too small, it accentuated Trevor's muscular physique. "I may give it back to you someday. Thanks for the loan—and jeans, too."

"Glad I could assist." Markus took Sidney's face in his hands and kissed her mouth. Then, holding her at arm's length, he ran his hands up and down her arms, studying her face.

Trevor cleared his throat. "I'm feeling a bit like a voyeur. Should I leave you two alone?"

"Sorry, Trevor. No—unfortunately." Markus took Sidney by the hand and led her to the table, motioning for Trevor to follow. "I say *unfortunately* because we have a lot to talk about and not much time to prepare."

"Prepare for what?" asked Sidney, taking the chair that Markus pulled out.

"For exfiltration. Moose and his team are here now, tidying things up. When they're through with what they have to do, I've been given the go-ahead to get y'all out of here."

"We're leaving tonight instead of tomorrow?" Sidney pushed down a wave of anxiety that made breathing difficult. *This is a good thing, leaving. So why am I anxious?*

"Yes. The sooner, the better."

"We heard the chopper land," said Trevor, pouring the remaining coffee into three cups. "How much time do we have?"

"Probably an hour, at best. As soon as Moose calls and gives me the all clear, we're heading to the arena where the helicopter is waiting. There'll be a short flight to El Paso. A doctor there will see to your arm. The next morning, a jet will be waiting at Fort Bliss for a zero seven hundred hours departure for the next leg—a flight to Langley. Last leg is another short helicopter ride to the Farm."

"The Farm?" Trevor set his cup down on the table and leaned forward. "As in, Camp Peary, the CIA training facility?"

"That's the place."

"You *do* have friends in high places. I wonder who they are." Trevor downed the rest of his coffee, drumming his fingers on the empty cup.

"There are a few safe houses established on the grounds," said Markus, sidestepping Trevor's remark. "The FBI has been notified and they'll take things over once the CIA is finished with their debriefing."

"And then what?" Sidney's mind reeled. "CIA. FBI. Safe houses. This seems like a movie, and I should be watching it, not living it. But—"

"But you are, and this *is* real." Markus said matter-of-factly. "The FBI will brief you on the witness protection program, in case that option is necessary, and I think it is. It won't be forever, just until the dust settles and all the bad guys are behind bars."

Markus's cellphone vibrated in his back pocket. Glancing at the caller ID, he said, "Go ahead, Moose."

The short conversation was loud enough for Sidney to hear clearly. Referring to Markus as "Dragon," Moose instructed him to have the witnesses ready to depart in thirty minutes, with Markus's succinct, monotone reply of "Roger that" delivered rapid-fire.

He met Sidney's penetrating gaze, holding it. "We don't have an hour after all—just half that. We've been given our marching orders. Pack one suitcase. Quickly."

"Dragon?" Her eyebrows arched upward. That explained the tapestry, the sign hanging above the entry gate, and the tattoo on his hip.

"My code—my *former* code name. We all have—I *had* one when... Hell, that's a conversation for another day." Impatient, Markus pushed back from the table. His chair toppled to the floor behind him. Setting it upright, he snapped, "Better start packing."

"Who will take care of Mocha?" Sidney called out as she hurried up the stairs.

"Victor. Otto. Heidi and Dieter will help. She'll be in good hands," Markus called back.

Turning away from the table, Markus almost bumped into Trevor who was standing with his arms folded across his chest, despite the sling. "Are you going to tell me what's *really* going on? I'm not talking about divulging classified information or top-secret BS. I'm talking about telling it to me straight—Dragon."

"There's nothing to tell."

"I disagree."

Markus paused, letting his breath out slowly. "That I worked for the CIA is unclassified. Dragon was my code name when I was part of a special division. Code names have a way of sticking to you for life. The rest—is classified. Now you know all you need to know, or, all I can tell you. I'm going to help Sidney pack. You need to get busy, too." Markus tried to ease past, but Trevor stepped in front of him, blocking his path.

"I have a lot at stake here—a mother and two brothers to consider. Witness protection program? I didn't ask for this."

"Neither did I when I agreed to help Sid, based on *your* email," he said through gritted teeth. "Sid didn't ask for this, either. But here we all are, in the same damn boat, dealing with it as best we can."

Markus and Trevor stood toe-to-toe, neither giving ground. Both men drew in deep breaths through their nostrils, puffing out their chests, forcefully expelling the air like two bulls in a standoff. Tension crackled the air between them as they waited for the other to speak first. After a long moment, Trevor took a slight step back.

"This is crazy. My mother needs me. I can't do this— this witness protection program." He cradled his damaged arm against his stomach as he turned to leave. "I won't do it."

"It's not a forced program. It's voluntary." Markus's words hung in the air as Trevor stomped up the stairs, Gunner at his side.

*****

With Sidney's suitcase in hand, Markus hurried out the door. Placing it into the back of the Jeep, he noticed that Trevor's backpack was already loaded. He glanced around to see him standing in the driveway, looking up at the midnight sky.

"The stars seem so bright out here. Like when I was a kid, and my dad would take us camping out at Possum Kingdom Lake." Trevor walked over and leaned against the Jeep. "Man, that feels like so long ago."

Markus leaned against the Jeep next to Trevor. "Out here, you can actually see the Milky Way."

"Yeah—there it is." Trevor pointed to the constellation.

"How's your arm?"

"It's been better." Trevor tugged at the sling, tightening the neck band.

"The flight surgeon will take a look at it when you land in El Paso."

"I remember you saying that."

"Right."

"Hey, I want to apologize for earlier." Trevor shot a sidelong glance at Markus. "I'm sorry I lost my cool."

"Apology accepted, but it's not necessary. I understand. And I'm sorry you're in this situation. Like you said, the situation *is* crazy. But I'm doing my damnedest to un-crazy it, if you will."

"What do you mean by that?" Trevor asked.

"By that, I mean to pay a visit to Fort Worth, to a certain prick named Winston Knight. I want to be the one to see his sorry ass go down."

"Sounds to me like this has become personal."

"It has become *very* personal. And, please keep this between us. I don't want Sidney to know about it—it would only add to her worry."

"I won't say anything." Trevor nodded toward the back of the Jeep. "I noticed you loaded only one suitcase. I'm assuming you're not coming with us but are headed straight to Fort Worth."

"That's right. But I'll meet up with y'all as soon as I can."

"What does Sidney think about you not coming?"

"I haven't told her yet."

Trevor raised his eyebrows. "Not that it's any of my business, but, why not?"

"That's a good question. Maybe I'm just a coward."

Maybe I just don't want to say goodbye.

At that moment, Sidney stepped out the door. "I guess I'm ready. You two look like you're in deep conversation."

"Deep and getting deeper." Trevor opened the back door, letting Gunner and Rex hop in. "I'll ride with the dogs this time."

"May we stop at the barn so I can say goodbye to Mocha?" Sidney slid into the front seat. "I'll make it quick. I know we're in a hurry."

"Not too big of a hurry that we can't stop at the barn. I'll be right back. I need to lock up." As he sprinted up the steps to set the alarm, he decided he would tell her at the barn that he wouldn't be joining the flight out. He'd wait until she'd said goodbye to her horse. But, no matter where he told her, it wasn't going to be easy.

Markus drove the half-mile stretch to the barn in quiet thought. He reached for Sidney's hand and caressed it with his thumb as his mind considered how she'd take the news. He slowed the jeep as he neared the barn.

Sidney stared at the paddock, fixing in her mind the sight of Mocha grazing and nipping at the short grass around the water trough. "Don't stop. I can't do it."

"Why don't you want to stop?" Markus asked, shifting the gears into park. "Don't you want to say goodbye?"

"I'm afraid I wouldn't be able to tear myself away, once I got my hands on her."

"Are you sure?" He could sympathize—he was having similar thoughts.

Turning to face him, she nodded, "Yes. I'm sure. I'll let this morning's time I spent with her be my last goodbye. Please, keep driving."

"If that's what you wish." *So much for telling her at the barn.* He shifted into drive, easing back onto the lane leading to the arena where the Black Hawk had begun running up its engines.

Rounding the curve as it swept past the tree line, he pulled alongside the fence, stopping short of the gate. He saw the crew doing their pre-flight checks, while Moose and his team stood off to the side, heads together in conversation.

"Well. Here we are." Markus stepped out and slammed the car door harder than he'd meant to. He hurried to retrieved the luggage from the rear compartment and then set the suitcase and backpack on the ground. "I'll have Moose load these in the chopper," he said as Trevor approached.

"I can handle my backpack. Don't think I can load the suitcase." Trevor paused before adding, "Good luck with your mission in Fort Worth. I'd offer my help, but…"

Markus gripped Trevor's shoulder. "I appreciate that. I do. I'll be in touch."

Trevor slung his backpack over his shoulder, wincing slightly. He sprinted toward the helicopter, Gunner on his heels. When Rex tried to follow, Markus put him in the back seat, giving the "stay" command. The dog sat with his head out the window and watched until the pair disappeared from view into the belly of the helicopter.

"You'll be in touch?" Sidney asked as she approached Markus. She stared at him, wrapping her arms around herself. "I don't understand."

"Moose is escorting you to El Paso. Once there, two CIA agents will join Moose and the team to escort you to Virginia."

"But, I… I thought you were coming," she stammered. "Why didn't you tell me earlier?"

Markus took her in his arms. "I don't know why not. I guess because I suck at goodbyes."

Sidney pushed away from his embrace. "But, why *aren't* you coming? And, what personal mission was Trevor referring to?"

He wavered on what to say, what to tell her. There was nothing he could say, except, "You're going to be safe, and everything will be fine. I'll meet you in Virginia as soon as I can."

"You're avoiding my questions." She took a few steps back, once again wrapping her arms around herself, as if creating a barrier.

A shrill whistle sounded. Moose approached at a jog, waving his arm and motioning them over. "Time to go," he barked, his voice competing with the whirring of the rotors.

"Grab this suitcase," Markus shouted, handing the case to Moose. "give us just a second here."

"Don't take too long. We need to get this bird in the air." Moose hurried off toward the helicopter.

Markus turned back to Sidney. "I'm not avoiding your questions. I just have some unfinished business I need to take care of."

"And you won't—can't tell me what it is."

"No. Not yet. This is one of those other times I mentioned earlier when I would need you to trust me."

"At what point do you start trusting me with the truth?"

Markus stood rooted in place. Saying nothing. Conveying nothing. How could he ever tell her the truth about his life? Some things were untellable.

Sidney stared at him for a long moment in an apparent quandary over what to say. Several times, she opened her mouth to speak, but the words were not forthcoming. Stepping further away, shaking her head, she stammered, "I... No... I can't... Goodbye..." She turned and ran toward the helicopter's open doors.

"Sidney—please!" Markus ran several strides after her, but stopped short. He watched Moose help her inside, and he stood transfixed as Sidney stared from the window at him. Markus waved—a half-salute, half-grasp of air before clenching his fist and letting his arm fall to his side. Sidney sat in the window, unmoving, not returning the wave. Backing away, Markus slung one arm over his eyes to shield them as the helicopter lifted off in a cloud of blowing sand.

CHAPTER 27

Alpine & Fort Worth

After pouring a brandy, Markus retreated into the coolness of his safe-room. Opening his email, he scanned through a few miscellaneous messages and made notes of things he'd need to take care of before leaving tomorrow for Fort Worth. He sent an email to Otto, asking him to come pick up Rex and watch him for a few days. The next was sent to Victor, asking if he'd feel up to starting his barn manager duties first thing tomorrow and taking over his hunting clients that would be showing up the day after Thanksgiving.

He received an immediate reply from Victor. The message read, "hell yes," and that he was bored to death. He and Aubrey were planning on coming out in the morning anyway to see her horse.

As Markus was replying with a list of specific instructions, an email from his contact in the Company popped up in the inbox. He opened the mail. The message was cryptic, saying only "Call ASAP."

He retrieved the flip phone from the locked box. "Yes? What is it?" he asked, a knot tightening his gut.

"It's not good news, I'm afraid."

"Is it about Sidney?"

"No. It's about her cousin, Jessica. She was found murdered in her home earlier this evening."

"Fuck." Markus downed the last sip of brandy. "How?"

"Wire garrote—rag stuffed in her mouth—hands tied behind her back. Sound familiar?"

"All too. Damn it—why wasn't anybody watching her? I specifically told you that she and her husband might be in danger."

"I made a formal request for an agent to be assigned to them. My request is stuck in the bureaucratic chain of command."

"Jesus Christ. I hope you or someone else can get it unstuck. Where's her husband now?"

"Still at police headquarters. He's the one who came home and found her."

"Alibi?"

"Tight. He was in meetings all day with clients. They've confirmed."

"All right. Well, get an agent assigned to him ASAP."

"I'm working on it."

"I'd highly recommend not telling Sidney about this until she's landed safely in Virginia. Moose and team have just exfiltrated her and Trevor to El Paso not thirty minutes ago."

"I'll pass your recommendation along. I'm sure it won't be a problem."

"Are Winston Knight's phones tapped? Anyone watching him?"

"Affirmative on both."

"Good. I'll be checking in regularly for updates on his activity. I'm leaving for Fort Worth tomorrow and want to arrange a surprise meeting. I'll fill you in on the details when I'm on the road. Anything else for me?"

"That's all I've got. Sorry to be the bearer of bad news."

"Yeah—you know what usually happens to the messenger."

Markus stared at his empty brandy glass, contemplated refilling it, but decided he wanted something stronger. After securing the room, he headed downstairs to the liquor cabinet.

*****

Fists pounding on the door and Rex's loud barking awoke Markus from an alcohol-induced deep sleep. He rolled off the sofa and onto the floor, landing on his hands and knees. *Who the hell could that be?* Reaching for his pistol, he knocked over his scotch glass sitting on the coffee table, spilling the last sip he had been too drunk to drink.

He tiptoed to the kitchen and peeked out the curtain. From that vantage point, he had full view of the driveway and of the porch leading to the side door. As he holstered his weapon, he told Rex to be quiet.

"Hold on—be right there." He stumbled to the door and then gestured with his arm to come inside. "Entréz, s'il te plait, Master Bates."

Elwood Bates followed him inside. "You okay? Looks like you've tied one on."

"Why do they say, "tied one on," when there's no tying involved—just—swallowing?"

"Good question. I'll Google it." Elwood peered around Markus to see a half-empty bottle of scotch sitting on the table next to an overturned glass.

Following the path of his gaze, Markus said. "Glenmorangie. The best. Care to join me?"

"Wish I could, but I'll have to pass. I've been calling your cellphone but no answer. I just wanted to let you know that we've loaded the cargo and we're off again to El Paso."

"Cellphone coverage is iffy out here. Where's Moose?"

"He and Cannibal stayed in El Paso with the two witnesses. It's just me, Cooper, and Rocky on this trip to pick up the cargo."

"All right—have a safe flight." Markus followed him onto the porch. "Do me a favor, Master. When you get back, tell Moose to call me when he can talk in private. It's important. And tell him to keep Sidney away from televisions and newspapers."

After locking the door behind him, Markus stumbled

back to the sofa. He plopped down. Stared at the bottle of scotch. Noted the height of the stairs. He didn't want to do either one, drink anymore, or climb stairs. He stretched out on the couch, punching a pillow into shape and stuffing it under his head. Tomorrow would be a long day of driving, long enough for him to clear his mind and come up with a plan. Within minutes, he was snoring softly, Rex lying on the floor close by.

*****

After handing Rex over to Otto and briefing him on the situation, Markus met with Victor at the barn for last minute instructions. By eight o'clock, he was in his Jeep driving east. He arrived in Fort Worth early in the afternoon; the pre-holiday traffic was light, with most downtown offices already closed for Thanksgiving. As soon as he checked into his hotel room, he called using his secured line to confer with his contact.

He asked for an update on Sidney and Trevor and was relieved to hear that they landed midday at Langley and were already safely sequestered at the Farm. "Great. Now, what do you have for me on Knight?"

"He didn't go to his office today but stayed at his ranch, and his office will be closed Friday. However, he's attending a black-tie affair at the Fort Worth Club Friday evening. Something called the Celebrity Cutting Horse Charity Fundraiser. The cutting horse competition is Saturday, but all the celebrities riding in the event and all the big movers and shakers have this exclusive party the night before."

"Can you get me an invitation or a ticket?"

"Already have—along with a tux. They'll be delivered to your hotel Friday morning. The invitation will be for a Mr. Jürgen Walker. Thought I'd mash together some of your former ID's."

"What would I do without you?"

"Let's not find out, shall we?"

"Let's not. And, one more thing before I let you go. Contact the local FBI and bring them onboard. Have them come to the hotel to wire me before I leave. I want this sting to go down without any errors or anything that son of a bitch can use to cry foul."

"You got it."

"And while you're at it, you might want to give Deputy Director O'Connor a heads-up," Markus added reluctantly. "He'll have to give this his blessing."

*****

Friday evening at six o'clock, Markus strode into the ballroom of the Fort Worth Club. The tuxedo he wore was not as tailored as he would have liked, but the roomy coat made concealing the wire easier. He handed his invitation to the pink lipsticked young woman at the check-in table.

She studied the invitation, then compared it to the names on her list. "Nice to have you with us this evening, Mr. Walker." She pointed to the seating chart displayed on the easel next to her. "You're at table number thirteen. Your nametag is on the chart at the place you'll be seated. The tables for the silent auction are along the rear wall, and the items for the live auction are on the table near the bandstand. Feel free to bid often and bid high."

He stepped closer to the easel to retrieve his nametag and to inspect the seating chart, scanning the table arrangements for the other guest's names. "How propitious," he smiled. "Thirteen is my lucky number."

"Maybe you'll get lucky tonight."

He chuckled. "I'm hoping so." *Table four—C. Winston Knight in the chair at the nine o'clock position.* Markus removed his name badge from the board and tucked it into his pocket.

Strolling past the tables bearing the items donated for auction, Markus surreptitiously kept one eye on table four. When the maître d' announced dinner would be served at six thirty, guests began making their way to their seats.

The chair at the nine o'clock position at table four remained vacant throughout the first course of barbecued quail. Second course salad plates were brought and removed. Most of the third course plates of beef tenderloin tamales with jalapeno and cheddar grits were served to all twenty tables before that chair was finally filled.

Winston's grand entrance turned heads as he apologized loudly to his table companions for running late. "At least I made it in time for the auction. That's what this is all about, right, raising money for the children's hospital?" He picked up the glass of wine in front of his plate, raising it in a toast. "Here's to sick kids everywhere."

Two rows behind and one table over, Markus watched the obnoxious spectacle, his jaw tightening with every minute that ticked past. He scooted his plate away, downing the rest of the cabernet in his glass. Clichéd chitter chatter took its toll on his patience. He was ready to get this started—ready for that asshole to get what was coming to him.

Excusing himself from the table, Winston stood and made a theatrical show of placing his napkin on the seat of his chair, telling the blond in the micro-mini next to him not to let anyone take his place. He strolled past table thirteen, smiling politely and greeting someone he recognized. Several seconds passed. Markus excused himself, too.

Winston sauntered out to the lobby, stopping momentarily to flirt with the young woman still attending the check-in table. When it became obvious his flirtations were unwelcomed, he put his hands in his pockets and casually made his way to the private restroom at the end of the hall, never paying attention to the other tuxedoed gentleman trailing him several steps behind.

Markus inserted a pick into the lock, easily opening the door. He slipped into the restroom behind Winston and relocked it. He gripped the knife that had been concealed in his pants pocket. It was now open and ready for business.

"This one's taken." Winston stood at the urinal, his back to Markus. "There's another bathroom next door."

Markus slammed his shoulder against Winston's back, sending him face first into the tile wall. He gripped Winston by the hair and smashed his face again into the cool, white marble while shoving his other hand that gripped the knife between Winston's legs.

"What the hell… You broke my nose! What's going on?" Winston struggled against Markus's weight, but Markus pushed harder.

"Keep your hands on the wall or I'll cut your balls off." Markus pressed upward with the knife.

Winston squirmed. "Easy—my hands are on the wall. If you're after money, my wallet's in my back left pocket."

"I'm not after money, I'm after answers."

"Answers about what?"

"About why you torched Trevor's mother's house. Why you killed Aleck Stavros. Why you murdered Jessica Cordoba. Start talking or I'll start cutting" He moved the knife a fraction, the cold blade drawing a thin red line of blood.

"I didn't burn anything or kill anybody." Winston's vehement denial echoed in the small room.

"Did you give the orders?"

"No!"

"Who did?"

"Take the blade off my balls and I'll tell you."

"It's the other way around, dick head. You talk, *then* I'll take away the blade."

"All right—all right. I ordered the arson. That asshole was having an affair with my wife."

"You dumb fuck—Trevor's gay." Markus increased the pressure on the knife. "Who ordered the killings?"

"I don't know anything about the killings. *El Cuchillo* gives the orders." Winston pounded his fists against the wall. "I'm talking, goddammit. Remove the fucking knife."

"Not yet. Who is *El Cuchillo*?"

Winston paused, shaking his head.

Markus pressed the knife harder, drawing more blood. "I'll castrate you right here, you son of a bitch. Who's *El Cuchillo*?"

"Rafael Cordoba," Winston shouted in a hot gush of words.

Jessica's husband? Holy fuck.

As if gut-punched, Markus tried to suck in a deep breath, but his body rejected the attempt. Backing away, he commanded Winston to keep his hands pressed high on the wall. He wiped the bloody blade on a paper towel and then closed his knife and pocketed it.

Unlocking the bathroom door, he motioned for the four FBI agents to enter. He heard one of them say that they'd recorded it all, good job, excellent confession. He saw people's surprised and curious expressions as they watched Winston being led away in handcuffs, blood trickling from his nose and dripping down his white tuxedo shirt.

The voices, the faces, the words, registered in a place somewhere deep in Markus's mind. He told himself he would review it all later—after he'd had time to dig through the contents of the cellphone he had borrowed from Winston's pocket.

CHAPTER 28

Fort Worth

Sitting at the desk in his hotel suite, minus his tuxedo jacket and bowtie, Markus connected his cellphone to Winston's through the power port. Opening an application on his phone that he nicknamed "Carnac, the Magnificent," he waited for the app to read, decipher, and bypass the security codes, thereby allowing access into all of the phone's personal data.

Within seconds, his cellphone's screen flashed Winston's security code.

1970? Really? No one uses their birth date.

He scrolled through the list of contacts, looking for Rafael Cordoba's number. Oddly, Rafael's name was not listed, although Jessica's was. Going back through the list, Markus noticed that one entry stood out—the initials, "EC."

El Cuchillo?

Markus opened the contact. Three numbers were listed for EC, a home, an office, and a cell number. He pressed the office number, but a recording picked up. A pleasant female voice thanked the caller for contacting Cordoba Imports, cheerily saying, "Please leave a message." He disconnected the call.

Bingo. EC, aka El Cuchillo, equals Cordoba.

Using his secure phone, he dialed his contact. "Sting was successful. Knight is now in FBI custody."

"Congratulations. We've already received word here. Good news travels fast."

"Since Knight's taped confession implicates Rafael Cordoba, I'm assuming he's been picked up for questioning."

A long pause without an answer, only breathing, came across the line.

"Don't fucking tell me he's fled." Markus shook his head in disbelief.

"He's fled."

"How in the hell... Never mind how in the hell. Any leads?"

"We're working on a few, but his cellphone number was tracked back to his home address via a GPS signal. Officers found the phone sitting on the kitchen counter. He'd made one phone call to his airplane hangar at Meacham Field earlier this morning, then left the cellphone behind."

"An obvious cat-and-mouse tactic. Do you have that number?"

His contact rattled it off. "Why'd you ask?"

Markus compared the number to the listing on Winston's phone. "Because *that* one is not his private number, I'm guessing. I have a different one." He shared the number listed for EC's cellphone.

"I'll turn it over to the agent in charge. But, how did you get that?"

"Insider information." A vague answer, he knew, but the more left unsaid, the better.

"Let me guess. You appropriated Winston's cellphone during your friendly chat with him in the bathroom but didn't turn the evidence over to the FBI."

"I can neither confirm nor deny any such accusations. Anything else for me?"

"Yes. We retrieved a copy of an email Jessica had sent to Sidney, which Sidney probably never got. It was printed out on Cordoba Imports letterhead, crumpled and thrown in the trash. One bloody fingerprint was pretty clear. It's being dusted now."

"What did the email say?" Markus bounced his knee up and down and tapped his pencil against the notebook.

"It said that Jessica had met with Sidney's attorney, Aleck Stavros, on several occasions. He was guiding her through the necessary steps of protecting her financial assets in case her misgivings panned out. She had become suspicious of Rafael when large sums of money started showing up in her personal account, money she couldn't explain. Aleck had advised her to have the bank begin an investigation into the mysterious deposits. Jessica apologized for not telling Sidney sooner, given the difficult situation she, herself, was going through."

"So, the Stavros murder probably had nothing to do with Sidney."

"Probably not. It appears more like the act of an enraged husband-slash-criminal on the verge of being busted for using his wife to launder money."

Markus mulled this over. "I bet if you dig deeper, Cordoba's alibi for the time of his wife's murder won't be as airtight as you thought."

"We've got agents on that, too, interviewing the clients who corroborated his alibi."

"Good. I'll check in hourly for updates, more often if something changes here."

After ending the call and pouring a scotch, Markus walked to the picture window overlooking downtown Fort Worth. From his view, he saw Christmas lights shimmering on buildings and draped on trees lining the sidewalks. For miles, lights glowed from houses already decorated for the holidays.

And all is merry and bright.

*****

Markus emerged from the steamy bathroom, a towel wrapped around his waist. After making coffee, he flipped open his laptop to check his email.

I'm beginning to dread these "Call ASAP" messages.

He dialed his contact. "Tell me it's good news this time."

"I'll let you decide. First, we've located Cordoba, thanks to the cellphone number you provided. He left Meacham Field on one of his company jets and flew to Acapulco, Mexico. We tracked him to a compound in Rio Negro—probably the cartel's headquarters."

"I'd say that's great news."

"And, it's been confirmed it was his bloody print on the letterhead. More blood was found on his desk and on a blue file labeled S. A. D. Its contents matched what you scanned and attached to me in an email."

"That file was taken from her attorney's office, I'm guessing at the time Stavros was murdered. But, the police report said a file was found next to the body. Any revelations about that?"

"The prisoner you interrogated, Anton, has turned state's evidence. He's confessed to the arson and to the Stavros murder. The file left next to Alek's body had Jessica Cordoba's name on it—miscellaneous notes detailing their meetings, along with photocopies of her bank statements. Anton said he didn't take that file because his boss already knew about it—the hit on Jessica had already been ordered. Anton also said his boss, *El Cuchillo*, had ordered the hit on Stavros as revenge for helping his wife who'd betrayed him."

"What a sick bastard." Markus paced the room before stopping in front of the picture window.

"We've known for a long time *El Cuchillo* was responsible for tons of black tar heroin making its way into the U.S. and Europe. We've intercepted other drugs, and more than enough weapons and ammunition to arm a small country. The *Rio Negro* cartel is also responsible for the majority of the human trafficking in and out of Mexico. We've just not been able, *until now*, to confirm the identity of the elusive *El Cuchillo*."

Looking out over the twinkling city lights, Markus gnawed on the inside of his cheek, letting his contact's words sink in. He closed his eyes, imagining the S. A. D. file being read by this animal who was as equally deranged as the animal who created the file in the first place.

"Is Whiskey Charlie still active?" Markus moved to the closet, dragging out his duffle bag.

"He's still active, but problematic to get hold of. Why? What are you planning?"

"I need someone to handle some specific logistics for me—logistics that'll require someone with his specialty."

"I know what he specializes in. Why are you even contemplating this?"

"Time is of the essence. Just do your best to find him. Have W. C. contact me right away on this secure line. I'll be in touch." Markus hung up the phone.

Well that was fast. He reached for his other phone as it buzzed on the nightstand. *Ah, Moose.*

"Hello, Moose. What's up?"

"Just checking in. I thought you might want a report on what's happening here."

"Absolutely. How's Sidney?"

"Last time I saw her, she was doing okay. The FBI's taken over the case and has moved her and Trevor to a safe house outside the state of Virginia. I'm not privy to where. There's been a lot of noise from the investigators about wanting to talk to you, too, whenever you finally decide to show up."

"That'll have to wait. How did she take the news about Jessi?"

"She was devastated. But she's a strong lady. She seems more concerned about Trevor than about her own situation."

"That sounds like her," said Markus, wanting to smile but aching inside. "I wish I'd been the one to tell her, but I appreciate you handling it. How is Trevor?"

"The surgeon was able to reattach his bicep to his elbow. He's expected to make a full recovery."

"Fantastic. Hey, before I hang up, I need to ask you to do me a favor."

"Sure thing. But, quickly, I wanted you to hear it from

me that I talked to Sidney about you behind your back. Nothing confidential. She came to me with lots of questions about you, about what you do and who you are—about your past. I told her a mostly sanitized version of the details I could share with her. She listened quietly, had a few pointed questions, and then that was the end of it."

"Okay. Thanks for telling me." *Mostly sanitized?* Markus tried to imagine what exactly it was she had asked Moose about his past—but at least he was on her mind. He'd settle for that, given what she'd said before she got on the helicopter.

"So, what's the favor?" asked Moose.

"Stress to your boss to appeal to the FBI not to bargain with Knight or offer him any kind of plea deal. There won't be any need for a deal."

"Knight's testimony against Cordoba and the cartel is extremely valuable. That request might not go over very well."

"Hear—my—words, Moose. There won't be any need for a deal."

After a pause, "I understand. Roger that."

"Thank you. I'll be in touch."

That son of a bitch Knight should be prosecuted to the full extent of the law.

Dressing quickly, he packed his belongings and checked out of the hotel. He stowed his briefcase and duffle bag in his Jeep and headed west, anticipating the call from Whiskey Charlie. The sparkling city bathed in holiday lights grew smaller in his rearview mirror as he drove through the chilly darkness of a moonless night.

CHAPTER 29

Mexico & The U.S.

Forty-eight hours later, a black-clad figure lay on his belly under the umbrella of an amate tree. He waited in the dark, hidden by the tree's massive roots that spread out across the ground like giant brown serpents. Surveilling the sprawling *Rio Negro* cartel's compound through the high-powered scope of his sniper rifle, he watched the figure known as *El Cuchillo* move about the mansion looming at the center of the complex.

Concealed behind the compound's high adobe walls and to the rear of the main residence was a cluster of smaller buildings, the storehouses of drugs and weapons, their contents' street value totaling in the millions. From his high vantage point, he patiently watched as a swarm of men moved in and out of the buildings, carrying packages to the armored vehicles parked in a queue.

The sniper waited, his breathing measured, his nerves calm, his mind empty of distracting thoughts. He ignored the black, spike-tailed iguana that scratched a track across the dewy ground in front of where he lay prone. The muzzle of his rifle rested in a "v" of the amate tree's roots.

Yes—that's it—come on outside where I can see you better.

Stepping outside onto the veranda, *El Cuchillo* greeted another man who could have been his twin. They wore the same type of expensive suit, and both slicked their hair back in long ponytails. *El Cuchillo*'s cellphone buzzed. He answered the call.

"I heard you were in federal custody, Winston." Rafael's smooth voice sounded bored. "How did you post bond so quickly?"

"This is not Winston."

El Cuchillo pulled the phone away from his head and stared at the display screen before replacing it to his ear. "Who is this?" he demanded.

"*This* is the last sound you'll hear before you die."

A sniper shot from 500 yards cracked the night wide open. The man standing next to the now headless *El Cuchillo* dropped to the ground and lay flat on his belly, his designer clothes splattered with blood and brain. The throng of men loading drugs and guns into the armored vehicles scattered.

But it was too late for any to save themselves.

Methodically, the sniper pressed a button on the radio frequency remote control. One, and then another, and then another of the dozen HMX plastic explosives detonated. As if struck by a massive earthquake, the ground heaved upwards, tossing armored cars into the air like they were children's toys. Bodies disappeared under piles of rubble as the mansion and the storehouses crumbled into heaps of masonry and metal. A choking dust cloud plumed into the sky like ash from a volcano, obliterating the stars.

Well done, Whiskey Charlie. You came through for me again.

Stowing his sniper rifle and the remote control, the black-clad figure picked up his bag and hiked five miles to the rental car he'd left parked in a clearing in the woods. Settling into the front seat, he adjusted the rearview mirror, catching a glimpse of his face concealed behind a black mask. The only discernable feature—his eyes—were cold, hard, and gray.

*****

Even at four in the morning, the streets of Acapulco were crowded with beautiful people streaming in and out of nightclubs. They cha-cha-chaed and mamboed their way along the sidewalks as they chose the next bar to grace with their presence.

Markus sat at a table at the far end of a crowded patio overlooking Acapulco Bay. He drank a third scotch while waiting for his cellphone to ring. Tuning out the Latin pop music blaring from the overhead speakers, he watched couples strolling along the beach, some hand-in-hand, some pausing momentarily in shameless, public displays of affection.

Completely unaware of the wicked world around them.

His cellphone buzzed. Markus answered the call. "Dragon."

"Whiskey Charlie. Was the mission successful?"

"Affirmative—at least to my satisfaction."

"Fine. I'll be at Designation X-ray at zero six hundred hours to pick you up. Transportation to the States has been arranged."

"Roger that. Oh, and if you don't mind, I'd like to keep your remote detonating switch."

"For future use?"

"Souvenir." Markus pocketed his phone. He threw back the final swallow of his whisky before slinging his duffle bag over his shoulder. He pushed his way through the high-spirited crowd of tourists seeking escape from reality.

Passing shops and boutiques selling cheap T-shirts, postcards, and sunscreen, he paused in front of a plate-glass display window and studied his reflection. There was a time when he had despised what he saw. After Sarajevo. After Sonja. A man on the verge of turning into the same kind of animal he was hired to kill.

If it hadn't been for Moose and his team barging in when they did, he would have died that day. Many times, he'd wished that he had. Besides Sonja and the gang members of the Russian cartel, the only other "person" to die that day was the alias John Walker, aka Jürgen Hoffer. Markus Yeager lived.

Taking a step nearer to the window, he looked closer at

the man staring back. After Sarajevo, he spent eighteen months in the hospital—eighteen months of recuperation and intense therapy. Though his body healed, scars, both physical and emotional, remained. But as he studied his image, he realized it had been almost two weeks since he'd had an episode of PTSD or the gray-outs that plagued him in the past.

Maybe I've finally accepted who I am—a sheepdog protecting my flock—capable of great violence against predators seeking to harm those I protect. Yet, seeing in his reflection neither a sheep nor a wolf, he considered the other possibility.

Maybe I'm like Rex. A hybrid.

Sidney's words echoed in his mind, the words she had uttered on that first day they met. "*If the devil had a dog, you'd be it.*" Either way, it was time he accepted who and what he was —and he hoped to hell Sidney could accept it as well.

Markus set off at a fast walk, hurrying to make it to Designation X-ray.

*****

Snow fell soundlessly against the warm windshield of the limousine. The driver announced to Mr. Smith they could expect a delay due to hazardous road conditions, but he'd do his best to get his passenger to his destination on time.

Markus reclined against the seat, his head turned toward the window. Few cars braved the roads' icy conditions, but a slew of sand trucks crawled along, spraying the roads with their ice melting concoction.

The flight from Acapulco to Dallas, then from Dallas to Virginia on a leased jet had given him time to come fully to terms with who and what he was. It had also given him enough time to decide what it was he wanted. He wanted back in the Company.

And, I want Sidney.

After an hour's drive that should have taken thirty minutes, the limousine turned into the exclusive neighborhood of Hidden Oaks. The opulent estates were home to

Washington's elite who commuted to D.C. during the week and back to Virginia for weekends and holidays. Markus instructed the driver to pull over.

This is close enough.

Twenty minutes later, Markus sat at the breakfast bar in the Deputy Director's kitchen, lights off, waiting for the Director to return home. Soon, headlights in the window swept across the room as a car pulled into the driveway. As it lifted, the garage door creaked noisily, and then the alarm beeped out a warning to enter the proper code.

Coming into the kitchen through the garage door, O'Conner flipped on the light. "What the—"

"Evening, Jim," Markus said, smiling.

"How did you get in here?"

"Same way as last time. You really should change your alarm code on a regular basis."

"And you really should get your alibi ironed out. I've been in Washington for two days, two *fucking long days*, explaining how a major player in an ongoing FBI investigation could have been assassinated—under *our* watch."

"And how'd that go over?"

"I'm not in the mood for your bullshit." He shot a severe look at Markus. "Let's talk in my office."

Markus followed O'Connor down the hall to an opulent, hickory-paneled room lined with law books and decorated with photographs of the many hunting dogs he had owned over the years. A confirmed bachelor, O'Connor devoted his life to his career and his spaniels.

Pointing to a red leather chair across from his desk, he said, "Take a seat. Scotch? Cognac? Your surprise visit calls for a toast."

"Thank you, sir. I'll have whatever you're having."

"Cognac it is." O'Connor passed a glass to Markus. "Here's to luxury vacations. I hear Acapulco is nice this time of year." He leaned back in his chair, his eyes and his expression unreadable. He was well known among contemporaries to wear a mask of calm in the face of a storm.

Taking a sip, letting the warmth of the amber liquid reach his belly, Markus hesitated before answering. "I can neither confirm nor deny I've visited Acapulco in the recent past."

"Don't play games with me, Markus. Reports coming out of Mexico say the *Rio Negro* cartel has effectively been gutted. Both brothers, Rafael and Javier Cordoba, along with one hundred or so of their *finest* employees, are suspected dead. The compound was vaporized. Nothing left."

"I can neither confirm—"

O'Connor bolted forward and pounded his fist on his desk. "Goddammit, Markus. This was a completely unsanctioned, unorthodox, unnecessary, not to mention *illegal* maneuver."

"Off the record, sir, it was a completely necessary, *and* successful, maneuver." Markus locked eyes with the Deputy Directory. "In this world we live in, where evil trumps good more often than we'd like to acknowledge, you and I both know there are some people who just need to be killed."

Easing back in his chair, O'Connor crossed his arms over his chest and stared up at the ceiling. The moment stretched into a long, uncomfortable silence before he spoke. "You've always been somewhat of a rogue—doing things your way—taking unnecessary risks."

"Again, sir, this was a necessary hit. If I were still on the payroll, this is *exactly* the type of operation you'd have selected me for. It's the same type of operation *we've* done before."

O'Connor leveled his gaze on Markus, his expression unreadable. "The speculation in Washington," he said, giving weight to his words, "and the speculation around Mexico, too, is that a rival alliance took out the *Rio Negro* cartel. I didn't argue. Given enough time, that theory could take flight."

"Give it wings. Let it go."

"What next, Markus? I can't protect you beyond this."

"I don't want protection. I want back in the Company."

O'Conner ran his hand down his face, tapping a finger across his pursed lips. "You're *persona non grata* right now. Lie low for a while until the stink fades away. Then, perhaps, I'll consider it. But, *strictly* on a contractual basis."

"I'll take it. Where's Sidney?"

"I need to make a few phone calls to clear this. Given that there is now no need for her to be in the witness protection program, I should be able get approval for you to travel to that location, unless the FBI wants to be pissy about it."

"Thank you, sir. And, I'll need to make one stop first."

"Where's that?" he asked as he dialed the number of the Director of the FBI.

"I need to pick up something in Alpine, Texas. I'd like to help put the pieces of Sidney's life back together—if she'll let me."

*****

The early morning rays of the sun spread across the jagged peaks of the Rocky Mountains, bathing them in warm hues of gold, lavender, and pink. Eighty some odd miles west of Denver, Markus steered his truck off the interstate and onto a small, winding lane leading to a secluded cabin overlooking Lake Dillon.

After parking the truck, he lowered the horse trailer's windows. Mocha and Blue stuck out their heads, nickering to each other. Tramping through knee-deep snow, Markus stood on the wide stone porch, Rex at his side. He knocked, counting the long seconds before the door opened. In that interminable moment of waiting, he thought again about what he would say, how he would react if Sidney rejected him.

He knew he would be all right—however devastated— and would survive if she turned him down. But, silently, fervently, he prayed to whatever gods might be listening that she wouldn't walk away, having been alarmed by the things about his past, his job, his life, that Moose had shared with her.

The door flew open. Sidney stood framed in the doorway, the window at her back aglow in the sun's warm rays.

"Markus. Thank God." She fell into his arms.

*****

Sidney leaned over in the saddle, patting Mocha on the neck. Having her horse with her again and knowing Rex was back to normal eased her mind. She thought about what Rex had done and knew it was only out of a desire to protect her, not because of blood lust. He was gentle with the barn cats at the stables and was aloof around strangers. But she knew that, if provoked into a defensive act, he would do what it took to protect her again.

And so would Markus, or Dragon, or whatever names he has used in his past.

The backcountry trails through the White River National Forest were hard-packed in snow, providing solid footing for the horses. Up ahead, a sleigh pulled by a matched pair of dappled gray Percherons glided over the trail, its passengers wrapped in blankets and singing Christmas carols.

"What a perfect scene for Christmas Eve," said Sidney, reaching out for Markus's hand.

"Right out of a Rockwell painting, only better, because we're here." Easing his mare closer, Markus took Sidney's hand and kissed it, despite the fact that it was ensconced inside a thick woolen glove.

"We should call Trevor when we get back and wish him a Merry Christmas. It'll be after midnight in England—officially Christmas day. It's been three weeks since he left. I miss him."

"We can call. It'll be good to talk to him and hear how he and Eli are doing."

Rex trotted alongside the horses, every now and then darting off into the woods to chase a squirrel or a rabbit. After a few minutes into his adventure, he would hurry back to the trail and take up his position next to Mocha and Sidney.

"I wish we could stay here forever. I've grown attached to our little cabin." Turning to Markus, she added, "I'm not attached because it's my safe house. I'm attached to it because it feels like home." She had similar feelings about this man—her safe harbor—her home.

"I love it here, too. It was nice of the Feds to let us stay for the remainder of December."

"It'll be nice, though, to find a place where the horses are with us and not boarded at a stable down the road."

"I agree. I've got a few more properties picked out for you to look at. Rolling acreage. Nice barns. White fences. I'll show them to you when we get back to the cabin."

The decision not to return to Alpine had been mutual. Going back to the place Sidney associated with such terrible memories would have added more time to the healing process. She'd only begun to sleep through the night without being awakened in the throes of night terrors. Markus's ranch was in good hands for now, and someday in the future, the decision to return might be a possibility.

But not right away.

"Where are the properties located?" Sidney asked.

"In eastern Kentucky, near the Appalachian Trail. Lots of opportunities for great trail rides"

"Sounds perfect. And we'd be close to Virginia, in case you needed to make a quick trip to Langley."

"I may have to, on rare occasions. Mostly, the jobs I'll be involved with will be out of the country. Sometimes life will be complicated, and I won't be able to tell you where I'm going. Are you sure you can handle that?" he asked, giving her gloved hand a squeeze.

Sidney turned in her saddle to face him. *Can I handle that?* It was a question she'd asked herself numerous times since she and Markus had a heart-to-heart discussion about things she'd learned from Moose.

She considered the question again, the hidden implications, and all it would mean for her future—for their future. She knew what she *couldn't* handle—the idea of Markus not present in her life. After the terrifying madness she'd been through, she knew she could deal with anything else life threw her way.

"I don't care how complicated it gets. I want to be with you, as long as you promise to love me for the remainder of our Decembers."

I can handle that, and more.

She reined Mocha around to head back to the stables, the flakes bigger and heavier than when they'd first set out on the trail. They rode hand in hand as snow fell silently on the ground, the tracks they had left earlier in that brief lost moment soon disappearing under the mounding drifts.

Acknowledgments

"A warrior is worthless unless he rises above others and stands strong in the midst of a storm."

The quote is from *Hagakure: The Book of the Samurai*, by Yamamoto Tsunetomo. The classic 300-year-old book is full of wisdom, teaching the honor code of bushido, which is the Samurai's "way of the warrior."

"On Sheep, Wolves, and Sheepdogs" is a notion explained in the book, *On Combat, The Psychology and Physiology of Deadly Conflict in War and in Peace*, by Lieutenant Colonel David Grossman, published in 2004 by Warrior Science Publications.

I would like to thank The Texas Wolfdog Project for graciously allowing me to use a photograph of their gorgeous wolf/dog hybrid, Domino, as the cover model for my book. Take a look at their website to learn about this wonderful organization and how they rescue, rehabilitate, and rehome these amazing creatures.
http://texaswolfdogproject.org/
https://www.facebook.com/TXwolfdogproject/

I would also like to thank graphic artist Carla Chadwick for designing this great cover and the one for my historical fiction, *Orphan Moon*.
http://carlachadwick.com/
https://www.facebook.com/carla.chadwick2?pnref=story

A Note From the Author

This is the *"Thank You"* page—the most important page of the book. Then why is it at the back, you might ask? I see it not at the back, but at the bottom of a stack of pages, supporting everything on top. Because, without all the people who've helped me and encouraged me along the way, the stack of pages that make up this book would surely topple.

First and foremost, I must thank my husband, Baron, for giving me his love, support, and encouragement. On top of that, he wrote for me a fictionalized, in-depth character study on which I based the male protagonist, Markus Yeager. Because of Baron's extensive military background, the value of his input on this book cannot be measured. And, when I would hit the proverbial brick wall of writer's block, he and I would saddle up the horses and go for a ride in the woods. We'd talk through difficult plot issues, and we'd brainstorm ideas with one another until I had a clear view of where to take the characters or a scene.

Okay, this is where I could get a little teary-eyed about my editor. And not just an editor, Ines Eishen is also a writing coach, encourager, cheerleader, taskmaster, and friend. From late-night email sessions, to afternoon Face Time sessions, to three-day wine-fueled weekend sessions, her editing advice took the manuscript to another level, polishing the rough spots and cutting the unnecessary parts. I'm grateful to her for many things, but above all, for our friendship.

To my advance team, my early readers, Claire Summers, Suzanne Tinsley, Helena Etwas, Gary Haley, Susan Bertram, Mildred Corbett, Beth Maybee, and Sherry Miles, I owe all of you more gratitude than I can put into words. Your keen input, comprehensive observations, and spot-on suggestions were priceless. Seeing the story and characters through your eyes was essential for me to understand what worked and what didn't. I learned something from each of you.

To my advance team, my early readers, Claire Summers, Suzanne Tinsley, Helena Etwas, Gary Haley, Susan Bertram, Mildred Corbett, Beth Maybee, and Sherry Miles, I owe all of you more gratitude than I can put into words. Your keen input, comprehensive observations, and spot-on suggestions were priceless. Seeing the story and characters through your eyes was essential for me to understand what worked and what didn't. I learned something from each of you.

And, to you my dear readers, I offer my sincere gratitude for taking the time to read my book. I hope you enjoyed the story and characters. Please leave a review on *IF THE DEVIL HAD A DOG'S* Amazon.com page and on Goodreads at **www.goodreads.com**. Search for the book by title or my name. Whether a glowing report or a kindly critique, your review is invaluable. Reviews drive new readers to a book and help new authors gain recognition and a higher ranking on Amazon. You can also leave feedback on my website at **www.TKLukas.com** and at the *T.K.Lukas.AuthorPage* on Facebook. If you would like to receive periodic updates about my projects and excerpts of works in progress, please leave your name and email address at the following link: **http://www.tklukas.com/contact-me-newsletter.**

Last but not least, Ryan, Erik, and Krista, I love you all. Now, someone please pop the Almondage!

About the Author

T.K. Lukas, an accomplished equestrian and author of the international best selling novel *ORPHAN MOON,* lives with her husband on a small ranch in rural Palo Pinto County in North Central Texas. Their three grown children are scattered across the globe. Along with international travel, she and her husband enjoy spending as much time as possible riding their horses through the woods, taking their dogs for walks, and watching their Belted Galloway cattle get fat. Visit her website, www.TKLukas.com and the *T.K. Lukas* Facebook page to keep up with her current projects and future releases.

(Baron on Blue and T.K. on Mocha)

Works by T.K. Lukas

Orphan Moon
    Published April 3, 2015 – Chevalier Publishing

* To answer many of your questions, **IF THE DEVIL HAD A DOG** is not the end for Markus Yeager and Sidney McQueen. A prequel as well as a sequel is on the drawing board. Sign up for my <u>newsletter</u> to keep abreast of the latest news and special offers.